ALSO BY CHELSEA SEDOTI

The Hundred Lies of Lizzie Lovett

As You Wish

IT CAME FROM THE SKY

a Novel

CHELSEA SEDOTI

sourcebooks
fire

Copyright © 2020 by Chelsea Sedoti
Cover and internal design © 2020 by Sourcebooks
Cover design and illustration © Philip Pascuzzo
Internal design by Danielle McNaughton/Sourcebooks
Internal images © Freepik, Shutterstock

Sourcebooks and the colophon are registered trademarks of Sourcebooks.

Published by Sourcebooks Fire, an imprint of Sourcebooks
P.O. Box 4410, Naperville, Illinois 60567-4410
(630) 961-3900
sourcebooks.com

Library of Congress Cataloging-in-Publication Data

Names: Sedoti, Chelsea, author.
Title: It came from the sky / Chelsea Sedoti.
Description: Naperville, IL : Sourcebooks Fire, [2020] | Audience: Ages
    14-18. | Audience: Grades 10-12. | Summary: Gideon and Ishmael Hofstadt,
    ages sixteen and seventeen, accidentally start a hoax that aliens have
    landed, turning their town of Lansburg, Pennsylvania, into a circus.
    Told through narrative, police interviews, text messages, blog posts,
    and more.
Identifiers: LCCN 2020005288 | (hardcover)
Subjects: CYAC: Hoaxes--Fiction. | Extraterrestrial beings--Fiction. |
    Brothers--Fiction. | Family life--Pennsylvania--Fiction. |
    Pennsylvania--Fiction. | Humorous stories.
Classification: LCC PZ7.1.S3385 It 2020 | DDC [Fic]--dc23
LC record available at https://lccn.loc.gov/2020005288

Printed and bound in the United States of America.
MA 10 9 8 7 6 5 4 3 2 1

For Steve Phillips and Evan Sedoti,
my favorite people to search for UFOs with.

To Whom It May Concern:

My name is Gideon P. Hofstadt and this is the 100 percent authentic, truthful, nothing-held-back account of what happened this past autumn. It's the story of how extraterrestrials came to Lansburg, Pennsylvania, and the chaos that followed.

There were sightings of unidentified flying objects.[1]

There were close encounters of the fourth kind.[2]

And, of course, there was The Incident, which you may have already heard about.

It's only right to begin this manuscript by clarifying one significant detail: there were never *really* aliens.

In the beginning—before the Seekers, before the media circus, before the promise of an extraterrestrial fountain of youth—there was only me and my brother.

Gideon and Ishmael Hofstadt, ages sixteen and seventeen, respectively.

Just us and an abandoned field.

And a mishap that became a lie.

And a lie that became the greatest hoax the world has ever seen.

---

1   Commonly referred to as *UFOs*.
2   Commonly referred to as *alien abductions*.

EVENT:
Inception

DATE: SEPT. 7 (THURS.)

It began with an explosion.

The explosion was intentional. The events that followed were not.

On the evening in question, I was in my lab—a converted outbuilding in a field on my parents' farm.[1]

I'd been given permission to use it two years earlier, when I was a freshman in high school. I could've taken over the spacious barn instead but was deterred by its proximity to the house. Besides, even though animals hadn't been kept there for decades, the smell of horses lingered.

I didn't enjoy the smell of horses. I didn't enjoy horses in general. The only animal I routinely tolerated was my cat, Kepler. Unlike most four-legged creatures, Kepler wasn't loud or dirty, and he shared my distrust of most people.

But I digress.

To prepare for that evening's experiment, I'd calculated the

---

1 Hofstadt Farm: 592 Olga Lane, on the outskirts of Lansburg, Pennsylvania, United States of America.

expected force of the explosion versus the distance from the blast site to the house, where my parents were engrossed in *Pitch, Please*, a reality show where contestants pitched ideas for America's next reality show. From their spot in the living room, they'd be oblivious to the blast. While Mother and Father were usually lenient about my science experiments, I imagined their tolerance didn't extend to bombs.

I gazed lovingly at my newly built seismograph, which was inspired by the online geodynamics course I was taking. Tonight's explosion would allow me to test the seismograph's sensitivity. As an added bonus, the blast might be large enough to register on other, nearby seismographs as well. Some of those seismographs, like the one at The Ohio State University, had publicly available data.

After doing my own reading, I could compare data from OSU's seismograph and...

Well, I didn't know, exactly. I supposed it would seem like an achievement to look at professional data and see a registered quake event I'd designed.

I opened a document on my laptop, noted the time, and observed that the seismograph seemed to be running properly. The explosion would be the final test, proof that my build was successful. And as soon as Ishmael returned, the detonation would commence.

But where was he? I'd sent my brother to double-check the explosives we'd set up in a field at the edge of the farm. It should have only taken a minute, but he still hadn't come back. It would be typical of him to lose interest in the experiment at the most pivotal moment.

I now realize I shouldn't have let him get involved in the first place. I should've wondered why he even *wanted* to be involved. But

I ignored the warning signs, because I enjoyed having an assistant. And yes, I also enjoyed having someone to lecture about science, even if he wasn't paying attention 82 percent of the time.

I paced back and forth—as much as one can pace in a twelve-by-fifteen-foot shed—getting increasingly anxious. I cleaned the lens of my telescope. I straightened bins of electronic components and checked the soldering I'd recently done on my Arduino. For a long moment, I gazed at my poster of the Andromeda galaxy.[1]

I'd just decided to go looking for Ishmael when the door flew open and he waltzed in, as if time was not, and had never been, of the essence.

He was eating an ice cream cone.

"You got ice cream? I told you to hurry, and you got *ice cream*?"

"Chill," Ishmael said. "It's from the house. It's not like I drove to Super Scoop or something."

"You know the rule about food and drink in the lab."

"Oh, come on," he said.

In my lifetime of being Ishmael's brother, I'd learned to pick and choose my battles. Food in the lab was a battle I *always* chose. I crossed my arms and waited.

"Seriously?" he whined. I watched strawberry ice cream drip down the side of the cone and threaten to fall on the clean floor. Finally, he sighed. "Okay, fine."

He turned back to the open door and tossed his ice cream cone into the field. I watched its trajectory with a scowl. "Was that necessary?"

---

1   Andromeda galaxy: the nearest major galaxy to the Milky Way, approximately 780 kiloparsecs from Earth.

"What?" Ishmael asked. "It's degradable, right?"

"You mean biodegradable."

"Whatever."

My blood pressure was rising. I just wanted to test my seismograph. "Can we get started now?"

Ishmael grinned, the ice cream already forgotten. "Let's do this."

I moved toward my equipment.

"Oh, wait!" Ishmael said. I turned back to him. With a dramatic flourish, he fastened the topmost button on his Hawaiian shirt— even in the chill of the September evening, Ishmael's personal style trended toward '80s beach movie. "All right. I feel professional now."

I ignored my brother's theatrics, because the moment had finally arrived. I forgot about him showing up late, with ice cream. I forgot about the questions he'd asked in the past two weeks, an eager glint in his eyes: *How big will this explosion be? Are you sure a bigger explosion wouldn't be better for your research? But, if you* did *want to make it bigger,* could *you?* I forgot everything except the task at hand.

I walked to the table where the equipment was set up and picked up the detonator.

"Dude," Ishmael said, "this is just like a movie."

It was *not* like a movie.

It was *science*.

"Are you sure I can't go outside to watch the explosion?" Ishmael asked.

"My answer is the same as the other twelve times you asked."

I wasn't expecting a large blast, and the explosives were set up decently far from us, but safety came first in all scientific pursuits.

"Can I press the button at least?"

"Shut up, Ishmael," I said.

I licked my lips. I took a deep breath. I looked affectionately at my seismograph, a machine I'd poured so much energy into.

Then I pressed the detonator.

The explosion rocked my lab. Shelves shook. A book fell off the table. Dust flew into the air.

And the sound.

It was *loud*.

Even after the noise subsided, my ears rang. A burnt smell filled my nostrils and dread twisted my stomach in knots. The explosion was larger than I'd anticipated. Much, much larger. How had my calculations been so inaccurate?

I looked at Ishmael. His eyes were wide, his face ashen.

"Shit," he said.

We turned and jetted for the door.

Ishmael beat me outside. I followed, racing across the field, choking on dust and smoke. When Ishmael stopped short, we collided. I moved around him to see what had caused his sudden halt.

There was a crater. The explosion caused a *crater*.

My brother and I stood side by side, gazing at the new geological feature of our parents' farm.

"Ishmael?" I said in an even tone that didn't betray my rising panic.

"Yeah?"

"Can you explain this to me?"

He hesitated. "I... Well, I thought the explosion should be a little bigger. You know. To help with the sizeograph or whatever."

"Goddammit, Ishmael."

In front of us, a patch of dry grass burst into flame. Ishmael and

I rushed over and frantically stomped the fire out. I was so focused, I didn't see my parents running through the field toward us. It wasn't until I heard their shouts that I looked up and saw their horrified expressions.

My father immediately joined the fire stomp. My mother gaped at the hole, one hand pressed to her chest. Across the field, I saw my sister, Maggie,[1] also making her way over to us.

By the time the fire—and the smaller fires it spawned—were extinguished, I was panting from exertion. My brother and father were hardly winded.

As I watched, Father's expression shifted from concern to rage. "What the hell happened here?"

"Vic—" Mother began.

"No," Father stopped her. "I want to hear what the boys have to say."

My heart sank. I was going to get my lab taken away. After the mishap last May, I was warned I was on my last chance before losing all out-of-school science privileges.[2]

"Let me see if they're okay first," Mother replied.

"They look fine to me," Maggie said, joining the rest of us. She nonchalantly pulled her brown ponytail through the back of her baseball cap, but there was no denying the gleam in her eyes. She was enjoying the spectacle.

Mother fussed over me, grabbing my chin and moving my face from side to side, as if making sure everything was still in place.

---

1   Magdalene Hofstadt, age thirteen.
2   The mishap involved the FCC contacting my parents regarding unlicensed radio broadcasts coming from our house—I'd been attempting to communicate with the International Space Station.

"Mother, really. I'm okay," I said, ducking away.

"Someone better start talking," Father ordered.

I opened my mouth to plead my case, but my brother beat me to it.

"We don't know what happened!"

Father crossed his arms, covering the Pittsburgh Pirates logo stretched across his chest. "You don't know?"

"Right," Ishmael confirmed.

"There's a hole the size of a pickup truck[3] in our field, and you *don't know* how it got here?"

"Well, see, we were in Gideon's lab doing, you know, science. And then there was this sound. Out of nowhere, boom! So we ran outside and..." Ishmael gestured toward the crater. "I think it came from the sky."

Mother gasped. Father narrowed his eyes. I silently pleaded for my brother to stop talking because I doubted there was even a 5 percent chance my parents would believe a mystery object had fallen from the sky.

"It came from the sky," Father repeated evenly.

"Right," Ishmael agreed.

"*What* came from the sky? I don't see anything here but a hole."

"Maybe it was, you know..." Ishmael floundered.

I wanted to make the situation go away. I *needed* to make the situation away. Which meant, unfortunately, assisting my brother. I looked at my parents and said, "A meteor. It could have been a meteor."

---

3   Later measurements showed the crater to have a radius of approximately 2.5 meters.

"Yeah, a meteor! It must have, like, fallen from the sky and exploded itself or something. That can happen with meteors, right?"

Technically, yes.

But before I could share that information, I saw a sight even more alarming than the crater: the chief of police walking across the field toward us.

INTERVIEW

ISHMAEL:

When I saw Chief Kaufman I totally freaked, because, like, how did she even get there so fast? And I kept looking at you for—

INTERVIEWER:

Do you remember what we talked about? About pretending I wasn't there?

ISHMAEL:

But you *were* there, dude. It's super weird to pretend you weren't.

INTERVIEWER:

Ishmael. This is supposed to be impartial. If the readers of this account know the person conducting interviews was intimately involved in the situation, they'll think the data is compromised.

ISHMAEL:

But *isn't it* compromised?

INTERVIEWER:

Please just do this my way.

ISHMAEL:

Also, can you not use the word *"intimate"*? It sounds sexual, which is pretty awkward.

INTERVIEWER:

It has nothing to do with sex. Intimate means close. I was *closely* involved with the situation.

ISHMAEL:

Then why can't you just say *closely*? Why do you have to make it weird?

INTERVIEWER:

Ishmael!

ISHMAEL:

Okay, fine. Whatever. Should I start over?

INTERVIEWER:

Just pick up where you left off.

ISHMAEL:

There's no reason to get upset, dude. Anyway, as I was *saying*... What was I saying? Oh yeah, I saw Chief Kaufman and was like, "Whoa, did you teleport here?" Then I realized she'd come over to see Dad and it was just, like, majorly bad timing that she got there during the explosion. I guess I wouldn't have said something fell from the sky if I'd known the police were gonna get involved, but by that time it was too late to take it back. But, I mean...it wasn't *that* bad of an excuse, was it?

EVENT:
Interrogation

DATE: SEPT. 7 (THURS.)

Chief Kaufman was sharp. *Too* sharp.

Father had been friends with her since their junior year of high school, when she'd petitioned to join the boy's baseball team—he was one of the few players who supported her. The petition failed, and some people say Kaufman's revenge for the slight was becoming the highest-ranking law enforcement official in town. Revenge or not, the job wasn't given to her unjustly. Since she'd become chief, Lansburg had the third-lowest crime rate of any town in Pennsylvania.[1]

While Father took the chief aside to speak privately, Ishmael and I retreated to our house. We waited in the living room, slumped on opposite ends of the floral-patterned sofa that had probably been in our family for as many decades as the farm itself.

Ishmael's eyes were fixed on the flat-screen television that hung above the fireplace—the only sign of modern life in the room. The sound had been muted, but the TV was still tuned to *Pitch, Please*,

---

1 It should be noted that the top two towns were Amish communities.

where a couple pitched a competition involving kittens and an obstacle course.

"This is bad," I announced.

"I know," Ishmael agreed. "It has to be animal cruelty or something."

"Not the *show*, Ishmael. Our current situation. Remember? The explosion?"

Ishmael waved off my concern. "It's fine, dude."

"*Nothing* is fine right now. Who knows what repercussions this might—"

I stopped abruptly when Mother burst into the living room, holding damp washcloths and a small pill bottle.

"Let's get you two cleaned up," she said.

She passed me a cloth and began wiping soot off Ishmael's face with the other.

"Mom, stop. I can do it myself," Ishmael said, pulling away.

"Take one of these at least," she replied, passing the pill bottle to him. "You need to recharge your electrolytes."

Ishmael rolled his eyes.

"You too, Gideon," she added.

"Mother. We've discussed this. I won't take those."

She ignored me and continued to move around the room, smoothing our hair and forcing glasses of water on us. When Ishmael tossed the bottle of myTality™ Recharge to me, I caught it because the other option was getting hit in the face. But I was *not* going to take any supplements.

After what felt like an eternity but must have been closer to thirty minutes, Father and Chief Kaufman entered the living room with Maggie in tow. My sister practically bounced up and down with joy over what was sure to be my and Ishmael's undoing.

"This is quite a mess," Kaufman said, giving me a discerning look.

She and Father sat in armchairs opposite the couch while Mother perched on the edge of the piano bench that, in my lifetime, had never been used for its intended purpose. Maggie hovered near the doorway to the kitchen.

"It's terrible, isn't it?" Mother said. "The state of the field. When I think of what could have happened..."

"Yes, Jane. Your boys are very lucky they're not in the hospital right now."

I liked nothing about how seriously she was taking the situation.

"Why don't you tell me exactly what happened?" Kaufman said, directing her shrewd gaze at Ishmael and me.

Though everyone knew Ishmael was the talker, the people person, Kaufman focused on me. I swallowed hard. I'd never done well in high-pressure situations. Nor did I excel at reading people. Perhaps the chief was merely being inquisitive. On the other hand, she could be building a case against me.

"Chief Kaufman...would you say that right now you're acting more as an officer of the law or Father's friend?"

She stared at me for a long beat. "Why would you ask me that?"

Why *would* I ask her that? I had quite possibly chosen the worst thing to say. I began to sweat.

"So, we were in the lab," Ishmael cut in, saving me, "working on an experiment."

Kaufman turned to my brother while pulling a pen and notebook from her pocket. "What kind of experiment?"

My heart sank. As soon as she heard about the seismograph, she'd guess the truth.

Luckily, Ishmael realized this as well. He leaned forward and smiled conspiratorially at Kaufman. "Okay, you caught us. There wasn't *really* an experiment. Gideon and I have been really busy lately. You know, it's my senior year, and both of us have jobs now. And Gideon's taking these online classes, like, for *fun*. We hardly have time to spend together. We were actually just hanging out in the lab. Bonding."

Maggie snorted and Mother shot her a sharp look.

"Bonding," Kaufman repeated.

Ishmael nodded and smiled again. The chief seemed to thaw a bit. It never ceased to amaze me, Ishmael's ability to charm anyone and everyone.

But then she said, "Is there a reason this bonding had to take place in a makeshift lab?"

I bristled at the word *makeshift*.

"Well, you know," Ishmael said, "sometimes we talk about things we don't want our parents to hear."

"Like what?"

Ishmael glanced at Mother and Father. "Well, like…Gideon was asking for relationship advice."

I was going to kill him.

"Gideon, do you have a boyfriend?" Mother asked eagerly, as if there weren't more important matters at hand, as if I wasn't currently the subject of a *police investigation*.

"Yeah, Gideon," Maggie said, her face glowing. "*Do* you have a boyfriend? Because I heard that you and Owen Campbell—"

"Must we discuss my love life right now?" I snapped. At the time, I was blissfully unaware of how much my love life would become intertwined with what eventually befell Lansburg.

Chief Kaufman said, "Right, let's move on. You were in the shed talking, and you heard an explosion."

Ishmael nodded. "So we ran outside and, well, you saw what it's like out there."

"Why don't you tell me what *you* saw," Kaufman replied.

"Well, there's a crater, you know? It's pretty obvious something fell from the sky."

"A meteor," I offered. "Or, technically, a meteoroid."

"You saw evidence of this *meteoroid*?"

I hesitated long enough for Ishmael to jump in. "Well, not *saw*, exactly. But there was a sound right before the explosion."

Kaufman raised her eyebrows. "What sound was that?"

"Sort of a falling sound," Ishmael said.

I cringed. Maggie laughed out loud.

"Maggie, go to your room," Father said.

"But—"

"Right now."

With a huff, Maggie stomped up the stairs. When she was gone, Kaufman said, "What exactly is a *falling* sound?"

"You know, like a whooshing," Ishmael replied confidently.

He was going to give me a heart attack. I needed to reel him in.

"Actually," Mother spoke up, "I might have heard a falling sound too."

What?

"Didn't you hear it, Vic? Right before the explosion?"

Father frowned. "I must have missed it."

What in the world was going on?

Chief Kaufman looked back and forth between my parents before jotting something on her notepad. Then she turned to Ishmael and me again. "Don't meteors usually leave residue?"

Finally, something I could answer with confidence. "Actually, this isn't unprecedented. Have you heard of the Tunguska event?"

Chief Kaufman shook her head.

"In the early 1900s there was an explosion in Russia that destroyed several hundred square miles of forest. It's generally accepted that a meteoroid falling to Earth burned so hot it burst before hitting the ground, creating a massive explosion but leaving no trace of itself."

Ishmael nodded hard enough for his hair to flop forward into his eyes. "Yes, something exactly like that must have happened."

"The Tunguska event, you said?" Kaufman asked.

I nodded and she wrote it in her notepad.

"And in the 1930s there was an event along the Curuçá River in Brazil where—"

"That's all right," Chief Kaufman said. "We don't need to cover every instance."

I was somewhat disappointed. It was rare for me to find people to discuss my interests with, and *nothing* interested me more than astronomy.

"I think I have enough for now," Kaufman said. She flipped her notebook shut and stood. "I'll look into this and call with any developments."

A wave of relief washed over me. Father walked the chief to the door, goodbyes were said, and I knew from the light in Ishmael's eyes that he thought we'd gotten away with something spectacular.

"We'll discuss this more tomorrow," Father told us. "I'm going to bed."

Mother stood to follow him. She watched him ascend the creaky, wooden stairs, and it wasn't until he was gone that she said, "Are you sure you're feeling okay? Is there anything I can get you before I go up?"

Ishmael and I shook our heads.

"I love you boys so much."

"Love you too, Mom," Ishmael said.

"I want you to take the myTality Recharge," Mother told me.

I sighed.

She moved toward the stairs, but stopped and turned back. "And boys?"

We looked at her.

"If there are more explosives on this property, I want them removed *immediately*."

EVENT:
Immediate
Aftermath

DATE: SEPT. 8 (FRI.)

I woke up with a sense that something was missing. My gaze flicked around the bedroom to my NASA posters, the scale model of the Saturn V, the mural of the solar system I'd painted on the wall when I was twelve. Everything seemed to be in place, except...

Data, I suddenly realized. I'd been so caught up in the explosion the night before, I'd forgotten my *experiment*.

I sat up quickly. Despite everything, I was still anxious to know if my seismograph had worked. If it had, the rest of the mess would almost be worthwhile. *Almost*.

Unfortunately, to check the seismograph, I'd have to go to my lab, which would mean passing my parents. I was sure they weren't any happier about the explosion after having the night to dwell on it.

There was no use putting off seeing them, though. I got out of bed, dressed in my usual T-shirt and cargo pants, and followed the smell of breakfast down our rickety staircase.

In the kitchen, Father stood at the stove. His favorite apron was tied over his workout clothes, the one with script across the front that said *What's cookin', Mr. Hofstadt?* Maggie already sat at our splintery farmhouse breakfast table, devouring a pile of pancakes.

Was my family going to proceed with the normal morning routine, as if unexplained explosions and police investigations were everyday occurrences on the farm?

"Morning," Father said, passing me a plate.

I sat across from my sister and began eating. The pancakes were flavorful, but dry. I eyed the syrup. Should I risk it? Syrup made pancakes significantly more appetizing, but it was impossible to use without getting traces on my face or hands. And I despised being sticky.

"What are your plans today?" Maggie asked.

I swallowed a bite of food, deciding that dry pancakes were the more practical choice. "It's a school day. My plan is to attend school, like I do every school day.[1] Why?"

"Just wondering if there's anywhere I should avoid. You know, places you might blow up next."

"That's enough, Maggie," Father said, pointing at her with the spatula.

Maggie smiled sweetly.

My intention was for there to be no more explosions, on that day or *any* day. Unless, of course, a future experiment called for it.

Mother buzzed into the kitchen, briefcase in hand. She wore a blazer with a purple shirt underneath, which meant she was anticipating a busy day. Purple was her power color, worn whenever she needed a boost of luck.

---

1   Technically inaccurate, being that there *were* days I hadn't attended school on a school day, e.g., days when I was sick.

INTERVIEW

Subject #2, Magdalene (Maggie) Hofstadt:

Of course I knew my brothers blew up the field. I figured it had something to do with one of Gideon's experiments. And I wasn't the only one who thought so, by the way. No one believed that meteor story. *No one.*

EVENT: Immediate Aftermath
(CONT.)

When I stepped through the doors of Irving High School, I still hadn't gotten a chance to check my seismograph reading. Maybe that was for the better. I should forget the explosion. It was much more important to concentrate on my studies—more important than ever, since Sara Kang's GPA had alarmingly surpassed mine, jeopardizing my chances of being valedictorian.

Unfortunately, it turned out ignoring the explosion wouldn't be simple. When I checked my phone between second and third periods, I had a text from Cass.[1]

> A METEOR CRASHED INTO YOUR HOUSE LAST NIGHT???

---

1 Cassidy Robinson, age sixteen, my longtime best friend.

I stopped in the middle of the hall and briefly shut my eyes.

Ishmael.

Ishmael, who'd never managed to keep his mouth shut about *anything*. How many people had he told? What exactly had he told them?

I fired off a text to Cass saying no, that was *not* the case, and I'd explain at lunch. Then I opened my phone contacts and sent another message.

TEXT CONVERSATION

Participants: Gideon Hofstadt, Ishmael Hofstadt

Are you telling people about last night? — GH

IH — no[1]

i mean

kinda

but just like 2

Two? Two what? People? Classrooms? Hordes? — GH

IH — ppl

Could you please not do that anymore? — GH

dude

IH — you srsly need to chill

---

1   To my chagrin, Ishmael had turned off autocorrect on his phone because it "suppressed his individuality."

EVENT:
Immediate
Aftermath

(CONT.)

I did not "need to chill."

I needed to evaluate the situation and prepare for every possible outcome.

In my brief moments of free time between classes, I researched legal implications of the explosion. Unfortunately, the information I found online was contradictory and muddled.

According to one website, making homemade explosives was only criminal in certain contexts. For example, if I was planning to sell the explosives, it was illegal. If the explosive wounded someone, it was *ultra*-illegal. Neither of those stipulations applied to me.

On the other hand, a different site claimed that in some states, one could receive jail time for "combining raw materials into a mixture capable of creating an explosion." I tried to search Pennsylvania-specific laws to no avail. The closest thing I discovered was that Pennsylvania allowed the sale of fireworks containing up to fifty milligrams of explosive material, which roughly equated to one roman candle.

The explosion in my yard was *not* caused by a Roman candle.

Basically, either Ishmael and I were in the clear, or we'd end up sharing a cell.

It was my own fault. I shouldn't have let my brother participate in the experiment. After all the practical jokes I've endured from him, I should've known his sudden interest in science had a punch line.

Truly, I shouldn't have even broken the rule[1] I'd put into place last year, after he spilled orange soda all over a circuit board I was working on. (He claimed it only happened because Kepler had clawed him.)

My worries weren't alleviated as the day went on. Six separate individuals approached me before lunch to inquire about the "meteor." This was especially concerning because there were some *weeks* when I didn't speak to six different people.

By the time I slid into my usual seat in the cafeteria, my body was a network of tension. Shoulders tight, head pounding, teeth beginning to ache. Stress made me clench my jaw, which in turn sent pain radiating outward.

There was no one at the lunch table yet, and I hoped for a quiet day. Sometimes our table filled up with random acquaintances. Other times, when everyone was off doing various activities, it was only me, Cass, and Arden.[2]

As I removed food from the paper bag Father packed, Cass slid her lunch tray onto the table next to me.

Her curls were pulled into a ponytail, and she wore a pair of

---

1   The Rule: Ishmael was not to come within fifty feet of my lab for any reason, at any time.

2   Arden Byrd, age fifteen, a recent transplant to Lansburg following her parents' divorce.

retro glasses. Her polka-dot dress looked like it was straight from the 1950s. Cass was of the opinion that costumes were more entertaining than regular clothes, so therefore her clothes should be as costume-like as possible.

"You know women were oppressed in the fifties," I said as she plopped into her chair.

"And as a black woman, I wouldn't even be allowed to sit at this table with you. Doesn't mean I can't appreciate the *fashion*." She gave me an expectant look. "But don't we have something *much* more important to discuss right now?"

"Such as?" I asked, playing dumb.

"Um, how about your house getting blown to smithereens?"

Cass gazed at me eagerly. I was 67 percent sure she'd be disappointed when she found out the truth wasn't as cinematic as she'd hoped.

"You must realize that's an exaggeration."

"But was there really a meteor?"

"Technically it would've been a *meteoroid*."

"Whatever. *Was* there one?"

I glanced around to see if anyone was within hearing range.

"Of course not."

Cass sighed dramatically. "Hells bells, Gideon Hofstadt! How dare you taunt me with the possibility of something exciting finally happening, only to cruelly dash my hopes?"

I couldn't help but smile.

My friendship with Cass was a mystery to most people. Honestly, I didn't know what made it work. Cass had other friends and was popular within her theater crowd. And I had other...well, maybe not *friends*, but *acquaintances*. People I attended Science Club with, anyway.

But despite our different interests and social groups, Cass was one of the few people who understood me. And in turn, she was one of the few people *I* understood. Friendships had been built on less.

Knowing it would thrill her, I said, "But there *was* an explosion."

"Go on," she said, sitting up straighter.

"It was my experiment. Remember the seismograph? I set off explosives to test it."

"Got a little overzealous, huh?"

"No," I replied as Cass began eating a slice of pizza, with no regard to how messy it was. I envied her. "*Ishmael* got overzealous."

"Well, praise Zeus[1] for the Ishmaels of the world. Life would be so boring without them."

"Boring, maybe," I said. "But less stressful too."

I told Cass about the nonexistent meteor, Kaufman's investigation, and the trouble I'd be in if the truth came out.

"Maybe the truth *won't* come out," Cass said. "Maybe Lansburg will become a famous meteor crash site, and the Discovery Channel will make a show about it, and *of course* I'll have to give them an exclusive interview."

"See, Cass, that's the difference between you and me. I don't *want* to imagine that."

"You didn't even hear the part where I'm discovered and get offered a movie role and become the third-youngest person to ever win an Oscar."

"I've always admired your logical thought processes."

---

1   Zeus: Greek god of the sky and ruler of Mount Olympus. Why Cass chose to praise him over Earth's other deities, I didn't know.

Cass threw back her head and laughed with the kind of abandon I'd never have.

"The worst part," I continued, once she'd calmed down, "is I never even got to check my reading to—"

I stopped talking abruptly when Arden appeared at the table and pulled out a chair. It wasn't that I didn't trust Arden. Not *exactly*. But we'd only met midway through the previous year. That wasn't enough time to really get a read on a person.

For me, anyway.

Admittedly, I've been accused of having "trust issues."

"Gideon, are you okay?" Arden asked, twisting a rope of her long, pale hair like she always did when she worried. "I heard what happened."

"I'm fine," I assured her.

"A meteor really crashed into your yard?"

I only hesitated for a moment. "Meteoroid. And yes, it seems that way."

"How horrible."

I felt a pang of guilt. Arden was already scared of half the things outside her front door. Now I'd given her something else to fear: objects falling from the sky.

"It wasn't so bad," I said. "It was over in a second."

Despite my assurances, Arden shivered and wrapped her cardigan more tightly around her shoulders. Even in summer, Arden often wore a sweater.

"How did you hear about the meteor, anyway?" I asked.

"I think you mean *meteoroid*," Cass said with a sly grin.

Arden shrugged. "Everyone's heard about it."

Well, wasn't that wonderful.

"Owen asked about it in third period," Cass broke in.

I was struck with the perplexing feeling I often got when Owen's name was mentioned. I both wanted to act as if I couldn't care less, and eagerly ask to hear everything he'd said and the exact tone in which he said it.

"Oh," I replied, deciding that was safe middle ground.

"He wanted to make sure you were all fine and dandy."

He already knew I was fine. He'd texted me himself, probably right after he'd heard about the explosion. But he checked with Cass to *doubly* make sure.

"That was nice," I said evenly.

"It *was* nice," Cass agreed. "Even if I'm still annoyed at him."

Cass had yet to forgive Owen for getting the lead role in the fall play—a role she desperately wanted. Never mind that it was a *male* role. Cass had been cast as leads, male and female, since freshman year. Her portrayal of Ichabod Crane in *The Legend of Sleepy Hollow* had been particularly epic.

"Owen likes you so much," Arden said dreamily, the meteor apparently forgotten.

"Well," I mumbled, "I...I have a lot of respect for Owen."

"Why don't you like him?" she asked for the hundredth time. "He's gorgeous."

I felt my face getting red. Cass smiled and raised an eyebrow at me, a look that clearly meant, *Are you ever gonna tell Arden about you and Owen?*

I ignored her.

It wasn't that Arden had ever *done* anything untrustworthy. It wasn't that she'd spread gossip. Still...I wasn't ready to be completely candid with her.

Luckily, or as it turned out, *unluckily*, I was saved from answering by a commotion at the other end of the cafeteria. From her vantage point, Cass was the first to see what was happening.

"Uh, Houston, we have a problem."

I turned and followed her gaze to a sight that filled me with immeasurable dread: my brother, standing on a chair, giving a speech.

I couldn't hear what he said over the noise in the room, but from the way he gestured, it was clearly an exciting topic.

"Please excuse me," I said stiffly to my friends.

I marched across the cafeteria, jaw once again clenched so tight I could've shattered teeth.

My rage increased when I got close enough to hear him. Fratricide[1] was becoming more appealing by the second.

"So I ran outside," Ishmael preached, "just in time to see a meteor whizzing through the air!"

The crowd around my brother made noises of approval and urged him to go on. Only one person standing in the back was unimpressed.

"Who cares about a boring meteor?" the guy mumbled, shuffling off to another section of the lunchroom.

Ishmael frowned after him for a moment before someone else asked, "Then what happened?"

"Right. Anyway, so I saw the meteor...the *fiery* meteor, and... Hey! What are you doing?"

---

1   Fratricide: the killing of one's brother.

"Show's over," I announced, tugging Ishmael off the chair.

"Gideon... *Ow!* Come on, what's your problem?"

I didn't speak until I'd pulled him safely away from the center of the room. "What are you *doing*?"

"I was... Nothing."

"Nothing!" I snapped. "I specifically told you to keep your mouth shut."

"Dude, you're being way too uptight," Ishmael said, shaking my hand off him.

Was I? I felt a twinge of doubt. It wasn't the first time I'd been accused of being uptight.[1]

"I just don't see what you could possibly gain by talking about this."

Ishmael seemed to consider it. "I dunno. I mean...does it really need to be about *gaining* something? Can't I just like telling stories or whatever?"

"Yes. You can like telling stories. But *I* like having a future. And my future involves attending MIT[2] and getting a job with NASA and making an important discovery that rocks the field of space exploration. Do you understand?"

"I actually don't understand at all."

I took a deep breath and spoke firmly and slowly. "Your story-telling could get me in legal trouble that derails my entire future. We could go to *jail* for this."

"Dude, that's definitely not going to happen."

---

1   Also: stuffy, rigid, tense, and boring.

2   MIT: Massachusetts Institute of Technology, one of the world's top-ranked universities; known for its emphasis on the physical sciences and engineering.

Ishmael's confidence that all outcomes would turn out favorable for him amazed me. In a way, I admired it.

"Just please tone it down," I said, a pleading note entering my voice.

"Okay, okay," Ishmael conceded. His expression clouded. "Apparently, meteors aren't that interesting anyway."

"Good. Then you have no reason to keep talking about them."

Without any real expectation that he would stay quiet, I returned to the table with my friends, which had unfortunately filled up with other people.

"What was that about?" Arden asked.

"Just my brother being his usual attention-seeking self," I replied.

In between bites of pizza, Cass said, "Ishmael's lucky he's so freaking cute. Otherwise he'd never get away with anything."

Interlude
Musings on Attractiveness

Do I think my brother often "gets a pass" because he's conventionally attractive? Yes. I do.

Despite his fondness for Hawaiian shirts and an aversion to combing his hair, Ishmael has always been good-looking.

And I...

I wouldn't say I'm *ugly*.

But I don't share my brother's above-average height, strong jawline, or unexpectedly graceful way of moving. I *certainly* don't share his unblemished skin.

I don't consider myself *ugly*, but I'm not handsome either.

Before you jump to conclusions, you should know I don't resent Ishmael for this. Being conventionally attractive has never been an ambition of mine. Unlike so many people who say "Looks aren't everything," I mean it. I would *never* trade my mind for my looks.

I'm not even claiming I have superior intelligence. But my mind calculates data in a way that's specific to me, the same as yours does in a way that's specific to you. And I love it. I love my mind. It means more to me than my appearance ever could.

Still, I'll concede that based on our looks, Ishmael and I have had very different life experiences. I've seen the way people treat him. Everything he does seems charming, and a smile can get him out of trouble.

And maybe in the context of the explosion and everything that followed, Ishmael's attractiveness benefitted me too. After all, from the very first moment, we were in the situation together.

INTERVIEW

Subject #1, Ishmael Hofstadt:

The thing is, at lunch, when Matthew said meteors were boring, I realized he was right. I mean, don't meteors fall practically every day? And what about meteor showers? Like, a thousand meteors all fall at the same time. That's why I changed my story...just *slightly*. I wanted it to be a little bit cooler, that's all.

EVENT:
Interview

DATE: SEPT. 8 (FRI.)

I went straight to my lab after school. For all of my attempts to put the previous night from my mind, I *had* to see if the seismograph worked. Kepler twisted around my feet, purring for attention, or maybe just expressing his own eagerness to see the results.

And there they were, the results of my experiment. The seismograph functioned perfectly. What's more, when I opened my laptop and pulled up OSU's seismography data, I saw that the explosion had registered there too.

I'd succeeded. Sure, there had been more trouble than expected, but isn't trouble worthwhile when it's in the name of science? Shouldn't the first priority *always* be the pursuit of information, of discovering new and exciting things about the world?

The thought gave me pause. I reached down and scratched Kepler's head while I sorted out what was bothering me.

Yes, discovery should come first.

But I hadn't actually *discovered* anything, had I? I'd only duplicated a machine whose earliest prototype came from 132 AD. Nor would I stumble onto new information with my seismograph. I'd contributed nothing to the world.

I was hit with a wave of melancholy. The feeling of not being quite *enough*. I wanted to invent something of my own. Discover something special, accomplish something no one had before. I wanted to contribute to science in a *meaningful* way.

Truth be told, I wanted glory.

My phone dinged with a text message, and my musings screeched to a halt.

IH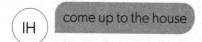

I ignored him. A moment later:

IH

I decided to comply only because it was getting chilly and I hadn't set up the space heater for the season.[1] Ishmael was the sort of person who'd interrupt important work to show you a YouTube video of a sloth playing guitar, or to see if you agreed that his fried egg was in the exact shape of Texas, so my expectations were low.

I crossed the field and approached the farmhouse from the back. In the kitchen, Ishmael sat at the table with a man who looked vaguely familiar. He was in his midtwenties, tall and lanky, wearing an ill-fitting suit. The jacket was too wide for his narrow shoulders and the cuffs hung over his wrists. While I wasn't immensely knowledgeable

---

1   My lab was kept running with a generator, so it had electricity, but heating and cooling options were limited.

about fashion, I did know wearing a suit that wasn't properly tailored looked less professional than not wearing a suit at all.

The suit-wearer had a notepad and pen on the table in front of him.

"Hello," I said cautiously.

He leapt to his feet, grinned, and extended his hand. "You must be Gideon. Adam Frykowski."

As we shook—him too eagerly, I might add—I searched my brain until his name connected.

"You work for the *Lansburg Daily Press*," I said.

Frykowski's face lit up. Just another of us poor human souls looking for recognition, for someone to acknowledge that they exist.

"I do!"

"You edit the obituaries[2]," I continued.

Frykowski's smile sagged. "Well, that's my main assignment, but I get others. Sometimes."

"Sit down, Gideon," Ishmael said from the table, businesslike. "Mr. Frykowski wants to discuss last night."

I sat, but raised my eyebrows. "I don't recall anyone *dying* in the explosion."

Frykowski joined us at the table, a fervent light in his eyes. "But there *was* an explosion?"

"Where are our parents?" I asked Ishmael.

"Mom's still working, and Dad took Maggie shopping for new cleats."

"Should we wait for them?"

"It's fine, Gideon," Ishmael assured me. "He only has a few questions."

---

2   The previous year I'd been fleetingly obsessed with population and spent hours comparing births versus deaths in Lansburg.

Clearly, Ishmael would talk to whomever he wanted no matter how I tried to contain the story. Better to be present during it so I'd at least know what tales he was telling.

"Make it quick," I said.

And the song and dance began again. Ishmael became animated. He told the greatly exaggerated story of how we were innocently minding our own business when something came from the sky and exploded in our field.

"And at first you suspected it was a meteor?" Frykowski asked.

"Meteoroid," I offered.

But what did he mean by *at first*?

"Did you actually *see* the meteoroid?"

Ishmael hesitated, probably trying to sort through the various versions of the story he'd told all day. "No," he finally admitted.

"You saw nothing until *after* the impact."

Ishmael nodded.

"Yet you're sure it was a meteor?"

Meteoroid. But I kept my mouth shut.

"Well," Ishmael said, "we kinda assumed."

"You assumed, but you don't have any *evidence* that a meteor hit the ground, is that correct?" Frykowski pressed.

I took a long look at him, a tight, anxious feeling spreading through my chest. Had I underestimated Frykowski? Was our story about to be blown open by an obituary editor, of all people?

Ishmael licked his lips. He was getting nervous too, which increased my own unease. "Well, no. We don't actually have any evidence."

"Meteors often leave fragments," Frykowski said.

"But not every time," Ishmael replied.

"Still, it's quite rare for there to be an explosion with no remaining evidence."

"It happened this one time in Tunsga...Tuska... Somewhere in Russia."

I needed to step in and help my brother. I needed to regain control of the situation. But I remained frozen, watching the interrogation play out with fascinated horror.

"The Tunguska event happened in 1908," Frykowski said. "Certainly, scientists investigating it today would have different insights."

"But there was this other time in Belize—"

"Brazil."

"Right, Brazil." Beads of sweat formed at Ishmael's hairline. "Gideon really knows more about it than I do."

"Listen," Frykowski said. His expression turned grave, as if he was finally getting down to business. "I don't think there was a meteor."

Speak, I commanded myself. But it seemed I'd forgotten how. What would happen when Frykowski exposed us as frauds? Would Ishmael and I be arrested? Would we get harsher sentences because, in addition to causing the explosion, we *lied* about it?

Ishmael swallowed hard. "So, like...what *do* you think?"

"My cousin attends your high school," Frykowski replied. "She overheard something interesting today."

I frowned at this new development. Who was his cousin? Had she been eavesdropping when I told Cass about the seismograph?

I glanced at Ishmael. He stared back with an innocent expression. A far *too* innocent expression. Oh no.

"What, exactly, was overheard?" I asked, finally finding my voice.

Frykowski leaned forward, his gaze intense. He looked back and forth between me and my brother. "I'd like you to be honest with me. Last night, did you have a close encounter with extraterrestrials?"

I nearly choked. I studied Frykowski's face for the hint of a smile, but his expression was dead serious.

This couldn't be happening.

My brother couldn't *possibly* have blamed the explosion on aliens.

I looked at Ishmael.

He smiled sheepishly.

He'd absolutely blamed the explosion on aliens.

To buy myself a moment of time before I full-on panicked, I said, "Since when does the *Daily Press* cover extraterrestrials?"

"Oh," Frykowski said, seeming surprised. "This isn't for the *Daily Press*."

"What *is this* then?"

"I run my own online news resource."

"You mean a blog?" I replied.

"You could call it that."

"Well, I hate to break it to you, but—"

"But we don't really want the whole alien thing to be public," Ishmael interrupted.

No.

No, no, no.

"So you *do* think the explosion was extraterrestrial in nature?" Frykowski asked.

At the same time that I was shaking my head, Ishmael said, "Mr. Frykowski, I'm *certain* of it."

TEXT CONVERSATION

Participants: Gideon Hofstadt, Cassidy Robinson

> Do you know anything about a blog run by a local reporter named Adam Frykowski? **GH**

Omg

YES

Its called The Light Binger

Light *Bringer **CR**

> Sounds religious. **GH**

Not religious

It means like bringing information to light

Conspiracies and stuff **CR**

> Does it have any merit? **GH**

Meaning??? **CR**

CR: If you're asking if the stories are real, uh, NO

CR: But it's totally entertaining

CR: Bigfoot sightings and stuff

GH: And aliens, I presume.

CR: So many aliens

GH: Fantastic.

CR: Why the sudden interest

CR: ???

GH: Well, Cass, funny story...

The following blog post was reprinted with permission of lightbringernews.com.

THEY'RE HERE: EXTRATERRESTRIAL CONTACT MADE IN LANSBURG

By Adam Frykowski
Posted September 9–7:16 a.m.

LANSBURG, PA—The explosion rang out on Thursday evening, carrying across the overgrown fields of the Hofstadt property.

Lansburg buzzed with talk of a meteor fallen to Earth, but less than twenty-four hours later, the truth was revealed: the explosion was the result of a beam of light shot from an unidentified flying object.

The only witnesses to the close encounter were Ishmael and Gideon Hofstadt, ages seventeen and sixteen. The teenagers were in a nearby converted shed when the explosion occurred.

"We ran outside when we heard a strange sound, sort of like a humming," says Ishmael Hofstadt. "Just a few yards away there was this bright light hovering in the sky. And a laser, like, shot straight down into our field. Then the light flew away."

This is not the first sighting of mystery lights in the skies above Lansburg. There have been at least twelve reports of UFOs from the year 2000 to the present, with three of them occurring this year alone.

Are these incidents connected? And if so, why did the aliens choose *now* to make physical contact, and why in such an explosive manner?

The Light Bringer continues to investigate.

Click here to subscribe to our newsletter!

EVENT:
Aliens Arrive
DATE: SEPT. 9 (SAT.)

Deviating from our usual morning norms, my brother was bright-eyed and alert as he steered our Jeep into town, while I couldn't stop yawning. Unlike Ishmael, who took joy from his job at Adrenaline X-treme,[1] I wasn't looking forward to my shift at the ice cream parlor. I never did. On top of that, I was still furious.

"How come you're so out of it?" Ishmael asked over the noise of the radio.

"I was up late reading Adam Frykowski's blog," I grumbled.

"Anything good?"

"Well, Ishmael, the Garden of Eden has been located, a twenty-eight-pound baby was born in New Philadelphia, and the Mothman is terrorizing West Virginians again."

"Cool," he said with a grin.

Cool. He thought the blog was *cool.* I wanted to avoid rehashing

---

1   Adrenaline X-treme: the extreme sports store where Ishmael regularly got bonuses for upselling customers, despite never having played an extreme sport in his life.

the argument we'd had the previous night, after Frykowski left, but Ishmael wasn't making it easy.

"Actually, since *we* were featured on the website this morning, I think the situation is decidedly *un*cool. Our family is going to become the mockery of this entire town."

"Not gonna happen," Ishmael said confidently, waving a hand at me.

"Ten and two," I reminded him.

"Maybe don't give driving advice until you can actually drive," Ishmael replied. "And seriously, no one reads that blog. Except you, apparently."

At least one other person had *already* read it. Cass texted the link only moments after it went live. She must have been eagerly refreshing the website.

"I just don't understand why you did this," I said.

"I told you, like, fifty times last night. I only said the alien thing to a couple people at school. I didn't think anyone else would find out."

I dug my fingernails into the armrest, attempting to harness my fury. "Yes. But when someone else *did* find out, you could have put a stop to it instead of—"

"Gideon, if you get caught in a lie, you don't just cave. That only makes things worse."

"I'm fairly certain the exact opposite is true."

Ishmael glanced at me and I resisted the urge to tell him to keep his eyes on the road. "Seriously, no one reads that blog. This isn't a big deal. Besides, it *could* have been aliens."

Suddenly, I was much less tired. I turned to my brother. "No, it could *not* have been aliens. It couldn't have been aliens because that would be illogical and impossible, but also because we know for a fact that *we* caused the explosion."

"Besides that part, I mean."

I rubbed at my forehead. A headache was already forming behind my eyes.

At least Ishmael was right about one thing: Frykowski's blog didn't appear to get much traffic. Most of his posts had fewer than three comments, and the only consistent user was someone called CIAyylmao2001, who mainly wanted to know why Frykowski wasn't covering the 9/11 conspiracy.

Maybe my alarm was needless. No one would see the alien article. And if someone *did* stumble on it, their judgment would be of Frykowski, not us. No one in Lansburg would assume the normally steady Hofstadt family thought their farm was under alien attack.

Soon, everything—the explosion, the meteor, the aliens—would blow over. There'd be a new scandal, and no one would remember the crater in our field or its mysterious origins.

Or so I thought.

Interlude
Lansburg, Pennsylvania

At first glance, Lansburg wouldn't appear much different from other rural American towns. Thirty miles south of Pittsburgh, it was founded by German settlers in 1823.

Though it began as a humble farming community, tourism kept Lansburg alive from the second half of the twentieth century to the present. No, it wasn't Disney World, but downtown Lansburg boasted a charming, old-world village—though I questioned the authenticity of Ye Olde Fudge Shoppe and the Pizza Haus.

Admittedly, Main Street *was* attractive, with its German architecture, cobblestone streets, and faux gaslights. Or perhaps I should say that *once* it was charming. Before the lava lamp was installed.

Yes, you read correctly. *Lava lamp.* But you likely already know about this. After all, the sixty-three-foot lava lamp prominently rising from downtown's central square was Lansburg's *real* claim to fame.

The lamp was the brainchild of Benjamin Irving, an eccentric inventor who retired to Lansburg in 1957. In the late '60s, when psychedelic decor was at peak popularity, Irving decided to build the world's largest lava lamp. Just to see if he could. Just so he could tell the world, *Yes, I did this odd, impossible-seeming thing.* Incredibly, the town of Lansburg agreed to have the monstrosity installed in the very center of town, surrounded by quaint shops with thatched roofs.

Taller than most of the surrounding buildings, the lamp, filled with pink "lava," even had an observation deck wrapping around it so viewers could get up close and personal with the rapidly heating and cooling gobs of paraffin. Or at least, they could *in theory*.

Unfortunately for Irving, the liquid in his lava lamp was based on the original formula. Along with paraffin and mineral oil, the lamp was filled with carbon tetrachloride. And in 1970, the United States banned carbon tetrachloride due to its toxicity.

In compliance with the new law, Irving's lamp was turned off, but that didn't deter him. Lava-lamp makers had already come up with a new formula to achieve the same result, and though the recipe was kept secret, Irving knew that given enough time, he'd be able to figure it out.

Sadly, he died before that happened.

The lava lamp remained standing but hadn't been in operation for almost fifty years. That didn't stop some of Lansburg from celebrating Irving as a local hero.

And it didn't stop tourists, who apparently didn't mind that the lamp wasn't lit and actively swirling with lava. Just seeing the giant structure seemed to be enough. Busloads came from Pittsburgh on weekends—mostly groups from retirement homes—and they happily took pictures in front of the dormant lamp before buying their great-grandchildren five-dollar T-shirts at Ye Olde Souvenir Shoppe.

Every few years someone petitioned to have the lava lamp removed, citing it as an eyesore to our picturesque town. But enough other people loved it for the tourism revenue. For better or worse, it seemed that Benjamin Irving's lava lamp would be a permanent fixture downtown.

I should have considered that for the people of Lansburg, people already accustomed to the bizarre, the idea of aliens might not have been such a stretch.

EVENT:
Aliens Arrive
(CONT.)

Super Scoop was located directly across the street from the lava lamp, where a tour group was already gathered. Like most Saturdays in the fall, downtown would get busy, but it would be a few hours before people flocked to the ice cream parlor.

Owen[1] was already behind the counter when I entered the store, wearing the old-fashioned white paper cap that looked absurd on everyone but him.

"*What* is happening at your house?" he asked when he saw me, looking both amused and baffled.

"What do you mean?" I ignored how my heart rate sped up in his presence and made my way through the 1950s-style ice cream parlor—yet another Lansburg anachronism—to the staff room so I could clock in.

"I'm just a little confused," Owen said lightly, "because a few

---

1   Owen Campbell, age seventeen. Handsome, friendly, intelligent. Well respected for being a top athlete, a star of the theater department, *and* student body vice president.

days ago everything was normal and now you've got explosions on your property and apparently aliens are the cause."

I stopped.

How had he heard about aliens? Did Ishmael blab to more people than he claimed, or had Owen read Frykowski's blog? Either way, it wasn't good.

"Well, yes...I can see how that would be confusing."

"And when I text you, I get one-word responses."

"Right," I mumbled absently, my mind still on aliens. "Wait, what?"

Owen shrugged, his previous good humor dimmed. He began needlessly wiping down the counter. "I kinda feel like you're ignoring me."

"I've just been busy. And I'm eighty-six percent sure—"

Owen groaned. "Please no arbitrary percentages right now."

"They're not arbit—"

"Gideon."

"Okay," I said. I looked longingly at the door of the staff room, wishing I could disappear through it. "I haven't been ignoring you. I promise."

I truly hadn't been. I just wasn't good at texting or calling and could easily go days without social interaction. I'd tried explaining to Owen that my introversion[2] had nothing to do with him, but he never seemed to believe me.

As if on cue, he said, "I wish I knew where I stood with you."

I glanced around the ice cream parlor, as if we might have suddenly gained an audience. Seeing no one, I took a step closer to Owen. "Please don't make this a relationship thing."

---

2   Introversion: a term popularized by psychologist Carl Jung, referring to people who are drained by social encounters and prefer solitary pursuits.

Anger flashed in his brown eyes. He threw down his dishcloth and turned to me. "Is that what this is about? There are *explosions* on your property, but you can't keep me in the loop because then I might think this is a *relationship?*"

"That's not what—"

"Here's some info: this *is* a relationship. Just because you're too scared to call it—"

"I'm not *scared*, I just—"

"Stop. I've heard it a million times."

I stopped.

I waited.

Owen sighed. He reached up and adjusted his cap, even though it was still perfectly seated on his perfect hair. Everything about Owen was perfect. It still felt surreal that *I* was the one standing there, arguing about relationships with him.

"I'm sorry," I said, reaching over and taking his hand. "Can we talk about this later? When we're not at work?"

"Fine," he agreed.

I turned and moved toward the staff room again, already a few minutes late clocking in.

"But, Gideon," Owen said as I pushed open the door. "Aliens? Seriously?"

I shrugged wryly and kept moving.

I'd tell Owen about the aliens, or lack thereof. I trusted him that much, at least. I was less enthusiastic about the relationship talk. Discussing my feelings was far more daunting than explaining aliens in my backyard.

Interlude
Owen Campbell

So yes, *all right*. Owen Campbell and I were dating. Or at least we were doing something very similar to dating. Something almost *exactly* like dating, except we never called it that. And also, we kept it a secret.

If most people knew about the secretive nature of my and Owen's relationship, they'd assume it was at *his* urging. That's because Owen's what many people would call "a catch." I'm not sure you need me to directly state this, but I am *not* a catch.

Yet *I* was the one keeping our relationship discreet, not Owen, and there were two reasons for it:

1. I found it uncomfortable to discuss sappy, emotional matters.
2. I didn't appreciate feeling *forced* into anything.

In a town the size of Lansburg, there weren't many dating options for *anyone*, let alone someone who wasn't heterosexual. Owen and I were the only two openly gay males at our school.

And what do you suppose happened when there were only two gay males within a small population?

Everyone tried to force us together.

Long before I spoke a word to him, I had friends, siblings, parents, even a *teacher* once say, "Why don't you and Owen Campbell date?"

As if a person being gay was the only requirement for me to like him. As if it didn't matter whether I was attracted to him, didn't matter if he was an asshole, or if our personalities didn't mesh.

I *was* attracted to Owen. He *wasn't* an asshole. And somehow, despite our differences, our personalities *did* mesh.

But that was beside the point.

For years, I resented Owen and scowled at the mere mention of his name. I constantly told people I'd rather spend my life alone than date someone I didn't like simply because he was my only option.

Imagine my distress when Owen and I started working together at Super Scoop and I found out I actually *did* like him.

I couldn't bear how smug everyone would be if they found out. There were few things I hated more than hearing "I told you so." I refused to give anyone the satisfaction.

Unfortunately, Owen didn't see it my way.

"You're more worried about what people will say than about *us*," he'd told me.

"I'm not *worried*. I just don't like being told what to do."

"Then we'll keep this a secret so…what? So you can hold on to your pride? Are you really that stubborn?"

Obviously, yes.

"Remember what you told me about basketball?" I'd

asked Owen. "Everyone's always saying you should play basketball just because you're tall. But you don't even like basketball, and you're sick of hearing it."

"Yeah..." Owen said. "Because *I don't like* basketball."

While, admittedly, Owen made sense, I continued to insist the relationship be kept quiet. Cass knew, of course, and many other people suspected, but for the most part it remained between only Owen and me, which was how I liked it.

But Owen's patience was wearing thin, and I knew a choice waited in my near future.

And okay, fine, *fine*. Maybe there was another, more personal reason I didn't want to be open about the relationship...

But that falls into the realm of "discussing sappy, emotional matters," which, as I said, I really prefer to avoid.

EVENT:
Aliens Arrive
(CONT.)

I got so wrapped up in the *relationship* part of my and Owen's conversation, it took me a while to return to the concerning fact that he'd heard Ishmael's alien story.

"There's a blog post," he said when I asked about it. "It's going around."

"It's ten in the morning. How much could it have gotten around?"

He was right, though. As my shift at Super Scoop went on, I received three texts and one email from acquaintances asking about the article. I couldn't imagine how many people were contacting Ishmael. He was probably having a grand time. He was probably scheduling appearances.

Cass came into Super Scoop around lunchtime. Owen was taking his thirty-minute break, and I was alone at the counter.

"So, you're running with this alien thing?" Cass asked eagerly, while contemplating the different ice cream flavors.

"I'm not running with *anything*. I'm waiting for the situation to die down." I took a bite of an unappetizing myTality™ Energizer bar Mother had forced on me.

"But, I mean, *wowsers*. Think of how amazing this could be," Cass said. "How theatrical."

Speaking of theatrics, Cass was wearing cowboy boots and an embroidered western shirt.

"Theatrics are best left for drama club," I said.

"That reminds me," Cass replied, "would you rehearse with me tonight?"

I hesitated. "Do I have to?"

"Well, no, you don't *have to*. But it's would be *nice*," she said.

"It's just that every time I help you rehearse, you yell at me for not doing it well enough."

"Only because you use that weird robot voice."

"That's just my voice, Cass."

Cass nodded, allowing that I was probably right.

"Besides," I went on, "I thought you hated the play."[1]

"I hate that Owen got the role of Pied Piper while I'm relegated to *love interest*."

Said as if *love interest* was the worst thing anyone could be. It was a nice reminder of why Cass was my best friend.

"Well, I'll help if you really need me to. But I'm just going to *read*, not *act*."

"Forget it," Cass said. "I'll ask Arden. And I want a double scoop of salted caramel."

---

1   The play in question was *Hamelin!*, a musical adaptation of the Pied Piper story.

I hesitated before moving toward the ice cream case. "I didn't realize you and Arden talked outside of school."

"Jeez Louise. We've been hanging out for a year. *Obviously,* we talk outside of school."

"Huh." I handed Cass her cone and rang up the purchase.

"What's wrong?" she asked.

"Nothing."

"Do you not want me to be friends with Arden or something?"

"You can be friends with anyone you want."

Cass took a bite of ice cream and gave me a long look. "You totally need to find coping mechanisms for your jealousy issues."

"This isn't a jealousy—"

"Fine, your *trust* issues. Whatever you wanna call it."

Owen returned from his break then, and Cass dropped the subject, thankfully—the last thing I needed was them ganging up on me about my perceived character flaws. They made small talk about the play, and Cass was polite, despite Owen having "stolen her role."

I took the opportunity to slip my phone from my pocket and check Frykowski's website.

There were sixty-two comments on the alien post.

COLLECTED DATA

BLOG COMMENTS

The following compilation is a selection of user comments from lightbringernews.com. Comments were originally posted on the article "They're Here: Extraterrestrial Contact Made in Lansburg."

skywatcher51:
I'm twenty miles south of Lansburg, but I've seen lights in the sky almost every night for the past month. Why isn't anyone else talking about this?

ThirdEyeFluoride:
@skywatcher51 you think the government is going to let us talk about what's been happening? you're seriously delusional. i'm surprised this post hasn't been removed yet.

annab311a:
I've lived in Lansburg my entire life, and I've never seen a UFO.

jojoyourboat:
DAE think the hofstats are weird anyway? lol. Im not even surprised this happened at that farm

CIAyylmao2001:
WHY IS EVERYONE TALKING ABOUT UFOS AND IGNORING WHAT REALLY MATTERS THAT 911 WAS A GOVERNMENT

SET UP AND WERE ALL AT DANGER OF ANOTHER ATTACK AT ANY MOMENT

THERE PLAYING WITH OUR LIVES, PEOPLE!!!!!!!!!!!!!!!!!! !!!!!!!!!!!!!!!!!!!!!!!

devlmdemedoit:

I just want to know, if aliens really are visiting, what do they want? Maybe we shouldn't assume they're going to attack us, guys.

concerned_earthling:

Anyone from the detroit area thinking of heading to Lansburg to see what's going on for yourself? If so, I'm interested in carpooling.

ZedzDedBaby:

is everyone hear a fucking moron? their r no aliens you assholes get out of your moms basements and go actualy do some thing and maybe you wont be so worried about stupid shit like ufos

cassiopeia-the-diva:

@ZedzDedBaby What did punctuation and proper grammar ever do to you?

MissusFry1962:

This is a very well-written article. I will check for updates to see what happens next. Love, Mom.

INTERVIEWS

Subject #2, Magdalene (Maggie) Hofstadt:

I was packing up after softball practice and Makayla came over and said she got a text from her cousin, who got a call from her friend, who wanted to know about the UFO at my house, and did I know anything about it? I *didn't* know anything about it. But let's just say, I was intrigued.

Subject #3, Cassidy (Cass) Robinson:

I *died* laughing when I read that ridiculous blog post. I knew Gideon wasn't exactly going to be mellow yellow about it, though, which is why I didn't mention it to anyone. I mean, anyone other than Arden, but I knew *she* wasn't going to blab. And my parents. Oh, and Mr. Jeffries, who lives across the street. But he's, like, eighty. I don't even think he has internet. What was he gonna do?

Subject #4, Victor Hofstadt (Father):

I go to the gym after Maggie's practice to squeeze in a quick workout. I'm not even there five minutes when one of the guys I train comes up and says, "So Vic, I hear your farm's got an alien problem." And right away, I know my kids are up to something.

Subject #5, Owen Campbell:

Gideon had been weird for days. I mean, he's always weird, but he'd been even quieter than usual. I thought it was something I'd done. Then I got five messages in an hour, all from different friends, all saying something along the lines of, "What the hell is going on at your boyfriend's farm?"

Subject #6, Arden Byrd:

I guess I heard about the aliens? I mean, no, I did. I saw people online talking about it, but I didn't know exactly what they meant. I went to your...I mean to *Gideon's* work to see if he was okay, but I saw through the window that Cass was already there, and I knew if I went in they'd do that thing where they stop talking when they see me. You used to do that a lot, you know.

Subject #7, Jane Hofstadt (Mother):

Yes, of course I heard the alien rumors. It was all over town by late afternoon. I was following up with potential myTality distributors and they kept asking what was happening on the farm. I told them I was quite sure there weren't any aliens. But the thought of aliens, or anything unfamiliar, can be anxiety inducing! So I made sure to provide everyone with samples of myTality Soothe.

EVENT:
The Hoax Is Born

DATE: SEPT. 9 (SAT.)

And now we've arrived at a pivotal moment. You know about the events leading up to it: the explosion, and the cover-up, and the blog post that put aliens on everyone's minds. Maybe then, you'll agree the next stage wasn't such a leap.

It was Saturday night, late. Normally, Ishmael would be out with his many friends or acquaintances or girlfriends. But he'd stayed home to avoid a girl who had a crush on him, because he was too cowardly to outright reject her.

I was in Ishmael's basement bedroom, perched on a small, metal storage locker. There was a couch in the room that Ishmael had dragged home from a mystery location, but who knew what germs had invaded the fabric? The cold, metal block seemed like a safer seating option.

Ishmael lounged on his bed, drinking a myTality™ Shake It Up, which was meant to deliver vitamins and protein through what was, essentially, a flavorless milkshake.

"I don't know how you drink those things," I said.

He shrugged, downed the rest of the shake in one gulp, and tossed the can into a trash basket already overflowing with soda bottles and fast-food wrappers. "I know you didn't come down here to talk about myTality."

"Of course not." I'd never venture into his lair without *very* good reason. "I want to discuss aliens."

After a slight hesitation, Ishmael said, "I guess you're still pretty mad?"

"*Mad* doesn't quite cover the complex range of emotions I've experienced the past few days."

"Don't you think it's kind of cool, though? People think *aliens* were here!"

"Ishmael," I said calmly. "No one thinks aliens were here."

"Sure they do."

"Even assuming that extraterrestrial life exists, there's absolutely no evidence aliens have visited Earth, and considering the Fermi Paradox—"

"But see," he interrupted. "No one knows that astrology[1] stuff except you."

I rubbed my eyes and tried to remain composed.

"Gideon?" Ishmael said after a moment.

"Yes?"

He licked his lips and shifted his weight. "I had this idea. I know you want to let the alien fuss die down...but what if we don't?"

I stared at my brother. "Well yes, Ishmael, that's *technically* an idea."

---

1   Astrology: a pseudoscience claiming that the orientation of the cosmos controls a person's personality and life path. Not to be confused with astronomy, an *actual* science studying celestial objects.

"It's just, have you imagined what it would be like if aliens really came to Lansburg?"

"But they didn't."

"Yeah, but we could *make* it happen."

"Ishmael, we can't make nonexistent aliens..." I stopped. "Wait. You're talking about a practical joke, aren't you?"

"Let's call it a hoax."

I gazed at my brother, dumbfounded. "Why would I *ever* agree to that?"

"Just hear me out," he pleaded.

If I didn't, he'd harass me until I caved. So I said, "Fine. But make it fast. The international space station is passing overhead tonight and I want to get my telescope set up."

Ishmael grinned and got to his feet, eager to give his pitch. He'd probably gotten sales tips from Mother. "Okay, well, I didn't exactly plan for any of this. But you have to admit, it's kind of amazing. Aliens in Lansburg! All because of one small explosion."

"Not that small."

He ignored me. "I've been spending all this time trying to think up a senior prank, and I have nothing. Like, I've done so many pranks at school that people are desensitized to them. So my senior prank has to be super epic, something the school—no, the *town*—will remember forever. Then this fell into my lap."

"How convenient."

"An *alien hoax*! Yeah, it's been done before, but not by us. You're smart and know about science. And I know how to pull off a prank. Is there anyone in the world who could do this better?" Ishmael plowed ahead before I could respond. "And I know you're thinking this is all about *me* and wondering what's in it for you. But doesn't part of you want to know if you can outsmart everyone?"

I opened my mouth to tell Ishmael an alien hoax was the worst idea I'd ever heard. But the words didn't come.

It *was* a terrible idea. We'd definitely get caught.

(Would we, though? Wasn't I clever enough to prevent that?)

And Ishmael was too unpredictable. There'd be no way to control him.

(Except when it came to pranks, he was surprisingly focused.)

And besides, what was *the point* of the hoax?

(To see if I *could*.)

(To *prove* myself.)

(For the *glory*.)

Something bubbled inside me, something that should have concerned me: excitement. It was the feeling I got before an experiment, when ideas began rushing at me.

Aliens, I thought. *UFOs. Lights in the sky. Abductions.* My brain began making checklists, compiling data. My thoughts sped up faster and faster until I had no control over them.

Could I pull it off?

Could I convince our town aliens were real?

Did I have the right knowledge and skill set to create a hoax unlike anything the world had seen before?

I took a deep breath and tried to reel myself in.

"You're forgetting something very important," I said. "No one who knows you will take this seriously."

Immediately, Ishmael began shaking his head. "But dude, that's where you come in. Who would believe *you'd* get involved in a prank?"

He had a point. I was known to be the voice of logic and reason. If I said Ishmael's claims were legitimate, certainly people would take notice.

This might really be possible. If I were to—

But no.

What was I thinking?

Why was I even entertaining the possibility of an alien hoax?

"It would be completely reckless," I told Ishmael. "Not to mention, a colossal waste of my time."

"Dude, it totally wouldn't be a waste. This could be like...like one of your science projects."

"This is nothing like a science experiment."

"Sure it is," Ishmael said enthusiastically. "It's just instead of chemicals or whatever, the experiment is about people."

I looked at my brother for a moment. While I had thus far spent my life focusing on the natural sciences,[1] social science wasn't without merit.

"A psychological experiment," I pondered.

"Right! A psychology experiment involving the whole town!"

I looked up. "No. Not psychology. *Sociology*."[2]

I could take notes. Collect data. Record conversations and gather relevant materials. It would be a legitimate research project. If I compiled information and documented results, sociologists might study my findings long into the future.

Suddenly, I had a realization that shot an electric jolt through my body. I'd read that to gain acceptance into MIT, one needed to be

---

1   E.g., physics, chemistry, biology, and, of course, astronomy.

2   Sociology: the science and study of society.

more than an exceptional student. The school favored applicants who demonstrated creativity and ingenuity. A sociological paper detailing the reactions of a town to an alien invasion might be the exact sort of innovation the admissions board was looking for.

To Ishmael and me, the aliens would be a hoax. To the rest of Lansburg, they'd be fact. The MIT admissions board could believe in aliens or not—that part hardly mattered. Either way, they'd have my research paper, which would be unlike anything they'd seen before. For once in my life, I would stand out.

My mind raced with possibilities. Where would we even begin? If this was an experiment, I'd use the scientific method. The first step of which was *ask a question*.

The question was simple: Could people be convinced that extraterrestrials were real and had made contact in Lansburg?

Could they?

And could I leverage their belief into an acceptance letter from my dream school, which would pave the way into a career at NASA?

Could I?

"So?" Ishmael asked.

I'm sure you're wondering about my state of mind. I'm sure you're having doubts about my decision-making skills. But how could I have passed up such a clear-cut opportunity to achieve my goals?

"This is a terrible idea," I said.

"Terrible...but also brilliant?" Ishmael asked, hope written all over his face.

"Possibly," I agreed. "Possibly brilliant."

My brother grinned. He knew he'd won. "Are we doing this? Are we making a hoax?"

I stood up. And before I could change my mind, I nodded solemnly. "Let's do it."

Ishmael whooped and punched a fist in the air. Then he asked, "What comes first?"

If he'd paid attention in science class, he would've already known that the next step in the scientific method was *do background research*.

"It's time to learn more about aliens," I said.

THE INTERNET SEARCH HISTORY OF GIDEON HOFSTADT ON THE EVENING OF SEPT. 9

aliens

alien abductions

alien hoaxes

most famous hoaxes of all time

ufos

ufo blue prints

weather balloons

project blue book

signs of alien abductions

alien electronic interference

famous alien encounters

phoenix lights

hudson valley sightings

books about aliens

communion

fire in the sky

close encounters

crop circles

betty and barney hill

the andreasson affair

how to keep your relationship secret without offending your boyfriend

alien conspiracies

movies about aliens

area 51

is my judgment impaired?

TEXT CONVERSATION

Participants: Gideon Hofstadt, Cassidy Robinson

I need a favor. — GH

CR — Your wish is my command

Remember how we discussed aliens earlier? — GH

CR — Lol
You think Id forget that?

How would you feel about doing a little acting? — GH

Oh holy cannoli

Seriously???

What are you planning

Gideon?

Please don't leave me hanging

CR

CR: Gideoooooooooooooooooooooo oooooooon!!!!!!!!!!!

GH: I'll come over tomorrow. I don't want to talk about it over the phone.

CR: Afraid of someone tracing this conversion?

CR: *conversation

CR: Wait

CR: ARE you afraid of that??

CR: Gideon?

EVENT: Another Awkward Breakfast

DATE: SEPT. 10 (SUN.)

Mother and Father should've been suspicious when Ishmael willingly got out of bed before 8:00. He and I had work to do, though. I warned him the night before that I'd be waking him early, and it was a testament to his commitment to the hoax that he agreed without a fight.

Father scrambled eggs while Mother made notes in her planner about upcoming meetings with myTality™ distributors. Weekend or not, Mother worked.[1]

"Will you be home today?" Mother asked Father. "A large shipment of products is coming, and I don't want the boxes left on the porch."

At the stove, Father paused mid-action. "*More* products? Janie, we've got a whole barn filled with myTality boxes. Maybe you should slow down."

---

1   Technically, Mother didn't *need* to work, thanks to my great-great-grandfather, who'd made a hefty sum of money with a patent for an ultraspeedy corn harvester, and also thanks to subsequent generations who'd made wise investment decisions.

"I won't have that negativity," Mother chirped. She reached into her purse and pulled out a pill bottle. "Here. Have a myTality Morning Burst. Vitamin C to help with your blahs."

"My *blahs* are just fine, thank you," Father replied.

I met Ishmael's gaze across the table. He raised his eyebrows at me. It was time to begin phase one.

"Would you mind if Ishmael and I drove to Pittsburgh today?" I asked casually.

Father glanced over. "For what?"

"I need electronic components for a Science Club project." It was a lie. I needed supplies for the hoax.

My parents glanced at each other. One of their most annoying talents was the ability to have entire conversations—complete with decision making—without speaking a word.

"I'm not sure that's a good idea," Mother said.

"Why?" I asked calmly. Throwing a tantrum was never a successful negotiation tactic.

"Because," Father said, "we don't trust your brother to drive all the way to Pittsburgh."

"But Father—" I began.

"If you want to drive long distances, get your license and prove that we can trust you."

Mother reached across the table and placed her hand over mine. "Honey, we know you're afraid of driving, but—"

"I'm not *afraid*," I said.

Ishmael snorted. I glared at him. We were supposed to be on the same team.

"I'm *not*," I repeated. "I just don't feel compelled to drive."

"Well, I don't *feel compelled* to let your brother drive all the way to Pittsburgh," Father replied.

I looked at Ishmael, wishing we could have our own silent conversations. But he only shrugged and smiled wryly, as if he couldn't help but agree with our parents.

"I have an idea," Mother said. "Why don't you go to Pittsburgh with me this afternoon?"

I narrowed my eyes. "Why are *you* going to Pittsburgh?"

A fervent glaze came over her face, which I immediately took as a bad sign. "The myTality conference, silly. Don't you remember? Oz[1] *himself* will be there!"

Father rolled his eyes, which Mother didn't miss.

"Oh, stop that, Vic. It's a very big deal. Oz rarely leaves the West Coast."

"Apparently, Californians are more susceptible to health-supplement scams," Father muttered.

Mother gave him a look. "Maybe they're more health *conscious*."

"Back to the issue at hand," I said. "Could you drop me off at the electronics store and pick me up after your seminar?"

"I don't see why not," Mother said brightly.

Before we could continue our discussion, the front door flew open and a voice called, "Yoo-hoo, Hofstadts."

"In here, Miriam,"[2] Father called.

Gram whirled into the kitchen, trailing the scent of perfume and cigars behind her. Her hair was dyed litmus-test red, and she wore

---

1   Oz, a.k.a. J. Quincy Oswald, the CEO of myTality™ and, from what I could gather, a charlatan.

2   Miriam Warren: my maternal grandmother.

her favorite fur coat. Not only was the coat inappropriate for early September, it was inappropriate for *any* occasion in Lansburg.

"Mom, you smell like an ashtray," Mother said.

"The poker game ran late. I haven't been home to shower yet."

"You haven't *slept*?" Mother's face was filled with disapproval. "Here, have a myTality Energizer."

Gram waved her hand at Mother. "Get that snake oil away from me. I *will* take some of those eggs if you don't mind, Victor."

"Coming right up," Father said.

Gram sat at the kitchen table and regarded my brother. "Ishmael, stop slouching over your breakfast. You're a young man, not seventy. What are you looking at, Gideon? You could straighten up too. And comb your hair before you leave the house."

"You're a beacon of warmth, as always, Gram," I said, and she threw her head back and cackled.

"How was last night's game?" Ishmael asked.

I listened to Gram with vague interest. Gambling had never appealed to me. My brother, on the other hand, was eagerly waiting for the day he'd be allowed to attend the underground poker games that enriched Gram's retirement fund.

"When are you gonna let me play?" Ishmael asked, for probably the hundredth time.

"Ishmael," Mother said, "we won't condone you losing money at a poker game we already disapprove of."

"I vote that you let him learn the hard way, Mother," I said.

Gram scowled at me over her plate of eggs. "I wish you'd stop that."

"Me? What?"

"That *mother* and *father* business. Creeps me out. You sound like a nineteenth-century Dickensian street urchin."

"What an oddly specific insult," I replied. "Also, a street urchin wouldn't *have* parents."

Gram had already moved on from the conversation, though.

The truth was that I'd switched to *Mother* and *Father* during my freshman year, because *Mom* and *Dad* sounded juvenile and needy. I no longer felt that way—I'd actually prefer calling them Mom and Dad again—but I'd gotten so much flack about it that I couldn't back down.

"Enough chitchat," Gram said. "I'm here for a reason."

"Aside from pointing out character flaws in your progeny?" I muttered.

Gram acted like I hadn't spoken. "Conversation at last night's game took a turn from the usual drunken sports blather."

I glanced at Ishmael.

Gram continued. "For some reason, half the town seems to think aliens have attacked the farm."

Mother and Father did the silent conversation bit again. Something told me they'd already discussed the matter at length.

Gram crossed her arms and raised a single drawn-on eyebrow, giving Ishmael and me a hard stare.

"I see," I said.

Ishmael took a deep breath. We were at the moment of no return. "Yeah, well, that did happen. Aliens. On the farm."

"Oh Christ," Father muttered from the stove.

Mother sighed.

Gram gave Ishmael and me a long, discerning look. "What are you boys up to? Is there some kind of profit in this?"

The greatest profit. Scientific discovery.

"No," Ishmael said. "It's just the truth."

"Funny, you didn't mention aliens the night of the explosion," Mother said.

"We were worried you wouldn't believe us," I replied, making myself entirely complicit in the alien scheme.

Father snorted. "That was a reasonable worry."

"Listen." Gram raised a ring-clad finger and pointed at us. "I don't know what your endgame is, but last night half the town showed up to talk aliens. I raked in more cash than I have in a year. So keep it up."

"Mom!" Mother gasped.

"Miriam," Father said, with only a bit more dignity. "We don't want to encourage this."

"Oh, get over it," Gram replied, waving her hand at my parents. "It's high time this town had something interesting happen."

I glanced at my brother. He couldn't suppress his grin.

To-Do List: Sunday Sept. 10

Gideon:

- Continue research
- Ready supply list
- Travel to Pittsburgh to procure supplies
- Meet with Cass and go over plan
- Create online identity to post comment on Adam Frykowski's blog
- Lay out strategy for coming weeks

Ishmael:

- Hang out with friends and spread the word about recent close encounter

INTERVIEWS

Subject #7, Jane Hofstadt (Mother):

Looking back, yes, I see that Vic and I made mistakes. Maybe we didn't adequately prepare our kids for the world. Gideon especially had too insular a life, I think. Oh, don't look at me like that. You *did*. In hindsight, allowing their alien hoax to continue was ultimately the wrong choice. But the boys were *teenagers*. We wanted to teach them consequences, that they wouldn't always have their parents to step in. We never imagined it would get so out of hand.

Subject #1, Ishmael Hofstadt:

Dude. I'm *plenty* prepared for the world.

EVENT: The myTality™ Seminar

DATE: SEPT. 10 (SUN.)

Mother thought she was sneaky. We were nearly to Pittsburgh when she said, "Why don't you attend the seminar with me, and we'll get your supplies after?"

I liked nothing about that suggestion.

"I'd rather not."

"I know how you feel about myTality," Mother said, glancing at me instead of focusing on the road. Perhaps I'd feel more comfortable getting my license if I wasn't convinced 67 percent of drivers had a death wish. "But if you gave it a chance, I think you'd change your mind."

"I don't think I would."

"It would mean a lot to me," she tried. "I'd like you to hear Oz speak. He's inspirational. And who knows when you might have the opportunity again."

With any luck, *never*. Granted, I didn't know much about

J. Quincy Oswald, but he was the leader of an MLM,[1] and that was enough for me.

"Mother," I said. "Please don't make me do this."

"I'm not trying to *punish* you. Nothing in this world is more important to me than the health of my children. And myTality offers a range of products to ensure that your health is stable long into the future."

That last bit was taken word for word from one of the myTality™ pamphlets she'd left lying around the house.

"I'd really prefer if you dropped me off at the store."

Mother took a deep breath. She reached up and patted her hair, which I noticed she'd taken extra care with this morning.

"Gideon, I'm worried about you. It's not healthy for someone to spend all day holed up in a lab. You probably have a vitamin D deficiency."

"Surely there's a myTality bar that can fix that," I said dryly.

She continued as if I hadn't spoken. "And I'm worried about your future."

"My future?" I gaped at her. "I'm at the top of my class. I'm going to MIT."

Except I wasn't *quite* at the top of my class anymore, and I'd frequently been skipping the extracurriculars that would pad my MIT application. Anxiety fluttered in my chest, but I pushed my worries away. If the hoax went according to plan and I wrote a groundbreaking sociological paper, a slightly lower GPA wouldn't matter.

"There's more to life than academics," Mother said.

---

1   MLM: multi-level marketing. Essentially, a kinder name for a pyramid scheme.

"Well, I also don't drink alcohol, do drugs, have unprotected sex, or engage in any other risky behavior. I'd say I have a brighter future than most people I know."

Mother shook her head. "This is exactly what I mean. Listen to your arrogance. It gets worse every year. And now you're wrapped up in this scheme with your brother..."

"There's no scheme."

"When you were little," she went on, "and your dad and I decided to leave the church, I thought we were doing what was best for you kids."

I raised my eyebrows. "I thought you left because Father García disliked you trying to turn parish events into business ventures."

"There was a time when the Catholics would have appreciated that," Mother said with a scowl. "Father García should get off his high horse."

"What's the point of all this?" I asked.

"The *point* is that the older you get, the more I see that you're in need of spiritual guidance. I think myTality could offer that to you. It's so much more than health products."

My jaw clamped firmly shut. My teeth instantly started aching. I was *arrogant*? In need of *spiritual guidance*? Who was this person, wearing my mother's skin and saying my scientific pursuits weren't good enough?

The situation was risky, though. If Mother was "worried about my future," I'd be kept on a tighter leash. Ishmael and I needed freedom to successfully pull off the hoax. Plus, though it was hard to admit, part of me was sad about disappointing Mother.

I was the good son. The prudent one. The studious one. The

one she could count on while Ishmael got detentions for practical jokes and came home from parties reeking of alcohol. I thought my parents were *proud* of me.

The conversation dredged up one of my least-favorite memories:

I was ten years old and the school principal arranged a meeting with my parents. Apparently, several of my teachers suggested I skip a grade.

I sat in the principal's office, feeling accomplished. He'd given me hard, undisputed proof that I was intelligent. I was going to graduate early and go to college early and there was no way NASA would reject me.

But instead of lavishing me with praise, my parents exchanged a look. Father—at the time I still called him Dad—asked that I step out of the room so they could talk privately.

Naturally, I pressed my ear to the door.

My parents expressed their concern that my "book smarts" and "social smarts" didn't align. That I was *already* unable to relate to and communicate with my peers. They were concerned that me skipping ahead would make my stunted social intelligence even more pronounced.

Then Mother confided to the principal that sometimes they worried about me.

"He's always been different," she'd said. "We know not every child is outgoing or affectionate. But sometimes it's as if Gideon... it's as if he doesn't *feel* anything."

I *did* feel things. I felt guilt and anguish and joy and all the rest. I might not *admit* those feelings, sometimes even to myself, but they existed. My own parents questioned that, though. They thought something was wrong with me.

I never ended up skipping a grade.

Years later, the memory still stung. But dwelling on the past wouldn't create a better future—or present—for myself. I pushed my old feelings of inadequacy and shame away and focused on what mattered: Mother felt I needed spiritual guidance.

"Fine," I said. "I'll attend the seminar. But promise we'll go to the store after?"

Mother beamed. "Yes, of course! I'll take you anywhere you need to go. Oh, honey, I'm so excited for what you're about to experience."

That made one of us.

Interlude
Multi-Level Marketing

I wish that MLMs played no part in this tale I'm telling. But they do, in ways larger and more baffling than I ever could have anticipated. Which means you need some background on them.

Like most legitimate businesses, MLMs begin with a product. The product can be anything: knives, greeting cards, dubious health supplements, etc. Unsalaried workers, often referred to as "distributors," attempt to sell these products for a commission.

That might sound reasonable enough. But MLMs differ from the average sales job: in addition to selling the products—which the distributor is expected to purchase large quantities of, in advance, with their own money— the distributor also attempts to recruit *more* distributors. These distributors recruit more, and *these* recruit more, and so on.

The people recruited under them became the original distributor's "downline." Each time someone on their downline makes money, a portion of the profit filters back to the top, to the distributor who began it all.

See the following chart for a visual representation:

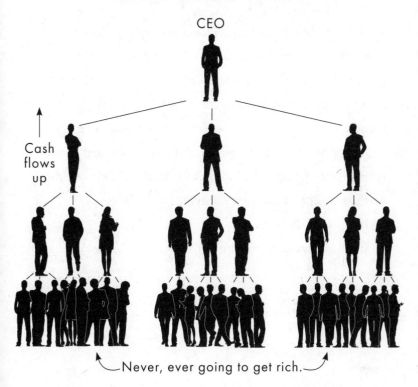

MLM STRUCTURE

CEO

Cash
flows
up

Never, ever going to get rich.

Generally, only the people at the top of the pyramid become wealthy. The lower tiers miss out on the luxury cars and fancy vacations they've been promised, and frequently end up in debt after spending thousands of dollars on products they'll never sell. I once read a study claiming that 99 percent of all MLM participants lose money.

Upward mobility, while *technically* possible, is highly

improbable no matter how much time and cash is invested. There's also debate about the legality of the business model. Over the years, countless MLMs have had lawsuits brought against them.

But the most highly criticized aspect of MLMs isn't the business practices; it's the cult-like mentality that consumes distributors. Otherwise levelheaded people become fanatical about the company, the products, and especially the original founder of the MLM. That person is often treated like a god.

And why shouldn't they be? After all, they had people selling their products, working free of charge, and also making up the majority of consumers buying the products.

It's absolutely corrupt.

It's also deviously brilliant.

EVENT: The myTality™ Seminar

(CONT.)

When Mother and I stepped inside the meeting room, I realized I'd underestimated the popularity of myTality™. I'd expected twenty middle-aged distributors raving about the health products and bragging about the size of their downlines. Instead, there were approximately five hundred people in the room.

Mother and I took seats in the middle of the crowd. She buzzed with excitement. "I'm thrilled to see Oz speak live. I've only seen him in webinars."

I pulled out my phone and checked the clock. It was already two minutes past the seminar's listed start time.

Why didn't events begin when they were supposed to? Maybe it was intentional. Start five minutes late and give stragglers a chance to arrive. But why cater to the chronically late? If people missed the beginning of an event, it was on them.

I grew more annoyed with the seminar, and my presence there, every passing second.

Finally, the lights dimmed. The crowd shifted in anticipation.

A voice came over the sound system, booming and echoing. "And now, the moment you've been waiting for. Clap your hands, stomp your feet, and give it up for the founder and CEO of myTality, *J. Quincy Ozzzzzzzzzzzzzzzzwald*!"

For god's sake. Was I at a "business seminar" or a football game?

Neon lasers began swirling around the audience. Instead of stepping onto the stage like a reasonable human being, J. Quincy Oswald appeared in the back of the room, lit by a spotlight. Techno music blared from speakers as he ran up the aisle toward the stage, arms spread wide to touch the hands of his adoring fans along the way.

What the hell *was* this?

I looked around the audience. People were rapt. They screamed and cheered and jumped up and down. They waved their arms in the air. Their eyes were bright and shiny, and a few of them had tears coursing down their cheeks.

I'm not exaggerating. *Actual tears.*

I turned to Mother, mortified at the thought of seeing such naked emotion on her face. She clapped and grinned and seemed utterly in her element, but thankfully refrained from crying.

I didn't get a good look at Oswald until he jauntily took the stage. He was younger than I expected and wore the uniform adopted by men trying to appear professional yet hip: jeans and a fitted sports jacket. Oh, how I despised that look. It felt like a communication error between the top half of the body and the bottom. To make matters worse, Oswald wore cowboy boots and a pair of sunglasses. Indoors. Perhaps the glare from so many lasers beams and spotlights was intense.

Immediately upon facing the audience, Oswald tore the glasses off and tossed them to the crowd near the front of the stage. He let out a loud *whoop* while running a hand through his intentionally messy hair.

"Now check this out," he began, speaking with a slight southern accent. He scanned the room theatrically. "They told me Pittsburgh wasn't a health-conscious town. But I'm seein' this crowd, and I tell you, they were *wrong*!"

More cheers.

I wondered who "they" were supposed to be.

"Each and every one of you is here because you have a *mission*. Your mission is to become the best possible version of you. Who wants more energy?"

"We do!" the crowd shouted in response.

"Who wants a longer life?"

More shouts, more cheers.

"Who wants to live *every moment* to the fullest?"

The crowd responded with the loudest affirmative yet.

J. Quincy Oswald walked slowly to the front of the stage, a grave set to his shoulders. He spoke more seriously than before. "And who wants to accomplish all that while earnin' enough income to enjoy a life of financial freedom?"

All around me people leapt to their feet, clapping and hollering. My jaw was firmly clenched and pain began to twist through my neck and head. And yet, for some reason, I couldn't bring myself to look away.

"Lemme tell you something," Oswald said. "You've come to the right place. Because myTality is in the business of makin' dreams come true."

Next to me, Mother's hands were clasped to her chest as if she were listening to a particularly awe-inspiring sermon. Did she truly buy into all this?

"Forget *mor*tality," Oswald went on, beginning a chant the audience seemed well acquainted with. "It's not *your*tality."

He paused dramatically, and I felt anticipation running through the crowd. Finally, he finished, the audience joining in at the end, "It's *my*Tality!"

A rousing scream from the crowd threatened my eardrums.

And thus began two of the most tedious hours of my life.

Oswald jumped around stage, a true performer, preaching and whooping and imploring the audience to better themselves. There was music. There were light shows. There were more chants and tears. A new product was unveiled, MyTality™ Gro-Rite, a pill that promised stronger, healthier hair and nails after only one week of use.

I heard more than I ever hoped to about the myTality™ product line. Supplements, vitamins, powders. Shakes and juices. Skin creams for aging, for acne, for radiance. Products that made you healthier. Made you happier. And most important, products that turned back the clock.

"Maybe people shouldn't fight acne if they want to look younger," I whispered to Mother.

She shushed me.

"Now I wanna ask you something, and I'm lookin' for an honest answer," Oswald drawled. "How old would you guess I am?"

People shouted numbers, as if they were taking the moment very seriously, though I was 84 percent sure they'd seen the skit before.

"Thirty-five!" someone called.

"Forty!"

"Thirty-eight!"

"Thirty-four!"

Oswald held up his hands for quiet. "Listen to this and hear me well: I turn *fifty years old* this year."

The crowd went wild.

There was absolutely no way J. Quincy Oswald was fifty. *No way*.

"You wanna know why I look so good?" he asked.

"Yes!" the crowd roared.

He waited until the room fell silent, drawing out the moment. "Because I *faithfully* use myTality products!"

I sighed deeply. The seminar was even more nauseating than I'd imagined.

And yet, I thought, *yet...*

Yet I was mildly intrigued by J. Quincy Oswald. By the way he held people rapt, made the crowd hang on his every word. I thought of the hoax, my own massive con. A small, dark part of me wondered if I might be able to learn something about trickery from Oswald.

The seminar shifted focus from health products to myTality™ being a "prepackaged, proven business opportunity." With myTality™, Oswald claimed, you worked *when* you wanted, *where* you wanted, and *how* you wanted.

Was anyone listening to his words? Or was it the cadence of his speech that captivated people? Was it the confident set of his shoulders? Was it the way he peered at the audience, as if trying to make eye contact with each individual attendee?

"You've heard the old saying," Oswald went on. "*Money doesn't buy happiness*. And that's true. But I've been dirt poor. I know what it's like to watch bills stack up, to wonder where my next meal is gonna come from."

Some audience members nodded in acknowledgment. A few sniffled. I glanced at Mother and raised an eyebrow, knowing full well that she'd never had to worry about money. She ignored me.

"So no," Oswald continued, "money won't buy happiness. But I'll tell you what it *can* do: it can buy you *freedom*—freedom to better yourself and *seek out* the happiness you deserve."

As the seminar drew to a close, Oswald made a big production of giving awards to our region's top-ten distributors. I nearly fell out of my chair when Mother was acknowledged as number seven.

When she got back from traipsing across the stage, where she received a wooden plaque directly from Oswald, I turned to her.

"Number seven out of how many?" I asked.

"Thousands."

"Huh," I replied, grudgingly impressed. "Congratulations."

"I've told you this is a real business venture for me."

She had. Yet I'd assumed she was bleeding our finances with all the products she had stocked in the barn. It never occurred to me she might be bringing money *in*.

Despite the new respect I had for Mother's business skills and my slight curiosity about Oswald, I was relieved when the seminar finally ended. As we filed out of the conference room with the rest of the crowd—most people shuffling along with expressions of dazed wonder—I pulled out my phone and skimmed my shopping list.

"We might have to make two stops, if you don't mind."

"That's fine," Mother said agreeably. "But first we're going backstage to meet Oz."

I sucked in a sharp breath through my nose. "Please don't make me do that."

"It's a perk of being in the top ten," Mother replied. "It's an honor."

I knew from her steely expression that her mind wouldn't be changed. I let her lead me backstage, where J. Quincy Oswald held court among a bevy of adoring fans.

"Jane Hofstadt," he said with a grin when he noticed her.

Mother looked like she'd been personally recognized by Jesus Christ. "You remembered!"

"I'd never forget a distributor with the drive and dedication you have," he said.

Mother blushed.

"And who do we have here?" Oswald asked, glancing at me.

"This is my son, Gideon."

"Nice to meet you, Mr. Oswald," I said politely.

He grabbed my hand, shaking vigorously. "I won't stand for any of that *Mr. Oswald* business. Call me Oz."

Under no circumstances was I going to call the man *Oz*.

"How'd you enjoy the seminar?" he asked us.

"It was...illuminating."

Mother placed a hand over her heart. "I've never felt closer to myTality than I do at this moment."

Seeing him up close, I was even more certain Oswald wouldn't approach fifty for at least a decade. He was young and handsome and clearly charismatic. I imagined those traits accounted for his success more than any business acumen.

What did that mean for the hoax? Was Ishmael's charm more essential than my scientific knowledge?

No, I told myself. *They're* equally *important.*

While Mother and Oswald exchanged platitudes, my mind wandered. I wouldn't take my brother's skills for granted, I decided, but I wouldn't diminish my own either. The hoax required both of us. It could only be a success if we worked together.

And it *would* be a success. It had to be. My whole future was suddenly riding on it.

INTERVIEW

Subject #3, Cassidy (Cass) Robinson:

I spent Sunday rehearsing for my epic performance. Not memorizing lines for *Hamelin!*, but... You sure it's all right to talk about this? Okay, cool beans. So yeah, I practiced for the stunt Gideon asked me pull on Monday morning. I was totally ecstatic about the hoax, which maybe makes me a bad person. But whatever. I needed some joy in my life after being cast as the love interest in *Hamelin!*. Ugh. Is there any role more insulting than the *love interest*?

Interlude
Hoaxes in History

Hoaxes aren't new. Over the course of human history, there have always been individuals with the desire to fool the people around them—or, for the truly ambitious, to fool the entire world.

Take George Hull, for instance. In 1869, he discovered the petrified body of a ten-foot tall man on his property. Soon to become known as the "Cardiff Giant," Hull charged spectators admittance to see the spectacle in person. But when the legitimacy of the "giant" was called into question, Hull admitted it was a prank.

Another infamous hoaxer was a man named Robert Kenneth Wilson, who, in 1934, sparked interest around the world when he took a photo of a strange serpent-like creature, eventually dubbed the "Loch Ness Monster." Today, of course, that photo is generally considered to be fake.

Then there's George and Kathleen Lutz. In 1975, they bought a home where six people had been brutally murdered. After moving in, the Lutzes experienced rampant paranormal activity, eventually leading them to write a bestselling book about their experiences. But ultimately, the haunting of the Lutzes' Dutch Colonial house in Amityville, New York, was revealed to be just another hoax.

More recently, in 2000, someone calling himself John Titor gained internet fame for insisting he was a time traveler from the year 2036. But when many of the predictions about world events were inaccurate, his followers became skeptical. It turned out that, *you guessed it*, it was yet another hoax, perpetrated by a Florida entertainment lawyer and his computer scientist brother.

And that's just the tip of the iceberg. There was the Piltdown Man; the Cottingley Fairies; the Dihydrogen Monoxide incident; the Sitka, Alaska, volcano eruption... Century upon century of hoaxes.

What makes some people take pleasure from tricking others? Is it a cry for attention? A desperate need to outsmart their peers? An attempt to achieve glory?

I won't deny that I felt kinship with past hoaxers. But I judged them too. I saw where they'd been sloppy, where they'd missed opportunities to take their hoaxes to the next level.

I wouldn't make their mistakes.

EVENT:
First-Period
Performance

DATE: SEPT. 11 (MON.)

Since Ishmael was a year older than me, we shouldn't have had classes together. But he'd failed health class the previous year, so we shared first period.

It mystified me that he managed to fail health class. The only thing preventing the class from being a complete breeze was that once a year Father brushed off his unused degree[1] and gave a guest lecture on fitness. Just the *thought* of it was humiliating.

Cass was also in the class. Usually she actively participated, answering questions before they were fully out of Mrs. Novak's mouth. Not because Cass had a great love of the subject material, but because she had a great love of *talking*. Talking about anything, at any time—from the zany contestants she'd seen the night before on *Pitch, Please* to whether Isaac Newton or Gottfried Leibniz was the true inventor of calculus.

I knew people would find it odd when Cass was uncharacteristically quiet on Monday morning. And when she fell asleep in the

---

1   See: exercise science.

middle of Mrs. Novak's lecture on the updated food pyramid, *every-one* noticed.

Cass slumped over her desk, face resting on her forearms, fuzzy cat-ear headband pushed askew—Cass had chosen a black, feline-like outfit for school that day. She breathed deeply and wheezed with each exhale. I was surprised she wasn't drooling.

"Robinson," Mrs. Novak said in her usual gruff way.

Cass remained asleep.

It was go time. I slid my phone partially from my pocket and opened the app I'd downloaded for gathering audio—I was committed to recording every detail of the hoax. For science.

Mrs. Novak repeated herself, louder. Still no response.

She glanced at me. "Hofstadt, wake your friend."

I leaned across the aisle and gently shook Cass's shoulder. "Hey, Cass?"

She blinked and groggily raised her head, looking around with confusion.

"Wha—" She took in our teacher's frown and crossed arms. "Was I asleep?"

"I'm glad you find my class so stimulating," Mrs. Novak said.

Cass glanced around the room, mortified. "I'm so sorry. This has never happened to me before."

"Stayed up too late partying, huh?" The stern look remained on Mrs. Novak's face, but I saw a twinkle in her eye.

"I wasn't partying, really," Cass insisted. "I just..."

She bit her lip. All eyes were on her. A few people smiled, like they were expecting a punch line.

"I..." Cass tried again. "I saw something bizarro last night, okay?

Lights in the sky. And there was a noise... Whatever. I don't want to talk about it."

"Wait," Justin Howard said. "Did you see the Hofstadts' aliens?"

Cass rolled her eyes. "There's no such thing as aliens. I saw some lights, that's all. It was weird, and yeah, I stayed up super late watching them. But it wasn't aliens."

People shot concerned glances at one another. Eyebrows raised. Whispered conversation began.

"What did the lights look like?" Sara Kang asked, leaning forward in her chair.

Cass took a deep breath. Then she began her monologue, a detailed description of the lights based on information I'd gathered from accounts of similar sightings.

It was both thrilling and unsettling to see people hang on her every word. I glanced at Mrs. Novak and even she, someone I'd pegged as a skeptic, listened intently and made no attempt to get back to the food pyramid.

We can do this, I realized. *We can make this hoax work.*

Step three of the scientific method was *form a hypothesis*.

Maybe something like: when presented with seemingly factual evidence, typically rational individuals will become convinced of the highly improbable, despite it going against their greater instincts and knowledge.

"This is bullshit," Sofia Russo[1] said suddenly, flipping her hair over her shoulder.

---

1   Sofia Russo: Cass's longtime theater rival. Their relationship mystified me—they thrived off competing with each other and, though their conversations were fraught with animosity, still somehow maintained a friendship.

"Language," Mrs. Novak reminded her.

"Isn't it weird that the UFOs just *happened* to appear to someone who's friends with the Hofstadts? *I* haven't seen any lights."

"Zeus knows, the whole world would've heard about it if you had," Cass said, smiling sweetly at Sofia.

Sofia smirked. "Maybe because, unlike some people, I've mastered speaking from my diaphragm."

Before Cass could voice a comeback, other people began asking questions about the lights. Some took her story at face value while others were hesitant. Only Sofia showed outright disbelief. Admittedly, it made me gain respect for her.

As I listened to my classmates debate the possibility of alien life, I considered what a strange predicament I'd put myself in. If the hoax succeeded and people bought into the narrative Ishmael and I were spinning, I'd lose respect for them. But if they didn't believe it and the hoax failed, I'd lose respect for *myself*.

THE NEXT FOUR DAYS

EVEN IF YOU PLAN SOMETHING METICULOUSLY, YOU can be startled by just how easily you achieve results. Somehow, the situation in Lansburg became very strange very quickly.

A brief recap of events following Cass's confession:

1. Cass's tale of extraterrestrial lights spreads through Irving High School.
2. According to Maggie, the middle school begins buzzing about aliens as well.
3. Adam Frykowski writes a follow-up article about UFO

activity in Lansburg, titled "'I Saw a Fire in the Sky': A Chronology of UFO Sightings in the Greater Pittsburgh Area." While the article is mainly an exploration of past sightings, it closes with Cass's story.

4. The comments on Frykowski's post rapidly pile up, with both Lansburg residents and outsiders adding to the conversation.

5. Frykowski's website is discovered by radio personality Robert Nash and featured on his nightly show, *Basin and Range Radio*.[1]

6. The day after Nash's show airs, there's a write-up about the "Lansburg Lights" in *Weird World News*, a national tabloid publication, increasing exposure across the country.

And after that, future sociologists, well, that's when the first abduction occurred.

---

1   A call-in show run out of Pahrump, Nevada, that is centered around aliens and other unexplained phenomena. It had been syndicated nationwide earlier in the year.

BLOG COMMENTS

The following compilation is a selection of user comments from lightbringernews.com. Comments were originally posted on the article "'I Saw a Fire in the Sky': A Chronology of UFO Sightings in the Greater Pittsburgh Area."

devlmdemedoit:
Has anyone tried to make contact with these UFOs? Can't we do something besides WATCH them?

hereafter:
This article is ridiculous. There isn't a single credible source listed. Why is the public putting any trust in Adam Frykowski?

skywatcher51:
@hereafter Don't read it if you don't like it.

ClAyylmao2001:
WHAT THE FCK PEOPLE HOW LONG IS IT GOING TO TAKE YOU TO REALIZE THOSE LITES HAVE NOTHING TO DO WITH ALIENS ITS THE GOVERNMENT KEEPING WATCH ON YOU????????? THERE EXERCISING CONTROL AND ALL OF YOU SHEEP ARE LETTING IT HAPPEN

COLLECTED DATA

kingcoyote:

i seen lights. 3 days ago i was outside putting the lid on the trash can to keep the raccoons out and i looked up and seen about 5 lights moving around and i no they werent airplanes or helicopters

cakesandmadness:

A girl at my school says she saw lights too and I don't know why she'd lie

♥dOnT_hAtE_mE_cUz_Im_FaMoUs♥:

@cakesandmadness Maybe bcuz she's a total drama queen?

qrevolution:

@kingcoyote So I'm not the only one that's noticed Lansburg is overrun by raccoons lately?

AliensAmongUs592:

This is an excellent article. We should all appreciate Mr. Frykowski for gathering so much relevant information in one place. I'm 65% certain I saw lights in the sky on my way home from work last night. I'll continue to follow this blog for further developments.

MissusFry1962:

Very informative. I can tell you did a lot of research. Love, Mom.

Interlude
Alien Abductions

Suspend your disbelief for a moment and pretend you believe alien abductions are possible.

Then, imagine this:

You're driving along a dark country road. It's a route you've taken countless times. But tonight, something is different. Tonight, a light appears in the sky ahead of you. You slow down and approach it slowly, an inexplicable feeling of dread getting stronger the closer you get.

As you near the light, your radio—tuned to a local station—has a burst of static. The stations rapidly change. And was that...? Did you hear a *voice* coming through the speakers? For a moment, it was almost as if you were receiving a *command*...

Now the light is directly above you. Without warning, your car shuts off completely, as if the battery died. The light becomes more intense, filling the vehicle, and a sound starts. A hum. Is it coming from above you? Is it from inside your own head?

Trying to restart your car does nothing. You panic. You fumble your cell phone from your pocket to call someone, anyone, to rescue you. Despite your terror, you notice the time: 9:07 p.m.

You open your phone contacts and hesitate. Who should you call? A friend? A family member? The police?

It turns out, you never have to make the decision.

As suddenly as it appeared, the light is gone. The radio plays softly. The night, once again, seems perfectly normal.

Except for the fact that your car is parked in the middle of the road, and you have your phone in hand. You glance down at it.

It's 9:48 p.m.

You'd only scrolled through your contacts for a few seconds. A minute at the absolute most.

So how did the time jump from 9:07 to 9:48? Where did those forty-one minutes go?

You brush it off. Better to not dwell on it.

But some things won't stay buried.

A few nights later, the memories come. The feeling of being powerless. Of having someone in your head, reading your thoughts. Instruments probing your body. Paralysis. And looming over you, a large, gray head with black eyes.

The eyes stay with you the longest. Make you wake up screaming.

Everywhere you go, everything you do, you think of those black eyes.

You feel altered, though you can't say *how* exactly. You simply know you're different. You know that in those forty-one minutes something happened to you, something you can't explain. No one would believe you even if you *could* explain.

One single night. Forty-one lost minutes. That's all it took to change your life forever.

That's all it took to destroy you.

Or maybe not. Maybe you *aren't* destroyed.

Yes, there's fear. There's pain. There's panic.

But maybe, you begin to think, maybe on the night you were taken, what you actually experienced was *enlightenment*.

(Other possible explanations include: overactive imagination, false memories, confusion, outright deceit.)

EVENT: Unexpected Escalation

DATE: SEPT. 15 (FRI.)

The school week began with Cass's admission about nighttime lights. By Friday, the entire town was buzzing about them.

In first period, Mrs. Novak assigned us a worksheet on the effects of smoking on the human body. Twenty minutes after class started, the door opened and Sofia Russo waltzed in.

"Russo," Mrs. Novak said. "You're remarkably late."

"Sorry," Sofia replied in a breathy voice.

"Sorry doesn't cut it. Go to the office and get a tardy slip."

"Wait, you don't understand," Sofia said.

Mrs. Novak leaned back against her desk. "Enlighten me."

Sofia straightened her shoulders and tilted her chin up. She was about to perform. Every time she walked onstage during a play, she did the same maneuver. It was a habit that kept her from getting lead roles, though she preferred to blame favoritism toward Cass.

Her pre-performance ritual complete, Sofia's eyes filled with tears. A shudder ran through her body. She wrapped her arms around herself, clasped her elbows in her hands.

Then she said, "Last night I...I was...taken."

"Taken where?" Mrs. Novak asked. Some of the sharpness had left her voice.

"Abducted," Sofia whispered.

What?

She wasn't...she wasn't saying she'd been abducted by aliens... right?

"Abducted?" Mrs. Novak repeated.

Sofia nodded and sucked in a deep breath. "I was...I saw the lights. I couldn't look away from them and they got brighter and brighter and then...*they* came. I could feel *them* in my head and..."

Sofia broke down sobbing and crumpled to the classroom floor.

The situation was so much like a highly dramatized performance of Cass's own alien confession that for a moment I had the sensation of being stuck in a time loop or transported to another dimension.

What was Sofia *doing*?

I glanced at Ishmael in the back row.

And wouldn't you know it, my brother *grinned*.

Mrs. Novak helped Sofia to her feet and asked another student to walk her to the nurse's office. Once they were gone, the classroom erupted with excitement and speculation. It seemed that 44 percent of the class agreed they wouldn't put it past Sofia to lie, but her performance went above and beyond.

Those tears seemed *real*.

When the bell rang, I hurried to catch up to Ishmael, who was meandering to second period as if nothing alarming had occurred.

"We need to talk," I said.

"Why?"

"*Why?*" I glanced around the hall to make sure no one was paying attention. "Because someone just claimed they've been abducted by aliens!"

Ishmael stopped walking and turned to me. "Look, dude. Sofia wasn't actually abducted."

I took a deep, calming breath. "Yes, I'm aware."

"What's the problem then?"

"Wait," I said, a terrible realization dawning. "Did you put her up to this?"

Ishmael squinted. "Of course not. You made that rule."[1]

"In that case, I have to wonder why you feel no concern about this development."

"Why are you freaking out so bad?"

I took a breath and tried to get ahold of myself. "This is an experiment. It's supposed to be closely controlled—by *me*, the scientist. If I lose control, my data will be meaningless."

Ishmael shrugged affably. "Yeah, but like, you're not totally giving up control. You're stepping back and watching the situation... evolve."

"Evolve," I repeated, staring at him.

"Right."

The hoax was *evolving*. It was taking on a life of its own.

Because of me.

Because of everything I'd set in motion.

Ishmael headed to his next class, whistling as he went, but I remained rooted in the hallway.

---

1   The rule: my brother was not, under any circumstances, to add to or amend the hoax without my approval.

Evolving.

Maybe there was no reason to be concerned.

Maybe I was more successful than I'd ever imagined.

INTERVIEW

Subject #3, Cassidy (Cass) Robinson:

Honestly, it was the best performance of Sofia's life. Later, in *Hamelin!* rehearsal, Sofia was backstage regaling a bunch of rats with the story of her abduction. Not *real* rats, obviously, the freshmen cast as rats in the play. When the rats heard their cue and scurried onstage to torment the townspeople of Hamelin, Sofia and I were alone. She gave me this smug smile and was like, "Guess I'm not so terrible at improv after all." And I said, "That wasn't *rehearsed*?" She shook her head. After that, I did the only thing that made sense. I congratulated her.

EVENT: Unexpected Escalation

(CONT.)

No one wanted ice cream in autumn.

Okay, that was inaccurate. *I* didn't want ice cream in autumn, or really 98 percent of the time. It was messy to eat from a cone and seasonally inappropriate once the weather changed. I was baffled that others disagreed.

I was at Super Scoop, wearily assembling ice cream cones for a myriad of elementary school kids who'd rushed in after their final bell. The late-afternoon light reflected on the lava lamp outside, giving the ice cream parlor a pink hue.

Technically, my manager, Laser,[1] was working as well. But she was in the back, watching TV.

Owen occasionally worked the after-school shift with me, when he wasn't in play rehearsals or baseball practice. Unfortunately, he was engaged with extracurriculars more often than not. Which, really, I should have been too.

---

1 Presumably, Laser wasn't her real name, and just as presumably her hair wasn't naturally neon blue, but I'd never questioned her about either.

At any rate, I was alone, with no one to help handle the elementary school rush, because Laser found it more imperative to watch a rerun of *Pitch, Please*—the pitch was for a battle of the bands–style show where every week a band member was replaced with a musician from a different genre.

The elementary school kids were noisy and I missed Owen and I'd already dropped ice cream on myself three times. Needless to say, I was tense even before the bell on the door chimed again.

Ishmael waltzed into Super Scoop. "Dude, we need to talk."

I waited for the last of the elementary schoolers to leave and said, "Talk, then."

My brother's eyes wandered to the ice cream case. "Can I get a strawberry cone?"

"Is *that* what we need to talk about?" I asked. "Strawberry ice cream?"

Ishmael frowned like *I* was wasting *his* time. "Gideon, this isn't a joke."

"*What's* not a joke?" My frustration was growing by the second.

"Seriously, can I have the ice cream first?"

I rolled my eyes but knew the conversation wouldn't progress if my brother remained fixated on ice cream. When he had the cone in hand, he finally got to the point. "I'm worried about this thing with Sofia."

"You're worried? Earlier today you thought it was great. You were *whistling*."

"Yeah. But then, like, I really thought about it."

I adjusted my paper cap and wished for the hundredth time that I worked a real job. In a lab somewhere, preferably.

"And what conclusion did you come to?"

"It's like you said. This is our prank—I mean, *experiment*. We're supposed to be in control of it. We're the ones who did all the research and stuff."

I raised an eyebrow. "Please, go on. Tell me about the research *we* did."

"You know what I mean," Ishmael said. "You did research and I...I made phone calls. And the whole *idea* was mine. But now Sofia's getting, like, famous from it."

"I admit, it makes me uncomfortable that someone is involved in the hoax without our consent. Alas, there's nothing we can do about it now. And as you said earlier, her abduction is a testament to our own cleverness."

"I said that?"

"Not in those words."

I moved around the shop, refilling chrome napkin dispensers and letting Ishmael mull over the situation. Finally, he burst out, "But it should have been me!"

I stopped and looked at him. "I'm sorry, what?"

"*I* should have been abducted. Not Sofia. Why would the aliens have chosen her instead of me?"

I took another long, deep breath. "Ishmael, you realize this is all fake, right?"

"That's not the point."

"We'll have to disagree about that."

I moved to continue working, but Ishmael reached over and pulled the stack of napkins from my hand.

"At first I thought Sofia's story was great. But then *all day* I saw people asking about her abduction."

"So, basically, you're upset because Sofia is getting more attention than you?"

"Not just that," Ishmael insisted. "Sometimes she got things *wrong*. Like, she called the aliens green when everyone knows they're *gray*! She's taking over our hoax and no one even remembers aliens visited *us* first."

I began to speak, intending to remind Ishmael again the aliens hadn't visited anyone.

But.

But.

He was right. I was proud the hoax was evolving, but the abduction should have been ours. Now, most likely on a whim, Sofia had created the basis for everything that might follow. *I* would have handled the abduction with care and precision. I would have made sure it was done right.

"You see the problem, right?" Ishmael asked.

"Yes," I agreed, feeling glum again. "I'm just not sure what to do about it."

Ishmael licked his strawberry ice cream cone and grinned. "That's the easy part. Obviously, I need to be abducted by aliens ASAP."

MAGAZINE ARTICLE

The following quiz was reprinted with permission from *UFO Hunter Quarterly*.

The Alien Abduction Checklist

Have you been visited by extraterrestrials? Mark an X next to each symptom you've experienced in the past twelve months.

___ Lost time, ranging from several minutes to several days

___ Sleepwalking, insomnia, nightmares, or dreams of flying

___ Waking with unusual stiffness in your back or neck

___ Hearing tapping or humming noises as you fall asleep

___ The feeling of being watched by animals with large eyes

___ Unexplained bruises, burns, or scars

___ The discovery of strange, metal implants in your body

___ Frequent electronic malfunctions in your presence

___ Streetlights going out when you walk under them

___ Sudden sinus problems, migraines, or rashes

___ Recurrent nosebleeds/waking to find drops of blood on your pillow

___ A sudden aversion to heights, snakes, spiders, large insects, or bright lights

___ A fear of being alone

___ Regularly double- and triple-checking the locks on all doors and windows in your house

COLLECTED DATA

___ An extreme aversion or terror upon seeing pictures of aliens or UFOs

___ A new, obsessive fascination with aliens or UFOs

___ Recently discovered psychic abilities

___ The feeling of being "special" or "chosen"

___ Seeing flashes of light from the corners of your eyes

___ Struggles with addiction

___ Sexual or relationship issues

___ Difficulty trusting or opening up to people

___ A history of alien abductions within your family

___ Having seen a UFO or strange lights in the sky

If you have experienced seven or more of these symptoms, there's a strong possibility you've been abducted by aliens.

We recommend you visit our website, where you can find information on abductee support groups in your area.

EVENT:
The Abduction of Ishmael Hofstadt

DATE: SEPT. 16 (SAT.)

"According to this list," Ishmael said, "you've probably been abducted by aliens."

We were in my lab, making plans for my brother's upcoming alien encounter. "According to that generalized and robust list, *everyone* has been abducted by aliens."

"But dude, relationship issues, difficulty trusting people..."

I continued flipping through my notes without looking at Ishmael. "A high percentage of people have those problems. It has nothing to do with extraterrestrials."

"Maybe if you showed this to Owen he'd understand why you're afraid to date him."

I stopped. My eyes went to my phone, which sat on the desk next to me, recording our conversation. "Owen is just a friend."

"Sure," Ishmael nodded. "Everyone totally believes that."

"Can we focus on your abduction?" I asked.

Ishmael nodded agreeably and looked back at the checklist. "So what symptoms am I gonna have?"

"The problem with these 'symptoms' is that they're almost entirely psychological. To make people *believe* you've been abducted we need physical evidence."

"Sofia didn't have evidence."

"Yes," I said, pulling from my reserves of patience. "But thanks to Sofia, we need to up the ante."

Ishmael scanned the list of symptoms again. "Metal implants? That seems like a good one."

"Does the lab look equipped for surgery?" I asked, gesturing around the room.

"What about sleepwalking?"

"That would do what, exactly? Prove to Mother and Father you've been abducted by aliens? They don't believe this anyway."

Ishmael put the list down and frowned. "About that. Don't you think they're being weird?"

"Weird how?"

"Like...they know we're lying. But they're not calling us out. They both get real quiet whenever aliens are mentioned."

I'd also contemplated this phenomenon. "I believe they're trying to let us learn a lesson."

"Huh," Ishmael said. "That's convenient."

"Back to the list. I think we only have two options," I said. "Nosebleeds—"

"You're going to give me a bloody nose?"

"I could help you *fake* a bloody nose," I corrected.

"We could do it for real."

"I don't want to do it for real."

"Why?"

I sighed. "Please, Ishmael. Can you just trust me?"

My brother held up his hands in surrender. "You're the boss. What's the other option?"

I hesitated, wondering if I was about to go too far. *No*, I decided. *Not when it's for the purpose of scientific discovery...and my acceptance to MIT.* "The other option is unexplained bruises, burns, or scars."

Ishmael frowned. "Oh."

For a long moment, the only sound in the lab was Kepler growling from the corner where he hunched, glaring at Ishmael.

"I guess you're not thinking of scars," Ishmael said finally, "because that would take too long. And probably bruises aren't weird enough?"

"Correct."

"Okay then. I guess I'm getting burned."

I hesitated. "You don't *have* to."

Ishmael shrugged and grinned. "It can't be *that* bad, right?"

BRANDING IDEAS

~~BURN DESIGNS~~
Ishmael's Awesome Alien Tattoo

Gideon's Ideas:

Simple and classic.
Boring.

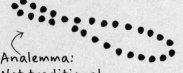

Circles are often connected
to aliens. See: crop circles
STILL BORING.

Analemma:
Not traditional,
but the astronomy
connection is interesting.

Kinda okay I guess

Ishmael's Ideas:

Lightning Bolt of
POWER

Absolutely not.

EVENT:
The Abduction of
Ishmael Hofstadt

(CONT.)

We didn't just want a burn. We wanted a *brand*. Since there hadn't been branding irons on our farm for decades, there was only one other choice.

I plugged in my soldering iron.

While it heated, I prepared a clean space on my desk and laid out tools.[1]

Ishmael's role in preparation was sneaking a dusty bottle of whiskey from the cabinet above the fridge. Neither of my parents were big drinkers, and I was 55 percent sure the whiskey had been purchased for a Christmas party, circa 1999.

Once the soldering iron was hot, I used the brass sponge to clean it while Ishmael drank whiskey straight from the bottle.

"Just enough to take the edge off," I reminded him. "Don't get drunk."

---

1   Tools: my notes, a brass sponge, a wet sponge, antiseptic, gauze, surgical tape, a mirror. I added flux to the lineup out of habit, before remembering it wasn't a normal soldering session and flux wasn't necessary.

"Yeah, dude. I *know*."

"If you get drunk, I'm going to be extremely upset."

"Hey, Gideon?" Ishmael said, sounding far more serious than I was used to. "I'm gonna let you burn me with a soldering iron. So I kinda don't want to hear it."

"Understood."

I was *fairly* confident in what I was doing. I'd gone online and researched scarification with soldering irons. For instance, it was important not to push too deep. As long as I kept the burns close to the surface of Ishmael's skin, it was unlikely that there would be a permanent scar. Six months to a year from now, the evidence of my brother's "abduction" should have faded.

Supposedly, the best way to get the design even and cause the least amount of pain was by using short, fast strokes. Plus, the analemma design we'd chosen was fairly simple.[1]

"Are you sure this isn't going to, like, get infected?" Ishmael asked.

"We're taking precautions," I replied.

I had no idea what the likelihood of the burn getting infected was, but considering it was being done with a soldering iron, which was not meant for human skin, in an unsterilized environment, yes, I thought infection was a risk.

Ishmael took a long, measured breath, then unbuttoned his Hawaiian shirt. I thoroughly cleaned the skin above Ishmael's heart.

"Are you ready?" I asked.

"Yep."

---

1   Analemma: a diagram showing how the sun moves annually relative to a fixed spot on Earth.

I picked up the soldering iron and hovered above his chest.

Here's a confession: I'd never been properly taught how to solder. I bought an inexpensive soldering iron and taught myself by watching tutorials online. I hadn't quite gotten the hang of it yet.

But this was different from soldering a circuit board. Surely, all I needed to brand Ishmael was steady hands. I hoped.

Ishmael leaned back and closed his eyes. Without further ado, I pressed the soldering iron to his skin.

His scream could've woken the dead. It could've been heard by all forms of extraterrestrial life in the galaxy. In *all* the galaxies.

I jerked the iron back while Ishmael's body bucked. Kepler yowled from the corner. Ishmael swore profusely, took a deep breath, then composed himself.

"Okay," he said calmly. "That hurt more than I expected."

"Are we shelving this idea?"

"Nope," he said. He leaned back again. "I know what to expect now. It's fine. Do it."

I took a deep breath. And I did it.

I hadn't expected the *smell*. The horrible stench of burning flesh permeated my lab. I took slow, steady breaths and told myself it was just another experiment, not something straight from a horror movie.

"Almost done," I said after what felt like an eternity, but was only about fifteen minutes.

Ishmael mumbled something unintelligible in response.

Finally, I burned the last curved line into his flesh. I sighed deeply. "Finished."

Ishmael opened his eyes. "Dude. I will definitely not be recommending this to anyone."

I set the soldering iron down and stepped back to examine my work.

I don't mean to brag...but it actually looked quite *good*. I handed my brother a mirror I'd borrowed from Maggie's room so he could see for himself.

"You know," Ishmael said, "I bet you could sell soldering-iron tattoos out of your lab."

I didn't respond. Because with Ishmael you never truly knew if a joke might turn into a scheme, and the last thing I needed was half of Irving High School showing up at the farm for me to burn designs into their flesh.

"Gideon," Ishmael said, still examining the markings on his chest. "I'm really starting to think we're brilliant."

I was too. But I said, "We're only brilliant if this is successful."

"We better call Adam Frykowski then."

TRANSCRIPT OF INTERVIEW CONDUCTED
BY ADAM FRYKOWSKI ON SEPT. 16

FRYKOWSKI:

I appreciate you contacting me. Do you mind if I record this?

GIDEON:

No. Do you mind if *I* record it?

FRYKOWSKI:

Uh...I guess not?

GIDEON:

Thank you.

FRYKOWSKI:

Let's start at the beginning. After the explosion on September
seventh, you saw no further signs of alien activity?

GIDEON:

Correct.

ISHMAEL:

Well, except for the lights.

FRYKOWSKI:

Lights?

GIDEON:

Lights?

ISHMAEL (TO GIDEON):

Yeah, dude, remember? A couple nights later I saw lights over the field.

GIDEON:

Ah, yes. How could I have forgotten?

FRYKOWSKI:

What night was this?

ISHMAEL:

Probably...the ninth? And a couple days later Cass Robinson—do you know Cass?—she saw lights too.

FRYKOWSKI:

What exactly were these lights doing?

ISHMAEL:

Um.

GIDEON:

Hovering, right? Didn't you say they were hovering?

ISHMAEL:

Right, hovering.

GIDEON:

That's how you knew it wasn't a plane, correct? Because planes
don't hover. Isn't that what you said?

ISHMAEL:

Right. That's exactly what I said.

FRYKOWSKI:

But you didn't encounter any beings?

ISHMAEL:

Not until last night.

FRYKOWSKI:

What happened?

ISHMAEL:

It was around midnight. The rest of my family was asleep, but I
kept having these weird thoughts, like I *needed* to stay awake. I
went out to the field, where the explosion happened—

COLLECTED DATA

GIDEON:

He was *drawn* to the field.

ISHMAEL:

Right, I was drawn to it.

GIDEON:

Almost like something else was controlling him.

ISHMAEL:

Exactly like that.

FRYKOWSKI:

And did you see anything strange out there?

ISHMAEL:

Not at first. But then a light appeared above me and I heard this humming sound. I was scared, but also...not. It felt right somehow. The light got closer and next thing I knew, I was lying in the field, curled up all fetal-like.

FRYKOWSKI:

Do you have any memory of what happened in between?

ISHMAEL:

There were eyes. Big eyes, leaning over me. That's all I remember. It felt like the whole thing took seconds, but when I looked at my phone, I lost almost an hour.

FRYKOWSKI:

You don't know what message the extraterrestrials were trying to give you, though?

ISHMAEL:

Not yet. But they'll be back.

FRYKOWSKI:

What makes you say that?

ISHMAEL:

They *marked* me.

GIDEON:

Mr. Frykowski, I hope you brought your camera.

EVENT:
Stargazing

DATE: SEPT. 16 (SAT.)

The house was quiet when I slipped outside. Everyone was asleep except Ishmael, who was probably sending pictures of his burn to everyone he knew.

I needed a break from aliens. I had a blanket tucked under one arm and I moved silently through the field, past my lab, to the edge of the property, where the explosion had occurred.

Owen stood at the edge of the crater, his hands tucked into his pockets, contemplating the torn-up ground.

"Hey," I said.

He turned and grinned at me. I melted.

A moment later we stood near the scorched Earth, kissing deeply. For the first time in a week, my mind felt clear.

"I've missed you," Owen said when we pulled apart.

"You've seen me at school and work."

"That's not the same."

It wasn't. There were too many people and distractions. When I was alone with Owen, I could just *be*.

I spread the blanket on the ground, and we lay on our backs, eyes fixed on the sky.

"Not much of a moon tonight," Owen commented, eyeing the small sliver in the sky.[1]

"I prefer this," I said. "Moonlight blocks the stars."

Owen reached down and twined his fingers through mine. I closed my eyes and breathed in deeply. Crickets chirped. Overgrown grass swayed in the light breeze.

"I heard about Ishmael's abduction," Owen said. I opened my eyes and looked up at the night sky.

When Owen realized I wasn't going to reply, he asked, "Do you even believe in aliens?"

While contemplating my answer, I picked out the stars in Pisces, almost directly overhead.

Alrescha.

Omega Piscium.

Kullat Nunu.

"That's complicated," I finally said. "When you think of how many chances there are for extraterrestrial life in our galaxy *alone*, it's hard not to believe something is out there."

"But?" Owen asked. He knew me well.

"But part of me thinks we're alone. The implications of that are quite frightening. Have you heard of the Great Filter?"

"Can we skip the science lesson tonight?"

"Okay," I agreed.

But I wanted to say more. I wanted to tell Owen how utterly alone

---

1   Waning crescent. Ten percent visible.

humans might be on our tiny chunk of rock. How, if there *were* aliens, they could be anything from microscopic organisms to godlike entities. We might not even recognize them. Did that count as a science lesson?

"Do you ever think about starfish?" I asked.

"Do I what?"

"You don't, right?" I asked. "You're aware of them, but they're irrelevant to your life. And even if you went out and found the smartest starfish in existence, you couldn't sit down and have a conversation with it. You couldn't *reason* with it."

"So?" Owen asked, impatience edging into his voice.

"If there are aliens, they might be beyond our human comprehension. For all we know, they'd look at us and see starfish."

"That's kind of depressing."

Yes, it was depressing. The universe fascinated me, but terrified me. It made me feel small and unimportant. It reminded me that, no matter what, I might always be a starfish.

"Have you thought about what could happen if this alien stuff goes wrong?" Owen asked, taking the conversation back to its starting point. "You and Ishmael could get in serious trouble."

"I really don't—"

"You could screw up your chances of getting into MIT."

I was doing this *for* MIT, though. Without the hoax, would the admissions board see me as extraordinary enough to accept? I wasn't like Sara Kang, my competition for valedictorian, who had perfect grades and tennis trophies and a charity she started, on her own, during fifth grade.

Jealousy welled up inside of me and I tried to push it aside. Letting envy consume me would only hurt my focus and productivity.

"Well, I don't intend to get caught," I told Owen. If the hoax went according to plan, no one would ever realize my involvement in it. My sociological paper would be through the eyes of an innocent bystander, simply observing alleged alien activity.

There was a long pause before he spoke again. "I guess what's bothering me is... Does it make you feel good to trick people?"

"What?" I sat up and Owen followed. "No. It's not like that."

"What it's like then?"

"I..." I looked around, as if there was something in the field that would save me. The arrival of a UFO would've been very convenient. "I feel like you're judging me right now."

Owen let out a breath of exasperation. "I'm not *judging* you. I just want to know what's going on in your head."

"You know more about me than almost anyone."

"If that's true, it's really sad," Owen said.

I looked back at the sky, where, despite the complexity of the universe, things seemed so very simple.

After a long silence, Owen said, "I don't know how much longer I can do this."

"I'm sorry," I said softly.

"Do you even care?"

"Of course I care. I just... This conversation is making me uncomfortable."

The same way I got uncomfortable every time I was expected to articulate my emotions. It inevitably ended with me feeling like I was only pretending to be a person. Like *I* was the alien, trying to participate in human rituals I didn't understand.

"Well, it makes me uncomfortable to not know where I stand with you—"

"You know where we stand," I said.

"Since when?"

"You want me to tell you those feelings in *words*. That's not how I express myself."

Owen rubbed his eyes. "Whatever. You win again. We'll drop it."

It was the part where I was supposed to say no, we should keep talking. That I *wanted* to. I should've told Owen everything, how much he meant to me, how I hadn't felt the same way about anyone else, how scared I was of losing him even though I knew it was unavoidable.

I couldn't bring myself to do it.

Instead, I gazed at the sky, and thought about everything above us that was unseen.

"Want to know something cool?" I asked, knowing he didn't want anything of the sort. "Neptune was mathematically predicted before it was visually spotted."

"Wow. Fascinating," Owen deadpanned.

I plowed ahead. "See, the orbit of Uranus was defying the laws of Newtonian physics. This mathematician realized the weird orbital behavior would make perfect sense if there was a similar-sized planet nearby. He did the calculations, figured out where the mystery planet would be, pointed a telescope at that spot, and lo and behold: there was Neptune."

"That's great, Gideon."

I pretended not to hear the hollow tone of his voice.

I pretended I knew how to be the person he wanted me to be.

Interlude
The Great Filter

Perhaps it's time that I, Gideon Hofstadt, address my thoughts on the existence of extraterrestrials.

First, the facts:

- The Milky Way Galaxy contains more than 400 billion stars.
- About 20 billion of those stars are like our sun.
- Approximately one fifth of those sun-like stars have an Earth-sized planet in their habitable zone—an area favorable to the formation of life.
- If only .1 percent of those planets actually *contained* life, there would still be *1 million* planets with life in the Milky Way.

With those odds, aliens *must* exist.

Yet...we have no evidence of them. Oh sure, there are claims by UFO hunters, but there's no *hard* evidence. According to the previously listed points, extraterrestrials should be an undisputable fact.

This is where the Fermi Paradox comes in. The Fermi Paradox essentially states this: there *should* be aliens out there—so where are they?

Something must be stopping intelligent life from colonizing the universe. A barrier, or *filter*, if you will. The Great Filter. An event in the timeline of a planet that life simply can't overcome.

If this is true, what does it mean for humans?

It could be that Earth has already passed the Great Filter. The conditions required for complex life to form might be more complicated than we realize. Maybe there are countless planets where life began, but only *humans* were able to progress to the point of actual civilization. If that's the case, Earth is one of the first—if not *the* first—planet with intelligent life.

It's a bleak thought. It would mean we're utterly alone, trapped on a tiny planet in an eternal universe.

The other option is that the Great Filter is still ahead of us. Meaning sometime in the future, an event will occur to prevent us from progressing to travel outside our own solar system. Maybe it'll be nuclear war. Or climate change. Or maybe we'll end up destroying the planet with our own technology. If this is true, we're closer to the end of our civilization than the beginning.

Basically, we're a lonely anomaly in a dead universe or we're on the verge of the destruction of the human race.

Neither option is comforting.

So, do I believe there are aliens out there?

The answer is, I don't know. But I want to believe.

I want to believe very badly.

NEWSPAPER ARTICLE

The following article was reprinted with permission of the *Lansburg Daily Press.*

SERIES OF UFO SIGHTINGS BAFFLES RESIDENTS

By K. T. Malone

September 17

LANSBURG, PA—Lansburg has always had a relationship with the bizarre—one simply needs to look at the lava lamp at town center to remember this. But in recent weeks, a new strangeness has rippled through town. Residents have reported seeing lights in the night-time sky—and more than a few people are convinced these lights are of extraterrestrial origin.

The start of the phenomenon can be traced back to the Hofstadt family, lifelong residents of Lansburg, who own property on Olga Lane. Jane Hofstadt, née Warren, is the great-granddaughter of Jefferson Warren, who is still celebrated for his contributions to farming technology.

On September 7, the two oldest Hofstadt children reported a mysterious explosion on their property. Days later, local blogger Adam Frykowski published an article on his website purporting that the explosion was caused by extraterrestrials.

While many Lansburg residents scoffed at the idea of aliens

among us, others came out of the woodwork, claiming they too had witnessed UFO activity.

In the past week, the recently dubbed "Lansburg Lights" have gained attention, attracting curiosity seekers around the region. Popular radio broadcaster Robert Nash even featured the Lansburg Lights on an episode of his nationally syndicated program.

Now the story has taken yet another turn. A new blog post by Adam Frykowski asserts that the oldest Hofstadt child experienced an alien abduction and has the scarring to prove it. The *Lansburg Daily Press* reached out to Victor and Jane Hofstadt for confirmation, but they declined to comment.

EVENT:
The Seekers Arrive

DATE: SEPT. 17 (SUN.)

For once, I was happy Owen didn't share my shift at Super Scoop. We'd left things in a weird place the night before. I was 77 percent sure we were both only pretending everything was normal.

But I was *not* happy that Ishmael was busy and Father had to give me a ride to work. He grumbled the entire way.

"This is the problem, Gideon. Refusing to drive doesn't only impact *you*. I have a training session this morning, and if you could've driven yourself here..."

Father occasionally worked at the gym—for fun. I considered pointing out that the entire reason he didn't have *regular* training sessions was so he could take care of me and my siblings, but decided it wouldn't be in my best interest.

"Look, Father," I said. "I have a large workload right now. When my schedule frees up, we can discuss me learning to drive."

"When your schedule frees up," he repeated, somewhere between amused and annoyed.

I hopped out of the car once we reached the edge of downtown and walked the rest of the way, passing Ye Olde Soap Emporium and Ye Olde Hot Dog Stand and other kitschy shops.[1]

As I approached the town square, I noticed strange activity in the vicinity of the lava lamp: it was surrounded by people. Not the usual elderly tourists, but people of *all* ages. The youngest looked only a few years older than me.

There was nothing obvious binding the crowd together. Their clothing indicated a range of social backgrounds and interests. Some carried cameras, but they were high-end ones with long lenses, not the usual tourist fare. There wasn't a single selfie stick in sight.

And were those *binoculars* I saw around one man's neck?

A few of the tourists gazed at our darkened lava lamp, but most were engaged in conversation with one another. A middle-aged man in a tweed jacket and bow tie, with hair sticking out in all directions, moved through the crowd, talking animatedly with everyone he passed.

Interesting.

I continued to Super Scoop. Laser was behind the counter, using the chrome siding on the milkshake machine as a mirror and darkening her already-dramatic eyeliner. She didn't glance up.

"What if I was a customer?" I asked.

"Then you'd be reminded that style isn't effortless."

Fair enough.

I donned my paper cap and glanced back out the window. "There's an odd group of tourists outside."

"Seekers," she said.

---

1   For the record, not only is "Ye Olde" inaccurate Old English, but "ye" should be pronounced "the."

"I'm sorry, what?"

"That's what they call themselves. It's short for Truth Seeker. Like, they try to unveil the mysteries of the world or some shit."

I froze. Laser mistook my pause for lack of understanding.

"They're *UFO hunters*," she clarified.

I hurried back to the window and took a longer look at the group. Yes, I saw it. A ragtag group of people. Their age or their social background wouldn't be what bound them. No. It was their *belief system*. Their belief in things that came from the sky.

"They showed up last night," Laser went on. "There's more of them than this. Probably a hundred? I don't know where they're staying."

Who cared where they were staying? All that mattered was that they were in Lansburg *at all*. I'd drawn them to town. I'd attracted nationwide attention.

I basked in my accomplishment and pushed aside the nagging thought of Owen sounding so disappointed in me. Asking me why I was doing it, if it felt good to trick people.

COLLECTED DATA

A Brief List of Beliefs Held by Seekers

- Aliens exist.
- The government knows aliens exist.
- Most UFO sightings are legitimate.
- The government knows UFO sightings are legitimate and wants to hide this from us.
- Area 51 is a government base in the Mojave Desert where there's evidence of alien life.
- The government will never let us see that evidence.
- There are a variety of additional phenomena the government has awareness of but continues to hide (e.g., the Bermuda Triangle and Bigfoot).
- The government regularly creates false events and presents them to the American people as true (e.g., the moon landing).
- The government has secret means of controlling the American people (e.g., chemtrails).
- The government, overall, should <u>never</u> be trusted.

EVENT: The Seekers Arrive
(CONT.)

It was several hours before I encountered my first Seeker up close.

My shift was nearly over. Cass—wearing a '90s grunge–inspired outfit—arrived at Super Scoop to get me through the last thirty minutes. After that we planned to meet Arden and go bowling.[1]

"I know Arden wants it to be this big event where we shop for homecoming dresses together," Cass said while I restocked ice cream toppings. "But the whole time she'll talk about how sad it is to go without a date. And like, I just can't deal. *I* don't have a date. *You* don't have a date, because god forbid you be ballsy enough to go with Owen—"

"I told you I'm not attending the dance."

"You are, but that's beside the point. *No one* cares about dates. Everyone goes in groups anyway because it's not the freaking 1950s."

"What does this have to do with shopping?" I asked.

"*Because*. If Arden and I go shopping, she'll whine about wanting a

---

1   Bowling: the ultimate we-live-in-a-small-town-and-have-nothing-else-to-do last resort. Also bowling: better than seeing a movie, where I'd become stressed about the implausibility of the plot.

date and I'll feel uncomfortable and won't know what to say, because the truth is, she could easily find a date if she lowered her expectations."

I raised my eyebrows. "I notice you're feeling unkind today."

"I didn't mean it like *that*," Cass said, tugging at the sleeves of her oversized flannel shirt. "She has this built-up idea of what romance means, and she's so obsessed with it that the real world won't ever live up. Not to mention, if she wants a boyfriend she should probably, you know, *talk* to guys."

"Huh," I said, draining a can of sickly sweet maraschino cherries. "I didn't realize romance was so vital to Arden."

Cass snorted. "Probably because you've hardly bothered to get to know her. Hey, why don't *you* go dress shopping with her?"

"I hate shopping."

"No kidding, cargo pants. We really need to have a talk about your wardrobe choices."

"I've told you several times," I said. "I appreciate the utilitarian advantage of extra pockets. Besides—"

The bell on Super Scoop's door chimed and someone came in, ending the conversation.

I glanced at the customer and was immediately apprehensive. It was the man I'd seen wandering near the lava lamp earlier, the one with the tweed coat and wild hair.

"Greetings," he said as he approached the counter, smiling and stiffly raising his hand in an awkward wave.

"Welcome to Super Scoop," I said. "What can I get for you?"

He didn't look at the illegibly scrawled but "charming" menu written on the chalkboard. Nor did he eye the ice cream case, with its fifty delightful flavor options.

Instead, he looked directly at me. "You're one of the Hofstadt brothers, are you not?"

"Maybe," I said cautiously.

"Who wants to know?" Cass asked.

"Arnie Hodges," the man replied. "I'm with a group of people who came into town last night."

"A Seeker," I said.

The guy laughed. "I've never called myself that, but it's true enough. I seek answers about our government's involvement in the alien agenda."

Cass's eyes lit up.

"I'm also a member of MUFON,"[1] Hodges added.

I refrained from rolling my eyes. "That's wonderful, Mr. Hodges, but—"

"I don't mean to be a bother," he interrupted, "but my sources told me one of the Hofstadts works at this ice cream shop, and it's important I speak to him."

"I'm Gideon Hofstadt," I conceded.

Hodges smile drooped. "You're not the abductee."

"Afraid not."

"But it happened on his property," Cass broke in excitedly. "And I saw lights too."

"You did? That's spectacular! Would you be interested in sharing your experience with me?"

"Totally," Cass said.

"Do you think you could do it over there?" I asked, pointing to a table by the window. "I'd hate for you to scare off paying customers."

---

1   MUFON: Mutual UFO Network. An organization dedicated to investigating UFO phenomena.

They complied with my request. As soon as they sat, Cass began speaking, her hands flying through the air in animated arcs. After a while, Hodges pulled a packet of grainy photos from his pocket—UFO shots, presumably—and eagerly shared them.

I watched them from behind the counter with a mild feeling of trepidation, Owen's question in my head again. Why *was* I so okay with tricking people?

When my shift ended twenty minutes later, I clocked out on the ancient machine in the staff room—Ye Olde Time Clock—and approached the table where Cass and Hodges were still engrossed in conversation.

"Are you ready?" I asked.

"Actually, Arnie is taking me to meet his friends."

I tried to remain composed. "You mean the people with binoculars looking for UFOs?"

Hodges laughed. "They may look strange from the outside, but they're a great group. They're just sick of being lied to."

"Lied to?"

"By the government."

"Ah. Of course," I said.

"Why don't you join us?" Hodges asked.

I looked at Cass. "Could I speak to you by the milkshake machine for a second?"

Once we were away from Hodges, I whispered, "What are you *doing*?"

"I'm totally infiltrating the Seekers," Cass said, as if it should've been obvious.

"You can't wander off with some, some... *MUFON* member."

"Seriously? This guy is the cat's pajamas."

"He's disturbed."

"He's harmless," Cass insisted.

"How could you *possibly* know that? He probably thinks he's been abducted by aliens."

"At least three times," she agreed. "The first time was when he was six."

"I'll go with you."

Cass shook her head. "No way. You'll be all skeptical and no one will talk to us. Look, he's only taking me over to the lava lamp. It's not even dark. I won't get murdered, okay?"

"Fine," I mumbled, recognizing defeat.

"Stop with the attitude," Cass said. "Isn't this what you *wanted*? Aren't I supposed to be stirring up drama?"

"Yes, but..." But I didn't know how to articulate the unease I was feeling. Finally, I said, "Just be careful."

"Definitely."

"And take notes."

Cass grinned. "Do I look like an amateur to you?"

A moment later, I watched Cass and her unlikely new friend leave Super Scoop and make their way to the lava lamp, where the crowd had thickened. Part of me, a *small* part, wished I was the sort of person who'd be so easily welcomed into a new group.

I pushed the thought away.

I was trying to complete an experiment, not win a popularity contest. And the experiment was going great. It was going perfectly.

INTERVIEW

Subject #6, Arden Byrd:

The day the Seekers showed up, I was supposed to hang out with Gideon and Cass, but they cancelled. I didn't find out why until way later. At the time, I thought they were ditching me. They'd done that before. I don't know, maybe I would've ditched me too.

THE NEXT SEVEN DAYS

THEY CAME IN CARS.

They came in trucks and campers.

A few seemingly came on foot.

First, it was the Seekers, lured by the seed planted on Frykowski's website and grown to fruition through the radio broadcasts of Robert Nash.

The Seekers drew the bloggers, East Coasters with their own websites chronicling supernatural happenings.

The bloggers drew the tabloids, and Lansburg appeared in low-quality black-and-white newspapers at checkout stands around the county.

The tabloid frenzy drew serious newspapers. They didn't come in the same numbers but sent a reporter or two to our sleepy Pennsylvania town. They covered the frenzy, writing about aliens in a tongue-in-cheek way. Yet there was something in that writing that said, while they didn't believe in extraterrestrials, they wanted to be present. Just in case.

The newspapers drew the camera crews. Lansburg's lava lamp became a fixture in the background of daily news reports.

Soon our modest town of fifteen thousand was overrun with outsiders. Hundreds of people flooded our motels, set up camps in our fields, filled our town square to capacity. Restaurants ran out of food. Grocery stores ran out of firewood, bottled water, and toilet paper—shoppers had to trek to the Walmart Supercenter in the next town over. Our streets became clogged by vehicles with out-of-town license plates.

And then, when I was positive the frenzy had reached its peak, when I became certain nothing else could surprise me, the media coverage grabbed the attention of the CEO of a popular health supplement MLM.

On September 25, J. Quincy Oswald drove into Lansburg like he owned the place.

EVENT:
J. Quincy Oswald

DATE: SEPT. 25 (MON.)

"We're so honored to have you here," Mother gushed.

Our entire family, plus J. Quincy Oswald, sat at the dining room table. The table Mother had frantically cleaned after getting Oswald's call. Our dining room was generally used for its intended purpose twice a year—the rest of the time it was a receptacle for clutter.[1]

"I'm just thankful I caught wind of the happenings 'round here before startin' my East Coast tour," Oswald replied.

His *tour*.

As if he were a rock star.

"How long are you staying, Mr. Oswald?" Maggie asked.

"Please, honey, call me Oz."

Oswald had already instructed us to call him Oz. At which my brother had grinned and replied, "Call *me* Ishmael."[2]

---

1   See: mail, softball equipment, myTality™ bottles, an assembled 3-D puzzle of the *Titanic* that Ishmael mystifyingly brought home one day.

2   "Call me Ishmael" is the opening line of the literary classic *Moby Dick*. I was quite sure my brother had never read the novel, but he never tired of repeating that line.

"I s'pose I'll be here for as long as it takes," Oswald went on.

Father passed the chicken noodle casserole Mother asked him to whip up—though she'd made him add some sort of myTality™ protein powder to the recipe. "As long as *what* takes, exactly?"

Father's gruff tone was the single thing that pleased me about the situation.

Oswald looked around the table with a self-satisfied smile. "I was gonna save this for dessert, but might as well jump right in."

"Please do," I said.

He sat back in his chair and raked his fingers through his hair in that calculatedly casual way of his. "Listen," he said. "This is gonna sound out-of-this-world nuts."

Ishmael and Mother leaned forward, bringing immeasurable shame upon our family.

"When I was a tyke, growin' up in the Texas backcountry," Oswald began, "my family lived in a trailer. We had *nothin'* back then. And we learned to be just fine with that. I always say, a man who builds his fortune deserves more respect than someone born into it."

It was likely the wrong time to inform Oswald that our own wealth had been handed to us by an innovative ancestor.

"That trailer, it was no good. My daddy was a drunk and my momma was hardly around. When I needed to escape, I'd grab my sleeping bag and camp out in the back. All those nights, I'd lose myself in the sky."

Mother put a hand on my arm. "I'm sure Gideon can relate."

"To Father being a drunk?"

"No." She swatted me. "The part about the sky."

Oswald was too wrapped up in his performance to pay us any heed. I wondered whether this was a tale he regularly shared, or if it had been crafted specifically for the occasion.

"One night, something occurred that I never told a soul," Oswald went on. "I was lookin' at the sky, and I saw a glow. A light blazed brighter the longer I stared at it. And then, something even *more* outstanding happened."

He paused dramatically, taking a moment to make eye contact with each of us.

"I heard a voice," he said.

Well, of course he did.

"The voice of God?" Mother breathed, as if that was a reasonable conclusion to draw.

"I surely thought so...at first."

I kept my expression neutral while studying my family members. Father was in disbelief; Ishmael and Maggie looked curious. But Mother... Was she enthralled, or was she trying to *appear* enthralled?

"So, like, if it wasn't God, who was it?" Ishmael asked.

"Extraterrestrials," Oswald replied simply.

Amazingly, he kept a straight face. There wasn't a tug at the corner of his mouth; he didn't blink. He looked as casual as if we were discussing reality television. Gram would've loved to have him at her poker games.

"Are...are you *sure*?" Mother asked.

Father rubbed his eyes like he'd traveled far beyond his tolerance for alien talk.

Oswald leaned forward and locked eyes with Mother. "Surer than I am of anything else in this world."

"I see," Mother said. "Well, that's...really quite interesting."

She didn't believe him. I was sure of it then, could almost feel her internal tug-of-war. She knew Ishmael and I had fabricated the alien story, and she knew Oswald lied about it now. She might love myTality™, but she wasn't entirely taken in by him.

"That night," Oswald went on, "my entire future was laid bare. I saw beyond the trailer I lived in. I saw beyond *my own life*. I was told that I had a place in the cosmos, that there was a mission for me. I could *change the world*."

While I maintained that Oswald was lying about extraterrestrials, there was a 75 percent chance he was being truthful about his perceived "specialness." He believed he was more important than the rest of us. He was a god; we were starfish. Psychologists would have a field day studying J. Quincy Oswald. He practically defined the word *narcissist*.[1]

"What exactly is this mission?" Maggie asked, sounding genuinely curious.

"To lead people to everlasting life."

I nearly spit out my bland, myTality™-enriched casserole.

"Don't you see?" Oswald went on. "That's what myTality was always about. I created a line of products to help people increase their wellness, but I was limited to Earth's resources. I knew that was only the start, though. Because that night, when I received the message, I was told the extraterrestrial Visitors would be back. When I completed the first steps in their plan, they'd return and give me what I needed to take myTality, and humanity, to the next level."

---

1   Narcissist: a person with an exaggerated sense of self-importance, the constant need for admiration, and a tendency to dwell on achieving power and success.

"And what's that?" Father asked.

Oswald smiled and sat back in his seat, letting silence linger. "The elixir of life. The ingredients and formula needed to ensure that none of us'll get old. None of us'll die. Humanity will become eternal."

Oh, for god's sake.

I looked to Mother to see what she made of this new development, but Ishmael spoke first. "You think the aliens are here to, like, give you the recipe?"

"I *know* they are," Oswald replied, oozing confidence.

There was another long silence. Then Father cleared his throat and said, "Well, I have to get to the PTA meeting."

He kissed Mother and left us to deal with Oswald on our own. Traitor.

"Oz," Mother said hesitantly. "You know how much I respect you and love the myTality business model. But—"

"I *do* know how much you love it. And it's no accident this started on your farm. I should've known that when the Visitors returned, they'd contact me through a myTality distributor."

Mother smiled unsurely.

"This could be an opportunity for you," Oswald said. "The Visitors involved you for a reason. They know you can help me, and in doin' so...maybe bring even greater success into your own venture."

There was a pause. Then Mother's hesitation disappeared. Her smile turned genuine. "What exactly do you need me to do?"

COLLECTED DATA

INTERVIEWS

Subject #4, Victor Hofstadt (Father):

I support my wife in everything she does. Those myTality products weren't my cup of tea, but Jane sure could sell them. With that being said, was I happy J. Quincy Oswald was in Lansburg? No. I was not. And I sure wasn't going to let him stay on our property, like Jane suggested. It's bad enough I had to spend half my day chasing reporters and UFO hunters away from the crater. No way was I adding Oz to the mix.

Subject #7, Jane Hofstadt (Mother):

Oh, Oz's alien story... That was silly from the start.

Subject #1, Ishmael Hofstadt:

But, like, how would the fountain of youth even work? Would you stay how old you were when you drank from it? Cause what if you didn't find the fountain 'til you were ninety or something? Then it's like, what's even the point? Or would it reverse time and you'd be young again? But then what if you drank too much and it turned you back into a baby? If that happened, would you look like a baby but have all your old-person thoughts like in that Brad Pitt movie? Or would you *think* like a baby too?

Subject #8, Special Agent Mike Ruiz:

I'm not at liberty to give an in-depth comment. But I can confirm that, at the time, Mr. Oswald's products were being investigated by the FDA.

EVENT:
J. Quincy Oswald
(CONT.)

J. Quincy Oswald overstayed his welcome. At least, *I* thought so. I was more than happy when, shortly after dusk, he said he should be going.

"You'll be in touch?" Mother asked, seeing him to the front porch. I trailed behind, ready to push Oswald forcefully into his car if necessary.

"You can count on it," he replied.

Outside, Oswald unlocked his monstrous, gold Range Rover. Funny that with all his talk of immortality, he didn't balk at driving an SUV that was notoriously bad for the environment. Apparently, Oswald planned to live forever while the world around him died.

Before he could leave, another car pulled into the driveway. Cass and Arden. We planned to hang out and do homework while they tried to change my mind about attending the homecoming dance.

They didn't realize I was aware of the last part.

Cass maneuvered her car around the Range Rover and she and Arden climbed out, looking at Oswald with open curiosity. He gazed back with a similar expression.

"Who do we have here?" Oswald asked.

"My friends," I said curtly. "We'll be going now. Nice to see you, Mr. Oswald."

But instead of allowing me to slip away with Cass and Arden in tow, Oswald stepped toward them, smiling his too-slick smile.

"J. Quincy Oswald," he said, holding out his hand. "But you can call me Oz."

Cass's eyebrows shot up. "The great and powerful Oz, in the flesh."

I'd given her a full recap of the myTality™ conference, and she'd decided instantly that Oswald and his followers were a source of great fascination.

"Well, I don't know 'bout all that," Oswald said with faux modesty.

"It was nice seeing you, Mr. Oswald," I repeated forcefully. "Good luck with your pursuits."

I motioned for Cass and Arden to follow me and began walking through the yard, in the direction of my lab.

"Can't we hang out in your bedroom?" Cass asked, hurrying to catch up. "The lab is so...lab-like."

"I'd like to distance myself from my house right now."

"The lab is fine with me," Arden said.

Once we'd left Mother and Oswald safely behind, Cass said, "So *that's* Oz."

"Please don't call him that."

"Come on. It's hilarious. You can't tell me it isn't hilarious."

"Do I look amused?"

"When do you *ever* look amused?"

Once we were settled in the lab—Cass claiming the comfortable desk chair, while Arden and I were relegated to the cold, metal, folding chairs—I began to relax. Kepler peered suspiciously from his hiding spot under my desk. Arden moved to pet him and he hissed, making her quickly draw back.

"I didn't expect Oz to be so..." Cass trailed off.

"Smug? Arrogant?"

"Hot."

I rolled my eyes. "He's the leader of a pyramid scheme, conning thousands of people out of their hard-earned money to line his own pockets."

"But he *is* handsome," Arden said.

"He seemed plenty taken with you too." I frowned, thinking of how eagerly Oswald had introduced himself to my friends.

Arden shook her head and her cheeks turned splotchy red. "With Cass maybe. Not me."

"Hey," Cass said, leaning forward. "Don't do that."

Arden shrugged. "It's true. I'm not trying to insult myself. It's just, look at us."

To be fair, Cass *did* draw the eye. She wore a sparkly tutu-like skirt and had her hair in a ballerina bun. Arden, meanwhile, was clad in her usual shapeless cardigan. And more important, Cass's shoulders were straighter. Her chin was raised higher. She carried herself like she deserved to be paid attention to, while Arden twisted her fingers anxiously through her long hair, shoulders pulled toward her chest, eyes downcast. Her posture screamed *don't look at me*, though I know she wanted to be seen just as much as the next person.

Still. I felt 92 percent sure Oswald *had* seen her. It was Arden his eyes lingered on.

"Look, Arden," Cass said. "So you're not wearing some weird outfit. You think that makes me any better than you? It's just clothes."

"That's not all it is, and you know it. Guys don't like me. Ever."

"Guys *do* like you," Cass said. "You just don't realize it. You need more confidence."

"Great," I said brusquely. "Maybe Arden can pop into the confidence store and pick some up."

Cass raised her eyebrows. "What's *your* problem?"

"I hate when people act like we can change our personalities, like it's that easy to become something we're not," I said, thinking of all the times I'd been coaxed to be more social, more emotional, more outgoing. As if the personality I was born with was deficient, and if I simply put effort into it, I could be a better person—a person who didn't resemble my true self.

"Let's not fight," Arden said. "Please? Can we talk about something else?"

"Yes," I agreed. I reached over and grabbed my calculus book from the desk. "Like homework. I really can't afford to miss more assignments if I want to stay in the running for valedictorian."

Cass looked at me with a bemused expression.

"What?" I asked.

"I don't know a ton about MIT, but I'd bet you anything they don't *only* accept valedictorians."

"Well, yes, of course," I said. For instance, they would probably overlook the fact that I hadn't been valedictorian if I showed them my brilliant sociological study that was getting discussed world-wide. "What's your point?"

"I dunno," Cass said, shrugging. "Maybe do homework because you want to learn something and not, you know, to get some title that doesn't even mean anything out of high school."

I frowned. "For the record, forty-two percent of MIT students—"

"*Or*," Cass interrupted, "you can forget all that stuff entirely and tell us what that Oz guy was doing here."

"J. Quincy Oswald is the *last* thing I want to talk about."

But Cass and Arden gazed at me raptly and I knew how entertained they'd be by Oswald's voice of God that became the voice of aliens. So I told them everything. Maybe it was better that I did. We spent most of the evening joking about the extraterrestrial fountain of youth and envisioning the mayhem that would ensue if people at Irving High School were granted eternal life.

I hadn't realized how much I'd needed to de-stress. How I needed a night of sitting around laughing with friends.

By the end of the evening, I was more amused by Oswald than concerned.

And that should've been concerning in itself.

COLLECTED DATA

TEXT CONVERSATION

Participants: Gideon Hofstadt, Ishmael Hofstadt

IH: dude

IH: but what about cow mutilations

GH: I'm sorry, what?

IH: i was thinking

GH: About mutilations? Why? Where are you right now?

IH: in my room

GH: Then why are you texting me?

IH: upstairs is so far

GH: Why were you thinking about cow mutilations?

IH: cause its maybe time to raise the stakes again

IH: and didnt you say cow mutilations are an alien thing?

GH: Under no circumstances are we mutilating ANY animal.

IH: oh

IH: well, we still need to raise the stakes

GH: Yes, I know.

IH: you do???

GH: I'm working on an idea.

Crop Circle Designs

EVENT:
Guidance

DATE: SEPT. 27 (WED.)

Being that I'd spent the majority of English lit doodling crop-circle designs, I assumed I was in trouble when Mr. Fiore called my name. He'd hated me since the first week of school, when I expressed displeasure that an entire quarter would be spent on poetry.

But all Mr. Fiore said was, "Ms. Singh wants to see you."

I was happy enough to leave class without discovering how Robert Frost[1] handled the apparently overwhelming choice of diverging roads.

I knocked on the guidance counselor's door and it swung open instantly, as if Ms. Singh had been waiting. She was young and hadn't yet lost passion for the job like some of the faculty at Irving High School. I'd met with her once before, at the end of the previous year, and while her eagerness was overwhelming, she was likable.

"Gideon, so nice to see you," she said, ushering me inside.

Though her office was too small for it, she'd pushed her desk

---

1   Robert Frost (1874–1963): an American poet. Once confused by Ishmael with Jack Frost, the personification of winter.

to one side and brought in a love seat and small armchair—using her own money and time, I imagined. A box of tissues sat on a coffee table next to a vase of fresh flowers, and motivational posters adorned the walls.

Ms. Singh gestured for me to sit on the love seat and took the chair across from me. It was so cramped that my knees bumped into the coffee table. I couldn't imagine how taller people managed.

"I want to check in with all the upperclassmen while we're still early in the year," Ms. Singh said. "It's time to get serious about the future, so I thought we could chat and make sure you're on the right track."

"Okay," I agreed. I never shied away from talking about the future.

"Last we spoke, you had your heart set on MIT."

"I still do."

Ms. Singh nodded pleasantly, but said, "Have you considered backup options?"

I frowned. I'd gotten that question enough from Mother and Father. "No."

"Well, I really encourage students not to pin all their hopes on one school."

But for me, there only *was* one school. I'd wanted to go to MIT since I'd found out MIT *existed*.

"I've worked very hard to make myself the ideal applicant," I said.

"I know you have. I looked through your file before you got here. Your GPA is excellent—"

"Not as excellent as Sara Kang's," I replied bitterly.

"You still have a shot at valedictorian if you put in extra effort this year."

"And if Sara Kang *doesn't* put in effort, right?"

Ms. Singh ignored the question and said, "Are you keeping up with your extracurriculars?"

"Yes."

It wasn't strictly true. I'd skipped the last several debate team meetings and hadn't volunteered in a while. But I was semi-active in science club. And I was still on track to becoming an Eagle Scout, despite it being a torturous experience. I enjoyed working toward some of the merit badges,[1] but the camping trips were agonizing. Tents and trees and nature. Not to mention s'mores, which were the stickiest, most stress-inducing food I'd ever eaten.

"I've done some research on MIT," Ms. Singh said. "They strive to take on well-rounded students."

"Which I aspire to be."

"They prefer applicants to have participated in a sport."

I knew that. I'd done my research too. "Unfortunately, that's not possible."

"Have you looked into all the options? Maybe track?"

I almost laughed out loud. I couldn't make it down the corridor without getting winded. "They *prefer* students to have a sport; they don't *require* it."

None of this mattered anyway. Surely my unconventional pursuits would be more attractive to the admissions board than whether or not I played football. I began to feel anxious. I should be

---

1   See: astronomy, electronics.

working on the next stage of the hoax, not spending time discussing my athletic ability.

Thankfully, Ms. Singh moved on. "What about your hopes for after college?"

"I plan to work for NASA."

She smiled. "An astronaut, huh?"

"An engineer."

People assumed wanting to work for NASA meant wanting to go to space. Not me. Astronauts were daredevils. Space travel involved innumerable risks. I'd rather keep my feet firmly planted on Earth.

"You know," Ms. Singh said thoughtfully, "I have a friend who works for Triple i."[1]

I tried not to visibly cringe.

"Triple i is interesting," I conceded. "But not NASA."

Triple i was all about space tourism and flashiness. It was where hip, young people worked, because sometimes space could be trendy. It wasn't comparable to NASA, with its long history of tradition and countless achievements.

"It might be worth looking into, though," she said. "I could put you in touch with my friend."

I thanked Ms. Singh because she really was trying to help, but I didn't want to talk to her friend. It was NASA or nothing. It was MIT or nothing. And thanks to the groundbreaking sociological paper I was writing, achieving those goals would be possible.

We chatted for a few more minutes, discussing my strategy for the rest of the year. She offered to get me information pamphlets.

---

1   Triple i: Interstellar Initiatives Inc., a private space-travel company.

Poor Ms. Singh didn't seem to know that the information in her pamphlets could be easily found online.

Still, I left the meeting feeling optimistic and imagining the glory and wonder my future would hold.

Of course, there were still several steps I had to take before I could *enjoy* that future. Beginning with researching crop circles.

EVENT: Suspicious Behavior

DATE: SEPT. 27 (WED.)

I liked doing research right before bed. I'd drift to sleep with new information still floating through my consciousness. I always hoped it would permeate my dreams.

But it was hard to concentrate on research with overly synthesized pop music blaring from the bedroom next door.

I threw my book about crop circles on the bed, stomped into the hall, and pounded on my sister's door.

"What?" she shouted.

I pushed the door open and stepped into Maggie's room.

"*Excuse me*. I didn't say come in."

I held up a hand to my ear, pretending I couldn't hear. She rolled her eyes, but reached over to her tablet and cut the sound.

"What do you want?" she asked.

"For you to have common courtesy and *not* blast your music."

"It doesn't bother Mom and Dad."

"They don't share a wall with you."

Maggie rolled her eyes again. "Whatever. I'll keep it down."

I was about to leave, because I'd never been entirely comfortable in my sister's lair. Each wall was painted a different neon color and they were covered with movie posters, photos, and various other bits of memorabilia. Softball trophies cluttered a dresser. The majority of her wardrobe was on the floor, along with who knew what else. The chaos of Maggie's room made me anxious.

But I hesitated when I realized what Maggie had been doing when I walked in. Not watching TV or playing a video game or texting friends. She'd been reading a book. An actual, physical book, made of bound paper. I was 91 percent sure I'd never seen her do that before.

"What are you reading?" I asked.

"Nothing."

Was it my imagination, or did she shift her leg to hide the book cover?

"Clearly you're reading *something*."

"It's none of your business."

If I were Ishmael, I'd have charmed the information out of her. But I didn't have that skill, so I resorted to a less sophisticated tactic: I leapt toward the bed and attempted to grab the book.

Unfortunately, I wasn't fast either. Maggie and I wrestled for a moment. I was on the brink of giving up when my hand finally closed around the book's spine. I pushed away from her and moved to the center of the room, examining what I held while Maggie scowled and called me an asshole.

"*Follow Me: A Study of the World's Most Charismatic Cult Leaders*," I read.

I looked at my sister.

"What?" Maggie asked.

"Why are you reading this?"

"Why not?"

"It's a weird interest to suddenly have."

Maggie laughed, loud and sharp. "Do you really want to talk about sudden, weird interests?" She yanked the book from my hand. "I found it in a box with a bunch of other books Gram left here and was curious. That's all."

"I see."

Maggie and I gazed at each other for a long moment, and there was a clear understanding between us. The understanding that neither of us trusted the other at all.

"What are you up to?" I asked.

"What are *you* up to?"

"Me? I'm not up to anything."

There was another silence, then Maggie smiled meanly. "You realize no one buys your alien story, right?"

"Judging from what I hear around town, you're wrong."

"Oh, please. Ishmael is known for practical jokes. You're known for being a science nerd. You think people aren't able to put the pieces together?"

"Why go along with it then?" I shot back. "Why are people making up alien stories of their own?"

Maggie shook her head and looked at me sadly, as if pained by my naivety. "You just don't understand human nature at all, do you?"

Of course I didn't. I never had, and even with the help of this sociological experiment, maybe I never would.

"I'm going back to my room," I said.

"Good."

"Please keep your music down."

Instead of responding, Maggie, a thirteen-year-old far better versed in human nature than me, curled up on her bed again, the book about cult leaders open in her lap.

INTERVIEW

Subject #2, Magdalene (Maggie) Hofstadt:

I kept thinking about how J. Quincy Oswald made me *want* to believe him, even though all that alien stuff was totally stupid. Probably everyone who signed up for myTality felt the same way. They didn't join the company for the products, they joined for *Oz*. Gideon always called myTality a cult, and I wondered if he was right, and what other cult leaders were like. That's why I read the book. Not that it was my brother's business. Besides, I saw what book was on *his* nightstand.

EVENT:
Crop Circles

DATE: SEPT. 28 (THURS.)

Getting eight hours of sleep was necessary to function at top capacity. For that reason, I'd always kept myself on a strict schedule. Unfortunately, you couldn't sneak into a neighbor's field to make crop circles while the rest of the world was awake.

It was past midnight when Ishmael and I dragged our supplies to David O'Grady's[1] farm. It would have been more convenient to stay on our own property, but that would raise suspicion. Due to its proximity, O'Grady's field was the next obvious choice.

I'll admit I never liked O'Grady. When I was very young, he once happened upon Father teaching me to play baseball. He called me "sissy-boy" when I ducked from the ball—as if I was supposed to stand there and let a projectile fly directly toward my face! Father immediately chastised O'Grady, but I never forgot those words, or how small they made me feel. Years later, once I learned more about bigotry, I wondered if O'Grady had *only* been talking about baseball.

---

1   David O'Grady, approximately seventy years old, our closest neighbor.

So there was no lost love between the farmer and me. But even so, I chose to make a crop circle in a cornfield that had already been harvested for the season. I wasn't out to ruin anyone's livelihood.

"It's funny," Ishmael said, dropping the two-by-four he carried and looking at the cornstalks surrounding us. "You'd think crop circles would be difficult to make."

"And yet they're not."

"It's totally not something I ever saw myself doing."

I yawned and rubbed my eyes. "Let's get this over with. I have a test in the morning."

Plotting the shape of the circles was simple with a computer and overhead maps. Ishmael assisted me in using string to mark the design in the field—we'd chosen one of the least complex ones. In no time, we were ready to begin the labor portion. Ishmael and I each had a wooden plank with rope attached. By holding the rope, we could drag the plank through the field, flattening cornstalks as we went.

It was absurdly simple, but exhausting. After nearly an hour of hard labor, we'd only completed the inner circle.

"Are you sure we shouldn't have gone with cow mutilation?" Ishmael asked. He stopped working and wiped his brow with the hem of his Hawaiian shirt.

I took the opportunity to stop too, doing my best to disguise how heavily I was breathing. "Is that a serious question?"

"Yeah, dude."

"Are you telling me you'd feel *comfortable* mutilating an animal? If I remember correctly, you won't even touch uncooked chicken."

Ishmael made a face. "Uncooked chicken is gross."

"Then how do you think you're going to mutilate a cow?"

Ishmael squinted. He looked up at the sky. He looked back at me. "I see your point."

"Thank you."

I went back to dragging the two-by-four around the field.

A while later, Ishmael stopped again. "Maybe we've done enough?"

"We're only half-finished," I wheezed. My T-shirt was adhered to my back with sweat and my legs wobbled. "Half a crop circle isn't a successful close encounter of the second kind."

"Second kind?"

I nodded, trying to get my breath back.

"What are the other kinds?"

"Exactly what you'd expect, starting with UFO sightings and getting progressively more ridiculous."

"Huh," Ishmael said thoughtfully. "Why don't you list them for me?"

"Are you trying to get out of working?"

Ishmael grinned sheepishly.

"Come on," I said, continuing through the field. "The longer you procrastinate the worse this will get."

Dawn was approaching before we finished—we hardly had time to spare. The O'Grady farm being operational meant activity began when the sun rose.

I couldn't tell how the crop circle looked. I'd have to wait for an overhead shot of it to know how successful we'd been. But I was sure one was coming. With all the fanfare over aliens, the news crew would send a helicopter. Or maybe one of the Seekers had a drone.

Exhausted, Ishmael and I picked up our planks and made our way back toward our house. I could get a couple hours of sleep before school started, at least.

I reminded myself the lack of sleep would be worthwhile. When people saw the crop circle, they'd react with wonder and excitement and maybe even fear. And I'd know *I* had created it. I'd made something no one in Lansburg would ever forget.

INTERVIEW

Subject #12, David O'Grady:

I don't leave cornstalks in the field just for giggles, you hear? They replenish the soil with organic material and prevent erosion during winter. Farming doesn't end when the harvest is done. But I guess I shouldn't expect the Hofstadts to know that. Their farmland doesn't do anything but sit there and look pretty.

Interlude
Close Encounter Types

Close Encounters of the First Kind

- Visual sighting of an unidentified flying object from less than five hundred feet away.

Close Encounters of the Second Kind

- UFO event that causes a physical reaction in the observer or in the surrounding area.

Close Encounters of the Third Kind

- UFO event where an extraterrestrial life-form is present.

Close Encounters of the Fourth Kind

- Human abduction by a UFO.

Close Encounters of the Fifth Kind

- Direct, cooperative communication between aliens and humans.

Close Encounters of the Sixth Kind

+ The death of a human or animal associated with a UFO event.

Close Encounters of the Seventh Kind

+ Creation of a human/alien hybrid.

EVENT:
More Lies

DATE: SEPT. 29 (FRI.)

Arden was waiting by my locker in the morning. I slowly approached her, hoping the stiffness in my joints from the long night of manual labor wasn't apparent.

"Gideon, have you heard?"

"Heard what?" I wished I had even a fraction of Cass's acting ability.

Arden's fingers twisted through her hair and she gazed at me with enormous eyes. "Mr. O'Grady found a crop circle in his field."

"Really? Wow."

"You should see the pictures," Arden gushed. "It's so cool— though it's kinda lopsided."

I didn't flinch. I was *not* going to be insulted. "I'm sure it's still quite remarkable."

"It is, for sure! Just not as fancy as the crop circles on TV."[1]

I refrained from telling Arden that making a crop circle might look easy but was actually very strenuous, and it wasn't a failing that

---

1   For the record, most of the crop circles on television are digitally rendered.

it turned out *kinda lopsided*. I would've liked to see anyone else in Lansburg make a crop circle remotely as good as mine.

All I said was, "How interesting."

"It *is*, isn't it?" She bit her lip and seemed to carefully choose her next words. "Gideon…you believe there are really aliens, right?"

To buy myself a moment, I motioned Arden to step aside from my locker and spun the dial on the combination lock. I hated lying to her face, but I didn't trust her enough to tell her the truth, and I couldn't let a momentary twist of guilt undermine the whole experiment.

"I believe the universe is full of mysteries. And right now, Lansburg seems to be a hot spot for them."

"But do you think beings are visiting from another planet?" she pushed.

I wished I was better at reading people. I knew Arden wanted, maybe *needed*, a specific answer, but I had no clue what it was. Instead of trying to fill in the blanks, I said, "Arden, what's going on?"

She hesitated. "You'll think it's silly."

"I won't."

"It's just…" Arden lowered her voice so no one would overhear. "Part of me really wants there to be aliens."

I stopped rummaging through my locker and gave her my full attention. "Why is that?"

"Wouldn't it be nice to know something else is out there? I'd feel…less alone, I guess."

I met Arden's gaze. For the first time, I felt like we were on the same wavelength.

"On the other hand," Arden said, "I'm afraid of what it means if the aliens *are* real."

196 | CHELSEA SEDOTI

"Me too," I admitted. I spoke evenly, remained collected, even though I wanted to shout, *Yes! Either way is terrifying! Yes, either way we have to confront our own cosmic insignificance! Yes, you understand!*

"Because if they're real," Arden went on, "why haven't I been taken?"

Wait. What?

Just like that, the momentary link we shared was shattered.

"What do you mean?"

Arden tugged her hair over her shoulder. "People keep seeing UFOs and some people have even been abducted. And I keep thinking... I don't know. It's probably scary, but it also means you're special, you know?"

I did not know. But I gestured for her to continue.

"I keep watching the sky at night," she said. "But I haven't seen or heard *anything*. What's wrong with me?"

What could I possibly say? *Arden, the reason you haven't been abducted is because no one has been abducted. The difference between you and the abductees is that you're not a liar.*

I couldn't bring myself to voice the words, though. I'd have to admit I lied to her from the start. I'd have to admit the *reason* I lied to her—because I was afraid to trust people, because opening up to her would make me vulnerable. Just the thought of being so candid made my heart rate spike.

So instead of being honest, I said, "Being abducted by aliens doesn't make a person special."

Arden snorted. "Easy for you to say. This all started at your house. It's like someone in a relationship telling a single person that relationships don't matter."

"They *don't* matter," I said.

I hated the expression on Arden's face. I suspected she might start crying and I *really* didn't know how to deal with that.

"Maybe you're focusing on the wrong thing. As long as there are aliens, you'll always have the potential to get abducted, right? Isn't that, ultimately, better than knowing we're alone?"

Arden thought about it. "I guess so."

"You *are* special," I told her. "Even if you never get abducted by aliens. You'll always be special."

Arden's eyes filled with tears, and I worried I'd made the situation worse. But she said, "Thank you."

She leaned over and hugged me. It wasn't just the first time Arden and I had hugged—it was the first time in a long time *any* friend had hugged me. Cass had learned my rules about physical affection long ago.[1]

I awkwardly patted Arden on the back, feeling the sharp jut of her shoulder blades. I didn't know how long the hug was expected to go on. Was I supposed to pull away or was she?

Before I was forced to figure it out, Arden disengaged.

"Thank you," she said again.

"Um. You're welcome."

Then she went to class. She moved away down the hall, silent and oddly graceful, slipping between people the way water slips over stones.

I watched her go, guilt welling up inside of me. How many times would I lie to her before the hoax was over?

---

1   Outside of a romantic context, physical affection made me uncomfortable.

EVENT:
Father Revolts

DATE: OCT. 1 (SUN.)

When I left my room in the morning, I noticed a strange phenomenon: my house was quiet. There was no clang of breakfast dishes. Music didn't play from the radio on the kitchen counter. The television wasn't tuned to ESPN. It was then that I realized how bustling the farm usually was.

I paused on the stairs and pondered it. What did it mean that some things could only be recognized by their absence? How much in a person's life might go unnoticed until it's gone?

I filed the thought away as something to dwell on later and continued to the kitchen. Father sat at the table. He was eating a Pop-Tart and reading a book about the history of the Pittsburgh Pirates. I didn't know where the Pop-Tart came from. Mother hated them. She said we might as well eat cake for breakfast.

"What's going on?" I asked cautiously.

Father kept his eyes trained on the book. "Good morning."

I looked at the stove. It was off. There were no pots or pans on it, no dishes in the sink.

"There's no breakfast?"

"There's a full fridge and pantry," Father replied.

"You want *me* to make breakfast?"

"I'm sure you're capable."

Of course I was. I'd followed complicated recipes during experiments. It wasn't the thought of making my own food that distressed me, it was the fact that Father *wasn't*.

"Is everything okay?"

"Well," said Father in an amiable voice that didn't match his words, "it looks like everyone in this house is going to do what they want, without me having any say. So you can all make your own goddamn breakfast."

"I see."

I walked to the counter and put a piece of bread in the toaster.

It wasn't the first time I'd made food for myself. For instance, there were times when Mother and Father took a solo vacation and left us with Gram, and she certainly wasn't going to wake up early and make breakfast for perfectly capable teenagers.

But aside from those rare occurrences, if Father was home, he cooked. He always said taking care of the house and family was his job, and it was important he do his job well. The current situation was unheard of.

My toast popped out of the toaster. I regarded it. Jelly sounded nice. But while *eating* jelly wasn't generally messy, slathering it on the toast in the first place could be an issue. Undoubtedly, someone[1] was careless the last time they opened the jar and slopped

---

1   See: Ishmael.

jelly down the side, or got it stuck in the threading on the lid. I'd likely end up with jelly covering my hand.

I grabbed the peanut butter instead, which at least didn't leave sticky residue.

I sat down across from my father. "Do you want to talk?"

Father put down his book. He looked at me for a long moment. "I'm not sure where to start."

I waited patiently.

"Your mom and I wanted to stay out of it," he said. "Let you and Ishmael get trapped in your lies."

I opened my mouth to speak, but he held up a hand.

"Don't start with me, Gideon. Don't tell me you saw aliens."

"I wasn't going to."

"Anyway," Father continued, "now we're apparently going along with this ruse."

I took a bite of toast and chewed carefully. "You are?"

"We are. Because *Oz* is here," Father said, his voice dripping with sarcasm. "And we're going to cater to him."

It suddenly became very hard to swallow. "*Why?*"

"Your mom is building a business. And having J. Quincy Oswald in her town, creating a new product line with her at the helm, will make all her dreams come true."

I was certain this new turn of events would lead to no good.

"And you're...okay with that?"

Father looked at a spot on the wall over my head for a long time. Finally, he said, "No. I'm not okay with it. But despite the fact that I gave up my career to raise you kids, despite the fact that I take care of *everything* around this house—I cook, clean, do laundry, spend half my day playing chauffeur—despite all that, I don't actually have a voice in what happens here."

I wanted to tell him how untrue that was. But I realized I didn't actually know one way or the other. It never occurred to me that he might be unhappy, that he might feel there was an imbalance in his and Mother's relationship.

"What do you want me to do?" I asked quietly.

"Do whatever you need to." He stood and made his way out of the kitchen.

There was a heavy feeling in my stomach. It was unnatural to see Father so unhappy. I wanted to give him something, some small token.

"Father?" I said, drawing him back into the room. "I was wondering if you might teach me to drive soon."

The look on his face indicated he wouldn't have been more surprised if a UFO descended right in front of him.

"Why now?" he asked.

"I just... I've put it off for too long. I'm ready to learn."

"Okay then," he said, his expression brightening a fraction. "We'll go out this weekend."

This weekend? "There's no rush if you've got other things going on."

"I'd rather do this sooner than later."

Well then. That was that. I was learning to drive.

Interlude
The Problem with Driving

Someday the issue of driving will be irrelevant. After all, we're moving in the direction of self-driving cars, and I'm 88 percent sure that, in the near future, they'll be the primary means of transportation.

For that reason, learning to drive was pointless. It would be a better use of time to learn a skill with long-term application.

"No one forced Isaac Newton to drive," I once told my parents. "Instead, he was given the freedom to make some of the most important scientific discoveries of all time."

Father gave me a long look. "Remind me, when was Isaac Newton alive?"

Isaac Newton lived from 1643 to 1727, which, yes, meant he never had to make the choice about driving one way or the other. It didn't exactly help prove my point. But the fact remained: driving was an unnecessary waste of my mental energy.

It was also dangerous.

More than one million people died in car accidents each year. On average, that was 3,287 deaths a day. And car crashes were the leading cause of death among people ages fifteen to twenty-nine.

Even the *best* drivers risked their lives when they got on the road—and I harbored the secret fear that my driving skills would be severely deficient.

People assumed that if you were science-minded, you must be good with all mechanics. I can assure you, that isn't the case. Manipulating a vehicle has more in common with athletic prowess than it does with *building* a vehicle.

Sadly, my spatial awareness left something to be desired. I had trouble gauging distances. The mere thought of maneuvering a car filled me with anxiety, and few phrases struck fear in my heart like "merging into traffic."

So, thus far, I had avoided driving.

I'd avoid even *mentioning* driving if I could—it's a topic that only serves to embarrass me. But, alas, like so many things that happened that autumn, my inability to operate a motor vehicle would turn out far more significant than I'd ever imagined.

EVENT:
Father Revolts
(CONT.)

Father left the room, gone off to...do whatever he planned to do. How would he fill his day if he wasn't taking care of us and the house?

A while later, the rest of my family wandered into the kitchen. Mother grabbed a myTality™ Power-Up and seemed entirely unconcerned with the lack of breakfast options. Maggie shrugged and got a bowl of cereal. Ishmael was the only one of us who seemed lost.

"Get a grip," Maggie told him. "You can pour cereal."

"I was just really hoping for waffles today," my brother replied glumly.

Mother sat at the table and opened her planner, aggressively flipping pages and making notes. I'd tried getting her to switch to using her phone to no avail. She said the act of physically writing down appointments etched them into her memory. But why did her memory matter if she kept track in a planner anyway?

"Will J. Quincy Oswald be in town for a while?" I probed.

"Hmm?" Mother replied, distracted. "Oh yes, quite a while, I think. At least until the launch of the new product. I'm meeting with him today."

"I see."

My phone buzzed with a text. It was from Ishmael. I glanced up and frowned at him. He widened his eyes and nodded at the phone, urging me to read.

TEXT CONVERSATION

Participants: Gideon Hofstadt, Ishmael Hofstadt

IH: go with her

GH: Where? To visit Oswald?

IH: yea

see what hes up to

keep tabs or whatever

GH: Why don't YOU go?

IH: youre the smart one

youll get more info

GH: You just want to keep your Sunday free.

IH: arent i supposed to talk to people

like spread more alien gossip

ill be rly busy

EVENT:
Father Revolts

(CONT.)

Maggie's head whipped back and forth between Ishmael and me. "Are you two texting each other?"

I put down my phone. "No."

"You guys are so weird."

"Be nice to your brothers," Mother muttered distractedly.

I glanced at my phone again. As much as it pained me, Ishmael was right. One of us should keep track of Oswald. Keep track of his movements...and maybe of his *methods* too. A small, perhaps traitorous, part of me still thought I might learn something from him.

"Mother," I said. "Could I join you today?"

She looked up from her planner with an expression that wasn't outright shock, but was very close. "Of course you can."

"Where's Oz staying anyway?" Ishmael asked.

"Well, your father wouldn't let him stay here—which would have been the hospitable thing to do. So he's out on Crescent Road."

There were no hotels on Crescent Road. There wasn't much of anything.

"Is he sleeping in a field?" I asked. Based on J. Quincy Oswald's snazzy clothes and high-end car, that struck me as incongruous.

"Not *in* the field. He rented an RV."

"Why not stay in town?" He could surely afford a room at Doe Lake Resort, the closest thing Lansburg had to a luxury hotel.

"That would be fine for *him*," Mother said. "But he wants to be close to everyone else."

"Everyone else?"

"The people with him. The other distributors."

I met Ishmael's gaze across the table.

Oswald had brought people with him. Or maybe they flocked to him after the fact. I thought back to the seminar, the rapt faces gazing at him, cheering and crying, their expressions of awe and worship.

Maybe he had a contingent of people who followed him everywhere.

Yes, that seemed right. I wasn't sure why it hadn't occurred to me already. *Of course* J. Quincy Oswald had groupies.

INTERVIEW

Subject #4, Victor Hofstadt (Father):

Kids should have time to be kids. That's what I always thought. I grew up with a single mom who worked sixty hours a week. I got a job to help her as soon as I was old enough. Baseball was my only break, and I guess that's why I loved it so much. I wanted my kids to have better lives than that. I wanted to take away their hardships, do everything for them, give them time to chase their dreams. I didn't realize that by giving them so much, I'd lose myself in the process.

EVENT:
A Visit to
Oswald's Camp
DATE: OCT. 1 (SUN.)

The field where J. Quincy Oswald set up camp was on the opposite side of Lansburg. Mother and I passed through the center of town on the way there.

More people milled around downtown than I'd ever seen before. Reporters carrying notebooks and wearing pristine hiking boots with their business suits, presumably planning a trek into the field to see the crop circle. Seekers with wild hair and rumpled clothes from nights spent sleeping in tents. The usual senior citizen tourist groups, curiously watching the news broadcast that was underway directly in front of the lava lamp.

I had done this.

I'd drawn these people to town. I'd given their lives interest and meaning, if only for a short while.

The tourists and UFO hunters and camera crews might never know I was the one who'd lured them to Lansburg, but that was beside the point. For once, I felt more like a god than a starfish.

"There's something I want to talk to you about," Mother said, pulling me from my reverie.

I glanced over. Her expression was firm and I immediately tensed. Here it was. The lecture I'd been waiting for, where she admitted she was angry about the havoc I'd caused.

"There's a distributor in Pittsburgh on my downline."

Or not.

"She has a son who's a little older than you," Mother went on. "He's studying for a culinary arts degree."

"Okay...and?"

"He's a nice boy. Very smart. And handsome."

Suddenly, I knew what she was getting at.

"No, Mother," I said simply. "I told you before, I don't need you to *matchmake*."

It had been a while since she'd done this, and I thought she'd realized I was never going to take the bait. *Never.*

"It's just that—"

"I'm capable of dating without your help."

Mother's eyes lit up with hope. "Are you seeing someone?"

"No," I replied shortly.

"You know, I always thought you and Owen Campbell would make a—"

"I know what you've thought."

Owen and I had come to a kind of unspoken truce since our argument—at least, I assumed we had, since we were both acting like everything was fine between us. But even if Owen weren't a factor, I couldn't imagine anything more excruciating than a blind date set up by one of my parents.

Mother and I were silent for a long time after that. I considered turning on the radio, despite the fact that 95 percent of what

212 | CHELSEA SEDOTI

played on it made me cringe. Eventually, she said, "I worry about you, Gideon."

I briefly closed my eyes.

"You're so isolated," she went on.

"I attend high school. It's impossible to be isolated while attending high school."

"How many people do you interact with while you're there?"

"I have plenty of friends."

"You have Cass."

"And Arden," I pointed out.

"You've never been very welcoming to Arden."

Mother was an extrovert. She couldn't understand that having a small social circle never made me feel like I was lacking. I didn't *want* tons of friends. She thought that made me broken, like something was essentially wrong at my core. And I hated that.

Different humans had different needs.

For instance: a man of average height and weight with an active lifestyle might require 3,500 calories a day to maintain weight and be functional. Whereas a similarly sized man who was entirely sedentary would require 2,200 calories. Though the men might have the same BMI,[1] each has specific caloric needs that fit their unique bodies.

Social interaction was the same.

Mother was bolstered by social events. I was the opposite. It didn't mean anything was wrong with me, just that she and I were made differently.

---

1   Body mass index.

"Will you at least consider it?" Mother asked.

"Consider *what*?"

"Going on a date with Alex. I think you'd like him."

Resentment welled up inside of me. Why couldn't she accept me for who I was?

"I just don't want you to be one of those people," she went on.

I raised my eyebrows. "What people would *those* be?"

"Someone who lives for their work and looks back one day and realizes how little life they've experienced."

I barked out a sharp laugh. Mother lived for work as much as I did. She never even *had* to work—it was her *choice*. She went from venture to venture, never able to settle down, because she needed to be in motion, needed to be accomplishing something. She was even willing to overlook an absurd alien story, just because it might help grow her business.

And I'd experienced *plenty* of life. It wasn't the same way Mother experienced it; it wasn't made up of personal interactions and social events. But I knew how the world *functioned*. I knew how nebula became star systems. I knew how hydrogen and helium formed the gas giants, while other atoms formed the terrestrial worlds. I knew Earth's ideal conditions for life and I knew the Drake equation said there must be other, similar, planets out there.

I knew about the universe, the wide scope of it.

That was life. Looking at the sky, seeing stars and planets and galaxies, seeing the intricate way they functioned together, the balance of it. *That* was an experience. I'd never trade it for a bunch of awkward first dates.

There was more to life than the *human* experience. It was so hard to grasp that most people didn't even try. But you could experience life on a universal scale. On a cosmic scale. You just had to open your mind to it.

I didn't tell Mother any of this for two reasons:

1. She'd probably take it as further proof of my oddness.
2. We'd arrived at our destination.

I'd seen some of the Seekers' campgrounds while traveling around Lansburg, and I assumed J. Quincy Oswald's setup would be similar. In some ways, it was. There were tents and campers, and a music festival sort of look. Or, at least, what I imagined a music festival would look like.

But while the Seekers had set up a commune, Oswald had a kingdom. And as with every kingdom, the king had a castle that set him apart from the peasants.

Calling J. Quincy Oswald's temporary home an *RV* was inadequate. It was a palace on wheels, the largest and gaudiest camper I'd ever seen.

Tents and lesser RVs surrounded Oswald's grandiose monstrosity, arranged in a series of concentric circles. It reminded me of drawings of wagon trains I'd seen in history class. When stopping for the night, the wagons pulled into a circle, blocking threats. A campfire was lit in the middle, where people could feel warm and protected and safe. Except here, the only thing that needed safekeeping was the great and powerful Oz.

You could tell how the different distributors were faring in their business endeavors. Those in RVs presumably were doing okay for themselves and were "steadily growing their downline," as Mother would've said. Those in tents, especially the ragged-looking ones at the edge of the circle, maybe not so much. One of the tents had a banner stretched across it, decorated with the myTality™ creed: *Forget* mor*tality. It's not* your*tality. It's* my*Tality!*

I followed Mother as she made her way through the campground. As she passed, people stopped to speak to her. She was recognized and treated with the utmost respect.

Oswald was king, but Mother wasn't just a lowly serf. She was his duke or earl or something. I didn't know if that made me proud or concerned.

Mother knocked on the door of Oswald's RV and it immediately swung open.

"There's my favorite distributor," he said. Mother beamed.

He motioned us inside, where the decor was as obnoxious as I imagined. White leather furniture, softly glowing track lights, marble countertops.[1] The interior of Oswald's RV probably cost more than most of the homes in Lansburg.

"So many people have come," Mother said, gesturing to the field outside.

"This is an opportunity no one dare miss," Oswald said solemnly. "You know we're gettin' a gift, don't you, Jane? We're first in line for something that's gonna revolutionize the whole world."

"I'm honored to be here for it."

Was it Oswald's confidence that drew so many followers to him? If you act like you're in charge, do you eventually *become* in charge?

---

1   The marble was especially absurd. In an RV, every feature should be chosen for its mass, flexibility, and collapsibility.

"And you, Gideon," Oswald said, placing a hand on my shoulder. "How must it feel to know it all began with you?"

"I'm rather indifferent to it, actually," I lied.

I saw a flicker on Oswald's face. For a brief moment, his mask dropped. He wasn't used to being met with apathy. Just as quickly, the moment passed, and his grin returned. "You youngsters never realize the significance of cultural change. You'll learn."

He led Mother to the table where papers and folders were spread out. Before joining them, I took a long look around the RV, hoping to find some sign of...anything, really. Personality. Life. A sign that Oswald wasn't buying into his own charade. But despite the luxury, the interior was sterile. There was nothing to tell me about Oswald as a person, or what might be happening below the surface.

I walked to the table, where Mother and Oswald were engaged in conversation. I tried to listen, but my brain shut down when it came to myTality™. I only got bits and pieces:

—*fountain of youth*—

—*have to set a price point*—

—*potential to become our most successful product*—

Notably absent from the conversation was discussion of the effectiveness of the "extraterrestrial elixir." No one at the table had illusions about the product, or the aliens being real—so I assumed, anyway—yet neither Oswald nor Mother seemed concerned that they were preparing to sell a lie.

Maybe I didn't have room to be self-righteous. Wasn't that what I'd been doing for weeks?

EXCERPTS FROM SELECT MEDIA COVERAGE SEPT. 27–OCT. 1

From the Lansburg six o'clock news (station WLPB-TV):

Here in Lansburg, speculation runs rampant as more UFO investigators flock to town—culminating with the arrival of J. Quincy Oswald, CEO of the much-debated multi-level marketing company myTality. Sources close to Mr. Oswald claim he's had direct contact with extraterrestrials, but no more information has been provided.

From lightbringernews.com:

The activity has ramped up considerably over the past weeks, with reports of UFOs, alien abductions, and the appearance of a crop circle in David O'Grady's field. *The Light Bringer* reached out to Mr. O'Grady for a comment, but he adamantly declined, citing that he "has nothing to say and wants these lunatics off his property." One has to wonder if there's something on the farm that Mr. O'Grady is trying to hide.

From *Basin and Range Radio*:

Live from the loneliest corner of the Mojave, you're listening to *Basin and Range Radio*, where we keep an eye on the night sky. This is your host, Robert Nash. Tonight, we return to a small Pennsylvania town that's been a hot spot for alien activity going on three weeks now. We've got Arnie Hodges, respected ufologist, waiting on the line to give us the latest updates.

COLLECTED DATA

From *The Finance Gurus* podcast:

ROB: Now we've talked a lot about J. Quincy Oswald on this show—

HARVEY: For any first-time listeners, he's the scumbag CEO of one of America's fastest-growing pyramid schemes. Whatever you do, kids, do *not* sign up with myTality.

ROB: Right now, he's got something else up his sleeve, though… You want to do the honors, Harvey?

HARVEY: Do I ever. Boys and girls, J. Quincy Oswald is currently in western Pennsylvania, communicating with aliens.

ROB: You heard right—*aliens*.

HARVEY: Now, we don't usually stray from personal finance on this show, but we've gotta take a moment to discuss what exactly Oswald is doing out there.

From *The Late, Late Show with Johnny Speck*:

Y'all have heard what's going on in Pennsylvania, right? And I don't mean the Steelers being favored for another Super Bowl win. Nope, I'm talking *aliens*. You heard me. Little green men. Look this up. I'm not lyin'. The whole town's supposedly been abducted by now, and all I've gotta say is, those rumors about the mushrooms in rural Pennsylvania must be true!

LANSBURG CLOSE ENCOUNTER STATISTICS AS OF OCT. 1

Information gathered from a variety of sources, including: blog posts, news articles, comments on news articles, general word of mouth.

150	people have seen lights in the sky
76	people have had visual contact with an unidentified flying object
60	people have sensed an extraterrestrial presence
82	people have been plagued by nightmares
32	people recall strange experiments being performed on them
29	people have visited the doctor, citing unexplained bruises or burns
48	people actually remember being abducted
38	people think myTality™ is the greatest company in the world
7	people think the current happenings are "bullshit"
3	people think Lansburg's lava lamp is somehow connected to extraterrestrials
1	person is certain the recent events are heralding the second coming of Christ

Interlude
Historical Comparisons of Mass Hysteria

Perhaps you're baffled by the situation in Lansburg. How could so many people believe they'd seen flying saucers or been abducted by aliens?

The simple explanation is mass hysteria—a phenomenon where a group of people shares frenzied emotions, such as excitement or anxiety. These people develop irrational beliefs or become convinced they're suffering from the same mysterious ailment.

What happened in Lansburg that autumn wasn't unprecedented. Allow me to give you a brief overview of some similar occurrences:

The Dancing Plague (Strasbourg, France, 1518): Numerous people inexplicably dance for days without rest—some of them ultimately dying from exhaustion.

The Salem Witch Trials (Salem, Massachusetts, 1692–1693): Young women experience strange fits that are attributed to witchcraft. The town is gripped by terror. Eventually suspicion and accusations lead to the execution of twenty "witches."

The Halifax Slasher (Halifax, England, 1938): A man prowls the streets, brutally attacking residents. A massive investigation is launched. Eventually, one of the "victims" admits he inflicted damage on himself for attention. Other victims confess they lied too. The Halifax Slasher never actually existed.

The Laughing Epidemic (Kashasha, Tanzania, 1962): Three teens begin laughing at a joke, and the laughter spreads through their school. This laughing epidemic lasts for weeks, extending to other, nearby schools as well.

The Mothman Sightings (Point Pleasant, West Virginia, 1966–1967): For more than a year, countless locals spot a winged, manlike creature around town. No explanation is ever found—though some claim the Mothman was an extraterrestrial.

Over the years there have been instances of mass fainting spells, of teens being "possessed by Satan," of people losing the ability to walk or speak. In one case in the Middle Ages, all the nuns in a convent spontaneously began meowing like cats.

In some occurrences of mass hysteria, like the Halifax Slasher, the events were undoubtedly faked. Other episodes were less clear. Were people being deceptive, or did they truly believe they were experiencing symptoms?

And if they believed it, even if that belief was false, did that make it the truth or a lie?

EVENT:
The Next Step

DATE: OCT. 1 (SUN.)

I sat in the swivel chair in my lab, head tilted back, gazing at the low ceiling. Kepler twisted around my feet, and I absently reached down to scratch his head.

"Kepler," I said. "The hoax is flourishing. Maybe I should consider it a success. I created something that can sustain itself independently. If God exists, isn't that what he did when he created the world?"

Kepler purred but didn't offer further input.

It must be so simple to be a cat. Part of me envied it. How comforting to think of nothing but food and sleep. But it was a vague envy. I'd never trade places with Kepler. I wouldn't abandon the complex structure of the human mind and willingly relegate myself to being a cat—or a starfish.

"On the other hand," I went on, "without me actively dictating the course of events, can I truly take credit for them?"

The door to the lab flew open and Ishmael sauntered in. He looked around. "Is someone here?"

My face heated. "I was just..."

He glanced down at Kepler. "Talking to the cat?"

"Well. Yes."

Ishmael shrugged. He plopped on the folding chair, and Kepler quickly made himself scarce.

"How was Oz?"

"Hard at work on his elixir. Apparently, the aliens contacted him about the ingredients. He'll unveil the product soon."

Ishmael screwed his face up in contemplation. "How's he doing it so fast?"

"Because, Ishmael, the 'formula' is probably sugar water."

"Ah, right. Do you want to know about my reconnaissance mission? I took notes like you wanted."

"Sure."

Ishmael handed me a sheet of paper. I sighed at the sight of his messy scrawl and began the process of deciphering it.

ISHMAEL'S INTEL

Okay. Im taking notes like you want but dont blame me if you cant read my writing.

- Hayden who works at Adrenaline X-treme with me: saw lights 2 times, 1st was on her way home from work at like 9 near her neighborhood. 2nd time she was leaving her boyfriends house at midnight and the light was right above her and she told him to come look so he saw too.

- Some guy by the lava lamp, he said his name, but I forget: saw 1 ufo the first night he was in town, 3 nights ago. Also saw an alien face in the lava lamp and said maybe it wasnt ever a tourist attraction but actually is filled with some alien preservative or something? I didnt really know what he was talking about and he creeped me out so I left.

- Mr Blake from the pharmacy: saw lights in the sky 3 times, a ufo 2 times and once the ufo had a beam of light shoot down.

- Gram: saw a ufo once. Grams for sure lying. I mean everyones lying. But gram especially.

- Matthew and Ethan from school: both saw lights a bunch of times and ethan had missing time once and matthew said streetlights keep turning off when he walks under them, so maybe they've been abducted. They also said Isabel, that girl on the student council, was abducted and shes shaken up about it, and Joaquin from the basketball team was abducted but he told Matthew and Ethan it was really cool and not scary.

- Sofia: says her abductions keep happening over and over and I guess all these people in the play with her (mice or something?) all have abduction stories too which is fine with Sofia as long as hers is the best.

- Old Mrs. Callahan: I wasnt even going to ask her anything cuz everyone knows she likes to tell stories to mess with people. But she grabbed me and told me all about her abductions that have been happening since she was 20 and how she always knew Lansburg had aliens. I know shes kinda senile, but shes been talking to a bunch of reporters, fyi.

- A bunch of guys at the bar: I guess they're in some club called muffon? I dont know. Anyway there were like 5 of them and they all saw lights and 3 saw a flying saucer and 1 had lost time and keeps having dreams about owls watching him. They had more stuff to say but the bartender noticed me and kicked me out cuz Im underage.

Okay I know you wanted lots of details but my hand hurts from writing so much. Can we just say there are a lot of people who saw ufos and stuff? Do you really need to know every single one?

EVENT:
The Next Step
(CONT.)

"Well," I said, staring at Ishmael's sloppy report, "you made an attempt."

"Dude, practically *everyone's* had some sort of alien experience," he said, ignoring my lackluster tone.

"What about the skeptics?"

"Well, *they* haven't seen UFOs."

I sucked in a breath. "Obviously. But what are they *saying*?"

Ishmael shrugged. "They won't believe anything unless they see it themselves."

I thought about that.

"Is there any way we could, you know…build a UFO?"

I gave my brother a long look that should've accurately established my feelings. But still, I said, "No, Ishmael. No, I cannot build a spacecraft."[1]

"What about lights?"

---

1   Note: this might have been possible with a sizable increase in funds.

I rubbed my eyes and considered. "Maybe something with drones? I don't know."

"What's wrong? You seem stressed."

"I suppose I'm wondering what exactly we're doing," I admitted.

"Uh, I thought we were doing the best senior prank ever."

"No, Ishmael, that's what *you're* doing." I thought for a moment, then asked, "Why do you love practical jokes so much?"

Ishmael frowned. Maybe he hadn't pondered his motivations before. I knew he acted on impulse, but part of me figured he still lay awake at night, running through his actions and trying to derive meaning from them. That's what I assumed everyone did.

"I dunno. That's just who I am."

"No one is born a clown."

"Practical jokes are fun. They make the world happier."

I snorted.

"Seriously. There's all this dark stuff, you know?" Ishmael ran his fingers through his hair, searched for words. "Like...there're so many murders and so much hate. Sometimes it's nice to do things just to make people laugh or make their lives more interesting. Twenty years from now everyone will still talk about the time aliens came to their town, and maybe that way they won't have to think about the bad stuff so much."

"So you're a hero then? Swooping in to improve the lives of the small folk of Lansburg, Pennsylvania."

Ishmael crossed his arms. "Don't sit there all high and mighty on your science throne, like your reasons for doing this are better than mine. I don't even *know* your reasons."

"For glory," I said after a slight hesitation. "I'm doing it for glory."

"I don't get it."

Where to even begin?

"Sometimes I think about the universe—"

Ishmael sighed.

"Hear me out," I insisted. "Sometimes I think about the universe, and how many galaxies are in it, and how many stars are in those galaxies. The scope of it is beyond comprehension. When I think about that vastness, why does Earth matter? And if Earth is insignificant, everyone *on* Earth is insignificant too."

"And?"

"And that means everything we do is inconsequential. Babies are born. People die. Some people become rich while others live in squalor. And on the cosmic level, *none* of it matters. I could achieve success or die in a freak accident before my seventeenth birthday, and either way, the universe is indifferent."

My brother frowned.

I went on. "Why should humans even try to accomplish anything? Yet we *do* try, because the desire to persevere is ingrained in us. I know my success is meaningless, but I can't stop *trying*."

Ishmael thought for a long moment. "I just... What exactly does this have to do with the hoax?"

"Don't you see? Even on a small scale, here on Earth, the likelihood of me accomplishing anything significant is unlikely. Honestly, Ishmael, if I was going to be one of the great minds of science, I'd already know it."

"But you're so smart, dude."

"I read a lot of books. That's all."

Ishmael opened his mouth to argue, but I wasn't being self-deprecating. It was the truth. There was a difference between intelligence and knowledge, and I feared I only possessed the latter.

"I'll never be Copernicus. I'll never be Tycho Brahe or Isaac Newton or even Carl Sagan. I'm just me," I said. "And this hoax may not be extraordinary in the grand scheme of the cosmos. But I can use it to leverage a better future for myself. It might be the only thing that gets me close to greatness."

"Yeah," Ishmael said quietly. "I get that."

I reached out and pounded a hand on my desk, startling Kepler in the corner. "Only the hoax isn't *ours* anymore, is it? Other people took it. *Oz* is making an alien elixir and *that's* what the press cares about. It destroys me to think of other people getting famous off this. And when you tell me about the skeptics, I don't want to sit back and let them have their skeptical thoughts. I want to push further. I want to make them *believe*."

There was a long silence. Then Ishmael said, "Well, dude. Let's make them believe then."

"How?"

"Well, there's always—"

"Please don't say cow mutilation."

"But you admit that would cause a—"

"Ishmael."

"Okay, okay," he said, holding his hands up. "Just don't give up so easy. What would Isaac Newton do?"

What *would* Isaac Newton do? Probably obsess about the Bible, try to turn lead into gold, complain about Robert Hooke, and in his spare time advance science and math a few generations.[1] Most certainly, he wouldn't waste time on an alien hoax.

Our alien hoax was pointless. It wouldn't impact the universe. It wouldn't even impact *Earth*.

But still.

It was *mine*.

J. Quincy Oswald could have his alien elixir. The people shouting in the streets could have their lights in the sky. The hoax still belonged to *me*.

"We need to make people take notice," I said, my feelings of inferiority beginning to drift away.

"What about, like, an abduction?"

"That's called kidnapping. It's illegal."

Ishmael rolled his eyes. "No kidding. But can we abduct someone without *really* abducting them?"

I suddenly sat up straighter. "Radio interference."

"What?"

I opened a desk drawer and rifled through, looking for the bag of electronics I'd purchased in Pittsburgh the day of the myTality™ seminar. "We can't abduct anyone. But we can make them think they *narrowly missed* being abducted. A close encounter of the second kind."

"Yeah, dude, that sounds awesome," Ishmael said, perking up. "But...what does that have to do with the radio?"

"Lots of abductions begin with car malfunctions. There's often radio interference. We can scramble radio signals on some quiet

---

1   In addition to being a brilliant scientist, Isaac Newton was a devoutly religious alchemist.

road, and with the current climate in Lansburg, people will assume they experienced extraterrestrial activity."

Ishmael bounced up and down in his seat. "That's perfect!"

"I thought it might come to this," I said, holding up the bag of electronics. "I already have the parts."

I just needed to figure out how to make them work.

RADIO JAMMER

RADIO JAMMER BLOCK DIAGRAM

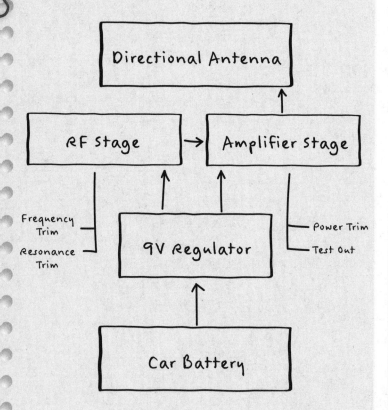

EVENT: Lights, Again

DATE: OCT. 2 (MON.)

I got back my most recent English quiz, which had a C written on it. I stared at the paper for a long time.

"What's wrong?" Cass—dressed like she'd stepped out of the 1980s—asked from her seat next to me.

I held up the paper. Her eyes widened in mock horror. "Oh, my stars, are aliens hurting your grades?"

They *were*. I was spending too much time reading about hoaxes and close encounters and mass hysteria. Granted, the quiz was only a small portion of our grades and we were studying poetry, a subject I'd never excel at. But I suspected I'd fallen behind in other classes too. What was wrong with me? Why was I letting a hoax become more important than school?

Because the hoax belongs *to you*, whispered a voice in the back of my head. *Of course it means more than randomly assigned homework.*

That didn't matter, though. Whether or not I cared about my English assignments, I had to do them. Otherwise Sara Kang would win and I'd graduate from high school with nothing to show for the hard work I'd put in.

At lunch, I arrived at the table first and began calculating the scores I'd need on subsequent English tests to offset the C. I was interrupted by Arden running up with wide eyes.

"Did you get my texts?" she asked.

"I haven't checked my phone all day."

My phone had become a hassle. Thanks to the hoax, I was getting regular alien-related texts from classmates who previously only contacted me for homework "help."[1] Ishmael had it even worse. The difference was, Ishmael adored the attention.

It was a paradox: I wanted to be successful and recognized for my work. But at the same time, I wanted to be left alone. Sort of like how I both thought highly of my own abilities and recognized how unimpressive those abilities actually were. When you got down to it, nearly everything about me was a contradiction. Maybe it was that way for everyone.

"What's going on?" I asked Arden.

She slid into her chair. I noticed she didn't have a lunch tray. She must have rushed over as soon as she stepped into the cafeteria.

"I saw them," she breathed.

"Saw what?"

Her face was flushed. Her eyes shone. Arden looked more animated than I'd ever seen her. "Lights, Gideon. I saw lights in the sky."

Oh no. Not Arden.

---

1   See: cheating.

I looked at her for a long moment. "Are you sure?"

"Of course I'm sure."

"Could it have been something else? A plane, maybe? Or Venus?"

A pained expression came over Arden's face. Her glow dimmed, her skin turning ashen as I watched.

"You don't believe me."

"It's just..." I didn't know how to finish, though.

"When *you* saw lights, you didn't doubt your own eyes."

"Yes, but—"

"And when Cass saw lights, you believed her too, didn't you?"

I didn't reply, because there was no need. Arden knew I hadn't challenged Cass's experience.

"So it's just me," Arden said. "You think I'm a liar. Or maybe you don't think I'm important enough to be visited by aliens."

What the hell? "Arden, no. That has nothing to do with—"

She turned away from me, shoulders slumped. "Just forget it."

This was what I deserved for lying to her. I should have included her in the hoax from day one. But how could I backtrack now? If I told her *I* lied, I'd also be saying I knew *she* was lying, and it would be too awkward to bear. By not being honest from the beginning, I'd effectively trapped myself.

"I'm sorry," I said, figuring the least I could do was listen to her story. "Can we start again? I really want to hear about this."

Arden shook her head listlessly. "Maybe some other time."

A moment later Cass appeared, her lunch tray loaded with food.

"Aren't you eating?" she asked Arden. "Here, have some of my fries. Zeus knows, I don't need all of these."

"I'm not hungry," Arden mumbled.

"You can't go all day without eating."

Arden pushed back from the table and leapt to her feet. "Stop telling me what to do," she said, loud enough for people at nearby tables to turn. Then she stomped away, her shoulders rigid with anger.

Cass looked at me. "Um, I kinda feel like I missed something."

"Accurate."

"What's going on?"

I didn't even know anymore.

COLLECTED DATA

INTERVIEW

Subject #6, Arden Byrd:

I woke up at midnight with a buzzing in my head, like my brain had turned into a million bees. Then this invisible string pulled me out of bed and over to the window. I pushed aside the curtains and the air was static and the world felt *alive*. There was nothing outside, though, just empty night. Then I realized my mistake. I'd looked *out*, when I should've looked *up*. I raised my eyes and there they were: lights dancing in the sky, twisting and turning like the aurora borealis. And in that moment, I felt like...like I'd been chosen.

EVENT:
Preparation

DATE: OCT. 4 (WED.)

I hunched over a mess of electronic components on my desk. The radio jammer was nearly finished, and soon I'd find out if I'd been successful.

"Now I'm going to use my oscilloscope to verify the jamming frequencies," I dictated to the phone, which recorded audio.

"Why are you saying everything you do?" Ishmael asked.

"We've been over this," I replied absently. "I'm recording everything related to the hoax."

"You must be blowing through your phone's memory."

I was. The hoax had taken over my life to the point where I was recording nearly every conversation I had.[1]

Ishmael craned his neck to see what I was working on. "You sure I can't help?"

"Considering that last time you 'helped,' you blew up the yard, no thanks."

---

[1] For full transparency, I admit not every conversation was recorded with *permission*. I was pleasantly surprised by how clean my audio recordings were, even when my phone was hidden in my pocket.

Ishmael shrugged and spun in circles in the swivel chair. It made me dizzy just looking at him.

"So," he said. "We're just gonna point this thing at cars and it'll screw up their radios?"

"In theory."

"What if they're not listening to the radio? What if they've, like, got a podcast on, or they're driving in silence?"

"Then it won't work."

"What if they have satellite radio?"

"Then it also won't work."

"What if—"

"Ishmael," I snapped, "this is the best I can do, okay? We're targeting cars leaving bingo night at St. Francis, and presumably those cars will be filled with old people, which will increase the odds of them listening to the radio."

"Okay, cool." Ishmael continued spinning. I was granted a full thirty seconds of silence before he said, "But are you sure—"

"I'm *really* trying to concentrate."

"Right. Sorry."

I took a deep breath and searched my mind. "Actually, there is something you can do."

"Are you just trying to get rid of me?"

"No."

Yes.

Ishmael stopped spinning. "Okay. What is it?"

"We need masks. And find something besides a Hawaiian shirt to wear."

"What's wrong with Hawaiian shirts?"

My jaw was clenched tightly and I knew I'd have another headache soon enough. "We're going to stand in the woods on the side of the road. Certainly, anyone passing by would find that extremely odd. Therefore, we'll wear dark clothes to hide ourselves and masks in case we get spotted despite the clothes."

"Ah, got it!" Ishmael said.

Dark clothes would be easy to procure. I was less sure about the ski masks. Most stores hadn't stocked winter items yet. There was always the Winter Wonderland Emporium on Main Street, but that was an expensive tourist trap.

"Get *cheap* masks," I told Ishmael.

"Dark clothes, cheap masks. Done."

He left the lab with a bounce in his step, enthusiastic about his task. I sighed and went back to work.

I tested the jammer on the small radio I'd borrowed from the kitchen counter. The frequency mixer didn't work as expected. I had assumed this would be straightforward, so what was the problem?

I was getting frustrated and antsy. I'd been in the lab too long. As much as I hated to admit it, sometimes I needed to step out of my own head.

When Cass texted and asked if I wanted to help her run her *Hamelin!* lines, it was a welcome distraction.

EVENT:
Running Lines

DATE: OCT. 4 (WED.)

Cass's house was a tribute to sleek, modern lines. The walls were white, the floor was tile, and there was a lot of glass. It was the opposite of the farm in every way; Cass's house looked like the future, while mine was firmly rooted in the past.

"Your house has *history*," Cass once said. "Think of all the generations of your family that have lived there. You're sleeping in the same place as your great-great-grandparents."

"Yes, and the plumbing hasn't been updated since the house was built, and there's water damage and peeling paint, and no matter how much you clean, the rooms always feel cramped and dusty," I'd replied.

There was *too much* history at my house. It was overbearing. I wanted to start fresh. Make my own history.

I walked up to the glass front door and rang the bell, knowing that inside Cass was pulling out her phone and looking at the video feed connected to the camera above me. Her house was equipped with the most modern alarm system innovations. My parents didn't even lock the front door most nights.

A moment later, the door swung open and Cass gestured me inside.

"I like your...pajamas," I said, raising my eyebrows at her baggy, purple unicorn costume.

"It's a Kigu," she replied. "Most comfortable outfit ever. You should totally get one."

"Yeah, I definitely see that happening."

Cass snorted and led me to the basement, her domain, a swirl of color and texture that contrasted sharply with the stark, spartan upstairs.

"We're working on the third act," Cass said.

"We?" I asked.

I entered the basement and stopped.

Owen sat on one of the couches.

"Oh. Hi," I said, feeling the strange fluttering in my chest that always happened when I saw Owen. "I didn't realize you were here."

He smiled. "I've hardly seen you lately. I told Cass she should invite you."

Despite the fact that Owen and I were...doing something that resembled dating, and I was happy to spend time with him, I felt like I'd been tricked. And it felt strange that they were hanging out without me. They were separate areas of my life. Yes, they were in theater together, and I knew their roles in *Hamelin!* intersected, but it still made me uncomfortable.

What if they talked about me? What if Owen shared all the arguments we'd had lately and Cass gave him unique insight into my personality that no one else had?

Owen walked over and kissed me lightly on the cheek. I tried not to flinch.

It was only a peck. Cass knew we'd done more than kiss on the cheek. But we'd spent so much time keeping our relationship private that it was bizarre to suddenly show affection in front of another person.

I moved to the couch and sat down. Owen sat next to me and Cass plopped into the opposite armchair.

"How's life on the farm?" she asked.

"The usual."

"The usual meaning normal or the usual meaning alien attacks?"

"Both?"

"What do you guys have planned next?" Cass asked.

Owen laughed. "Like Gideon would share his secrets."

The room fell silent for a moment, and I must have made a strange expression, because Owen glanced from me to Cass, as if realizing I *did* share my secrets with her. A wounded look came into his eyes.

He was being unfair. Of course I talked to Cass about things I wouldn't discuss with him. Cass had been my best friend since childhood and Owen was a fairly recent addition to my life.

"How's the play going?" I asked.

Owen didn't take the bait, but Cass sized up the situation and assisted my topic change.

"It would be infinitely better if I was the lead."

Owen tossed a pillow at her. "Don't be jealous. I personally support a *male* getting the *male* lead for a change."

"And I totally respect you as an actor," Cass said. "I just wish the female lead had some substance."

"Maybe you should add your own," I suggested.

"I've considered giving her some kind of awesome possum backstory," Cass admitted.

Owen handed me his script. "You can read along. Cass and I mostly have our lines memorized."

I flipped through the pages and took in the highlighted lines, the notes Owen had written in the margins. In the same way that I could look back on my own experiment notes and see how I'd come to specific conclusions, I could track Owen's process and see how he built his character. How his mind worked.

To me, *that* was romance.

That was what counted.

That connected me and Owen more than any over-the-top public display of affection.

I felt a rush of emotion that I couldn't define. There was a swelling in my chest and my hands tingled, and more than anything I wished Owen and I were alone right then so I could pour out my feelings to him, all the things he'd been wanting me to say but I hadn't been able to.

"Gideon?" Owen said.

I was startled out of my musings.

"What's your problem tonight?" Cass asked. "Come back to Earth and help me turn this character into more than a damsel in distress."

Interlude
The Pied Piper of Hamelin

In case you're unfamiliar with it, you should know *"The Pied Piper of Hamelin"* is a bedtime story you tell your children—if you want to make sure they never sleep again.

Allow me to give a brief synopsis:

The town of Hamelin has a rat problem. Because this takes place during the Middle Ages, one cannot simply call the exterminator. The poor townspeople despair.

But wait! Hope isn't lost! A stranger rides into town, a man referred to as the Pied Piper.

This Pied Piper fellow tells the townspeople he can fix their rat problem. By playing a (magical) tune on his (magical) pipe, the Piper will charm the rats and lead them out of Hamelin forever. All he requires is monetary compensation.

The townspeople agree. Despite the Piper coming across like a swindler, he does indeed charm the rats. He plays his pipe and the rats pour out of Hamelin and follow him to the river where they drown.

The town rejoices! But the townspeople are opportunists—now that the rats are gone, they see no reason to pay the Pied Piper.

The Piper is enraged. And one night, while the town sleeps, he gets revenge. He walks through the streets of Hamelin playing a new song on his pipe. This time it isn't rats that pour into the streets behind him. It's children. All the children in Hamelin.

They follow him through town, up a mountain path, to a dark cave. In the cave, there's a pool of water. And there, the Pied Piper drowns each and every one of them.

The end.

EXCERPT FROM IRVING HIGH SCHOOL'S ADAPTED *HAMELIN!* SCRIPT

The town of Hamelin is burning, lit by the spiteful glow of flames. In the distance, agonized screams of anguish can be heard. GRETA dashes into the street, tears streaking down her angelic face. She stumbles and falls to her knees.

GRETA:

Oh, please, won't someone please save me?

From offstage comes the melodious tinkling of pipe music. The PIED PIPER enters stage left, and rushes toward GRETA'S languishing form.

PIED PIPER:

I am here, my love!

The PIED PIPER envelops GRETA in his masculine clutch.

GRETA:

I knew you would come.

PIED PIPER:

I would never leave you, my darling.

COLLECTED DATA

GRETA:

The mayor has turned the town against you. They think you're behind the disappearance of the children. But I never doubted you.

PIED PIPER:

Nor have I ever doubted your love.

GRETA swoons.

PIED PIPER:

But we must leave this place now.

GRETA:

Where will we go?

PIED PIPER:

I will be happy anywhere, if you are by my side.

The PIED PIPER dips GRETA and kisses her passionately. Even as Hamelin burns around them, she succumbs to his loving embrace.

EVENT:
Running Lines
(CONT.)

I stared at the page, trying to remake the words in front of me. No matter how hard I tried to rearrange them, they remained as they were. Not only was it some of the worst writing I'd ever encountered, it ended with:

The PIED PIPER dips GRETA and kisses her passionately.

Kisses her.

Passionately.

It wasn't just a kiss—oh no, that would be far too simple and not appease the romance-obsessed play-goers in the audience. No, it had to be a *passionate* kiss.

"Um," I said.

Cass and Owen looked at me.

"What?" Cass asked.

"You have a kissing scene?"

"Yeah?" Cass stared at me like she didn't know what my problem was. Like there was no reason I should have a problem at all.

"Neither of you thought maybe that was something you should *tell* me?"

Cass and Owen exchanged baffled looks.

"I didn't even think of it," Owen said.

"You're kissing my best friend *passionately* and you didn't think it might be weird?"

"Gideon..." Owen looked almost like he might *laugh*. "It doesn't mean anything. It's *acting*. I'm obviously not attracted to Cass. No offense," he added, glancing at her.

"None taken. I'm not into you either, by the way."

I looked back and forth between them. They were acting so casual.

"I'm sorry, I just find it a little awkward that my best friend is going to be *passionately kissing* my..."

Owen and Cass stared at me with great interest.

"Your what?" Owen asked, when it was clear I wasn't going to continue. "You weren't going to say boyfriend, were you? Because you've made it very obvious that this isn't official."

Well, yes. That was accurate.

Logically, I knew *Hamelin!* was a play, not real life. It was fake life. A fake kiss in a fake world between people who weren't romantically involved. And even if it *was* a real kiss in real life, I'd have no room to be uncomfortable. Because I'd been the one holding back. I'd been the one preventing my and Owen's relationship from progressing.

Logically, I *knew* that. I was a logical person. Logic always won. Life would be meaningless without logic.

And yet.

And *yet*.

Unhappiness surged through me.

I took a moment to steady myself. Whether my feelings were logical or not, they didn't need to be on display for Cass and Owen.

"Okay," I said.

"Okay what?" asked Cass, looking at me like I'd just said the Earth was flat.

"Okay, fine, there's a kiss. I'm sorry I acted strange."

Owen reached over and squeezed my knee. "I promise, there's no reason to be jealous."

"I'm not jealous."

Interlude
Jealousy

I was jealous.

I was jealous and I hated myself for it.

It's not that I thought Owen would leave me for Cass. But still, I was disturbed at the thought of him kissing someone else.

And...

Well, I promised I'd be truthful in this account.

Owen kissing Cass bothered me because it was a glimpse of things to come. *This time* it was for a play. *This time* it was a kiss with someone he wasn't attracted to.

This time.

What about all the times in the future?

I had no illusions about my and Owen's future. According to an article I read, less than 2 percent of high school relationships ended in marriage.

While I had a year and a half of high school left before escaping to college, Owen was a senior. He'd leave in less than a year, while I was stuck in Lansburg. How could our relationship survive that?

Especially when...when I wasn't sure how much I meant to Owen in the first place.

Do you recall what I said about people trying to force Owen and me together? Regardless of whether or not we liked each other, if there were only two openly gay kids at a school, surely they must date?

For me, that wouldn't have been reason enough. But I happened to like Owen. A lot.

Was it the same for him, though? Doubtful. He was smart, popular, attractive, talented. The kind of person everyone liked and respected.

The truth is, I wanted to keep our relationship quiet because if people knew someone like Owen was dating someone like me, there'd be jokes. Maybe the jokes would be enough to make him step back and wonder what he was doing with me.

And he'd realize he was with me because I was there. The very thing I hated so much—being pushed toward him simply because there were no other options *must* have been why he dated me.

I knew I had redeeming qualities, and I was sure one day I'd find a man who appreciated them. But certainly that man wouldn't be as impossibly perfect as Owen. He and I were mismatched. Our relationship was entirely unbalanced.

That was why I wouldn't make our relationship public. Why make it official in the first place when I knew the eventual outcome?

And that was why it hurt to think of Owen kissing Cass. I knew it was the beginning of a long string of people he'd kiss, people who weren't me.

If heartbreak was inevitable, wasn't it better that we never named the thing between us? Wouldn't it hurt less when he left me? You can't truly lose something you never had in the first place.

INTERVIEWS

Subject #3, Cassidy (Cass) Robinson:

I felt for Gideon. But he was being a total drama llama. I wasn't gonna, like, drop out of the play because he was jealous.

Subject #5, Owen Campbell:

Honestly, it was probably the first time I felt sure Gideon actually *liked* me.

EVENT:
Radio Jamming

DATE: OCT. 6 (FRI.)

The radio jammer was complete. I wasn't positive it would function in the field, but I was ready to find out.

I dressed in dark slacks and a black sweater, then went downstairs to Ishmael's room. He lounged on his bed, eating a bowl of cereal.

"Is that your dinner?" I asked.

"What else am I supposed to eat? Dad still refuses to cook."

It had been nearly a week, and Father's strike was in full swing. Aside from his involvement in Maggie's softball games, he'd pulled back from all his responsibilities. As far as I could tell, he spent most of his time at the gym.

"Did you get everything?" I asked Ishmael. My own backpack was packed, double- and triple-checked, and ready to go.

"Yeah, hold up," he said.

He put down his bowl and stood. He wore black jeans and a plain gray T-shirt, but as I watched, he shrugged into a black trench coat.

"What do you think?" he asked. "I definitely look like a spy, right?"

He looked like someone who was *trying* to look like a spy. "Where'd that come from?"

"I borrowed it from Xavier."

"I sincerely hope you didn't tell him why you need it."

"Dude, give me some credit."

"What about masks?"

"Got 'em," Ishmael said, holding up his own backpack.

"I guess we're ready, then." But I hesitated. "Well. Maybe I should check my supplies one more time."

"Don't be nervous," Ishmael said.

"I'm not nervous."

"You're totally nervous. But don't worry, this is gonna be great."

Right. It would be great. It would go off without a hitch. The radio jammer would work flawlessly.

I straightened my shoulders. "Okay. Let's go scramble some radio signals."

LEGALITIES

According to the FCC[1] website:

Federal law generally prohibits radio broadcasts without a license issued by the FCC. Anyone found operating a radio station without FCC authorization can be subject to a variety of enforcement actions, including seizure of equipment, fines, and other criminal penalties.

And that, of course, was just the tip of the iceberg.

There were possible legal ramifications from the initial explosion. The hoax itself fell under reckless endangerment. When Ishmael and I made crop circles in Mr. O'Grady's field, we'd committed criminal trespassing and destruction of property.

I was racking up misdemeanors left and right—all of which came with potential long-term consequences.

So you see, at that juncture, I couldn't quit even if I'd wanted to. The hoax had come too far. I *had* to control it, remain on top of the situation. Otherwise, instead of leading me to MIT, the hoax might land me in a jail cell.

---

1   FCC: Federal Communications Commission.

EVENT:
Radio Jamming
(CONT.)

I hated the woods. If we could have gotten away with driving to our desired location, I would've done it in a second, but we couldn't risk anyone spotting our Jeep. So we drove as near as we dared, parked in the empty Shop-n-Save lot, and cut through the forest.

I'd chosen the spot for three reasons:

1. It was isolated.
2. There were no streetlights.
3. It was the only road leading from St. Francis, where the monthly Bingo Extravaganza was taking place.

But as we trekked through dense thickets of trees, I began to wish I'd chosen a spot that was easier to get to.

"Wait," I called to Ishmael.

He stopped and glanced back, a bizarre figure in his trench coat.

"I want to check something."

I unfolded my map and compared it to the satellite view on my phone.

"Dude," Ishmael said. "It's just up ahead."

"I want to be one hundred percent sure."

"How can someone so smart be so bad with directions?"

I bristled. "As I've told you before, intelligence comes in many forms. Spatial awareness has never been my forte. That doesn't mean—"

"But *I'm* great at directions," Ishmael said. "Can't you just trust me for once?"

Of course I couldn't trust him. But it was cold, my nose was running, branches kept scratching my face, and I was getting bitten by bugs.

I despised the outdoors so, so much.

"Okay," I agreed. "Lead the way. But if we're close, we should put the masks on first."

"Good call."

Ishmael unzipped his bag and fumbled inside for a moment before pulling out two items.

"Which do you want?" he asked.

"Aren't they the same?" I used my cell phone to shine light on them.

And froze.

My brother held two plastic Halloween masks.

"Ishmael. What is this?"

"Masks, dude. Do you wanna be Elvis, or this guy?"

He shook the second mask.

"That *guy* is John Fitzgerald Kennedy, the thirty-fifth president of the United States. But I don't want to be *either* of them."

Ishmael looked truly baffled.

262 | CHELSEA SEDOTI

"Ski masks, Ishmael," I hissed. "I wanted you to get *ski* masks."

Understanding dawned. "Oh! That actually makes a lot of sense."

I rubbed my eyes. It hadn't even occurred to me to be more specific with him.

"With Halloween so soon, there're masks everywhere," Ishmael said. "And you said cheap ones, so I thought—"

"It's fine. What's done is done."

"We could do this a different night. I can get ski masks like you wanted."

"No." I shook my head. "We're already here. Give me JFK."

He tossed the mask to me and I pulled it over my head, breathing in plasticky fumes.

I despised Halloween masks. They were itchy, uncomfortable, and belonged to a holiday I abhorred. I hadn't celebrated Halloween since I was nine and voiced my distress over dressing up foolishly and knocking on the doors of strangers just to be gawked at and handed candy I wouldn't even eat.

The mask made it hard to see, and was it my imagination, or was it getting harder to breathe[1]? I tried keeping pace with my brother, but in the darkness, with the trees closing in, it became increasingly difficult.

Finally, Ishmael halted. We were just inside the tree line. Ahead of us, moonlight lit the twisting path of Turtleback Road. For a moment I lamented that we didn't time this to coincide with the new moon. But that would've made our trek through the woods more perilous, so perhaps it was for the best.

---

1   In enclosed spaces, it's possible to die from asphyxiation due to the buildup of carbon dioxide from one's own respiration.

Quickly, I pulled out the jammer, attached it to the car battery that would power it, and pulled out the antenna.

We waited for the first car to approach. The only noise came from the woods—the rustling of some creature creeping through the underbrush, the chirp of insects. I tried not to think about the nature surrounding us.

After ten minutes, when I could feel Ishmael shifting around and getting antsy next to me, the hum of a car engine came from the direction of the church. A moment later, headlights swept across the road.

I fumbled with the radio jammer, held it up, and pressed the "on" switch just as the car passed.

Nothing happened.

"We'll get the next one," I said.

But the next car also passed us without so much as a flash of brake lights.

"Are you sure it's working?" Ishmael asked.

"Am I inside the cars?"

"No, dude, you're standing right next to me."

"Then no, I'm obviously not *sure* it's working. But it worked when I tested it on the Jeep earlier."

"Maybe no one's listening to the radio?" Ishmael said.

"Maybe."

In the distance, I heard the approach of another car. I waited patiently, and when a nondescript, white sedan rolled into view, I pressed the switch.

The car swerved. Not much, not fully into the opposite lane. But enough to tell me *something* had happened in the vehicle.

As I watched, the car slowed, and I could almost feel the way the driver's mind was working, how they must be trying to puzzle out what just occurred. I pictured them frantically flipping through radio stations, trying to figure out if it was a broadcast error or a problem with their vehicle. Or aliens.

"Yes!" Ishmael said.

"Keep your voice down."

After a moment, the driver hit the gas and sped into the night.

Another car rumbled through the fall evening. I raised my arm to turn the jammer on, but dropped my hand when I saw the lime-green Cadillac.

"It's Gram."

Ishmael bounced up and down, his Elvis mask wobbling. "That makes it even better. Zap Gram!"

"I'm not going to zap Gram."

Ishmael grabbed the jammer from my hand. "I'll do it."

"No," I snapped.

I tried to grab it back, and for a moment we tussled. Elvis and John F. Kennedy, standing on the side of the road late at night, fighting to get control of a radio jammer.

I won by default. Gram's car passed before Ishmael could zap her.

"You're such a killjoy," he mumbled.

I shushed Ishmael when I heard another car approaching. It was a minivan, and though it didn't swerve, for a brief moment the brake lights came on.

We zapped two more cars that didn't have a discernible change. The next one stopped entirely in the middle of the road for approximately ten seconds. The one after that also swerved.

"This is *so* working," Ishmael said excitedly.

Then I heard the sound of an engine that wasn't like the others. A louder, more aggressive rumble, a vehicle that had something to prove.

When the gold Range Rover appeared, taking up most of the road, I wasn't surprised.

"It's Oz," Ishmael said. "I'm gonna zap him."

"Don't."

But Ishmael shrugged me off and zapped Oswald's car anyway. I figured it was my punishment for winning the battle over Gram.

The Range Rover faltered and the brake lights sprang to life. Then the SUV stopped.

I was surprised it worked. J. Quincy Oswald struck me as the type of person who only listened to self-help podcasts—or maybe audio recordings of his own voice.

I kept my eyes trained on the gold SUV. Despite being an off-road vehicle, it looked more out of place in the middle of the woods than the lava lamp did in downtown Lansburg.

Unlike the other vehicles that stopped, Oswald didn't quickly drive away.

I waited.

"What's he doing?" Ishmael asked.

I didn't know, and didn't like it, whatever it was.

A moment later, my dislike of the situation grew by 73 percent. The driver's door swung open and J. Quincy Oswald stepped into the night.

He'd traded his cowboy boots for simple slip-on shoes, and he'd lost the sports jacket. The sleeves of his button-down shirt were rolled to the elbow. It was the most human I'd seen him look.

"Hello?" he shouted into the night.

"Shit," Ishmael muttered.

Oswald circled to the front of the Range Rover, lit by the glow of the headlights. He tilted his face to the sky. "*Hello?*" he called again, louder.

I glanced at my brother to see if his expression was as confused as mine must've been, forgetting he still wore the Elvis mask.

"I know you can hear me," Oswald screamed at the stars. "I know you're there, and I'm listenin'. I'm ready for whatever you give me."

Oh, boy.

Was he putting on a show because he knew someone was in the woods, watching him? Was he treating the empty road as if it were a stage?

Or.

Or.

Was this real?

For the first time, I considered that maybe J. Quincy Oswald wasn't performing, wasn't trying to con people. He might actually, truly believe aliens spoke to him. That scared me far more than his lies ever could.

Oswald fell to his knees in the road, directly in the path of his SUV, which he'd put in Park but hadn't turned off. Still beseeching the sky he shouted, "I've done everything you asked. The elixir is almost ready. Please, give me more instructions."

He was serious.

No. He *wasn't* serious. It was an act. It *had* to be.

"This dude is out of his mind," Ishmael whispered.

Before I could shush Ishmael, before Oswald could continue his attempted communication with extraterrestrials, a new element entered the equation.

A pickup truck pulled up behind Oswald's Range Rover.

"Do *not* zap it," I whispered through gritted teeth.

Oswald was so engrossed in the cosmos that he didn't notice a man get out of the truck behind him. It was David O'Grady, the farmer whose field we'd made the crop circle in. I'd heard he was *not* happy about that. I'd also heard that several Seekers tried to sneak on his farm to see the crop circle, and he'd chased them off with a gun. According to rumor, David O'Grady was always armed.

"What's going on here?" O'Grady rasped.

"Communication from the far reaches of the universe," Oswald replied reverently, still looking up.

O'Grady sighed and hitched up his pants by a belt loop. "I'm gonna have to ask you to pull to the side of the road. You're blocking traffic."

Oswald held up his hand to O'Grady, halting him. "I'm receivin' a message."

Ishmael snorted. I elbowed him. And, quite unfortunately, I caught him off balance. He stumbled and fell to the ground, creating a loud crash in the quiet night.

O'Grady's head snapped in our direction. "Who's there?"

I quickly pulled Ishmael to his feet. "Run!"

We tore through the woods, O'Grady on our heels.

"Shit, shit, shit," Ishmael said as we ran.

I didn't say anything. I couldn't have spoken even if I wanted to, because my chest was about to explode. When had I last run so much? When I was eight and forced to by some sadistic PE teacher?

Despite his age, O'Grady kept pace with us. I risked a glance behind me, but the JFK mask hindered my view.

Ishmael pulled farther and farther ahead of me. He never glanced back and didn't realize how dire my situation was. I tried to push myself harder, but my legs ached and lungs burned.

O'Grady was going to catch me. He was going to catch me and everything, the entire hoax, would be revealed.

The thought made my heart pound even faster.

I glanced back again and saw with horror that O'Grady was only ten feet behind. It was dark under the canopy of trees, but I could make out his features. He looked at me, right into my eyes. He'd *seen* me, and in just a few seconds he'd be close enough to reach out and grab me.

Then something miraculous happened.

David O'Grady tripped.

He fell to his knees and cried out in pain.

I looked in the direction Ishmael had gone, my legs still pumping. While my body tried to flee, my brain wondered if I should stop and help the farmer. Who leaves an old, injured man alone in the forest?

Of course, this old, injured man had a gun and a bad temper.

Even as I was trying to decide what to do, O'Grady began getting to his feet. That settled it. I kept running.

I ran and ran and eventually caught up with Ishmael, not because I became faster or gained lung capacity, but because Ishmael stopped to wait for me.

We'd reached the edge of the forest by that point, nearly back to the Shop-n-Save parking lot, and I stopped. I couldn't push myself any farther. I gasped for breath. My face felt hot and flushed and strange.

Then I remembered I was wearing the ridiculous mask. I ripped it off and immediately felt better. I sucked in deep breaths of cool night air and wiped away the sweat dripping into my eyes.

"See," Ishmael said. He jogged in place, pumped up and ready for more excitement. "I knew running track would pay off."

INTERVIEWS

Subject #9, Chief Lisa Kaufman:

Yes, interfering with radio signals *is* illegal. No, I'm sorry, at this time I can't say whether or not anyone will be pressing charges.

Subject #10, Mary Howard:

I'm one of those people, I don't believe something unless I see it myself. Except for God, of course, who I haven't seen with mine own eyes, but I've sure *felt*. I didn't pay heed to those alien stories, though. Thought it was a buncha oddballs looking for attention. Until the night of the Bingo Extravaganza. I was driving home when all of a sudden, the radio started to...flicker. I don't have a better word, but it came in and out real fast, until it was just static. And in the static, I heard something. Now, I guess it was a voice, but I won't say for sure it was talking to *me*. I'll just say the voice was there, and I surely heard it. I was so startled I slammed on my brakes! And then I saw the light in the sky. Right ahead of me, bright as anything. I'll speak the honest truth: it's the most scared I ever was in my life. I didn't wait around to be taken to no spacecraft. I got out of there right quick. Little ways down the road, the radio started working again, and that's how I knew I was safe. After that night, I didn't doubt the aliens anymore.

Subject #11, Miriam Warren (Gram):

Yes, I was driving down Turtleback Road that night. And yes, sure, I saw the UFO... Or had radio static... Or any other thing you're saying happened. Whatever it was, it happened to me too.

Subject #12, David O'Grady:

There wasn't a problem with my radio. I stopped my truck because I saw that health nut bozo in the middle of the road, shouting at the sky like he was talking to God. I thought maybe he snapped, maybe I should call an ambulance or something. Don't know what I was thinking exactly. Just that I'd seen that Oz around town and I'd heard what he'd been running his mouth about, and the sooner he left Lansburg the better. I got out of my truck, with a mind to wrangle that man. That's when I heard a person by the side of the road. When I ran that way, they moved into the forest. I chased. Don't know what I thought I was gonna do. Sometimes I forget I'm not so young anymore. Ended up that I tripped, landed on my bum hip. Never got close enough to nab the person, but I got a glimpse of him, and I'll tell you, I'll be damned if it didn't look like John Kennedy. Worst part is, while I was getting to my feet, Oz came up, insisting *he* call an ambulance for *me*. Lemme tell you something: in all my years, I never once needed an ambulance, and some little stumble in the woods ain't gonna change that.

NEWSPAPER ARTICLE

The following excerpt was reprinted with permission of the *Lansburg Daily Press*.

RADIO INTERFERENCE ON TURTLEBACK ROAD: PROOF OF ALIEN LIFE?

By K. T. Malone

October 7

LANSBURG, PA—Friday evening's Bingo Extravaganza was much like any other. The monthly event, held at the St. Francis de Sales Parish Hall, has long been a favorite among Lansburg residents, and October's festivities didn't disappoint.

After Henrietta Callahan won the grand prize—dinner for two at Doe Lake Resort—the crowd dispersed. For many bingo players, that was when the evening took an unusual turn.

Several Lansburg residents tuned into their favorite radio programs for the drive home, only to discover their radios no long worked properly. For a period of at least an hour, cars driving down Turtleback Road experienced radio interference such as static, distortion, or complete loss of signal.

Ufologist Arnie Hodges has made Lansburg his temporary home as he investigates the recent phenomena in town. Hodges claims radio interference is a common sign of an extraterrestrial encounter and encourages everyone who experienced it to contact a hypnotist about recovering repressed memories.

Though frightening to those involved, the event only had one injury: David O'Grady, farmer and longtime Lansburg resident, tripped and fell near the site of the radio interference. When asked why he had left the road, O'Grady said he'd been chasing a mysterious figure who bore a resemblance to past president John F. Kennedy.

EVENT: Driving Practice

DATE: OCT. 7 (SAT.)

I dragged myself downstairs in the morning, feeling the aftereffects of my race through the woods: I hadn't gotten enough sleep, my legs were sore, and I was covered in bug bites. If Ishmael felt even remotely as terrible as I did, he didn't show it. He was already at the breakfast table, energetically chomping through a bowl of cereal.

Father sat across from him reading the paper, but tossed it aside when I entered the room. I noticed it wasn't his usual sports section, but an article titled "Media Flocks to Lansburg."

"You need breakfast before we go?" he asked.

I looked at him blankly. "Go where?"

"Driving. Your first lesson is today."

Oh. Right.

Exactly what I was in the mood for.

Twenty minutes later, I sat in the driver's seat of the Jeep. The vehicle felt approximately four times as large as it did from the passenger's side. I wished desperately for a car that was less unwieldy.

I hadn't had a say in the Jeep, though. When Gram bought the Cadillac, she offered her beat-up Jeep Wrangler to Ishmael and me. Yes, I should have been grateful for a free vehicle. But besides the daunting size, the Jeep was in deplorable condition because Gram was, quite possibly, the worst driver in Pennsylvania.

The men and women who frequented her poker games still teased her about the time she dropped a lit cigarette while driving and, in her distraction trying to find it, plowed into a bus stop.

I didn't find the story funny for two reasons:

1. What if someone had been *at* the bus stop?
2. I was deeply afraid of making an error just as grievous.

"Did you adjust your mirrors?" Father asked, watching me from the passenger's seat.

"I believe so."

"You *believe* so?"

"I have excellent visibility with the rearview mirror. The side mirrors... I'm unsure of the optimal position. For instance, how much of my own vehicle should I be able to detect?" My fear was making me obnoxious, but I couldn't stop myself. "Surely the Jeep should only take up a small fraction of the frame, yet that's what's giving me perspective, and without perspective the mirrors are useless."

From the back seat, Ishmael loudly crunched through a bag of chips. "I'm so glad I came for this."

Father gave Ishmael a look. "I can still send you into the house."

"Sorry. I'll be good."

"You should see a small sliver of the car, but mostly road,"

Father told me, twisting in his seat to look behind us. "What about the maple tree? Can you see it in your right mirror?"

"Not really."

"Not really, or no?"

"*Not really*, Father. I see a fraction of it, but not the tree in its entirety."

"Gideon. You need to relax."

I scowled. "I'm relaxed."

Ishmael snorted.

"Adjust your mirror to see the tree," Father said.

I did as he asked, taking longer than necessary.

"Now turn the car on."

I shakily turned the key and my heart dropped. What if, upon coming to life, the Jeep malfunctioned and flew straight into the side of the house?

That was an illogical thought. I *knew* it was illogical. Why did I forget everything I knew to be true when it came to motor vehicles?

"You know which pedal is which, right?"

I sighed. "Yes, Father. Of course I do."

The mechanics of the Jeep weren't the issue. I understood *the theory* behind driving, and I had basic knowledge of how the vehicle functioned.[1] It was just a machine, after all. But I still feared that somehow I'd get confused and press the wrong pedal. I worried my foot might slip as I tried to step on the brake and I'd plow into the car ahead of me.

Knowing something was entirely different from *doing*.

---

1   I'd only gotten one question wrong on my permit test, and it was a question about motorcycles that wasn't in the DMV study guide.

"I should change shoes," I said.

Father sighed deeply. "Why?"

"These soles are smooth. I don't have any traction."

"Dude," said Ishmael, "you're not mountain climbing."

"But—"

"Your shoes are fine," Father said.

"Just drive barefoot," Ishmael suggested. "I do it all the time."

Father turned and looked at my brother. "Why are you driving barefoot all the time?"

Ishmael shrugged.

"Could we discuss that later?" I snapped.

Father scrubbed his hand over his face as if he was just so, so weary. "This is going to be a long day, isn't it?"

I suspected he was correct.

Interlude
Mistakes I Made
My First Time Driving

1. Failed to use my turn signal on two occasions because I was too nervous to shift my hand on the wheel.

2. Chose to make three right turns to reach a destination because I was too nervous to attempt a left.

3. Slammed on the brakes approximately forty feet behind the next car while stopping at a traffic light because I was unable to properly gauge distance.

4. Ran a stop sign because I was focused on the speedometer and wondering how to efficiently regulate my speed.

5. Gripped the wheel so tightly that for the rest of the day my hands were sore.

EVENT: Another Interrogation

DATE: OCT. 7 (SAT.)

My relief at the end of my first driving lesson was short-lived. As I pulled into the driveway, my body still stiff with tension, I saw that another vehicle waited there: Chief Kaufman's police cruiser.

"Do you have plans with Kaufman today?" I asked Father, hoping she was there for a social visit.

"Nope."

I felt a trickle of apprehension entirely separate from my apprehension about trying to park near the cruiser without hitting it—the last thing I needed was to get into a fender bender with a police vehicle. Had Kaufman gotten wind of my and Ishmael's antics with the radio jammer? I was 71 percent sure we hadn't left evidence behind, and with our masks, O'Grady shouldn't have realized it was us. But still...

"Who's that guy with the chief?" Ishmael asked suddenly.

I was fully concentrated on putting the car in park, but from the corner of my eye I saw Father peer out the window. "I don't know. Let's find out." He opened the door before I had a chance to engage the emergency brake, which was *not* proper safety protocol.

The man climbed from the passenger's seat of Kaufman's car at the same time I exited the Jeep. The first thing I noticed was his suit. It immediately put me on alert. In Lansburg, suits were reserved for weddings and funerals—with the exception of Adam Frykowski and his desperate attempt to appear more credible. The man with Kaufman didn't need to *try* to appear credible. He was middle-aged, impeccably groomed, and exuded confidence. His suit, for the record, was tailored to perfection.

"Morning," Kaufman said. She nodded to the man. "This is Agent Ruiz."

My heart turned to ice. "Agent?"

Ruiz reached out to shake my hand. "I work for the FBI."[1]

Oh no. They definitely knew about the radio jammer. Why else would an FBI agent be in Lansburg? How had they pinned it on Ishmael and me so quickly, though?

Even Father seemed alarmed at this new development. He warily introduced himself to Ruiz, then said, "Maybe we should take this conversation inside."

I studied Ruiz as we made our way into the living room. He didn't seem particularly hostile. If he'd come to accuse of us committing a federal crime, would he be so relaxed?

"What's this about, Lisa?" Father asked once we were all seated.

"We have a few questions for the boys."

Ishmael smiled confidently. "Hopefully we have answers for you."

Ruiz pulled a small spiral notebook from his pocket and looked

---

1   FBI: Federal Bureau of Investigation.

at me and Ishmael. I braced myself. "I'd love to hear a little about the alien activity that's been going on."

What?

He wanted to know about the *aliens?* The FBI couldn't be taking the abductions seriously, could they?

While I pondered whether the hoax had gone so far that it had fooled the government, Ishmael talked and talked. As always when holding court, he was in his element. He took Ruiz through the timeline of activity, from the explosion in our field to the present. I dimly wondered if lying to a federal agent was a crime.

Ruiz made notes and nodded often, stopping occasionally to clarify names and dates or get details about the people involved. Eventually, he asked, "How long have you known J. Quincy Oswald?"

"I wouldn't say we *know* him..." Ishmael said.

My brother and Ruiz continued to talk, while I fought to keep a scowl off my face. Why was Oswald always popping up? Our entire hoax was becoming centered around him and his ridiculous alien juice. The FBI was getting involved now, and if the situation got big enough, *NASA* might even become interested.

And who would be there to take the credit if NASA rolled into Lansburg?

J. Quincy Oswald, of course. The great and powerful Oz.

He was reaping the benefits of everything I'd worked for. He was going to go down in history as one of the first people who'd experienced true extraterrestrial communication—

I stopped.

I mentally shook myself.

What was I thinking? I was acting like this was *real*, like the farm actually had been some sort of UFO landing pad.

There were no aliens, I reminded myself. Or maybe there were. Maybe somewhere in the universe there was proof we weren't alone. But not in Lansburg.

"That's it for now," Ruiz said, flipping his notebook shut.

I realized I'd missed a good portion of the conversation while fuming about Oswald.

"Thanks, boys," Kaufman said.

"No problem," Ishmael replied. "Let us know if you have any other questions."

"Yes. We're happy to help," I added hollowly.

We saw them to the door and said goodbye, but my trepidation didn't depart with Kaufman's police cruiser.

As soon as Father left the living room, I turned to Ishmael. Keeping my voice low, I said, "What was *that* about?"

"What do you mean?" he threw himself down on the couch and picked up the remote.

"Why is the FBI here?"

"You heard him. They want to know about the aliens." Ishmael scrolled through channels until he landed on a rerun of *Pitch, Please* where contestants pitched a show that would follow a group of flat-earthers on a journey to discover the edge of the planet.

"Since when does the FBI investigate aliens?"

My brother didn't look away from the TV. "I dunno. I'm not, like, an expert on what the FBI does."

A thought struck me. "Do they know this is a hoax? Is *that* why Ruiz is here?"

"No way. We've covered our tracks."

Had we? So well that trained investigators couldn't uncover errors we'd made?

"I don't like this," I said. "Something isn't right."

Ishmael waved me off with his usual cavalier attitude. "Seriously, dude, you worry way too much."

EVENT:
Another
Interrogation
(CONT.)

I did *not* worry too much. I worried the exact, reasonable amount. Without worrying, you might not plan for every possible contingency. But how do you plan for an FBI agent showing up at your house?

Later that evening, I was still dwelling on the encounter. I couldn't concentrate on the book I was reading about Ptolemy's contributions to astronomy, and even my favorite astrophysics podcast was unable to hold my attention.

I ended up in my lab poring over newspaper articles, blog posts, YouTube videos, and forum comments about the Lansburg Lights. So many websites mentioned the phenomenon that it was becoming hard to sift through. I tried to imagine the materials through Agent Ruiz's eyes. Did he see an interesting mystery? Legitimate alien activity? A clever hoax?

One thing was certain—it was no wonder he'd asked about J. Quincy Oswald. Oswald was referred to in countless news sources. Some articles mocked him. Some praised him. But all were eager to see what would come of his "extraterrestrial fountain of youth."

I, meanwhile, was hardly mentioned at all.[1]

Tightness began to form in my jaw. It felt like something had been stolen from me.

I tried to remind myself that I shouldn't *want* my name in articles. It would mean I'd been busted, that the hoax had failed.

Maybe my plans were flawed from the start. Maybe it was absurd to do an experiment I could never take credit for. I assumed *knowing* I was successful, and having a sociological report to impress MIT, would be enough. Maybe it wasn't. Maybe, like Oswald, I wanted complete praise and recognition.

I took a deep breath. I needed to get a grip. It had been a long day. Surely the situation would look better after I'd gotten a good night of sleep.

Before leaving the lab, I pulled out my phone and sent an impulsive text.

Thinking of you. GH

I immediately regretted it. I never sent sentimental messages like that. What would Owen think? But a moment later my phone buzzed with his response.

OC Hang out soon? I miss you.

A smile slipped onto my face. Just like that, life seemed manageable again.

---

1   Twice, to be exact. And only one of those articles referred to me by name.

Outside, I stopped for a moment to take in the dark sky. I spotted the Pleiades, the Seven Sisters, and counted the six stars that were visible to me.[1]

And what was beyond the Pleiades? What secrets was the universe hiding in places that our most powerful telescopes could never reach?

Was there life out there? Or was the human race steadily hurtling toward its downfall, its Great Filter, like others that had come before? And if we were on the eve of destruction, did it even matter?

We humans imagined our lives were so meaningful. Not just our day-to-day lives, but the bigger picture. The disasters, the wars, all the victories and tragedies, large and small. Our homes, our towns, our countries felt meaningful. *Earth* felt meaningful.

But in reality, Earth was only a speck. The entirety of it could fit into the red spot on Jupiter. And that was just in our solar system. What if we took into account everything outside the Milky Way?

When it came down to it, it *was* possible that humans were nothing more than the starfish of the universe.

Yet I couldn't stop trying to be more.

I pulled myself out of my musings and continued toward the farmhouse, wondering if other people had the same thoughts or if I too was truly alone.

When I passed the crater in the field, something caught my eye—a twinkle in the moonlight. I stepped closer and saw a discarded soda can. Probably left by someone who'd snuck onto the farm to see the sight of the initial extraterrestrial contact. I wondered

---

1   In ancient times, the Pleiades served as an eye test—a person's vision was determined by how many of the seven stars they could see.

if Father had caught them and chased them off, or if Mother had to call Chief Kaufman to make them leave.

A flush of shame crept over me. I'd created so much trouble for my family. But it was too late to turn back now.

I picked up the soda can and kept walking. As I passed the barn, I heard voices from inside, and a light flickered between the rotting, wooden slats. I paused. The barn was rarely occupied. Mostly it served as storage for the thousands of dollars of myTality™ products Mother accumulated.

The door was ajar and I peeked inside.

The building was filled with preteen girls. They sat cross-legged on the floor in a loose circle, cushioned by old hay. There were maybe fifteen of them, most of whom I recognized from Maggie's softball team. Maggie herself sat on the side of the barn and the other girls stared at her raptly.

"What's going on?" I asked cautiously.

Fifteen sets of eyes turned to me.

"Gideon, please leave," Maggie replied in an unnaturally calm voice.

"Tell me what you're doing first."

"This is a private meeting."

The other girls nodded, as if Maggie had said something sage-like.

"Okay," I said, creeped out by so many people staring at me, by the blankness on their faces. "Just... Never mind. Bye."

I ducked away from the barn and continued to the house.

What was Maggie up to? Something disturbed me about her demeanor. She was tranquil. Self-assured. She acted like she was in charge, and not only did she *know* it, she *relished* it.

I was in my room before I realized that, for a moment, Maggie reminded me of J. Quincy Oswald.

INTERVIEW

Subject #2, Magdalene (Maggie) Hofstadt:

It's not that I *respect* cult leaders. I don't think anything's okay about Jim Jones convincing his followers to drink cyanide punch or David Koresh stockpiling weapons for his "Army of God." I don't think Charles Manson's "Family" should have gone on a two-day killing spree or that we should celebrate the sarin gas attack masterminded by Shoko Asahara. Obviously, all that stuff is horrible. I'm just saying, isn't it interesting, what some people are able to convince others to believe?

EVENT: Progress Check

DATE: OCT. 9 (MON.)

"October ninth progress update," I said for the benefit of my audio recording.

Ishmael and I were in my lab, gazing at the desk that was covered with notes and documents, lists and drawings, newspaper articles and plans.

"The media attention is piling up." I tapped on a stack of papers. "Exhibit A is composed of articles from credible sources."

"No Adam Frykowski blog posts then?" Ishmael joked from his chair next to me.

"Correct. Now, exhibit B is—"

"More Seekers have shown up, you know," Ishmael interrupted, bored with my research. "And more of Oz's myTality distributors."

I scowled. "Oswald *again*. I want to get rid of him."

"Like...kill him?"

I sighed hard enough to make the papers in front of me flutter. "No, Ishmael. I don't want to *kill* him. I just want him to go home to California. Or anywhere."

My brother gave me a searching look. "What's your problem with the guy?"

"Is it not apparent?"

"I know he's annoying or whatever. But you *super* hate him. Like, way more than there's reason to."

Where to begin?

I hated Oswald because he was a liar. A cheat. A con man.

But most of all, I hated how easy life was for him. How we lived in a world where his unique blend of personality traits was revered. No matter how smart or talented someone was, no matter how much time and energy they dedicated to a project, there would always be a J. Quincy Oswald who could use his charm to take it away in an instant.

I didn't know how to sum that up for Ishmael, though. So I simply said, "He's my nemesis."

"This isn't a comic book, dude," Ishmael said. He idly opened a container on my desk and began sifting through loose electronic components inside, as if he had any idea what he was looking at.

"Nemeses aren't just for superheroes. For instance, take Isaac Newton and Robert Hooke—"

"Could we maybe not make this conversation about Isaac Newton?"

"It's *not* about him," I insisted, moving the electronics box away from Ishmael and firmly closing the lid. "It's about Oswald."

"You get that you're turning the hoax into some weird competition between you and Oz, right?"

"Yes, but...how could I *not* compete?"

Ishmael shrugged. "You just don't."

"You're telling me you don't feel *any* element of competition right now?"

"This isn't about I win or he wins. It isn't sports or something. And even sports competitions are friendly."

I knew countless people, Father included, who would *not* agree that sports were friendly competitions. This was likely one of the reasons Ishmael never became the baseball player Father hoped he'd be.

I thought for a moment. "What about last year, when Braden took out classified ads listing Irving High School for sale?"

"What about it?"

"Didn't it bother you? *You're* the one known for pranks."

"So? It was an awesome prank," Ishmael said, grinning. "It made me laugh. Why would that bug me?"

"Because…" I sputtered. But I didn't entirely know what to say. "What about when you and Kyle both applied to be delivery drivers for Pizza Haus and he got hired? You wanted that job so badly."

"It was just a job," Ishmael said. "Besides, Kyle was totally more qualified."

"How does one become 'more qualified' for a job at Pizza Haus?"

"He had a paper route before. He was used to doing deliveries."

I looked at Ishmael for a long moment, trying to detect a lie on his face, but I didn't see one. He truly didn't have the urge to compete. He didn't live with the same bitterness I did. He probably never looked at his peers and silently itemized the ways he didn't measure up.

"Gideon," Ishmael said after a moment. "You know you don't need to, like, prove yourself to anyone."

"But I *do*."

"Is this about the universe again, and how you feel insignificant?"

Wasn't *everything* about that? I didn't say so, though. I said, "Can we focus on Oswald?"

"Sure," Ishmael agreed. "What do you wanna do?"

"I don't know. To start, I want more information about what he's up to."

Was he just trying to make money with the new product or was there something more? My mind flashed to him in the middle of the road, shouting at the sky. I still entertained the possibility that part of him actually believed aliens were visiting.

"We can go over there right now," Ishmael said.

I glanced at my phone. "It's late."

"Do you have a bedtime or something[1]?"

"I don't want to wake Oswald up," I said. "I don't relish the idea of talking to him at all."

Ishmael shook his head like I was hopeless. "We're not gonna *talk* to Oz. He'll never even know we were there."

"We... What?"

"We're gonna spy on him," Ishmael said, his eyes lit with the gleam I knew too well.

"No," I said simply.

Ishmael flashed his most charming smile. "You know I'll convince you. Why don't you give in now and make this go a lot faster?"

---

1   The average teenager requires 9.75 hours of sleep to function optimally. Given the early start time of high school, having a bedtime was both practical and necessary.

EVENT:
The Infiltration

DATE: OCT. 9 (MON.)

Ishmael spent several minutes encouraging me to drive to Oswald's camp. I refused for two reasons:

1. Learner's permits only allow one to drive with a licensed passenger age twenty-one or older.
2. One practice session was not nearly enough for me to be comfortable behind the wheel. At all.

So Ishmael drove, giving me helpful tips along the way. Such as, "If you hit a yellow light, it's best to gun it" and "No one really pays attention to turn signals."

It was late when we neared Oswald's field, which was how I'd come to think of it. Based only on the power of his presence, he'd claimed the field as his own.

"We should walk the rest of the way," Ishmael said, maneuvering the Jeep down an unpaved side road.

"I didn't exactly wear appropriate footwear," I complained.

Ishmael shook his head. "Everyone says you're the smart one. But look at which of us came prepared."

"It's not so much that I didn't *prepare*. It's more that, even during the drive over here, I wasn't convinced we were actually going through with this."

My brother gave me a sad look. "Come on, dude. You know me better than that."

Ishmael got out of the Jeep and I followed. We entered the woods together, my shoes immediately sinking into the muddy ground. A moment later, my foot caught on a tree root and I stumbled.

"Shhh," Ishmael hissed.

"I didn't do it on purpose," I whispered back.

We crept up on the outskirts of Oswald's camp. I'd expected a livelier scene. When I passed the Seekers' camps at night, it always seemed like a party was going on. Campfires lit, people wandering and talking, music playing. What else were you going to do when living in a field with limited resources?

But Oswald's camp felt military. Everything was neat and tidy and arranged with precision. There was no music. There were no campfires. The only people wandering around looked to be on the way from one task to another.

"Are they all out somewhere?" Ishmael asked.

"I think they're just...weird."

"At least you know other people in Lansburg go to bed as early as you."

I ignored my brother's jab and scanned the field in front of us. I nodded toward the enormous camper in the middle. "That's Oswald's."

Ishmael snorted. "You think you need to tell me that?"

"What's the plan?" I asked.

"We try to see inside."

That seemed like an exceptionally bad idea. But there wasn't time to tell Ishmael that. He began weaving through tents, not being particularly stealthy about it.

Not to mention, he wore one of his Hawaiian shirts—its primary color was hot pink. If he hadn't already crossed half of the field, I would've asked if he still wanted to brag about being prepared.

When Ishmael reached Oswald's RV, he turned back and pressed a finger to his lips for quiet, as if I might announce our presence with a trumpet. Then he peeked into a window, the bottom of which was level with his eyes. Feeling undignified, I stood on my tiptoes to peer inside as well.

The curtains were sheer enough to see through. The tastefully understated track lighting bathed the interior in a warm glow.

"This camper is nicer than our *house*," Ishmael whispered.

Our house was built a century ago and sparingly updated. It wasn't exactly challenging to find nicer dwellings.

Inside the RV, Oswald had his back to us. He raised a hand and tilted his head back, taking a long swig of a drink.

I watched eagerly. I wanted to see after-hours Oswald, inebriated enough to drop the charade.

He turned slightly and revealed the bottle in his hand.

Not alcohol, but a myTality™ Shake It Up. Anger welled up inside of me. Did the man *ever* stop performing?

Oswald wandered around the camper, looking around absently, like he was waiting. Nothing was out of place. Not a scrap of paper, not a discarded water bottle. It was pristine, even by my standards.

I rested back on my heels, annoyed and disappointed. I wasn't sure what I'd expected. Maybe I thought we'd catch Oswald filling bottles marked "alien juice" from gallons of distilled water. Reading *How to Win Friends and Influence People*. Something. *Anything*.

"Oh shit," Ishmael said, reaching over and tugging on my sleeve.

I immediately boosted myself back onto my toes and peered into the window.

Oswald wasn't alone. A girl had emerged from what I assumed to be the bedroom area of the RV, wearing nothing but a sheet wrapped around her body. She crossed to Oswald, who set down his myTality™ health shake and wrapped his arms around her.

I stepped back from the window.

"This isn't exactly what I was hoping for," I whispered.

"But dude—"

"Stop watching." I pulled him away. "You're being creepy."

"*Dude*," Ishmael said more insistently. "Did you even check out that girl?"

"*Of course* I didn't. What's wrong with you?"

Ishmael shook his head and pulled me back to the window. "Not like *that*."

Reluctantly, I rose on my toes a third time.

"Look," my brother said. "How old do you think she is?"

I watched until the girl pulled back from Oswald's embrace. She was very, very pretty. And very, very young.

"Let's go," I said. Ishmael nodded and followed me willingly back through the woods.

"How old?" Ishmael asked again once we were back in the Jeep and headed home.

"Young. Really young."

"Like...underage?"

"I don't know," I said, feeling as disturbed as my brother sounded.

Ishmael got lost in thought for a long moment. "It's just, I'm wondering if we should tell someone."

"Like who?"

"Chief Kaufman, I guess."

"What would we say? When we were *spying* on J. Quincy Oswald in his RV, we saw him with a woman who *might* have been underage and we think *possibly* they were going to have sex, but we don't really know for sure?"

"Well, actually, I think they probably already had sex because she was wrapped in a sheet."

"That's not the point."

"Yeah, I know," Ishmael said. "I guess we don't actually have much to tell anyone, do we?"

"We don't."

I frowned and gazed out the window, thinking. Venus was bright in the sky ahead of us.[1]

"Hey, Gideon," Ishmael said quietly after a little while. "Even if that girl wasn't a minor, she was still, like, half Oz's age."

"So?"

Ishmael chose his words carefully. "So it might not actually be *illegal*, but it would be immortal."

"You mean *immoral*," I said.

---

1   Due to its brightness, many UFO sightings have been attributed to people misidentifying Venus.

"Right. Anyway, I was just wondering. If Mom knew about this, would she still be so obsessed with myTality?"

I opened my mouth to say no, of course she wouldn't. She'd find the situation disgusting. But... Why didn't she find the company off-putting to start with? It was scamming people out of hard-earned money.

Did I take issue with that? If people were naive enough to give their money to myTality™, did they deserve whatever they got?

I wasn't sure.

"I don't know how Mother would feel," I said finally.

I was afraid I wouldn't like the answer.

INTERVIEW

NANCY CLEMENTS:

I'd been a myTality distributor for, oh, maybe ten months at that point. I hadn't quit my day job, but I'd made enough money to know myTality was a viable career path. Not that I needed much convincing. From the very first time I tried the products, I saw a powerful, positive change in my life. I was fifty-three years old and realized I had no control of my own mortality. I'd put my health and happiness in other people's hands. Oz made me understand it belonged to *me*.

INTERVIEWER:

But surely you don't think the products *work*?

NANCY CLEMENTS:

They *do* work.

INTERVIEWER:

Have you gotten measurable results?

NANCY CLEMENTS:

I thought this was an impartial interview?

INTERVIEWER:

Right. Of course. I apologize.

NANCY CLEMENTS:

I just want to be clear that myTality changed my life.

INTERVIEWER:

Perhaps we should focus on the night in question.

NANCY CLEMENTS:

I didn't hear anything that night, honestly. It wasn't until the next morning that the distributors knew something was wrong. We woke up to Oz hollering about someone invading our camp— and that was strange in itself, because Oz never hollered. Not out of anger, anyway. A group of us ran over and saw them clear as day: footprints leading up to the RV. And Oz, he told us how the aliens visited him the night before, and they told him there were terrible, powerful men on Earth who wanted to steal the formula for the elixir. And those men wouldn't make the elixir public like Oz. They wanted it for secret, nefarious purposes.

INTERVIEWER:

What purpose might that be?

NANCY CLEMENTS:

Warfare.

INTERVIEWER:

How would one use this "fountain of youth" in warfare?

NANCY CLEMENTS:

Well, *I* don't know. The aliens weren't visiting *me*.

INTERVIEWER:

I see. Please, go on.

NANCY CLEMENTS:

That's all of it. Oz knew spies were watching our camp, and he knew he had to guard the formula. He was... He seemed scared, to tell the truth.

INTERVIEWER:

And what about the girl who'd spent the night with him? Was she there that morning when all of this was going on?

NANCY CLEMENTS:

I don't think I'm supposed to talk about that.

EVENT:
Family Dinner

DATE: OCT. 10 (TUES.)

In the past week, I'd learned to appreciate dinners of the past. Those wonderful occasions when Father made healthy and delicious meals, and my family ate and conversed without awkwardness and tension.

It wasn't that Mother *never* cooked. But she did it rarely enough that her meals always turned out...questionable. Especially when she added myTality™ protein powder to her recipes.

Gram had come over, so the table was crowded. Father sat with us but ate a TV dinner instead of Mother's chili. Generally, I was opposed to TV dinners. They provided few nutrients, which was the entire point of eating. Food was fuel. I wouldn't fill up a car with watered-down gas.

But considering the less-than-desirable chili, Father's micro-waved chicken-fried steak was almost appealing.

Gram frowned at her bowl. "It pains me that my daughter never learned to cook."

Mother smiled tightly. "Well, Mom, I guess I was busy working."

"I worked too and still managed to put dinner on the table."

"You ran a poker game. That's not the same as running a business."

Gram snorted. "Business? You call that pyramid scheme a business?"

Maggie interrupted, and whether she was trying to put a stop to the conflict or just being rude, I didn't know. "I'm never learning to cook."

"What a practical life choice," I said.

"It *is* practical. Why spend time cooking when you can find people to do it for you?"

I looked at my sister for a long moment. Did she mean she'd only eat in restaurants or that she planned to have...*minions*?

I waited for someone to scold Maggie for her cavalier attitude, but the table was silent.

"So, Gideon," Gram said, changing the subject. "I heard you're finally learning to drive."

"Finally? It's not like I'm thirty."

"Being afraid to drive is nothing to be ashamed of. It's wrong not to own it, though. Stop making excuses and let yourself be afraid."

"Wow, you're like a sentient self-help book," I muttered.

"Don't get sassy with me." Gram pulled a cigarette from her purse and moved to light it.

Father came to life. "Miriam, I've asked you not to smoke in the house."

"This was my house from the day I was born until the day I let you two take it over. I'll do as I please."

"I respect the time you lived here," Father said, "but when you transferred the house out of your name, you lost your right to make the rules."

Gram looked at Father for a long moment. "It's always such

a conundrum. I hate when you stand your ground, but I wouldn't respect you if you didn't." She sighed and hoisted herself to her feet. "I'll go outside."

"You shouldn't be smoking anyway," Mother called after her.

With Gram gone, my family lapsed into awkward silence.

"So..." Mother said, clearly searching her mind, "homecoming is soon, isn't it?"

"Yep," Ishmael replied. "It's going to be awesome. The theme was originally some boring Enchanted Forest thing, but now they changed it to be, like, space themed."

"That should make you happy, Gideon," Mother said.

"I'm not going."

"Why not?"

"When has a dance *ever* made my list of *fun things to do*?"

Mother reached across the table and placed her hand on mine. "Maybe you'd feel differently if you had a date."

"That has nothing to do with it."

Maggie hid a smirk behind her napkin, and even Father began paying attention. How wonderful that my family could become reunified over my social preferences.

"Gideon," Mother said, "you need to experience life."

"We've had this conversation before," I replied, tension forming in my jaw.

"But nothing changes. We want to know you're ready to deal with the world when the time comes for you to leave here, and socializing is part of that. Maybe..." From the way Mother hesitated, I knew I wasn't going to like whatever came next. "Maybe you'd be open to seeing a therapist?"

I was not *at all* open to it.[1]

"Is there anything I can say to make you feel like I *don't* need a therapist?" I asked, keeping my voice even so I didn't betray my panic.

Mother and Father glanced at each other.

Before they came to a telepathic decision, I blurted, "What if I attempted to be more...social? I'll go on that date you wanted me to."

Mother's face lit up. "I think that would be lovely."

"Can we drop the therapist conversation then?"

She hesitated. "Maybe we could put it on hold—*if* I saw you were truly making an effort."

Why should I *have* to make an effort? Why couldn't I be an introvert without being treated like I was broken? Why was Mother so set on turning me into something I wasn't?

I couldn't bring myself to voice my thoughts, though. Instead, I said, "Fine. Set up the date."

---

1   While I found psychology to be an important field, I was 90 percent sure I'd collapse from embarrassment if I had to discuss my feelings with a stranger.

ARTICLE

The following article first appeared in the October 10 issue of the national tabloid *Weird World News*.

JFK RETURNS!

The town of Lansburg, Pennsylvania, is on the fast track to becoming the paranormal capital of America. Recently the site of multiple alien abductions, Lansburg has now become home to another phenomenon—former president John F. Kennedy has been spotted roaming the streets.

Is he an apparition, risen from his grave to share a final message with us? Was his assassination a hoax, and he's lived out the remainder of his life in small-town Pennsylvania? Or could it be that the barrier between dimensions runs thin in Lansburg, and Mr. Kennedy crossed over from a universe where he was never killed?

Most important: How is this new phenomenon related to the current extraterrestrial invasion?

It's been theorized that the sixty-three-foot lava lamp at Lansburg's town center acts as a lightning rod for paranormal activity. If that proves true, we might soon see these lava lamps spreading across the country like wildfire.

EVENT:
A Plea for Help

DATE: OCT. 11 (WED.)

With the influx of Seekers, media, and myTality™ groupies in Lansburg, Super Scoop was busier than ever. Meaning my job had become considerably more annoying. Did the people flocking to town have an affinity for ice cream, or was *Ye Olde Ice Cream Parlor* simply located in a convenient spot? I considered collecting data in an attempt to answer that question, but decided I had enough on my plate.

Besides having to deal with increased social interaction, there was another issue with the constant stream of people in Super Scoop—I previously used my downtime at work to do homework. Without those free hours, I was falling behind. Especially in English.

I hated English class. I *despised* it. It was bearable when we worked on grammar or learned how to write proper citations. But I struggled with English literature. The work became subjective. Subjective!

It was *schoolwork*. There should've been a right answer and a wrong answer. We should've read a passage and drawn conclusions from it, *actual* conclusions, not just a sense of how it made us *feel*.

Books were filled with *symbolism*. (Why not just *say* what needed to be said?) Entire lessons were devoted to the inner workings of a character's mind. (How could anyone guess what was in someone's mind—especially a fictional character?) There were meandering conversations about why an author wrote a particular work, and what it meant. (Why not just ask them?)

Worst of all was poetry. The bane of my existence.

During a lull between customers, I attempted to analyze "The Death of the Ball Turret Gunner."[1]

"It's amazing how complicated a five-line poem can be," I complained to Owen.

Owen grinned. "Come on. It's not that bad."

"Mr. Fiore tried to interest us in poetry by talking about music," I said. "Because all music is poetry with melodies attached."

"I remember that," Owen said. He'd been in Mr. Fiore's class the year before. "Did you do the project where you brought in your favorite song lyrics?"

"Yes," I grimaced.

I didn't have a favorite song, hence no favorite lyrics. I did an internet search and chose a random Beatles song. I got an okay grade because Mr. Fiore said I *technically* did the assignment. But he "questioned the passion I put into it" and felt I'd "missed the point."

"I loved that assignment," Owen said. "It made me see poetry in a whole different way."

"I hated it."

Owen laughed. Not meanly, but in an *oh, Gideon* way, the way

---

1   A poem by Randall Jarrell, published in 1945.

that said he knew me well. It gave me a warm, contented feeling, and I laughed too.

We continued serving ice cream to people, most of them Seekers. You could tell by their T-shirts proclaiming *I want to believe* or showing pictures of the American flag on the moon with the words *It never happened.*

When the bell on the door chimed again, I glanced over, expecting another conspiracy theorist. Instead, I almost dropped my ice cream scoop.

It was J. Quincy Oswald. In my workplace. Infiltrating yet *another* aspect of my life.

"Oh, wonderful," I mumbled.

Oswald scanned Super Scoop wildly, as if something might jump out at him. Finally, his eyes locked on me. He pointed. "You."

Without missing a beat, Owen said, "Can we help you, sir?"

"Perhaps an ice cream cone on this lovely fall day?" I deadpanned. "I'll throw in sprinkles for free."

"I don't eat food with synthetic additives," Oswald replied, eyeing the ice cream contemptuously. His gaze moved to me. "We gotta chat."

My heart rate kicked into high gear. Did he know Ishmael and I had been at his camp? Did he know we saw him with the girl?

"All right," I replied, sounding more confident than I felt. I attempted to inconspicuously wipe away the sweat that had broken out on my forehead.

"Somewhere private," Oswald said, glancing around furtively.

Aside from a mother wrangling two toddlers, Super Scoop had emptied. Who did he think was listening?

"We can use the staff room."

"Gideon..." Owen said apprehensively.

"It's okay," I replied, hoping it was true. "We'll just be a minute."

Oswald followed me into the closet-sized staff room, his gaze jumping from the ancient time clock to the unused cubbies to the bulletin board pinned with fliers for a band Laser "worked" for.[1]

"How can I help you?" I asked Oswald.

"Are there cameras in here?"

"No. Why?"

He looked at me gravely. "There are people in this town who wish me harm."

Yeah. And he was standing in a cramped room with one of them.

"What people?" I asked.

"People from branches of the government you haven't even heard of."

"I see. That sounds..." I trailed off.

Implausible? Ludicrous?

"Stressful," I finished.

Abruptly, Oswald leaned forward and took my face in both of his hands. For a horrified moment I thought he was going to kiss me. Instead, he peered deeply into my eyes.

Have I mentioned that I found maintained eye contact immensely uncomfortable? Especially when said eye contact was with a maniacal health-supplement guru who claimed aliens gave him the fountain of youth?

"Yes," Oswald said finally, nodding as if confirming something. He released my face and stepped back. "I knew I could trust you."

---

1   She apparently operated the sound system, but to me it sounded more like she was a glorified groupie.

The tension in his shoulders loosened and his easygoing smile reappeared. I, meanwhile, was more apprehensive than ever.

"You and I, Gideon, we're connected."

I didn't like the sound of that.

"Last night I received a message," he went on.

"From?"

"The Visitors."

"Aliens, you mean?"

Oswald plowed ahead without responding. "I was told to seek you out. You have a role to play in this story."

In *this* story? He meant in *his* story. He was trying to turn me into a minor character in his alien melodrama. But this was *my* alien melodrama.

"What role would that be?"

Oswald leaned forward. "Last night I was taken to the ship. There were seven Visitors waitin' for me—I've never seen so many at once. They spoke of the danger I'm in. They said I have to finish the elixir and get it to the masses as quickly as I can. And they said there's only one person who can help make that happen. *You*."

"I'm flattered they've heard of me," I said dryly.

Oswald didn't pick up on my sarcasm. "They've heard of everyone and everything."

I glanced around the staff room, as if something in there could save me from what was surely the most absurd conversation of my life. Unless I wanted to clobber Oswald with a mop, I was out of luck.

"Okay, I'll bite," I finally said. "What do the Visitors claim my role is?"

"They didn't say."

"Convenient."

"They'll tell me when the time is right," Oswald said. Again, he looked deeply into my eyes, and very briefly I experienced the power of persuasion he had over most people. I felt almost...drawn in. I felt like I was being *seen*. "I need you to swear something to me, Gideon."

"What's that?"

"Swear that when the Visitors reveal your role, you'll be ready to fulfill it."

"I can't possibly promise you that," I said.

He put his hand on my shoulder. "You have to. There's no one else who can do this."

I stepped back and swung the staff room door open. "Okay, fine." I'd tell him what he wanted to hear if it meant getting rid of him. "I'll do my best."

"Your best is all I ask for," Oswald said, flashing his movie star smile. "I'll be seein' you."

He sauntered out of the staff room and through Super Scoop, pausing only to smile at the mother with the toddlers. She smiled back at him, utterly charmed.

I watched him go, my annoyance growing by the second. How dare Oswald come into my place of business with his alien elixir nonsense? How dare he assume I'd be willing to help him at a moment's notice? And how dare *I* let myself, for even the briefest, most fleeting moment, feel pride at being singled out by him?

EVENT: Social Blunders

DATE: OCT. 11 (WED.)

Dusk was approaching when Owen and I left work. Soon the faux gaslights lining Main Street would flicker to life. A group of Seekers gathered around the lava lamp, their attention fixed on Arnie Hodges, the ufologist, who stood on a step stool, preaching.

Owen stopped to watch.

Snatches of Hodges's speech drifted to us. More of the same things I'd read in countless blog posts. *The time has come. The aliens have revealed themselves. The secrets of the universe are about to be unveiled.*

I wondered how the Seekers would react when the alien activity stopped—because it *would* have to stop. Soon, maybe. Ishmael and I hadn't chosen an end date for the hoax, but we couldn't keep it going indefinitely. What would happen when we weren't manipulating events? How long until claims of abductions and mysterious lights would begin to decline? How long until people got bored and drifted away from Lansburg?

"You ever wish we could see that thing in action?" Owen asked, interrupting my thoughts.

"What?"

He nodded toward the town square. It took me a moment to realize he was looking at the lava lamp, not Hodges or the Seekers.

"I've never really thought about it," I said with a shrug. "I know what a lava lamp looks like. It wouldn't be different, just bigger."

"*Knowing* how something will look and actually *seeing* it aren't the same."

"Let's agree to disagree," I said. But I smiled and nudged Owen with my elbow. I loved how his perspective of the world was so much different than mine.

We began walking down the street together, leaving the lava lamp behind.

"Need a ride home?" Owen asked.

"If you don't mind."

As we wandered the cobblestone street, past quaint tourist shops, something occurred to me.

"Oh, just so you know, my mother roped me into doing this thing."

"What kind of thing?"

"She wants me to hang out with this person. The son of someone on her downline."

Owen stopped walking. "Hang out?"

"Right."

"Like...your mom arranged a playdate?"

"Ah, well, more like an *actual* date."

Owen stared at me for an endless moment. "What the fuck?"

"What?"

"You're going on *a date* with someone?"

"Not because I *want* to," I said. I was confused. I thought Owen and I would laugh about the situation. "It's important to my mother."

"Could you maybe have told your mom, 'Hey, I'm actually in a relationship, so I'm not interested in dates right now?'"

"I suppose I *could* have..."

Owen shook his head, and it wasn't the same way he'd done it earlier. There wasn't any bemused exasperation. "You get mad because I have to kiss a girl onstage, but it's totally cool for you to go on dates with other guys? You don't even go on dates with *me*."

"One, it's not *any* girl you're kissing. Two, we *do* go on dates—"

"You mean stargazing and fooling around in your field where no one might accidentally see us? That's not a date, Gideon."

Wasn't it? But those moments were...well, some of the best I'd ever had. They were the moments I looked forward to the most. They were everything to me.

"You know what?" Owen said. But he seemed at a loss for words. After a long time he sighed and said, "Maybe you should find your own ride home."

INTERVIEWS

Subject #5, Owen Campbell:

Look, I know where Gideon was coming from. *Now* I know. But at the time... I mean, how are you supposed to handle your boyfriend casually dropping that he's going on a date? What was I supposed to do, give him pointers?

Subject #6, Arden Byrd:

I still can't believe you went on a date with someone else.

Subject #3, Cassidy (Cass) Robinson:

I can't believe you *told Owen* you were going on a date with someone else.

Subject #7, Jane Hofstadt (Mother):

I never would've set up the date if I'd known Gideon and Owen Campbell were involved—I *especially* wouldn't have done it if I'd known what a mess it would end up causing. Of course, it *did* keep a member of my downline happy...

EVENT:
Social Blunders

(CONT.)

I couldn't concentrate.

I tried working on my poetry assignment. I tried tinkering with my seismograph. I tried browsing the internet for new information on the Lansburg Lights.

But no matter how I attempted to distract myself, my thoughts returned to Owen.

I shouldn't have told him about the date.

No, that was wrong. I shouldn't have agreed to go on the date at all. It made Owen feel like I didn't care about him. But the date meant nothing to me, and I assumed Owen would understand that.

Wasn't it the same with *Hamelin!,* though? He and Cass knew their kiss meant nothing, but *I* still got upset about it.

I felt afraid then. There was something wrong with me. Why couldn't I navigate social situations like other people did? Why hadn't I realized how horribly the date would upset Owen?

The door to my lab sprang open, interrupting my thoughts. Ishmael strolled inside.

"So, anyway, dude, check this out."

"Don't you ever knock?"

"You're not going to like this," Ishmael plowed ahead, "at least not right away. But hear me out."

I instantly knew I was going to *hate* whatever Ishmael told me.

"I've been thinking about the hoax and how we need a next stage, you know? Something *big*. Something to keep people interested. Especially since Oz has the whole fountain of youth thing going on."

"Okay..." I said cautiously.

"So I took matters into my own hands."

"I don't know what that means, and I'm afraid to ask."

"I'll show you," Ishmael said.

I waited for him to pull out his phone and show me something online, but instead he left the lab, gesturing for me to follow. I found that even more frightening.

"What's the—" I began.

I abruptly stopped, because there was no need to ask questions. Ten feet away, standing in the middle of the field, was a cow.

"Ishmael," I said.

"Yeah, dude?"

"Why is there a cow here?"

"It's the next stage of the hoax!"

I whirled toward my brother, not bothering to keep my anger in check. "We're not mutilating a cow! How many times do I need to repeat that?"

"Actually," Ishmael said, rubbing the back of his neck in an *aw shucks* way. "I agree with you. I was all into the idea at first, you know? But while we were on our way here, Muffin and I—"

"Muffin?"

"Yeah, that's what I named her. Anyway, Muffin and I, like... bonded."

"Wonderful, Ishmael," I said. "That's just wonderful."

"I looked into her eyes, dude, and I realized, she's like, a person."

I rubbed my own eyes. "She's not a person. She's a cow."

"Okay, not *person*. I mean she's a *being*. She has thoughts and feelings. And I realized, no way could I kill her."

I didn't have a clue how to break down the current situation into something manageable.

"Why then," I began slowly, "if you decided cow mutilations weren't on the agenda, did you still bring her here?"

Ishmael shrugged. "We were most of the way home. And believe me, walking her here was *not* easy."

Something occurred to me that I should've asked from the start.

"Ishmael, where did you walk her here *from*?"

"I thought I already said. The O'Grady farm."

The O'Grady farm, where we'd made a crop circle. Owned by Mr. O'Grady, who'd chased us during our radio interference scheme.

I sat on the ground, not minding the dirt for once, and put my head in my hands. "No."

"No what?"

"No, no, no."

"Gideon?"

"You didn't do this," I moaned. "Please, tell me you didn't steal David O'Grady's cow."

"Um...where else would I have gotten a cow? You can't exactly buy them at the pet store."

"You committed theft!" I snapped.

Ishmael frowned. "I think we both know this isn't the only crime we've committed recently."

"No," I said. "Not *we*. You don't get to use the word *we* right now. I had nothing to do with *Muffin*."

"Besides, O'Grady has a bunch of cows. I doubt he'll miss one."

There was absolutely no way that was true. No way.

I looked at the cow. Part of me still couldn't accept what I was seeing. "You have to take her back."

Ishmael immediately shook his head. "No way. It took hours to get her here, dude. I mean, I used a rope for a leash, but it's not like taking a dog for a walk."

"No," I said. "I wouldn't assume a cow was leash trained."

"Right. It was hard. I'm not taking her back."

"You are," I said, looking up at my brother from where I still sat on the ground.

"I'm not."

"Ishmael. You *have* to take the cow back."

The cow let out a long, loud *moo*. I cringed and hoped my parents didn't have any of the windows open.

"She doesn't even want to live there, dude. Mr. O'Grady is gonna slaughter Muffin. Do you get that?"

"He raises milk cows, not meat cows," I said, digging my hands into the ground, resisting the urge to pull up grass by the fistful. "And you took Muffin with the intention of killing her for a hoax, so I don't really think it's appropriate for you to act high and mighty right now."

"*You* take her back then." Ishmael stubbornly crossed his arms over his chest.

My head pounded with rage. I squeezed my eyes shut and told myself to calm down. I'd never understood violence. I'd never been in a physical fight, not even a small tussle. It seemed so counterproductive. But at that moment, I desperately wanted to punch my brother in the face.

"Fine," I said, getting to my feet. "I'll take the cow back. But don't *ever* ask me to do something for you again."

The rope Ishmael used to lead Muffin to our house still hung around her neck. I grabbed the end of it and tugged gently. Muffin didn't move. I pulled harder. Still nothing. I dug my feet into the ground and pulled with all my strength. The cow swayed slightly, but her feet didn't shift an inch.

"She's really heavy," Ishmael said.

My heart already pounded from exertion. "Yes, I noticed."

"If she doesn't want to move, you won't be able to make her."

"You managed," I said.

"I told you," Ishmael reached out and rubbed Muffin's head. "We bonded."

Indeed, Muffin *did* tilt her head toward my brother, seeming to lean into his affection.

"Can't we keep her?" Ishmael asked.

"*Where?*"

He looked around dramatically. "I don't know, Gideon, maybe on our *farm*."

I gazed up at the sky for a long moment. When I spoke again, I'd slightly regained my composure. *Slightly.*

"Okay, Ishmael. Let's walk through this. First of all, you have no idea how to care for a cow. Second, this cow doesn't belong to you. Third, how exactly would you prevent Mother and Father from discovering we've mysteriously acquired cattle?"

"Not *cattle*. Just *one*. One... What's the singular for cattle?"

"Cow."

"But cows are only girls. Isn't there a word that isn't for a girl or boy?"

"I don't think so, Ishmael. I don't know. I'm not really well-versed in livestock."

"What about livestock? Can you have one livestock?"

"Ishmael!"

He continued to pet Muffin thoughtfully while I tried not to have a complete meltdown. The cow's big, brown eyes rolled toward me. Her gaze felt accusatory. Possibly hostile. Even animals liked Ishmael more than me.

Most animals, anyway. As my brother and I stood there, Kepler sidled around the side of my lab, tail swishing. He stopped abruptly when he saw us. Apparently, Kepler's dislike of most living creatures included cows. Once he got over his surprise at Muffin's presence, he ran very suddenly toward her, hissing.

The cow backed away and let out a strangled *moo*. Kepler yowled in response and swiped in her direction.

And then the worst possible thing happened: Muffin the cow—who had a makeshift leash dangling from her neck but wasn't tethered to anything—took off running.[1]

Muffin raced across the field at a speed of at least twenty miles per hour. The average human can run twenty miles per hour. I wasn't

---

[1] Cows are often thought of as slow, plodding animals. That's inaccurate. When they want to, cows can *move*.

the average human, but my brother was. He probably could've run faster than that, due to his time on the track team. Ishmael *should have* been able to catch up with Muffin.

But for a full five seconds after she bolted across the yard, he stared after her, stunned. Finally, he sprang to life, flying after Muffin, shouting her name as he went.

I nudged Kepler toward the lab, avoiding his still-extended claws. Then I watched Ishmael chase the stolen cow across our property. Muffin gained more and more ground. I was thankful she'd run *away* from the house instead of toward it.

Soon, the cow reached the tree line and disappeared into the woods.

Ishmael stopped running. He bent over and put his hands on his knees, his body heaving as he sucked in air. I made my way across the field.

"I wasn't fast enough," he said, gasping, once I was within hearing range. "I've just...doomed Muffin to death, probably."

"I think that's a bit of a leap."

"You think she'll be able to survive in the woods, all alone?" Ishmael snapped. "She doesn't know how to hunt."

"She wouldn't be hunting, being that cows are herbivores. The word you're looking for is *forage.*"

"You know what I mean."

"She ran in the direction of O'Grady's farm. Maybe she's going home."

"You think so?"

I hesitated. I wished I was the kind of person who could lie and insist everything would be okay in the end. I did my best anyway.

"I'm sixty-three percent sure Muffin will find her way home."

"Okay," Ishmael said. "Okay, thanks dude."

But while I couldn't give my brother assurances and false hope, there was something I *could* do: keep quiet.

I didn't lecture Ishmael or point out that the entire predicament was really his own fault.

INTERVIEW

Subject #2, Magdalene (Maggie) Hofstadt:

I knew something was up the night Mom made hamburgers for dinner. Ishmael made a big deal about not eating his. He said he couldn't believe we'd eat defenseless animals. Mom asked if Ishmael was going to become vegetarian and he said no. Apparently, other animals were okay—it was only cows he'd developed sympathy for. Later, when I found out about Mr. O'Grady's missing cow, it wasn't hard to put two and two together.

TRANSCRIPT OF INTERVIEW CONDUCTED
BY CHIEF LISA KAUFMAN ON OCT. 12
(RECORDED WITH PERMISSION)

KAUFMAN:

Thank you all for meeting with me.

FATHER:

You're welcome. Is there anything I can get for you? Coffee?

MOTHER:

Or perhaps some myTality tea?

KAUFMAN:

No, thank you.

MOTHER:

Are you certain? You look tired.

KAUFMAN:

I'm sure, Jane. Thank you, though.

GIDEON:

Chief Kaufman, are you recording this conversation?

KAUFMAN:

I'm not.

GIDEON:

Do you mind if *I* record it?

KAUFMAN:

Do I mind if... Why would you want to do that, Gideon?

FATHER:

Ignore him. He won't be recording anything.

GIDEON:

I'm trying to document everything relating to the alien encounters in Lansburg, including all conversations with the authorities.

FATHER:

Gideon—

KAUFMAN:

It's fine, Vic. He can record if he wants to. This isn't about aliens, though.

MOTHER:

Well, if you're here to ask questions about Oz, I'm afraid—

KAUFMAN:

It's not about him either.

MAGGIE:

This isn't about my softball team, is it?

FATHER:

Your softball team? *What* is going on with this family?

KAUFMAN:

I'm just here to ask some questions.

FATHER:

Go ahead.

KAUFMAN:

How well do you know the O'Grady family?

MOTHER:

They're our neighbors, and we occasionally see them socially, but I wouldn't say we're close.

KAUFMAN:

So you haven't heard that one of their cows is missing?

ISHMAEL:

Uh, excuse me. I have to... I'm just gonna grab a drink of water

real quick—

FATHER:

Sit down, Ishmael.

MOTHER:

One of their *cows* is missing?

KAUFMAN:

Not just any cow, but their prized milk cow, Prudence. Apparently,

she's won the blue ribbon at the state fair three years in a row.

GIDEON:

Blue ribbon. How about that.

FATHER:

I know that cow. O'Grady brags about her all the time.

MAGGIE:

The cow escaped?

KAUFMAN:

Actually, Mr. O'Grady believes she was stolen.

COLLECTED DATA

ISHMAEL:

Well, it wasn't us. I mean, what would any of us want with a cow?

KAUFMAN:

I wasn't accusing you, Ishmael.

ISHMAEL:

Oh.

KAUFMAN:

Since you're neighbors, I thought one of you might have heard or seen something over at the O'Grady farm. But maybe there's something you want to tell me?

ISHMAEL:

No, ma'am.

KAUFMAN:

Have any of you seen or heard anything?

GIDEON:

No.

MOTHER:

I haven't.

FATHER:

Me either.

MAGGIE:

Nope.

KAUFMAN:

Ishmael?

ISHMAEL:

Sorry, I thought that was clear. I haven't seen anything either.

MAGGIE:

Chief Kaufman, why would someone steal a cow?

KAUFMAN:

Jealousy, I suppose. Someone who's been competing with Prudence?

MOTHER:

Is there evidence the cow was stolen and didn't just run away?

KAUFMAN:

This is an open investigation, Jane. I'm afraid there are things I'm not at liberty to discuss.

MOTHER:

I understand.

KAUFMAN:

Okay, thanks for your time. If anything comes up, please give me a call.

ISHMAEL:

Just one thing, Chief.

KAUFMAN:

Yes, Ishmael?

ISHMAEL:

Have you considered that this is maybe tied to the recent UFO activity?

KAUFMAN:

I have not.

ISHMAEL:

Don't you think it might be a thing? Because I've heard before how there are sometimes cow abductions—

FATHER:

I'm sure Chief Kaufman will get right on that.

ISHMAEL:

I'm being serious.

FATHER:

Sorry we couldn't help more, Lisa. We'll let you know if we hear

anything.

COLLECTED DATA

INTERVIEWS

Subject #4, Victor Hofstadt (Father):

Word around the gym was that the cow ran away, but O'Grady was calling it a kidnapping. Said it was part of a conspiracy to keep him from winning the blue ribbon a fourth year. I didn't know about all that. But I will say, the entire time Lisa questioned us that day, I was looking at my sons and thinking that there *better not be a goddamn cow on this property.*

Subject #9, Chief Lisa Kaufman:

I got a criminal justice degree from Temple University, fast-tracked through the force, and became the chief of police for a town of fifteen thousand people. And despite that, I'd spent the past month investigating UFO sightings and reports of kidnapped cows. Yes, it's safe to say that I was feeling disillusioned with my career.

Subject #1, Ishmael Hofstadt:

What kind of name is *Prudence*?

EVENT:
Building Trust

DATE: OCT. 12 (THURS.)

When Cass texted that she was coming over, she didn't say she was bringing Arden.

"Hello," I said, holding the lab door open for them. "Arden, I didn't know you were coming."

A troubled look crossed her face. "Should I go?"

"Of course not."

Except her presence meant Cass and I couldn't discuss the hoax. We couldn't discuss my rivalry with Oswald. We couldn't discuss Owen, and we certainly couldn't discuss anything that had to do with my *feelings*. Not that I had any intention of pouring my heart out to Cass. I was 91 percent sure I'd never actually done that before.

I knew what Ishmael would tell me. Or Father. Or Mother. Or anyone more adept at social situations. They'd say, "Maybe it's time to start trusting Arden."

It had been a year. She'd done nothing to break my trust in that time. I should risk it. I should open up to her. I should act like a normal human being.

But I looked at her, standing in my lab with her wide doll eyes, looking sweet and sad and in need of acceptance. And I just couldn't relax completely.

Cass threw herself down on the swivel chair and pulled off the scarf she'd tied around her head to compliment her bell-bottoms, embroidered shirt, and love beads. Kepler darted out from under the desk and ran through the ajar lab door, hissing at Cass as he passed.

I vaguely listened to Cass and Arden discuss something apparently hilarious a kid at school had done. They were clearly enjoying themselves. Was Cass beginning to prefer Arden's company to mine?

I'd never been Cass's only friend. She hung out with other people on weekends. She texted other people all day. But I always knew I came first. Cass said it was because deep down, no matter how much she might sometimes be the center of attention, she never really felt like she fit in. "Except with you," she said once. "Like, people are always trying to find their place. And you're it for me. You're my place."

I'd never say anything so sappy to another person. I'd never even let someone know something so sappy had impacted me. But that was the great thing about Cass. In response, all I did was awkwardly shuffle my feet and fix my eyes on the horizon. And yet she knew everything I was trying to say.

You see, Cass was my place too.

And now, Arden was around. And maybe it was like adding another room to the cozy house Cass and I had created. But maybe not. Maybe it was like having an earthquake tear the house apart. Maybe Cass was finally going to realize how strange I was, how much easier it would be to have a different person as her best friend.

I looked back and forth between them and something struck me. The feeling I had, the feeling that Cass and Arden were becoming a team that had no place for me, must be how Arden felt constantly. Every time she hung out with me and Cass. Every time she *didn't* hang out with us but knew we were hanging out without her.

A wave of guilt washed over me.

And I suppose that was what made me offer something to Arden, a kernel of insight into my life.

"I'm going on a date on Saturday," I said during a lull in conversation.

Arden's face lit up. You'd think I'd just told her I'd been nominated for a Nobel Prize. "With Owen? Where are you going?"

Cass raised her eyebrows.

"Ah, actually, not with Owen."

Arden looked puzzled. Cass, less so. It occurred to me that Owen might have already told her about the situation.

I explained, "It's a blind date my mother set up. With the son of some myTality person."

Arden's expression became even more confused. "How does Owen feel about that?"

"Not great, I imagine," Cass said.

I gave her a long look. "You imagine, or you *know*?"

Cass shrugged.

"Cass," I said, my voice rising.

"Settle down, eager beaver. Owen and I don't spend all our time talking about you, if that's what you're worried about."

It *did* worry me. I hated the thought of them talking about me. Cass knew me better than anyone, except maybe Ishmael. And Owen knew a different part of me than Cass did. I hated thinking of them comparing notes. Like by doing so they could put together a Gideon puzzle, make me into a complete person. Most certainly, it wouldn't be one they particularly liked.

"I wasn't worried about that," I lied.

"You know what's interesting about you, Gideon?" Arden said. "You hate the thought of people talking about you when you're not around, but you also want to be famous for your sciencey stuff."

I opted to ignore that she'd called my work *sciencey stuff*. "All people are contradictions, Arden. That's what makes them so unstable."

And frustrating.

And terrifying.

Give me rocks. Give me water or air. Give me elements that could be broken down into things that *made sense*. Things that would always be exactly what they seemed.

"Okay," Cass said. "This conversation is getting a bit heavy, and I can't deal with that right now. Let's talk about something fun. Gideon, are you excited for your date?"

"That's, perhaps, the least *fun* topic you could have chosen."

Cass grinned. "Not for me."

"Is the guy cute?" Arden asked.

"I have no idea."

Cass and Arden both leaned forward like I'd said something appalling.

"How do you not know?" Cass asked.

"It's a blind date."

"Yeah," Arden said. "But you didn't look him up online?"

"No."

"Trust me, he's looked you up," Cass said.

"There wouldn't be much to find."

I avoided social media like the plague. There were probably photos of me online somewhere—on my parents' social media accounts, or Cass's. But those weren't attached to my name.

"I wonder if that creeped him out," Arden said. "Can you imagine looking up someone online and finding nothing?"

"Personally, that would make me respect a person," I said.

Cass rolled her eyes.

"What do you know about this guy?" Arden asked.

"Not much. Mother knows *his* mother. She said he's handsome, which, coming from her, could mean anything."

Cass swung around to the desk and turned on my computer. "Let's look him up now."

"Let's not."

"Come on. It'll be fun," Cass said.

Arden nodded in agreement. "Aren't you curious?"

I wasn't, for two reasons:

1. There was more to a person than their looks.
2. It wasn't a real date anyway.

"Please?" Cass said.

"Pretty please?" Arden chimed in.

I sighed. I supposed it wouldn't hurt to do a quick search. I gestured to my laptop. "Fine."

"What's his name?" Cass asked, pulling up a search engine.

"Alex," I said.

Cass looked exasperated. "Um, are you aware of how the internet works? I need more than a first name."

"Spiro or Spiros or something like that."

Cass typed away. A second later she said, "Holy crap."

"What," I asked, moving to peer over her shoulder. "Is he awful?"

Then I saw the picture Cass was looking at. My stomach sank.

My blind date was gorgeous. Not handsome-for-an-acne-riddled-teenager gorgeous. Not cutest-boy-in-school gorgeous. But *model* gorgeous.

"Oh god," I said in horror.

"Oh god," Arden breathed reverently.

"Are you sure this isn't an actor or model or something?" I asked.

"His profile says he lives in Pittsburgh."

"There could be more than one Alex Spiros."

Cass scrolled through the pictures on his profile. Most of them were selfies.[1]

"Not only is his name Alex Spiros, his hometown is Pittsburgh, and... Yep, here we go."

Cass stopped scrolling on a picture of Alex with a middle-aged woman, presumably his mother. She wore a myTality™ T-shirt.

"Godammit," I said.

"How can you *possibly* be disappointed right now?" Cass asked. "This guy is hot."

"But look at the pictures," Arden pointed out. "He's at, like, clubs and concerts. Not exactly Gideon's type."

---

1 Let the record state that, in my lifetime, I have taken exactly zero selfies.

"With looks like that, he's everyone's type," Cass argued.

Arden frowned and shook her head. "Gideon, you don't need to like him just because he's cute."

I sighed. "Thank you for that vote of confidence, Arden, but I'm not sure if *me* liking *him* is the issue we're facing."

Cass made a huffing sound. "Don't even go there."

I looked around dramatically. "Go where? Where am I going?"

"That low-self-esteem crap."

"Okay," I said. "Let me break this down for you. I do not have low self-esteem. I esteem myself just fine. But that doesn't change the fact that I'm objectively not attractive."

"See," Cass said, "to me, that's *exactly* what constitutes low self-esteem."

"It doesn't matter to me, though," I said. "I genuinely don't care if I'm attractive or not."

"How can you not care?" Arden asked, bewildered.

Cass rolled her eyes for what must have been the twentieth time. "If you don't care, why are you grumbling about this Alex guy being too good-looking for you? You have plenty to offer him. Yeah, he's conventionally attractive. And no, you're not exactly the underwear model type. But there are lots of different ways to be attractive."

"I guess."

"Look at me and Arden," Cass said. "Do you agree that we have radically different looks?"

I looked at Cass in her hippie costume and Arden hiding behind her hair.

"Yes."

"Right," Cass agreed, "but we're both hot, aren't we?"

Arden's face reddened. "Well, *you* are—"

"Hey," Cass interrupted. "That no self-deprecation rule goes for you too."

"You're both beautiful," I agreed. And I wasn't just trying to pacify Cass. It occurred to me, in that moment, how seldom I actually *looked* at my friends. The same way I didn't notice the woods surrounding my house or the lava lamp on Main Street. I was so used to seeing Arden and Cass that they'd become part of the landscape. But they *were* beautiful.

"And you are too," Cass said. "And you're interesting. And ambitious. And unique. If Alex doesn't like you, fuck him. But don't for a minute think you don't deserve to be on that date."

I smiled at Cass. "If I were the kind of person who believed in using physical affection to show gratitude, I'd hug you right now."

Cass snorted. "And if I were the kind of person who enjoyed backhanded compliments, I'd hug you back."

"Well, I do like hugs, and I love you both," Arden said. And she pulled us together into an embrace.

For once, I didn't flinch away.

TEXT CONVERSATION

Participants: Gideon Hofstadt, Owen Campbell

Will you please answer my calls?

I want to explain myself.

You know I'm not actually interested in this guy.

Owen, please?

You can't avoid me forever.

Okay, you're very talented, maybe you can.

Look, I'm sorry, okay? Maybe I didn't make that clear, but I'm really, really sorry.

GH

Does that mean you're not going on the date?

OC

Well...I can't really back out now.

Stop texting me, Gideon.

OC

Copy of a flyer found taped to a light post outside Super Scoop.

THE MYSTERIES OF THE ⭐ UNIVERSE REVEALED!

You **know** we aren't alone.
You **know** a deeper cosmic message is just out of reach.
You **know** the life you're living isn't your *best* life.

Finally, the answers to all questions, great and small, are within your grasp!

When: Friday, October 13
7:00 p.m.

Where: Lansburg town square

Extraterrestrial Visitors have revealed their plan to J. Quincy "Oz" Oswald, founder and CEO of the famous myTality™ health-product line. Now he's going public with the secrets he's learned!

Are you ready to achieve personal fulfillment and work toward the future you deserve?

Don't miss out!

To learn more, visit mytality.com/elixireternia

EVENT:
Oswald's Rally

DATE: OCT. 13 (FRI.)

A sad fact of my life was that no one had to convince me to attend the rally J. Quincy Oswald held on Friday night. I had to keep tabs on him. You should *always* know what your nemesis has up his sleeve.

My brother was neglecting to conduct his due diligence and instead went to a party at his friend Devin's house. I knew better than to ask Father to help with anything involving Oswald, so I asked Cass for a ride instead.

"I wouldn't miss it for the world," she said.

That was how I ended up standing in a crowd of Seekers and myTality™ distributors, with Cass on one side of me and Arden on the other. Cass wore a shiny silver dress and tinsel laced through her hair.

"The outfit is a bit much," I told her.

She glanced down, flexing a foot adorned in a sparkly, plastic shoe. "I'm going for a space-age look."

"I know what you're going for."

"I can't believe how many people are here," Arden said, pulling into herself more, as if that would help her avoid the crowd. I didn't blame her. Being surrounded by people on all sides always set off the panic sensors in my brain.

Nearby, Arnie Hodges stood on his step stool and spoke to the people surrounding him, like he was Oswald's opening act.

"They want us to believe no alien spacecraft crashed in Roswell, New Mexico," Hodges preached. "They want us to believe there aren't alien corpses in freezer units at Area 51. They want us to believe Project Blue Book, a government study of UFO activity, never turned up evidence of alien life. But are we going to sit back idly and believe whatever they tell us?"

"No!" shouted the crowd around him.

Compared to the myTality™ distributors and Seekers, I saw only a few locals in the crowd: Adam Frykowski in his too-big suit, taking notes on a steno pad; a couple kids from school; some families I knew in passing; and Laser, standing outside Super Scoop, puffing on an e-cig and glaring at anyone who got too close.

Our town had been completely taken over by outsiders. I'd never been fond of small-town life, but it was disorienting to suddenly not know most of the people wandering Lansburg's streets.

At five minutes past 7:00—fashionably late again—Oswald appeared in front of the crowd. He wasn't on anything as unassuming as a step stool, like Hodges. No, Oswald towered over us on the observation platform that ran the circumference of the lava lamp. The stairs leading to the platform had been locked off for years and I wondered if he got permission to go up there or if he'd gone rogue.

"People of Lansburg," he drawled into a bullhorn. "Welcome."

The myTality™ distributors cheered enthusiastically, the

Seekers slightly less so. Oswald let the applause wash over him, as if it was giving him fuel.

"We come from different walks of life," he said. "We've got unique hopes and dreams, battle individual demons. But tonight, we unite under one purpose. We're here to unveil the mysteries of the cosmos and revel in the magnificent new gift humanity has been given."

"He sure has stage presence," Cass said with admiration.

"And he's so handsome," Arden breathed from my other side.

I refused to acknowledge either statement.

"Now I wanna tell you my story," Oswald said.

Many people in the crowd nodded eagerly.

Oswald took a deep breath and cast his gaze around, conveying that he was sharing some great, personal secret. "When I was a boy, I was lost. I was lonely. I floated through my days without a plan."

More nods. Some sprinkled clapping.

"Then one day, I woke. I realized the only person in charge of my destiny was *me*. If I wanted more from life, I had to reach out and take it, because no one was gonna hand it to me."

Well, I didn't disagree with that.

"You know what I did after that awakenin'? I studied. I saved money. I started a company that brought in over a million dollars in its first year alone." The myTality™ distributors cheered. Oswald went on. "I *took control*. I *changed my life*. Now, my destiny belongs to no one *but me*!"

Oswald paced back and forth on the observation deck giving his words a moment to sink in. The crowd was enthralled.

After a perfectly timed pause, he raised the bullhorn again. His voice came out distorted but still had that powerful timbre that made people pay attention. "Now, I've told people this story, and you know what they've said? They've said, *But Oz, I'm not as smart as you.* They've said, *I'm not as driven as you.* They've said, *I don't know* how *to change.*"

He stopped and faced the crowd head-on again, looking solemn. "Tonight, I'm telling you the honest truth. I'm not smarter or savvier than *anyone*. I'm like each and every one of you, with one exception: I had help along the way." He raised a finger and pointed at the sky. "I had an extraterrestrial influence."

The crowd went wild, distributors and Seekers alike. He'd hooked them all. Even Cass and Arden cheered along.

"Could you please contain yourselves?" I asked them.

Cass laughed, the tinsel in her hair sparkling in the glow of streetlamps. "If you want me to sit through this, you have to let me have fun."

Arden only shrugged, but there was no denying the happy flush in her cheeks and the way her eyes shone.

"I was visited by aliens," Oswald preached. "And they told me there was a greater path for me. These Visitors gave me formulas for health products that could cleanse our bodies, and in doing so allow us to work toward spiritual enlightenment. But they also told me something bigger was coming. Something that would change the whole world and allow us to live in harmony with the universe."

The crowd seemed to take a collective breath, hanging on Oswald's every word, waiting for this reveal.

"And now, in this humble town, the Visitors have come again. They've made good on their promise," Oswald said. "They've given me the fountain of youth."

The myTality™ distributors clapped and whooped with excitement. The Seekers and Lansburg locals were slightly more hesitant.

"Imagine havin' perfect health," Oswald said. "Imagine never again feelin' the restraints of time. Imagine knowin' that the future stretched before you eternally and in that future you'd have the power to do anything you wanted to do, *become* anything you wanted to *become*."

Around me, people slowly nodded.

"By combining ingredients found on Earth with others that come from the farthest bounds of the cosmos, I'm mixin' up a product unlike anything our world's seen before." Oswald paused dramatically. "It's called...*the Elixir ETernia*."

TRANSCRIPT OF OCT. 13 RADIO BROADCAST OF *BASIN AND RANGE* RADIO

NASH:

Live from the loneliest corner of the Mojave, you're listening to *Basin and Range Radio*, where we keep an eye on the night sky. This is your host, Robert Nash. Tonight, we're talking to a very special guest. Listeners, please welcome J. Quincy Oswald.

OSWALD:

Thanks, Rob. I'm thrilled to chat with you. And please, call me Oz.

NASH:

Now, Oz here has experienced direct contact with extraterrestrials. Why don't you tell us about that?

OSWALD:

Most people know me as the founder of myTality, a successful line of health products. But don't be fooled—I may not have spoken openly about the Visitors before now, but they've been present in my life.

NASH:

More than *present*. They're sending you messages.

OSWALD:

Sure are. I've been in communication with the Visitors since adolescence. My most recent abduction was just last week, from right here in Lansburg, Pennsylvania, which I'm temporarily calling home.

NASH:

We all want to know, what exactly *happens* when you're abducted.

OSWALD:

It begins with waking to a kind of glow around me. Light fills the room 'til it consumes everything—even me. When I reach full awareness again, I'm in a spherical room with white walls. There's nothing in the room but the chair I'm sitting on. I'm not restrained in any perceivable way, yet I can't move.

NASH:

Mm-hmm, go on...

OSWALD:

I'm approached by a Visitor. Sometimes one, sometimes several. They have skin like soft gray leather, and their eyes are large and black. They have mouths, but they never speak to me with them.

NASH:

But they *have* spoken to you in some way?

OSWALD:

They most certainly have. They have a device almost like a needle attached to a long tube. They push that needle into my head right at the temple, maybe all the way to my brain. They're able to communicate with me then.

NASH:

These Visitors, as you call them, they've given you a mission?

OSWALD:

They've taught me how to combine Earth ingredients with alien technology to create what one might call "the fountain of youth." An extract that, when regularly taken, will prevent aging.

NASH:

And you've been tasked with making this product?

OSWALD:

The prototype is complete and I'll be ready to unveil the finished version in a few short weeks.

NASH:

Did you hear that, listeners? Soon enough, we can *all* experience this alien miracle product! Why don't you tell everyone what you call it?

OSWALD:

The health drink is called myTality Elixir ETernia.

NASH:

With a capital ET on ETernia, is that right?

OSWALD:

You got it.

NASH:

And where can our listeners find this product?

OSWALD:

It can be purchased through any of our myTality distributors for the low cost of $15.99 per ounce. Of course, if someone signs up for our compensation plan and becomes a distributor themselves, they'll get a lifetime discount...

EVENT:
Oswald's Rally
(CONT.)

Cass and Arden declared me "boring" when I refused to talk to Oswald after his sermon. He'd descended from the observation deck and was immediately swarmed by people trying to get close to their new prophet.

"He's busy anyway," I said. Besides, I'd rather not risk him cornering me again.

"Let's just go over for a minute," Cass insisted.

"*Why?* What could you possibly have to say to that man?"

"He's probably the strangest person to ever pass through Lansburg. And these days, that's saying a lot. How could I *not* be fascinated?"

I was even losing my best friend to Oswald. He was taking *everything* from me.

"Fine. Go talk to him. I'll meet up with you later."

I stalked away from Cass and Arden before they tried to convince me otherwise.

Laser still vaped in front of Super Scoop, though the crowd around her had thinned. I moved in that direction.

"Can you believe this shit?" she asked, gesturing with her e-cig. She snorted. "Alien fountain of youth."

"Indeed," I said, pleased that I wasn't the only anti-Oswald person in town after all.

I moved toward the door of Super Scoop, but Laser blew out a plume of vapor and held up a hand to stop me. "He doesn't want to talk to you."

"What?"

"You're going in there because Owen's working. And I'm warning you, he doesn't want to talk to you."

"I see," I mumbled, and slunk off in the other direction.

I was mortified. I didn't realize Laser paid attention to what went on between Owen and me. If she knew about our relationship and our fight, everyone must.

The whole town probably thought I was a jerk. A jerk bad boyfriend who couldn't create alien scandals nearly as enticing as J. Quincy Oswald did. A jerk who had no social skills, who couldn't drive, who probably wasn't going to get into MIT because his grades continued to slip.

Shame churned inside of me. It was bad enough to fail. Having everyone *know* about my failure was something else entirely.

"Gideon," someone called from in front of Ye Olde Fudge Shoppe.

I looked over to an unpleasant sight.

"Agent Ruiz," I said, trying to keep my tone even, to hide that my heart rate had doubled. "Did you come to watch the spectacle?"

"I did," he said in his own even tone.

"What did you think?" I said as if we were acquaintances making small talk.

"I'm more curious what *you* thought," Ruiz replied.

"Well, I don't think there's a fountain of youth, that's for sure."

"But the alien parts—you believed that, right?"

I hated how casual Ruiz seemed, when I knew he was anything but. There was an intensity in his eyes that betrayed the truth. I needed to watch myself around him.

"In a sense," I said carefully.

"What sense?"

"Should one of my parents be here for this conversation?"

Ruiz chuckled. "I'm not interrogating you."

"In that case, I think I'll be on my way."

"Okay then. Nice seeing you." He smiled at me weirdly. *Suspiciously*.

I hurried away with no idea where I was headed, just needing to move. Ruiz knew about the hoax. Maybe he couldn't prove anything yet, but he was keeping tabs on me. He'd been sent to find out what was happening in Lansburg, and it hadn't taken him long to discover Ishmael and I were at the center of it.

I was going to get caught. I hadn't set up the perfect hoax. I hadn't done *anything* perfectly, maybe *ever*.

With every step I took, my embarrassment and anger increased. Everything was getting away from me. *Everything*.

COLLECTED DATA

INTERVIEWS

Subject #3, Cassidy (Cass) Robinson:

Just because I wanted to talk to Oz didn't mean I was going to become one of his disciples. Obviously, I got total jeepers-creepers vibes from the guy. But I *did* want to study him. He was probably the best actor I'd ever met.

Subject #6, Arden Byrd:

I didn't expect him to pay attention to me. There were so many people waiting to see him. People who *loved* him. But listening to him tell a whole crowd the truth about his life, no matter how it made him look... I guess it inspired me. And I wanted him to know I'd had an experience too. Nothing like his. But I saw the lights. I *felt* something. I thought, even if I didn't get a chance to talk to him, maybe Oz would glance over and our eyes would meet for a second. Maybe he'd look at me and know that, in some small way, I was like him.

EVENT: The Date

DATE: OCT. 14 (SAT.)

It was my greatest hope that Father would forget we had another driving lesson planned for Saturday morning. He didn't.

"Can't we do this next week?" I asked. "I have that thing tonight."

"What thing?" he asked, hovering in my bedroom doorway, running shoes already laced and baseball cap perched on his head.

"That *date* thing."

Father raised an eyebrow. "You need ten hours to prepare for a date?"

"Maybe."

"Gideon, get in the car."

I sighed and turned off my laptop, where I'd been skimming Adam Frykowski's write-up of Oswald's rally. I was less interested in what Frykowski had to say and more interested in the blog comments. But they trickled in at a surprisingly slow rate. Though the post had gone live hours before, there were only six comments total. Was Frykowski losing his followers?

"Is Ishmael coming?" I asked, following Father downstairs.

"Ishmael didn't get home until three in the morning."

"So he's sleeping?"

"No. He's scrubbing the floors as punishment for breaking curfew."[1]

My second driving experience was as harrowing as the first. Father decided we should practice parking. He had me drive to the St. Francis parking lot where, thankfully, there wasn't a mass going on.

"Wide open space," he said, gesturing around. "Nothing to worry about."

Yeah, as long as every time I parked I made sure there were no other vehicles within fifty feet of me. Nor did having an empty parking lot help me effectively maneuver the Jeep between the painted lines of a parking space. By my twentieth try, Father was frustrated.

"The lines are *right there*. Line the Jeep up with them. It's not that hard."

"Clearly, Father," I replied, "it *is* that hard. I'm sorry my spatial awareness isn't up to your high standards, but I don't appreciate—"

"Just try again."

"I can't do it," I snapped.

"You *can*."

"You're getting angry at me for something I literally *cannot* do. Do you know how that makes me feel?"

"It's not that you *can't*," Father said through clenched teeth. "It's that you're too worked up to try. You're as capable of parking a car as anyone else. You just can't stop *thinking*."

---

1   Note: I'd never been punished for breaking curfew. It was a benefit of rarely leaving the house.

"Well, pardon me, but I always considered that an asset."

By the time Father decided we could quit for the day, we were both irritated and speaking to each other as little as possible. Admittedly, it was still childish the way I slammed the Jeep's door and stomped into the house.

"So it went well then?" Ishmael cracked when I passed him. He was vacuuming under the couch cushions, presumably stage two of his punishment.

I ignored him and stormed into the bathroom. I needed to splash cold water on my face, cool myself off. I turned on the tap, took a deep breath, and glanced in the mirror.

And froze in horror.

My face was redder and more broken out than usual. My frustration with driving had triggered the worst acne attack known to man.

Certainly, I was just overheated. Once I cooled down and spent some time far away from the Jeep, I'd look better.

But an hour later, when Ishmael crawled past my bedroom door, dusting the baseboards with a rag, he looked at me with concern.

"Dude, why are you so broken out?"

I cringed. "It's still bad?"

"I mean... You don't look *awful* or anything, but..."

I reminded myself that I'd never been vain about my looks. Who cared if my face was horribly broken out? It was irrelevant.

"Hopefully it clears up before tonight," Ishmael said.

"Before tonight?" But as soon as the question was out of my mouth, I remembered. "Oh god. The date."

"It's not a big deal," Ishmael said, unconvincingly. "I mean, the guy probably gets acne too."

Based on his social media pictures, I was 86 percent sure that wasn't the case.

No, looks weren't everything. But my self-esteem had taken several blows recently, and I didn't relish the idea of going through a date with the worst breakout of my life.

"What am I going to do?" I moaned.

"Doesn't that spot-treatment stuff work pretty fast?"

"I don't have any, since Father refuses to run errands. Could you go to the store for me?"

"I'm not allowed to leave until I finish everything on my list," Ishmael said, holding up his dust rag as if it was proof. "I've got to clean the grout in the bathroom next."

Of course he did. Of course this would happen on the day he was being punished. I considered calling Cass and asking her to give me a ride to the store, but remembered she was in rehearsal all day. Opening night of *Hamelin!* was approaching, and they were squeezing in all the practice they could. I was on my own.

Except...

Something occurred to me. I jumped to my feet and hurried past Ishmael.

"You okay, dude?" he called after me, but I didn't pay attention. I went outside, crossed the yard, and let myself into the barn.

Where I was met by a sea of thirteen-year-olds.

"Could you please knock before you come in here?" Maggie asked.

I stepped through the circle of Maggie's friends and made my way to the other side of the barn, where boxes upon boxes of myTality™ products were stored.

"You don't own the barn, Maggie," I said, scanning labels for the box I wanted.

"No," Maggie agreed. "I don't own anything. And that's what allows me to be truly free."

I glanced back at my sister. "What are you talking about?"

"You wouldn't understand." Maggie spoke with a knowing voice that was nothing like her normal tone.

"But we could teach you," piped up a girl on the other side of the barn. Several other girls nodded in agreement.

Maggie gestured serenely to the circle. "Would you like to join us, Gideon?"

"I'll pass."

I turned back to my search and finally found what I wanted. A box of myTality™ Clear-It-Up products. I pulled it off the stack and rifled through while Maggie and fifteen of her closest friends watched me attentively. Finally, I located the spot-treatment cream.

I left the barn quickly, hoping it wasn't obvious how embarrassed I was, wondering how many times I'd be humiliated before the day was over.

INTERVIEW

Subject #2, Magdalene (Maggie) Hofstadt:

Cults play on the familiar. Have you ever noticed that most cults have a religious aspect? If someone's raised in a Christian house, and they come across a cult with Christian influences, they don't have to *relearn* anything. Their old belief system fits into the new one. Another example would be if there was a whole town that believed in aliens. Starting an alien-based cult wouldn't be as hard as, say, starting a werewolf-based one. How it works is that cults help people believe something they wanted to believe anyway.

EVENT:
The Date

(CONT.)

The instructions on the tube of myTality™ Clear-It-Up spot treatment said to dab a small amount on "the infected area."

So basically, my entire face.

I spread the cream liberally over my cheeks and forehead, praying it would work. Then I went back to my room and scoured the internet for articles about Oswald and the Elixir ETernia.

The response was mixed. Naturally, the myTality™ distributors thought the elixir was as groundbreaking as Kepler[1] discovering the planets moved around the sun in elliptical orbits. Conspiracy theorists and ufologists were more hesitant—but not outright *skeptical*. It irritated me that no one was calling Oswald a phony.

How did he do it? How could he stand in front of a crowd, say he'd discovered the fountain of youth, and have people *believe* him? I could hardly get anyone to trust me about things that were *true*.

I spent so long stewing and reading everything I could find about Oswald that I didn't notice the growing dusk. I was startled

---

1   Johannes Kepler, the astronomer, not my cat.

when Ishmael burst into my room, saying, "Shouldn't you be getting ready for—"

He stopped short and I looked at him expectantly.

"Dude. What did you do to your face?"

"What?" I asked, holding a hand to my cheek. "Is it better?"

"Um. Maybe you should look in a mirror?"

I bolted into the bathroom. In my haste, I skidded on the wet floor—Ishmael must have just finished mopping. I grabbed the sink to stop myself from falling, pulled myself back into a standing position, and looked in the mirror.

My entire face was bright red.

Not my usual acne-prone red. Not even the terrible red from a few hours earlier. No, it was the red of the worst sunburn ever. The red of poison ivy rash. The kind of red that doesn't even look natural.

"Oh god."

Ishmael came up behind me. "It looks painful."

"Just to my ego."

"Do you think you should go to the hospital?"

"No," I said. "I think I should never leave the house again."

"What about your date?"

"I'll text him and cancel."

Except I didn't have his number. Not to mention, he was driving from Pittsburgh and probably on the way already since he was supposed to pick me up in—I pulled out my phone and glanced at the time—fifteen minutes.

"This is bad." I turned to my brother abruptly. "Do something. Fix this."

Ishmael winced. "This might be beyond repair."

366 | CHELSEA SEDOTI

It was Oswald's fault. Everything was his fault. His stupid myTality™ product had ruined my skin as effectively as he was ruining my life. I *hated* him. I hated him more than I'd ever hated anyone before.

I grabbed the tube of spot treatment from where I'd left it by the sink and tossed it angrily to the ground. When that didn't make me feel better, I stomped on it. The cap burst off and the rash-causing cream shot all over the bathroom floor.

"Hey!" Ishmael said. "I just cleaned in here!"

"Ishmael, my date is going to be here in a few minutes and I look like I have an infectious disease!"

My brother bit his lip. "I have an idea."

I followed him into Maggie's bedroom. He didn't bother knocking, but it was empty anyway.

"What are you doing?" I asked.

He gestured to a basket sitting on the dresser. A basket filled with makeup.

"Don't girls use that concealer stuff to hide acne?"

I was willing to try anything. I rifled through the basket until I found a bottle of tan liquid.

"How do I use this?"

Ishmael shrugged. "How should I know?"

I opened the bottle and poured some into my palm, then smeared it across my forehead.

"It's kinda unfair," Ishmael pondered out loud. "Why should girls get to use makeup to cover their flaws and guys just have to deal with it? I mean, I *could* wear it, but people would give me shit. Wouldn't it be nice to normalize men wearing makeup?"

I spread more makeup over my chin and nose, then my cheeks, which were more inflamed than the rest of my face.

"Don't you think, Gideon?"

I rubbed the makeup in, expecting it to absorb into my skin like lotion. It didn't. It was a different consistency—thicker and goopier—and it only smeared. I began to rub more frantically at my face, which had become messy streaks of red and tan.

I looked worse than before I started.

"What are you doing in my room?" came a voice from the doorway.

I spun around to find Maggie with her hands on her hips, nothing remaining of her Zen master attitude.

"What happened to your face?" she gasped. Then, after a pause: "Are you using my *foundation*?"

"Please help me fix this," I said in response.

She stalked over to the dresser and grabbed the makeup. "You wasted half the bottle!"

"I didn't know how much I was supposed to use."

"None," Maggie snapped. "Because it didn't belong to you."

"I take full responsibility for the idea," Ishmael said, holding a hand up.

"What do I do?" I asked Maggie.

She studied my face closely and cringed. "The color doesn't even match your skin tone."

"Can you fix it?"

"Yeah, after you wash your face."

I moved toward the hallway quickly, heading back into the bathroom. And that's when the doorbell rang.

INTERVIEW

Subject #7, Jane Hofstadt (Mother):

I don't think it's fair to blame myTality Clear-It-Up for Gideon's rash. Plenty of people used that product without incident. I suppose sitting in the hot barn all summer might have caused some chemical change? But Gideon shouldn't have applied so much at once. It says right there on the label to do a spot test to make sure you don't have an allergic reaction. You can't blame myTality for user error.

EVENT:
The Date
(CONT.)

Some people don't realize being early is as much of an inconvenience as being late. Alex Spiros was one of those people. I hadn't changed my clothes. I hadn't combed my hair. I hadn't brushed my teeth. And my face was covered in a paste of makeup.

I ran to the bathroom and washed as quickly as possible. But when I dried my face, streaks of tan still appeared on the white towel. I glanced in the mirror, knowing I hadn't gotten all the color off, but checking for any obvious spots. Naturally, scrubbing my face had made the redness even worse.

"*Gideon*," Father called from downstairs. From his irritated tone, I assumed it wasn't the first time he tried to get my attention.

There was nothing to be done about my appearance. I took a deep breath and steeled myself. It didn't matter how strange I looked. I wasn't interested in Alex Spiros anyway. After the date, I never had to see him again. Besides, I had more to offer than looks. I was clever. I was talented. I was going to *be* something one day.

I made my way downstairs, my siblings following behind me, eager to watch the train wreck.

In the living room, Alex sat on the couch, talking to Father.

"So," Father was saying. "How about the Pirates missing out on the playoffs this year?"

"I don't follow baseball," Alex replied. "It's kind of an antiquated sport, isn't it?"

Father tried to hide his distress.

And, to his credit, Alex tried to hide his own distress at the sight of me.

When he heard us enter the room, Alex turned, and his eyes landed on Ishmael first. He looked pleasantly surprised. Then his gaze skipped to me, and he seemed to instantly realize *I* was his date. Distress flashed across his face, but he quickly recovered.

Alex was just as attractive as his photos. He was tall and broad, expertly groomed, and wore a tight shirt that showed off his build. I'd never felt less desirable in my life.

"Hi. I'm Gideon," I said.

"Alex."

He shook my hand politely. We stood awkwardly in the living room.

"You met my father, I see," I said eventually. "This is my sister and brother—"

"Call me Ishmael," my brother broke in.

I rolled my eyes.

"So, uh, you want to head out?" Alex asked.

I nodded. We said goodbye to my family and made our way to Alex's car. I slid into the passenger's seat and tried to ignore the overwhelming odor of cologne.

Once we were on the road, Alex broke the silence by saying, "I heard there's a decent pizza place in town. I thought we could eat there."

"Sure," I said, trying to keep the dread from my voice. I didn't hate pizza, but it was on my list of overly messy foods.

Alex and I drove quietly for a while. Too long of a while. I needed to say something. I needed to somehow let him know the entire date wasn't going to be as torturous as the start of it.

"Just so you know," I said. "My face doesn't always look like this."

Alex glanced at me. "Oh. Um, okay. Cool."

Or maybe silence was the better option after all.

INTERVIEW

Subject #4, Victor Hofstadt (Father):

As a parent, you want what's best for your kids. And I try to be optimistic, I do. But anyone could've seen Gideon's date wasn't exactly going to be a home run.

EVENT:
The Date

(CONT.)

Alex finally spoke as we drove down Main Street. By the time we reached Pizza Haus, he'd proclaimed our lava lamp "weird," the Seekers "creepy," and Lansburg as a whole "sadly nostalgic."

While I didn't entirely disagree with those assessments, I didn't like hearing them from a stranger's mouth.

Being that it was Saturday night, Pizza Haus was packed with people from school. They all stared. I didn't know whether they were surprised to see me on a date, or if they couldn't look away from my blotchy complexion.

"You like green peppers?" Alex asked, scanning the menu. "What about sausage and onion?"

I didn't have time to voice my opinion before he gestured a waiter over to take our order.

"So," I said in the following silence. "You go to culinary school."

He nodded. "I want to have my own show one day."

"Like a cooking show?"

"Yeah."

"Don't you need to be an established chef before you get your own show?"

Alex shrugged. "Things don't work like that anymore. They want you for your personality, not your skills."

"I see." I balled up a napkin tightly in my fist.

"What about you?"

"I plan to study at MIT, then work for NASA as an engineer."

"Isn't NASA kind of dead?" Alex asked. "Triple i is where it's at these days. I mean, how many useless probes is NASA going to send into space? Private space travel, now *that's* interesting."

I gritted my teeth. "Well, I don't quite agree with that. Obviously."

"To each his own."

Another painful silence. Alex pulled out his phone and checked a message. I wondered if we could agree to spend the rest of the date like that, each buried in our respective devices.

"So," I said. "Your mom is a myTality distributor."

"Yeah. She does okay for herself."

"It's pretty absurd, isn't it? The whole myTality thing."

"What do you mean?" Alex asked, a blank look on his face.

I tried to make my expression neutral. "Never mind."

"I drink one of those shakes every morning. I get a lot of energy from them."

"How nice."

Conversation proceeded in uncomfortable starts, stops, and missteps until our pizza came. And then an entirely new challenge was in front of me.

I despised eating pizza with my hands. Grease would drip down my chin and toppings would slide off and sauce would seep out, until

I was covered in pizza goop. Luckily, there was a solution—I ate pizza with a fork and knife. It earned me strange looks, though.

"Are you going to eat the whole slice like that?" Alex asked, watching me struggle to saw through a piece of pizza with a look of fascinated horror on his face.

"I am."

"*Why?*"

"I don't like messy food."

"I get it," Alex said, though from his expression he clearly didn't. "I can be a little OCD too."

I opened my mouth to tell Alex the following three things:

1. I did not have obsessive compulsive disorder.
2. Even if I *did*, he wouldn't be able to tell based on the way I ate food.
3. He was, in all likelihood, *not* "a little OCD too."

But before I could speak, I heard a devastating sound: Owen's voice. Saying my name.

I looked up and saw him approaching my table. In my surprise, I managed to finally cut through the crust, while at the same time inadvertently using my knife as a lever. A chunk of pizza launched from my plate and into the air before landing right in front of Owen.

I wanted to be put on a rocket and shot into the farthest, darkest corner of the galaxy where no one would be witness to my humiliation.

Rather than comment on the pizza I'd catapulted at him, Owen said, "What happened to your face?"

"I had a mishap," I mumbled.

Then Owen looked over and registered who I was with. His expression turned guarded. "I'm interrupting."

"No," I replied. "We were just... This is Alex."

"Nice to meet you," Alex said.

"You too," Owen replied. He nodded toward a group of other theater kids streaming through the door. "I have to go. See you later."

Before he could move away, Sofia Russo bounced up to us. "Gideon! I didn't know you had a boyfriend."

"He has several, actually," Owen said bitterly.

Yes, I definitely would've welcomed the opportunity to free float in space. I finally saw the appeal of being an astronaut. Maybe it wasn't the daredevil nature of it that drew in people. Maybe it was just nice to know you couldn't embarrass yourself when Earth was 500 kilometers away.

Alex and Sofia glanced between Owen and me. With every passing second I felt more uncomfortable. Finally, I couldn't take it anymore. I stood.

"Look," I babbled to Alex, "this date was a mistake. I shouldn't have agreed to it. And clearly we're not... We don't have much in common. I'm sorry, but I need to go. Okay? Sorry. Really."

I reached for my wallet to throw some money on the table. But in my haste to leave the house, apparently I'd left it behind. My night couldn't possibly get worse.

I didn't know what to do—would apologizing for not having money make the situation more or less awkward? Could *anything* make it more awkward?

"Sorry," I mumbled again.

Then I hurried out of Pizza Haus, shame making my myTality™ rash burn even brighter.

INTERVIEWS

Subject #3, Cassidy (Cass) Robinson:

I wasn't surprised Gideon called and asked me to pick him up from Pizza Haus. I knew the date was going to be a total tragedy. Not because he wasn't "good enough" for Alex. But because he went into it with a bad attitude. I'll tell you what *did* surprise me though: when I showed up and saw what he'd done to his face.

Subject #5, Owen Campbell:

I actually felt bad for Gideon. He looked awful, and obviously the date wasn't going well. But I was still pissed off too. And it was really uncool to leave Alex sitting there alone. So I asked if he wanted to join me and my friends. What else was I supposed to do?

THE NEXT SEVEN DAYS

YOU COULD SAY THAT OVER THE NEXT WEEK, I had a bit of a crisis—or a breakthrough, depending on how you looked at it.

On Sunday, while I lay in bed running every detail of the Worst Date Ever through my mind, I concluded that I needed to get my life together. I decided to do the following:

1. Complete all schoolwork, including my paper on "The Death of the Ball Turret Gunner." I'd put it off, mainly because I did *not* think it was about abortion, like Mr. Fiore insisted, and rather that the author—who had

    served in the Army Air Corps during World War II—meant it to be taken literally.

2. Ask teachers for makeup work to improve my less-than-stellar grades.

3. Attend my extracurriculars again.

4. Begin compiling and analyzing data I'd collected from the hoax so I could move forward with the actual report.

5. Download the MIT application forms and begin filling them out—it was never too early to start.

6. Avoid thinking about my blind date or Owen or J. Quincy Oswald or *anything* unrelated to my future goals.

I'd allowed myself to get distracted by pride and feelings. I'd also gotten foolishly caught up in the hoax itself—as if *it* were the end goal, not my sociological study. I needed to get back on track, remember what mattered, work hard to secure myself the best possible future.

And for the most part, my efforts were successful. I made progress. I felt good. I felt like the kind of person MIT would accept with open arms.

Right up until I let Cass talk me into attending the homecoming dance.

IRVING HIGH SCHOOL HOMECOMING FLYER

3... 2... 1...
BLAST OFF!

You're invited to an out-of-this-world
HOMECOMING DANCE

WHERE: Irving High School Gym
WHEN: Saturday, October 21st, 8-11 p.m.
ATTIRE: Semiformal, or your best space suit!

EVENT:
The Homecoming Dance

DATE: OCT. 21 (SAT.)

I'd been to a total of one high school dance. It was homecoming fresh-man year, which Cass *also* convinced me to attend. She spent the evening frustrated because I wouldn't do any actual dancing (I don't dance), wouldn't take a million pictures with her (I was having an especially bad breakout), and hardly interacted with her new theater friends (they were loud and overwhelming and I didn't know what to say to them). It surprised me that Cass wanted a repeat of that night.

The only reason I agreed was because I was attempting to act... normal. Like a high school student on track for a bright future, not a teenager who spent hours researching aliens and feeling resentful of the leader of an MLM.

Cass and Arden got ready at Cass's house—I opted to skip that particular pre-dance ritual—then picked me up. We weren't able to leave for thirty minutes due to Mother fawning over us.

Admittedly, Cass and Arden looked excellent. Arden wore a tasteful black dress and she'd let Cass do her makeup, which was subtle and elegant. Having had my own makeup experience recently, I understood how difficult subtle makeup could be. Cass, on the other hand, did not go for an understated look. She'd found a flapper dress and was a whirlwind of fringe and beads. She looked straight from a 1920s speakeasy.

I'd only put 14 percent as much effort into my own appearance. I was just happy my skin had returned to its normal color.

When we arrived at Irving High School, it wasn't the crush of students in their homecoming finest that immediately vexed me.

It was the decorations.

I'd forgotten the dance was "space" themed. Foil stars hung from the ceiling, illuminated by Christmas lights. Off to one side, a punch bowl held a toxic, bright green concoction. From the middle of the ceiling, where a disco ball would normally go, a giant papier-mâché UFO was suspended.

"Look at that," I said to Cass and Arden with a scowl. I pointed to a booth where groups were getting photos taken.

"What?" Cass asked.

"That backdrop. I assume it's meant to be the surface of Venus, but the idea of us being on Venus is ridiculous."[1]

Then I saw something even more egregious. Someone had made cardboard cutouts of the solar system and hung them on the far wall. I pointed it out to Cass and Arden.

"Why are Neptune and Uranus the same size? Why is Pluto there, but not Ceres? Why is Saturn *pink*?"

"Not everything has to be literal," Arden said.

"But whoever made those planets wasn't even *trying*."

---

1   For starters, the surface of Venus was roughly 864°F.

384 | CHELSEA SEDOTI

Cass laughed. "Maybe they had more important things to think about. Like, you know, basically *anything*."

We moved through the dance, stopping to talk to people along the way. Rather, Cass stopped to talk to people while Arden and I held back. I did my best to avoid looking at the solar system wall. If I pretended it wasn't there, maybe it would stop bothering me.

After an hour, I started to relax. Even when Cass was off socializing, Arden stuck by me. The punch, despite the slimy green color, tasted good enough. And Ishmael's over-the-top antics on the dance floor were entertaining. My brother wore sunglasses and a blazer over his signature Hawaiian shirt. Though he was perfectly capable of dancing well, he chose not to, instead trying—and succeeding—to get laughs from everyone in the vicinity.

To my surprise, my mood steadily improved.

Until I saw Owen.

It wasn't the fact of his presence that bothered me. I'd actually tried to get ahold of him all week. The problem was, he wasn't alone. He had none other than Alex Spiros with him.

I reached out and grabbed Cass's arm.

"Ow, what?" she asked. She followed my gaze and I felt her body stiffen. "Oh. Damn."

"Who's with Owen?" Arden asked. "Wait, is that..."

"It's your blind date, isn't it?" Cass said.

I nodded because I didn't trust myself to speak.

Part of me was angry. Part was sad. Another part of me figured it was inevitable. Owen had finally found someone who was his match, someone attractive enough to stand next to him.

Except, I seethed, Alex wasn't *really* Owen's match. Because

Owen was a great person and Alex Spiros was a douche. Was that what Owen wanted? The whole time he was with me, was he secretly hoping for some...some *TV chef*?

"I'm going over there," I announced.

"That might be the worst idea you've ever had," Cass said.

Arden nodded. "Why don't we leave? We can see a movie or something."

"A movie sounds great," Cass agreed.

I ignored them and made a beeline toward Owen and Alex, who stood at the edge of the dance floor.

"Well, this is unexpected."

Owen's face fell when he saw me. Alex gave me a small nod and looked supremely uncomfortable. Good.

"Gideon," Owen said. "I didn't think you'd be here."

"I guess this would be okay then? It wouldn't count if I didn't know about it?"

I didn't bother looking at Alex. He didn't matter. I focused on Owen and watched a range of emotions play out on his face. Unfortunately, I had no idea what any of those emotions were.

"Look," he said finally. "I'm not doing anything wrong."

"You don't find anything about this situation a bit *awkward*?"

"*Everything* with you is awkward." Owen's voice rose, and people around us turned to look. "*You* weren't going to come to the dance with me, were you?"

"No," I snapped. "Because you're not speaking to me!"

"Don't try to make this my fault. I wasn't speaking to you because you went on a date with another guy."

"And look how that turned out."

"So you don't want to date me, but no one else can either?" Owen asked, and I wasn't having trouble reading his emotions anymore. He was furious. "You need to get a grip. The universe doesn't revolve around you."

"The universe doesn't revolve around *anything*!"

Then I felt someone at my elbow, pulling me away. I glanced over, expecting Cass, but it was Ishmael.

"Owen, Alex," he said pleasantly. "Nice to see you both. Unfortunately, Gideon and I need to be going."

My brother dragged me to the darkest corner of the gym, where we were mercifully hidden from the stares. "Dude," he said. "That was a bit much."

Before I could respond, Cass and Arden joined us.

"That was so uncharacteristically dramatic," Cass said. "I'd applaud if I didn't know how upset you must be."

"I'm not upset."

"Sure you're not," Cass replied dryly. "You always shout in public when you're *not* upset."

"I'll take you home," Ishmael offered.

"I can do it," Cass said.

"I really don't mind."

"Both of you stop," I snapped. "You don't need to escort me anywhere. I'm not going to make a scene. Again."

"Don't get mad at us," Cass said.

"Look dude, I know this hurts. But it's just part of life. Owen's a great guy, but you'll find someone else."

Cass nodded. "And he would've been here with you, if you'd let him."

Arden had been silent throughout the conversation. She looked back and forth between Ishmael and Cass rapidly. Finally, she fixed her gaze on me. "All this time you were lying to me? You and Owen really *have* been dating?"

Her pitiful tone and accusing gaze put me over the edge.

"Yes, we've been dating. No, I didn't tell you. Because it's none of your business. It's *no one's* business. It was always going to end up here, with me getting left for another guy, at some stupid dance, where people can't even tell the difference between Neptune and Uranus! Why should I have told you *anything,* Arden? Why does any of this even matter?"

"What the hell is wrong with you?" Cass snapped. "This isn't Arden's fault. It's no one's fault but your own."

She was right, of course. I needed to apologize to Arden, whose eyes had already filled with tears. But I couldn't. I couldn't even bring myself to meet her gaze.

So instead I turned and stormed out of the dance, leaving everyone behind me under the glow of fake stars.

TEXT CONVERSATION

Participants: Gideon Hofstadt, Victor Hofstadt

GH: I need a ride.

VH: Right now?

GH: Could you pick me up?

VH: You're at a dance with everyone you know, and you can't find someone else to drive you home?

GH: Please, Dad.

VH: On my way.

EVENT:
The Homecoming
Dance
(CONT.)

For a while, neither of us spoke. Finally, as we left the populated part of Lansburg and started down side streets that led to the farm, Father said, "What happened?"

Normal Gideon would've said "*nothing.*" But I didn't feel normal. I felt like, for once, I had to let my feelings out.

"You know that guy I went out with last week? Alex? He showed up at the dance with Owen Campbell."

"I see," Father replied. "So you like Alex, huh?"

"No." I hesitated. "I like Owen."

Father let out a breath. "Thank god for that."

I looked at him, surprised.

"I wasn't impressed by that Alex kid," he explained.

I snorted. "Me either."

Father reached over and turned down the radio. The sports talk he was listening to faded into a hum.

"How does Owen feel about you?"

"He used to like me. We were kind of dating. But I ruined it."

Father didn't respond, and I knew he was waiting for me to say more. I couldn't remember the last time I'd been so open with him. He probably worried that if he spoke the moment would pass.

"I didn't want our relationship to be public. I thought it was only a matter of time before he dumped me, and if our relationship was public, our breakup would be public too. I couldn't stand the thought of everyone...pitying me."

"Why'd you assume Owen would dump you?" Father asked.

"Let's face it, I'm not incredibly desirable. I'm not even very *likable*."

"That's ridiculous. If people don't like you, it's because you don't *let* them like you. You keep everyone at arm's length."

"I don't know how to be any other way," I said, frustration and sadness welling up inside of me.

"Pride can be a hard thing to overcome," Father said, reaching over to squeeze my shoulder. "But everyone needs to let themselves be vulnerable sometimes."

I stared out the window for a moment, watching trees and farmland stream by. Finally, I said, "I know you and Mother think I'm broken."

Father looked at me sharply. "What are you talking about?"

"You think I can't feel anything. And you'd rather I was some star baseball player, and Mother would rather I was, I don't know, an *extrovert*."

"We know you feel things. What worries us is that you keep those feelings bottled up. And neither your mom nor I have *ever* been disappointed by who you are."

"Sure," I said dryly.

"Gideon," Father said. "I once had to pick up your brother from detention after he set up a Slip 'N Slide outside the principal's office. And you think *you're* the one we're disappointed in?"

I laughed. He had a point.

We turned onto Olga Lane and our house came into view, old and rickety as always, but also comforting. It looked warm and safe and like it could shield me from the awful thoughts bombarding me.

"I'll always be proud of you," Father said as he came to a stop and put the car in Park.

"Even right now?" I joked, knowing I was a mess of rage and sadness and shame.

But Father didn't laugh. Instead, he looked straight at me and said, "*Especially* right now."

TRANSCRIPT OF OCT. 22 TELEPHONE
CONVERSATION BETWEEN GIDEON
HOFSTADT AND CASSIDY ROBINSON

GIDEON:

Hello?

CASS:

I know it's early—

GIDEON:

It's *very* early.

CASS:

—but it's important.

GIDEON:

Look, I don't want to talk about last night—

CASS:

This isn't about you.

GIDEON:

Oh.

CASS:

Have you talked to Arden?

GIDEON:

It's five o'clock in the morning.

CASS:

That's a no?

GIDEON:

Of course I haven't.

CASS:

You haven't talked to her since you left the dance?

GIDEON:

No. Cass, what's going on?

CASS:

Arden is missing.

GIDEON:

She's *what*?

CASS:

She ran out of the gym last night after you did. I talked to Ishmael for, like, two seconds, then I went after her. But when I got outside she was gone.

GIDEON:

She probably went home.

CASS:

That's what I figured. But her mom called a few minutes ago asking if Arden spent the night here. She never went home, Gideon. No one knows where she is.

INTERVIEWS

Subject #6, Arden Byrd:

Cass said, "Gideon's just upset. He didn't mean any of that." But really, he confirmed something I'd suspected for a while: he'd never see me as a real friend. I knew if I tried to say that to Cass, I'd cry, so I ran out of the gym. I didn't know where I was going. I ended up on Main Street and was starting to calm down and wonder how I'd get home. That's when the light appeared in front of me.

Subject #14, Arnold (Arnie) Hodges:

Yes, I saw the girl wandering down Main Street that night. Knew why she disappeared too. She was abducted.

NEWSPAPER ARTICLE

The following article was reprinted with permission of the *Lansburg Daily Press*.

LOCAL TEEN MISSING AFTER HOMECOMING DANCE

By K. T. Malone

October 23

LANSBURG, PA—Authorities are searching for a Lansburg teen who vanished after Saturday night's homecoming dance.

Arden Byrd, fifteen, was last seen around 9 p.m. leaving the Irving High School gym. The last people to interact with her say she was in a distressed state and didn't tell anyone where she was going.

Emma Byrd, Arden's mother, contacted police the next morning when she discovered her daughter had not returned home. "I knew something was wrong right away. Arden has never stayed out all night."

Though a contingent of people have come forward saying Arden's disappearance has ties to alleged extraterrestrial activity, police chief Lisa Kaufman said there is no basis to these claims.

"We're treating this like any other missing persons case," Chief Kaufman said. "The police department will consider any phone calls about alien abductions to be pranks."

Arden is 5 foot 2 and 102 pounds, with blond hair and green eyes. She was last seen wearing a knee-length, black formal dress.

Anyone who has information about Arden's whereabouts is asked to call 911 or contact the Lansburg Police Department immediately.

The following article was reprinted with permission of lightbringernews.com.

LOCAL TEEN ABDUCTED BY ALIENS!

By Adam Frykowski
Posted October 23–9:35 a.m.

LANSBURG, PA—Authorities are searching for a Lansburg teen who vanished after Saturday night's homecoming dance.

Unfortunately for the authorities—and the teen—they're searching in the wrong places.

Arden Byrd, fifteen, left the Irving High School gym at 9 p.m. and vanished into the night.

But Arnie Hodges, expert ufologist and MUFON member, tells a different story. He says the teen was abducted by aliens. Several of the men and women who were with Mr. Hodges in the town square at that time corroborate this.

Police chief Lisa Kaufman, who declined to comment on this article, claims there is no evidence Byrd was abducted by extraterrestrials. But here at *The Light Bringer* we know the path to enlightenment has never started with closed minds.

If you have information about Byrd, or any other recent abductions, please share with us at contact@lightbringernews.com.

Click here to subscribe to our newsletter!

EVENT: The Disappearance

DATE: OCT. 23 (MON.)

It said something about Lansburg—or maybe society as a whole—that people got more worked up about aliens than a fifteen-year-old girl disappearing.

Arden remained missing throughout Sunday. I assumed by Monday morning there'd be news, but aside from an article in the paper and on Frykowski's blog, nothing had changed. I wanted to stay home, to *do* something, but I didn't know what. So I went to school.

"This is my fault," I told Cass at lunch.

"It's no one's fault."

"You know people are saying she was abducted by aliens."

"Well, *we* know aliens had nothing to do with it." Cass glumly picked at her french fries. I would've known how upset Cass was even without the lack of appetite—she was dressed in jeans and a plain sweatshirt.

"And that's my fault too."

"What is?"

"That people are brushing off Arden's disappearance because they think it's an alien abduction."

"They're idiots," Cass said, but I knew she felt guilty for her part in the hoax too.

Why hadn't we considered that events might spiral out of control, that someone might end up in genuine danger? And no one cared, because they'd been playing at danger for weeks. With half of Lansburg claiming to be abducted by aliens, of course no one would take a missing girl seriously. Especially a missing girl who'd claimed to see a UFO herself.

After school, Chief Kaufman came over and questioned me and Ishmael. I told her everything I'd said to Arden at the dance, though repeating it intensified my guilt.

"What do you think happened?" Ishmael asked.

"We don't know yet. But we haven't seen any sign that Arden's in danger."

"And what sign would that be?" I asked. "Do victims usually have time to leave notes saying *FYI, I was taken by a serial killer*?"

"It's highly unlikely Arden had a run-in with a serial killer," Kaufman said gently.

"Our town has been swarming with strangers for weeks. If it ever was likely, I'd think it was now."[1]

Mother perched on the piano bench on the other side of the room, yet spoke to Kaufman as if whispering in her ear. "Gideon is feeling a lot of guilt about this."

"Understandable," Kaufman said. "But in all likelihood, Arden is just holed up at a friend's house."

"Arden doesn't *have* other friends," I said.

---

1   Realistically, serial killings only account for 1 percent of murders committed in the United States.

Later, when Kaufman left and Mother and I were alone, she wrapped her arm around me. "Whatever happened to Arden, it's not your fault."

But it *was*. Arden never would've left the dance if I hadn't been cruel to her.

When Chief Kaufman questioned Cass later that day, Cass snapped, asking where the search helicopters were, if someone was making flyers and organizing search parties.

"We're not at that stage yet," Kaufman said. "All signs point to Arden walking away of her own free will. She probably needed time to herself."

"Clearly, you don't know Arden," Cass replied.

She'd been missing for thirty hours by that point, and there seemed to be no leads. How was that possible? How could someone vanish without any trace?

I called Arden's phone over and over, but it went straight to voicemail. I texted that I was sorry, that I hadn't meant to snap at her, that I shouldn't have kept secrets. I didn't know if she'd ever read the messages, but I had to hope.

That evening, Ishmael drove me into town for my late shift at Super Scoop. I ranted the whole way.

"No one even cares."

"*We* care," Ishmael said.

"No one's even worried about her."

"*We're* worried."

"What's wrong with people?"

"I don't know, dude."

The sight of the Seekers surrounding the lava lamp increased my fury. I wanted them gone. I wanted all evidence of aliens removed from town. I wanted people to get their heads out of their asses and realize something was actually *going on*, something more important than fake-abduction mass hysteria. I hated all of them.

Or maybe I really just hated myself.

EVENT:
An Epiphany

DATE: OCT. 23 (MON.)

It was late when I left work. Moths buzzed around the gaslights and the moon cast an eerie glow on Main Street. The square was empty for once—the Seekers had retreated to their various camps.

Ishmael texted that he was going to be late. To kill time, I wandered to the lava lamp.

Two nights before, Arden had walked down the same road. According to Arnie Hodges, anyway—and he was hardly a reliable source of information.

As I got closer to the lamp, I was startled to see someone on the observation deck. Not just *on it*, but leaning precariously over the side. For a moment, I thought it was Oswald, still preaching after his constituents had gone home. Then I took in the gangly figure, the ungraceful movements. Definitely not Oswald.

Curious, I made my way to the previously blocked-off stairs. I climbed up, ignoring how the unmaintained metal squealed under my feet.

The observation deck seemed higher once I was on it. I looked out over Lansburg, at the quaint shops and cobblestone streets. The cool October breeze lifted the hair from my forehead.

A shuffling sound came from the other side of the deck, and I rounded the lava lamp, my face only a foot away from the unlit paraffin and carbon tetrachloride and who knew what else. A figure appeared in front of me. I squinted in the dark, then realized who was leaning over the railing, lost in his own contemplation.

"Frykowski."

He whirled, surprised, and I reached out to steady him before he pitched over the rail. Up close, I could smell alcohol.

"Hofstadt," Frykowski said drunkenly, his mouth trying to draw out both the *d* and *t* in my last name.

"Do you have a death wish?" I asked, watching him and discreetly beginning to record audio with my phone at the same time. "You shouldn't be up here while you're drunk. You shouldn't be up here *at all*."

"I'm not drunk," he slurred. But he stepped away from the railing. With his back against the lava lamp he slid into a sitting position and slouched there.

"Why are you up here?" I asked.

"Hofstadt," he replied. "What do I have to do to get ahead?"

"I don't know what you're talking about."

"Sit with me." He patted the floor next to him.

I glanced down at the street. I'd see Ishmael when he pulled up in the Jeep. So I sat.

"All I ever wanted was to be a journalist," Frykowski said.

"Aren't you one?"

He laughed bitterly. "I edit obituaries and write a shitty blog no one reads."

Accurate.

"Your blog gets decent traffic," I said, attempting an encouraging tone.

"For two seconds, Hofstadt," he said, reeling drunkenly toward me. "My two seconds of fame. Now they're back to not caring about me."

"Who?"

"Everyone." Frykowski scowled. "Don't you get it? I started things. *I* did. *I* connected your explosion to aliens. *I* put it out there for the world to read. And they read it, and they came, and they fucking *took* it from me. Don't you *see*?"

Shockingly, I did.

"Now all the big boys are in it," he went on. "*Weird World News* is writing about Lansburg. That asshole radio guy from Podunk, Nevada, is doing broadcasts. The Lansburg Lights have even gotten mentioned on the *national* news. The whole country is reporting on us, Hofstadt."

"It's true," I said.

"And you know how many comments my last blog post got? Two. *Two!*"

I made a mental note to check his site later.

Frykowski looked me straight in the eye. "Tell me…with all this media attention, why should anyone care about me?"

Almost against my will, I found myself nodding in commiseration.

"I'm nothing," Frykowski said. "They made me into nothing."

"It makes you wonder why you even try," I said.

"Exactly!"

"No matter what you do, other people take credit for your success."

People…or *one* person. One person who swept into town in his shiny palace on wheels.

Frykowski patted me on the back. "See. You get it."

If Oswald hadn't shown up, the situation would still be in my control. Hell, if myTality™ didn't exist, Mother would've never sent me on the Worst Date Ever, and I wouldn't have gotten in a fight with Owen, and Owen wouldn't have gone to the dance with Alex, and I wouldn't have yelled at Arden, and she'd be safely at home.

Everything was Oswald's fault.

"In the end," Frykowski said glumly, "guys like us are nothing."

"Yes," I said, distractedly. "Wait. I mean *no*."

I wasn't *nothing*. I wasn't a *starfish*.

I tried to make sense of my racing thoughts, my anger and confusion.

"Maybe you're content being nothing," I said. "But I'm not ready to give up."

I'd come too far to be taken down by the owner of an MLM. A guy who wore cowboy boots with blazers. A guy who'd skated through life on charm.

I stood.

"Come on," I told Frykowski. "I can't leave you up here."

I helped him to his feet. He swayed against me, and his weight pushed me closer to the railing. I hurriedly righted myself and guided Frykowski to the stairs before he killed us both.

"Your problem," I said as we made our way off the deck, "is that you gave up too fast. You let people make you think you're not good enough. Your worth shouldn't have come from them, though. It should come from *you*. And if there's someone in the world who's out to defeat you, well, defeat them first."

By the time we reached the bottom of the stairs, Ishmael had pulled the Jeep up in front of Super Scoop.

"Keep your feet on the ground," I told Frykowski.

"Hofstadt," he called as I hurried across the square toward my brother. "Was this on the record?"

I didn't respond.

When I opened the passenger door of the Jeep, Ishmael eyed me warily. "You look...riled up."

"Ishmael," I said. "This is very important. We need to go to Crescent Road. I'm going to confront Oswald."

COLLECTED DATA

BLOG COMMENTS

The following compilation is a selection of user comments from lightbringernews.com. Comments were originally posted on the article "LOCAL TEEN ABDUCTED BY ALIENS!"

CIAyylmao2001:
IF YOU THINK SHE WAS TAKEN BY ALIENS YOUR A FUCKING IDIOT FRYKOWSKY. ALMOST ALL ADBUCTIONS IN THIS COUNTRY ARE DONE BY ARE OWN GOVERNMENT HAVE YOU EVEN HEARD OF PROJECT MK ULTRA??????? SHES PROBABLY LOCKED IN A LAB RIGHTNOW BEING GIVEN LSD AND UNDERGOING MIND EXPERIMENTS

MissusFry1962:
Adam, it's not kind to make light of a tragedy. This was a nicely written piece, but I think you should remove it from your website. Love, Mom.

EVENT:
An Epiphany
(CONT.)

The myTality™ camp was dark when Ishmael and I arrived. As before, there were no bonfires, no celebrations.

"I just don't get what exactly you're confronting Oz *about*," Ishmael whispered.

"About being a fraud."

"But, dude...aren't *we* frauds?"

Instead of responding, I pulled out my phone and set it to record audio.

When we reached the palace on wheels, the monstrosity at the center of camp, Ishmael moved toward the window we'd peered through on our last visit.

"Let's see if he's here."

"No. I'm done lurking in the shadows." I took a deep breath and raised my hand to knock.

"But dude," Ishmael said. "How can you tell him we know *he's* faking without letting him know *we* were faking?"

I stared at my brother grimly.

"Oh," he said sadly. "The hoax is ending."

Yes, it was ending.

If Oswald turned us in, the consequences would be dire. Ishmael and I had committed a multitude of crimes—trespassing, reckless endangerment, livestock theft. Agent Ruiz would probably be more than happy to slap handcuffs on me and call the alien mystery solved. What would that mean for my future? I felt sick at the thought of saying goodbye to everything I'd envisioned for myself. But I had to stop Oswald. I *had* to.

I knocked on the door.

Oswald answered a moment later, in casual attire. No boots, no blazer.

"Gideon, Ishmael," he said, surprised.

"Can we come in?"

"I'm always thrilled to see you, but now's not a great time."

"It is for me." I was done letting him call the shots.

Oswald looked behind us into the darkness of the camp, as if someone might be lurking there.

"Okay," he said, finally. "Come on."

We entered the camper. Ishmael hovered near the door, looking uncomfortable, while Oswald leaned casually against the wall and smiled, easygoing as ever. "How can I help you boys?"

"This has to end, Oswald."

"Pardon?"

"Your messages from the cosmos. The Elixir ETernia. The whole scam. It's over."

He laughed. "Whoa there. I'm not sure where this is comin' from."

"There are no aliens and you know it."

Oswald's expression immediately turned sad. "Oh. I see."

"You do?" I asked cautiously.

"They never really visited you, did they?" He put a hand on my shoulder. "That must hurt."

"What? No. They've never visited *anyone*."

Oswald smiled condescendingly. "They've sure visited me."

"You're ly—"

I stopped abruptly when I heard a noise from the bedroom. A cough.

Ishmael and I glanced at each other.

"Who's here?" I asked.

"No one," Oswald replied quickly, but there was no denying the flash of alarm on his face.

"Your *girlfriend*?" I sneered. "That *teenager* you were—"

"Now how do you—"

"Get rid of her," I demanded.

"What?"

"We're having a private conversation. I want her gone."

From the corner of my eye I saw Ishmael staring at me like I'd gone rabid.

"You don't come into my home and tell me what to do," Oswald said. "You need to—"

Before he finished, I stormed to the bedroom door and yanked it open, preparing to... Well, I wasn't 100 percent sure what my plan was.

I stopped abruptly.

I tried to process what I was seeing.

"Arden?" I said, hesitantly.

INTERVIEW

Subject #6, Arden Byrd:

I ended up on Main Street and I was starting to calm down and wonder how I'd get home. That's when the light appeared in front of me. It was Oz's Range Rover. This might sound silly, but Range Rovers always seemed like cool-people cars. Like anyone who drives one doesn't have the same problems I do. The window rolled down, and Oz asked why I looked so blue when I was dressed so nice. And he just...he saw me. He saw right into me. And he *cared*. He asked if I wanted to go somewhere to talk, and I did. And when I was in his RV with him, I never wanted to leave again. It was almost like, for the first time, I felt alive.

EVENT:
An Epiphany
(CONT.)

Arden sat on the bed, wearing boxer shorts and a myTality™ T-shirt that was five sizes too big. She looked at me with huge eyes.

"You've got to be kidding," Ishmael muttered behind me.

I spun toward Oswald. "What did you do to her?"

Oswald took a step back and held his hands up. He opened his mouth to speak, but before he could, Arden was on her feet, wrapping her hand around my elbow.

"Stop, Gideon. He didn't do anything."

"This can't be happening," Ishmael lamented, rubbing his eyes like he could erase the scene in front of him.

"Arden, we need to go."

"No."

"The whole town is looking for you. People think you've been murdered!"

"I'm staying here," she said stubbornly.

"The *police* are involved. This is a big deal. This is a *crime*."

Doubt flickered across her face.

"Do you really want Chief Kaufman to find you here with him?" I pressed. "How do you think *she'd* react?"

Arden's gaze went to Oswald who, for the first time, didn't seem slick. The color had drained from face and his skin looked like wax.

"You should go with your friends," he told her weakly.

"I want to stay with you."

"Arden, sweetheart, you really need to go."

"Don't you call her that." I seethed. "Don't you call her anything, ever again."

His words had done their job, though. Arden went back into the bedroom and gathered her things—her purse, and the dress she wore to the dance.

"Do you want to put shoes on?" Ishmael asked hesitantly.

"No."

I quickly ushered Arden to the Jeep and got into the back seat with her, shoving aside piles of junk Ishmael had amassed there.

"Are you okay?" I asked, as we pulled onto the road.

"I'm fine."

"Did he..."

"He didn't do anything that I didn't want him to do."

From the front seat, Ishmael groaned. "This is so screwed up."

"Arden," I said. "We need to go to the police station."

Her expression turned panicked. "What? No."

"Your mom is terrified. People think you could be *dead*. You don't understand what a big deal this is."

"Who would care if I was dead?"

"*I* would."

Arden's eyes filled with tears. "You didn't even trust me enough to tell me about Owen. And now I'm supposed to believe you're my friend?"

"I'm sorry, Arden." I took her hand. "I'm a jerk."

She sniffled.

"But it's not *you*, it's—"

"Cliché, dude," Ishmael interrupted.

"It *is* me, though," I said. "I should've told you the truth, and I can't even explain why I didn't. It just seems impossible to talk about my feelings and make myself vulnerable. Maybe I'm not even really honest with myself."

Tears snaked down Arden's face. "I just wanted to be included. I wanted you to *like* me."

"I only like about five percent of humanity. But one of the few people I like is you."

Her tears didn't stop, but a faint smile appeared on her face.

"I'm so sorry for what I said at the dance. I was angry and took it out on you. I hope you can forgive me."

"It's not just you, you know. It's everyone and everything. Sometimes I don't think I'll ever belong anywhere."

"Me too, Arden. Me too."

After a pause, Arden took a deep breath and said, "I don't regret what happened with Oz."

"But—"

She held up a hand to stop me. "I know it doesn't make sense to you. But he makes me feel good about myself."

"That's part of his act."

"I don't care."

"You know you can't see him again, though," I said. "You know this was wrong. He's an *adult*. He *used* you."

Arden ducked her head. "Maybe. But I won't turn him in."

"You *have* to."

"I'm gonna have to agree with Gideon," Ishmael said from the front of the Jeep.

"He was there for me when no one else was. Maybe he *was* using me. But what I did was *my* choice, and I'm not getting him in trouble for it."

The Jeep was silent for a long time. Eventually, Ishmael said, "Uh...I kind of need to know where to drive."

I looked at Arden. "We need to go to the police station."

"I said—"

"Don't mention Oswald if you don't want to. But people are looking for you. You need to tell the cops *something*. Say you ran away and...I don't know. Stayed at a motel."

Arden thought about it. Finally, she nodded. "Okay, fine."

It *wasn't* fine, though. Arden thought she went with Oswald willingly, but I knew how he manipulated people. He was an adult who took advantage of a mixed-up teenager, and there was nothing *fine* about that. I hoped Arden would eventually see that for herself.

"Gideon?" Arden said softly. I turned to her. "Thank you for apologizing."

"I meant it," I replied. "I promise."

She sniffled and rubbed her nose.

"There's a box of tissues back there somewhere," Ishmael offered.

Ishmael's accumulated jumble in the back seat included a

discarded Hawaiian shirt, fast-food wrappers, and for some inexplicable reason, a green teddy bear. Arden and I fumbled through the mess for the tissues.

A moment later, Arden pulled something off the floor. She frowned. "Is this a...JFK mask?"

I decided, for the first time, to be fully honest with Arden. She deserved that much, even if it had taken far too long for me to get there. "That's actually a funny story..."

As we drove to the police station, I told Arden about the night in the woods with the radio jammer, the lengths Ishmael and I had gone to in order to keep the hoax alive. She laughed at our antics, but as we pulled into the parking lot and Ishmael steered the Jeep into a spot next to Chief Kaufman's cruiser, Arden grew solemn.

"So...the aliens were a prank from the start?"

I stiffened, suddenly realizing my admission would mean I knew Arden had lied about her own encounter. "Yes, it was a prank. I'm so sorry."

"I think part of me already knew," Arden said.

I raised my eyebrows, surprised by her calmness. "You did? But then, what about..." She looked at me expectantly, waiting for me to go on. "The night you saw...you know. Lights in the sky."

"What about it?"

I hesitated, unsure of how to continue without insulting her.

Arden spoke again before I was able to: "Just because *you* lied about UFOs doesn't mean I did."

"But that's not—"

"Stop," she said firmly. "I know what I saw that night. I won't let you take it from me."

I stared at her for a long moment, marveling at the determination in her voice. Where had this strength come from? Had it been hiding all along behind her hunched shoulders and downcast eyes? It's amazing what you learn about a person once you stop shutting them out.

Okay," I said. "I believe you."

She smiled at me, and that moment, in the back of the messy Jeep, in the dark parking lot of Lansburg's police station, I knew our friendship would never be the same as it was before—it would be so much better.

INTERVIEW

Subject #9, Chief Lisa Kaufman:

I suppose they thought no one would notice that Arden came into the station wearing a myTality shirt.

EVENT: Stargazing— Again

DATE: OCT. 25 (WED.)

There was a time when an evening wouldn't pass without me looking at the sky. But with the recent chaos in Lansburg, I'd spent more time dwelling on what was happening on Earth. Certainly, that added to my tension. Stargazing had always been a way for me to decompress.

So on Wednesday night, I went to the edge of the field, near the crater Ishmael and I created. The spot where the strange whirlwind began. Kepler followed, twisting around my feet.

Already, weeds sprouted from the crater. Wind was beginning to erode the sides. One day soon, all evidence of the initial explosion would be gone.

I sat down, pulled Kepler onto my lap, and looked up at the sky.

I located the stars that made up Orion's Belt,[1] and from there was able to pick out the rest of the constellation. Orion was the hunter of the night sky, and more than ever, I wished I had his mythical strength.

---

1   Alnilam, Alnitak, Mintaka.

Two days had passed since Ishmael and I rescued Arden and took her to the police station. Chief Kaufman questioned us for a long time. Arden was like steel. She claimed she'd been at a friend's house and swore I hadn't known where she was until she called me to pick her up. Ishmael and I stayed silent, as promised.

Later, after Arden was reunited with her tearful mother, I asked Ishmael if he thought Kaufman believed the story.

"Not a chance, dude."

An article about Arden's disappearance appeared in the online version of the *Lansburg Daily Press* the next evening. The Seekers still insisted she'd been abducted by aliens. Arden hadn't returned to school yet, and I hoped people would be kind when she did, not treat her like a sideshow.

I'd been honest with Cass about Arden's whereabouts—with Arden's permission—and she was less shocked than I'd been.

"I should've considered she was with Oz," Cass said.

"Why in the world would you have considered that?"

Cass shrugged. "I saw the way she looked at him at his rally."

"She needs to go to the police."

"Obviously. We'll keep trying to convince her."

Not that Cass had much time for anything. The opening night of *Hamelin!* was on Thursday and she was busy preparing.

Overhead, Aldebaran glowed red, the brightest star in Taurus. As always when looking at the night sky, I felt insignificant. Earth was only a speck in the Milky Way. The Milky Way galaxy was only a speck in the universe. And who knew how many other universes there might be.

But for once, my own insignificance didn't scare me. Maybe I *was* more of a starfish than a god. Maybe nothing I did would ever matter on a cosmic scale. But my life didn't play out on a cosmic scale. And though it might be humble and meaningless, it meant something to me.

I thought back to a few nights before, when Frykowski had stirred something in me. He was so willing to accept failure. I wasn't. That night, I'd *acted*. Yes, I'd set out to confront Oswald and it turned into something much different than expected. But that didn't change that I'd stepped up and refused to be pushed around. And in the end, I got Arden out of it.

Maybe sometimes, if you did the right thing, you achieved something even better than your intended result.

It was time to think about the other areas of my life as well. Like making things right with Owen. Was I really going to give up and assume Alex had more to offer than I did? Maybe I owed it to myself to try one more time. And even if Owen and I were over for good, he at least deserved an apology.

If astronauts could hurtle into space at thirty thousand kilometers per hour, facing incalculable risks along the way, certainly I could tell a boy how I felt about him.

EVENT: *Hamelin!*

DATE: OCT. 26 (THURS.)

People stared as I walked into Irving High School's auditorium. Not because it was surprising for me to attend a play—I attended all the shows to support Cass, despite theater not being a favorite pastime of mine. The difference was that I didn't normally arrive with an enormous bouquet of roses.

"You sure you won't carry these for me?" I pleaded to Maggie.

"No way," she said. "Isn't stepping out of your comfort zone kind of the point?"

It was, of course.

I'd resorted to asking Maggie to see the play with me when no one else could. Ishmael was working, Arden was still holed up in her house, and everyone else I would've gone with was *in* the play.

Gram had dropped Maggie and me off at the school. During our harrowing car ride,[1] I asked if we could pick up flowers on the way. Gram scowled and said, "Flowers make silly gifts. Who wants a present that's gonna die?" But she drove me to the florist.

---

1   A total of three red lights were run.

"People are staring," I said as Maggie and I sat near the front of the theater.

"You're overreacting. They probably think the flowers are for Cass."

Maybe I *should* have brought Cass flowers. After all, she'd been my best friend for a long time, and I'd never given her flowers at the end of a performance. On the other hand, if I brought flowers for Cass *and* Owen, wouldn't Owen take the gesture less seriously?

How did anyone *ever* manage to navigate social situations? There were so many rules I couldn't figure out.

While we waited for the play to begin, I adjusted the bouquet and tried to distract myself from my discomfort.

"So, how's your cult?" I asked Maggie.

"I don't know what you're talking about."

"Liar."

"It's not a cult. It's a group of people who happen to believe in the same thing."

"Right," I agreed. "Whatever *thing* you tell them to believe."

Maggie couldn't suppress a satisfied smile. "Maybe it's what they wanted to believe anyway."

"And what belief is this? What are your little meetings about?"

"Aliens, obviously."

"What makes your cult different from the Seekers? Or Oswald's followers?" I asked.

"We agree the aliens are here to give us a message. But it doesn't have anything to do with the fountain of youth or government conspiracies. The aliens are here with a message of love. If we open our hearts to them, we'll achieve true harmony."

"I know you don't believe a word of that."

Maggie shrugged.

"Why are you doing this?" I asked.

Maggie thought for a long moment. "Honestly? I just wanted to see if I could."

"You wanted to see if you could *manipulate* people?"

"How is it different than what you and Ishmael are doing?"

I opened my mouth to respond, but realized I had no answer. Thankfully, before I had to admit that, the lights dimmed and *Hamelin!* began.

INTERVIEW

Subject #2, Magdalene (Maggie) Hofstadt:

Another thing about cults is, you have to keep the members isolated. They should feel like no one outside the group understands them. Which is basically how people my age feel anyway.

EVENT:
Hamelin!
(CONT.)

Hamelin! was everything I feared. The writing was cringeworthy, the story was diluted into nothing but a romance, and Cass's character, as she'd complained, was subpar. She did her best to liven Greta up, but it only helped so much.

Owen was fantastic as the Pied Piper, though, spirited and magnetic, while still bringing a touch of darkness the story needed. Even Sofia Russo, as leader of the rats and antagonist to the Piper and people of Hamelin, performed well.

As the kiss scene approached, I prepared myself for pangs of jealousy. But as I watched Cass and Owen deliver their ridiculous dialogue before sharing an equally over-the-top kiss, I realized I'd been a fool. It was just pretend. There was never any reason to be upset.

When the play ended, after the actors had taken their final bows, the audience slowly moved toward the lobby. It was tradition after a performance for the actors, still in costume, to greet people, take pictures, and soak up praise.

"That was painful," Maggie said as we moved with the crowd. "I could teach the Pied Piper a few things about being a leader."

I was too focused on the crush of people around me to respond. I couldn't be in crowds without feeling like the air was being sucked out of my lungs. A man bumped into me. I felt the hot breath of the woman behind me on my neck.

I *hated* crowds.

Trying to juggle an enormous bouquet of roses—while keeping them from getting crushed—made the situation much worse.

In the lobby, the crowd thinned. I made my way to a corner and waited for the cast to emerge.

I checked my phone and saw Arden had texted during the play.

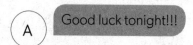

Good luck, indeed. I needed it.

When I looked back up, the rats had infiltrated the lobby, moving through the crowd in their gray leotards and rat-eared headbands, drawn-on whiskers beginning to smear. Cass appeared and was immediately swept up by her parents. She caught my eye from across the room, tilted her head to the right, and gave me a thumbs-up.

I looked in the direction she'd indicated.

Owen.

Dressed in pied, yet somehow not looking absurd. Instead, he looked confident. And handsome. And utterly unapproachable. It didn't help that he was among a group of guys from the baseball team.

"There's Owen," Maggie said.

"I see."

"Are you going over?"

"In a minute," I replied.

"Coward."

She was right. I was a coward. When it came to Owen, I'd been a coward from the very start.

It was time for me to be something else.

I took a deep breath and marched over to Owen.

For a moment neither he, nor his friends, noticed me. I hovered awkwardly at the edge of the group, wondering how to break in. Clear my throat? Say something to announce myself?

In the end, it didn't matter. One of Owen's friends looked over. Another followed suit. Soon the whole group stared at me.

"Gideon," Owen said.

"These are for you," I blurted out, thrusting the flowers into his arms.

"Thank you."

Was he surprised? Happy? Embarrassed?

"They're for doing a good job in the play. I mean, not that I knew you'd do a good job when I got them. Not that I thought you'd do a *bad* job either. I assumed you'd be great, and you were. So."

Everyone continued to stare.

"I also wanted to apologize," I went on haltingly. "For, you know, for being an asshole. You deserve better than that, and... yeah."

I began to feel like I'd done the absolute wrong thing. Maybe Owen never meant for this to happen. Maybe his friends weren't as comfortable with his sexuality as he thought. Maybe Owen was still furious and enjoyed watching me embarrass myself.

I said the last part before I could convince myself not to. "I also want to say, you mean a lot to me. Not just as an acquaintance or coworker, but romantically."

I cringed as soon as the words were out of my mouth. *Not just as an acquaintance or coworker...* Had a less-passionate phrase been uttered in the history of the universe?

"Do you want to take a walk?" Owen asked finally.

"Yes," I said, relieved. "That would be good."

EVENT:
The Talk

DATE: OCT. 26 (THURS.)

The halls of Irving High School were deserted. I always liked seeing the school that way—devoid of the hustle and bustle of the average school day. It was the only time I felt truly comfortable there.

Owen and I walked side by side, him still in costume and carrying the roses. Though they'd annoyed me all evening, I wished I had the flowers back. They'd been a shield. Without them, I didn't know what to do with my hands.

"When I said I wanted our relationship to be public," Owen said after a while, "I didn't mean I needed some grand romantic gesture."

My face burned. "I shouldn't have brought the flowers."

"I love the flowers. I'm happy you brought them. I just hope you know I never expected you to make big scenes. I just wanted to, like, see a movie with you."

"I hate movies."

"You know what I mean."

I stopped walking and turned to Owen. "You know what I told you, about not dating publicly because people tried to force it on us?"

"Yeah."

"Well, it's not true. I mean... It *is* true. But it's not the main reason."

"I figured."

I took a deep breath and braced myself. "Owen, you must realize being with me is...beneath you."

"What?"

"Don't act confused. You're handsome and popular and excel at everything and I'm...just me. I spend ninety-seven percent of my free time in my lab. With my cat. And that's not going to change, because I don't *want* it to change. I don't want to be popular or social or anything other than what I am. But the fact remains that guys like you don't end up with guys like me."

"Gideon—"

"Let me finish," I said. "When you go to college next year, what happens? You'll find someone else and move on. And I'll...still be in my lab. I'll still be me. What's the point of getting attached when it's just going to end?"

"You're an idiot," Owen said.

"I... What?"

"That's a risk with *every* relationship. The only way to avoid it is to never date at all. And personally, I'm a little insulted you think I'm just with you while I wait for something better to come along."

"You never felt that way?" I asked meekly.

Owen sighed. "Your pride gets in the way of everything, you know that? No, I never felt that way. I never considered you temporary. I *like* you."

"I like you too," I said. And then, after a pause, "I want to be your boyfriend. Officially."

"Even though, in your words, romance is 'a concept designed by greeting card companies, when human mating is just biology.' Or something like that."[1]

I winced. "I did say that, didn't I?"

"You did."

"I was wrong. That happens sometimes."

Owen smiled slightly, but there was sadness in it. "I've waited a long time for you to say all this."

"Am I too late?" I asked, a catch in my voice. The world seemed to still, like even Earth stopped rotating on its axis in anticipation of his response.

"I'm still mad at you."

"You should be."

"And I'll never go back to the way things were," he said firmly.

"I wouldn't ask you to."

"But I'm willing to give this a chance. On the condition that we start over. And hang out in public, like a normal couple."

My heart soared. The Earth resumed its normal operations. "*Are* we a couple then?"

"I don't think we should decide that yet."

"Okay," I agreed.

We stood in the hallway and stared at each other. Maybe we'd work things out. Maybe we'd start a relationship—a *real* relationship, not like before. Or maybe I'd end up with a broken heart. But the risk was a part of it. A part of life.

"Can I kiss you now?" I asked.

---

1   My exact words had been: an artificial emotion created by advertisers to make a biological necessity marketable as greeting cards.

"Out in the open, where anyone might walk by?" Owen gasped in mock surprise.

In response, I leaned forward and kissed him, awkwardly maneuvering around the bouquet of roses crushed between us.

It wasn't the most graceful kiss of my life. But it felt the most honest.

EVENT:
Oswald's Plan

DATE: OCT. 28 (SAT.)

According to their website, MIT had received 20,247 freshman applications the previous year. Of those, they admitted 1,452 students to the freshman class.

I sat in my lab with my laptop open, looking over the steps of the application process and wondering how I'd possibly been so cavalier about my acceptance. Even with all the effort I'd put in, my odds weren't great.

It hit me that I needed to think about backup schools. I needed options.

I sat back in my chair and tried to imagine a life where I didn't attend MIT. It wasn't as devastating as I would've once thought. I'd be upset about being rejected, but it wouldn't kill me. If nothing else, in recent months I'd learned that not everything needed to be exactly what I'd envisioned. There were many different ways life could turn out favorably.

A knock on the lab door jarred me from my reverie. I shut my laptop, opened the door, and froze.

It was J. Quincy Oswald.

At *my lab*.

"Oswald," I said.

He grinned. "You ever gonna call me Oz?"

"No," I replied flatly.

Oswald wasn't deterred. He pushed into the lab and settled in my desk chair, casually crossing his legs.

"What do you want?" I asked.

I felt at odds. How dare he waltz into my space like he belonged here? How dare he even *speak* to me after what happened the last time we saw each other? Yet, at the same time, I was curious. What did he want? Did he intend to discuss Arden, try to convince me not to go to the police?

"You and I gotta talk," he said.

I didn't move from where I stood by the door. "I'm listening."

"The time has come."

"The time for what?"

"The Visitors have revealed your role."

Oh. That.

He really still thought I'd help him?

I admit, when I first encountered Oswald, I bore him a small, grudging amount of respect. He was clearly skilled, even if I found his use of those skills contemptible. But he'd shattered that respect when I found Arden in his RV. I couldn't look at him with anything but disgust.

"Stop," I said bluntly.

I caught him off guard. His laid-back attitude faltered. "Pardon?"

"Stop with the alien talk. We both know it's bullshit."

"Now, Gideon, if you look into your heart I think you'll find—"

"I'm serious, Oswald."

The door to the lab was still ajar and Kepler slipped inside, meowing. I waited for him to hiss at Oswald and bolt, but instead he slowly approached.

"Hey there, little guy," Oswald said. He lowered a hand to the floor. Kepler cautiously sniffed it. And then, to my immense surprise, he allowed Oswald to scratch his head.

The cat who hated everyone and everything allowed my nemesis to pet him.

It was too much.

"You need to leave now."

Oswald straightened, suddenly all business. "I'm launching the Elixir ETernia a week from today."

"So?"

"I plan to unveil it at a gathering in the town square," he plowed ahead. "Local businesses are donating time and services. We'll have food, music, lights, a sound system—I won't mess with that bullhorn again. It'll be the biggest event this town has seen in years."

I shrugged to let him know how unimpressed I was with his planned festivities. "Okay. And?"

Oswald leaned forward and gazed intently at me. "And at the moment the Elixir ETernia is presented to the world, at the exact moment of the unveiling, I want the lava lamp to turn on."

There have been many things said about J. Quincy Oswald. Bad things and good things. True things and false. But having known him personally for a brief time, I will confirm this: for all his faults, Oswald also had a little bit of genius.

The lighting of the lava lamp, dormant for decades, would be dramatic and memorable. Cass would *swoon* over the theatrics of it. I could imagine Oswald with the night sky behind him, the sky that held so much mystery and promise, holding up the elixir, backlit by the unearthly pink glow of the lamp. Every newspaper in the country would have that photo on the front page.

No one would mistake Oswald for a starfish.

I tried to keep my expression neutral. The last thing I wanted was for him to know I was impressed. "This has nothing to do with me."

"No town official will turn that light on," Oswald said.

"With good reason. Who knows if it even *can* be turned on anymore?"

"The equipment is still in the room beneath the lamp. It's dusty, but looks operational."

I was galled. He'd already broken into the boiler room to investigate. This wasn't just a whim.

"So turn it on yourself," I said.

Oswald smiled with faux modesty. "Unfortunately, my knowledge of machinery is limited. A few of my distributors took a stab at it, but they couldn't make heads or tails of the heating element."

I finally saw what he was getting at.

"But you could," Oswald went on. "I *know* you could turn that light on."

Well.

Maybe.

I wasn't exactly a mechanical expert.

But I wouldn't mind getting in there and checking out the

equipment. I knew how regular lava lamps functioned, and I'd be curious to see what modifications were made when it was scaled up.

Except, wait, *no*.

I wasn't on Oswald's side.

"What makes you think *I* could do it? You don't know anything about me."

Oswald rolled the chair closer and looked into my eyes like he was going to hypnotize me. "I know you caused the explosion that started all this. I know you somehow scrambled radio signals. I know you made crop circles. Are you telling me you can't figure out how to turn a lava lamp on?"

I was floored. He outed me for practically everything that had happened over the past months. Beneath his swagger, he was observant.

"If you're saying I faked events," I began slowly, "you're also admitting you faked your own."

Oswald smiled but didn't speak. We stared at each other for a long moment. Eventually he said, "So here we are. What do you want to do?"

There was only one thing I wanted since he'd arrived in Lansburg.

"Admit aliens never visited you," I said.

I was 90 percent sure he'd never do it, that he'd keep his secrets forever. But with his usual confidence, Oswald said, "Aliens never visited me."

"Admit the Elixir ETernia is fake."

"The Elixir ETernia is fake."

"And admit you're only in it for the money."

Oswald grinned. "Can't do that one."

I began to protest, but he held up a hand to quiet me.

"I like the money. But that's not why I do it."

"Why then?"

He thought for a long moment. "Because I only feel alive when people are watching me."

"So you do it for the glory," I said softly.

"For the glory," he repeated. "Not a bad way to put it."

It turned out J. Quincy Oswald and I had something in common after all.

"Okay," I said. "I'll look at the lava lamp."

But I wouldn't do it for Oswald. I'd do it because I wanted to know if the lamp *could* be turned on, and if *I* could be the one to do it. I'd do it for the *glory*.

And yeah.

Maybe I had another motive too.

TEXT CONVERSATION

Participants: Gideon Hofstadt, Ishmael Hofstadt

IH: so wait, i dont get it. we ARE gunna help Oz?

GH: Yes.

IH: but do you still hate him

GH: Yes.

IH: and youre still mad about how he scams people?

GH: Yes.

IH: then why turn the lava lamp on?

GH: Come up to my room when you get home tonight.

IH: cant you give me a hint at least!

Ishmael, don't you think it's time someone took J. Quincy Oswald down?

is this like a new prank?

It's the ultimate prank.

coming home right now

Taken from the "In Your Community" page from the November 2 issue of the *Lansburg Daily Press.*

UPCOMING EVENTS

SATURDAY, 7:00 P.M.

J. Quincy Oswald invites all Lansburg residents and visitors to the launch of his new product, the Elixir ETernia. The event will be held in the town square at 7:00 and include music and vendors. Food will be available for purchase from local restaurants.

SUNDAY, 10:00 A.M.

The Knights of Columbus will host a pancake breakfast at St. Francis de Sales Church following 9:00 mass. Proceeds will be donated to the Find Prudence Fund, a community effort to locate David O'Grady's award-winning cow. More information can be found at the parish office.

SUNDAY, 6:30 P.M

The Keep Lansburg Lovely committee is meeting at 6:30 p.m. at Irving Community Center to discuss recent litter problems around the town square. A vote will be held at 7:30 p.m. to determine if new trash cans should be purchased. Refreshments will be provided.

INTERVIEW

Subject #2, Magdalene (Maggie) Hofstadt:

It's true that cult leaders need to be charismatic. But more important, the followers need to think the leader has inside information. It doesn't need to be an all-knowing, God-spoke-to-me sort of thing—though a lot of times, it is. It can be as simple as the cult leader living in the location where certain important events took place. Like an explosion that kicked off a string of UFO sightings.

THE NEXT SIX DAYS

YOU MIGHT BE WONDERING WHY I SO READILY agreed to help J. Quincy Oswald, the man whom I considered my nemesis.

Because I *did* plan to help. We should be very clear on that. I intended to do exactly what he asked. I'd figure out how to turn the lava lamp on, and I'd give him his moment of glory and fame.

And then I'd expose him for the fraud he was.

Oswald wanted a sound system for the Elixir ETernia launch—so much of his sales pitch was body language, and relying on the bullhorn instead of a microphone must have severely limited his wild gesturing. I would use the sound system for my own purpose. I'd use it to play the recording I made with my phone when Oswald came to my lab.

On Saturday night, Oswald would unveil his product. And immediately afterward, as he basked in the glow of the lava lamp and his followers cheered, they'd hear a recording of him admitting the product was fake. That aliens never visited him. That it was all a scam.

As soon as Oswald left my lab that night, I began making a list of everything I needed to do, everything that would make my plan work perfectly.

GIDEON'S NOTES FROM OCT. 29 TO NOV. 3

<u>SUNDAY</u>

Had in-depth discussion with Ishmael.

> Ish: You know, dude, this means we'll be outed too.
> Me: Then you can finally take credit for the hoax.
> Ish: Good point.

Ishmael is on board. His task: get as many people as possible to the town square on Saturday. Not just Seekers and myTality™ acolytes, <u>everyone</u>. The entire high school, Father and his workout buddies, longtime Lansburg residents who attend Bingo Extravaganzas. <u>EVERYONE</u>.

> Ish: I got this.

My task: research lava lamps and exactly how they work.

It turns out, the internet has a very passionate lava lamp community. I'm not an expert, but I got the info I needed. More convinced than ever I can do this.

MONDAY

Arden returned to school. Lots of whispers as she passed in the hall, but she says no one directly harassed her.

Cass: If anyone <u>does</u> bug you, tell me right away.
Me: Apparently Cass is exploring a new career as a bodyguard.
Cass: You don't think the job would suit me?
Me: Maybe not in that outfit.

Outfit: gauzy green top, glitter makeup, seashell hair clips.

Me: What is this supposed to be anyway?
Cass: Mermaid chic, obviously.
Arden: I'm so glad to be back here with you guys. I thought my mom was going to keep me home forever.

Don't want to keep anything from Arden anymore, so told her about my plans for Oswald. Long, awkward silence.

Me: If you don't want me to go through with it, just say the word.
Arden: You'd change your plans for me?

Me: Yes.

It's true. I wouldn't like it, but I'd do it.

    Arden: He really admitted he lied about the
        aliens?
    Me: You can listen to the recording.
    Arden: No. I don't want to hear it.
    Cass: You okay?
    Arden: I know what he did was wrong. And I
        understand that people deserve to know the
        truth. But I don't want to be there when it
        happens, okay?
    Me: Of course.

Hoping this means Arden is coming around, that
soon she'll be willing to talk to Chief Kaufman about
her experience with Oswald.

TUESDAY

After school: Oswald let me into the boiler room
underneath the lava lamp. Only took 30 min. to get
basic idea of how the heating element functions. <u>No
one</u> from Oswald's camp has the mechanical aptitude
to figure it out for themselves???

In regular lava lamps: "lava" is heated by a lightbulb.

In our giant version: light and heating element are separate.

Makes sense. No lightbulb could heat such a huge amount of liquid.

Boiler is simple. Has a switch to turn it on and window displaying temperature—with dial showing if furnace is going "in the red" so emergency shut-off can be engaged.

Setup means I can start heating the lamp on Sat. afternoon, well before unveiling. If calculations are correct, might be able to get lava moving at the same time the lamp lights up—even possible turning on the light will give last push of heat needed. Still, warned Oswald the two won't coincide exactly.

> Me: The lamp will light up right away, but it'll take a while before the paraffin heats up enough to start swirling.
> Oswald: But the light will be pink, right?
> Me: Yes.

He seemed satisfied.

Spent approx. 2.5 hrs. tinkering/making list of items needed.

A bit paranoid I can't do a test run. Even in the

dead of night, it would be impossible to turn on the lamp, see if I got it running properly. People would notice. Sat. night will have to be first time.

Made plans to return Thursday, after Oswald picks up supplies. Made conversation as he locked the boiler room behind us.

Me: Is everything else in place for Saturday?
Oswald: Are you worried?
Me: It's just, if you're looking for help with the sound system, I know someone. They do AV work for a band. They probably have access to equipment.

Oswald was interested.

Wrote down info, hoping he wouldn't be put off that my contact went by "Laser."

WEDNESDAY

In lab, hunched over computer, trying to get work done. Ishmael burst in.

Ish: Did you see last week's episode of Pitch, Please?
Me: I don't know. Maybe?
Ish: The contestants wanted to make a show

about weird dance competitions, like starting the world's biggest conga line, right?

Me: And this is your life goal if becoming a magician doesn't work out?

Ish: No, dude. I was thinking about the conga line, and it made me think about my friend Easton. You know Easton, right?

Me: What about him?

Ish: Once, he was in the mall, and saw this line forming, okay? And he just got into it. Even though he didn't know what it was for.

Me: That seems like an immense waste of time.

Ish: Right. Especially 'cause it turned out to be a line for little kids to meet Spider-Man, which Easton totally wasn't into.

Me: What are you getting at?

Ish: It's like...when people see a line, part of them wants to know what it's for so much, they'll get into it just to see. So that conga line thing is brilliant.

Me: Good for them. Maybe they'll win the reality show.

Ish: Dude. You know what else it reminded me of? That scene in Cass's play. The one where the Piper guy leads all the kids out of town.

I stopped working and gave Ishmael my full attention.

Ish: Wouldn't it be cool if the Piper led the whole
    town to the <u>lava lamp</u>?

<u>THURSDAY</u>

Not worried I might get into trouble. All that
matters is defeating Oswald. <u>Proving myself</u>. So close
to making that happen.
    Tying up loose ends now. Everyone knows their
roles. Plans are down to the minute. Have listened to
Oswald's audio recording multiple times to ensure it's
clear. Luckily, Oswald has great diction. Transferred
the file onto two flash drives to be safe.
    After work: went to lava lamp with Oswald to make
final preparations.

    Me: Are you nervous?
    Oswald: About what?
    Me: That the unveiling might not go according
        to plan.
    Oswald: Things always go according to plan for
        me, Gideon.

That's what he thinks.
    Can't stop imagining the look on Oswald's face when
the recording starts, when he knows he's been bested.

For the first time in his life, he'll realize he isn't a god after all.

FRIDAY

Felt I deserved a break. Especially after the blow of getting English paper back with C- written on it. Apparently, Mr. Fiore <u>did not</u> agree "The Death of the Ball Turret Gunner" was meant to be literal, nor did he appreciate my objections: Isn't poetry <u>meant</u> to be interpreted by the reader?

To get mind off poetry/tomorrow's event, took Arden to see Hamelin! Afterward, went to dinner with Cass, Owen, and some other theater people. Owen and I held hands underneath the table.

Sofia Russo: You guys are so cute together.

Felt that the comment infringed on my privacy. But also, she's right.

SATURDAY

All systems are go.

EVENT:
The Incident

DATE: NOV. 4 (SAT.)

The sun was still in the sky when Ishmael and I set out for the town square, but it would be dark soon enough. Dark enough for the lava lamp to have maximum impact. Dark enough that none of Oswald's people would notice when I slipped over to the sound system—conveniently monitored by Laser—to add my own touch to the evening's festivities.

Ishmael had taken longer than usual to get ready. "What's your problem?" I asked, standing in the doorway of his room while he traded one Hawaiian shirt for another.

"I just want everything to be perfect," he replied. "This is a big night. There are a lot of moving pieces, dude."

I watched my brother for a long moment. "Ishmael, is it possible I've rubbed off on you a little bit over the past few weeks?"

"With the way you're scheming, I think maybe it's the other way around."

My brother and I grinned at each other. He clapped me on the back as we made our way up the basement stairs.

"Aren't *you* nervous?" Ishmael asked, as we climbed into the Jeep.

I thought about it for a moment. The usual tension I felt during big moments—certainly during big *experiments*—wasn't present. And, in a way, wasn't this my biggest experiment of all?

"You know, I'm *not* nervous," I said.

My plan was going to work. I'd never felt so confident.

Subject #9, Chief Lisa Kaufman:

People started gathering hours before the event was scheduled. Most of my officers ended up at the town square, directing traffic and keeping the peace. At 6:00, I made the call to block off Main Street from vehicle traffic. The crowd was already spilling out of the square.

At Irving High School, the curtain was about to rise on *Hamelin!*. I texted Cass.

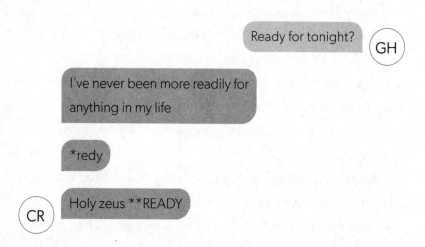

Ready for tonight? GH

I've never been more readily for anything in my life

*redy

CR Holy zeus **READY

I relayed the information to Ishmael.

"And Owen's fine with all this?" he asked, keeping his eyes on the road. We passed by Mr. O'Grady's field and I wondered about the state of our crop circle.

"He doesn't want to participate, but he's fine with Cass doing it," I replied.

Owen and I had a long talk about the hoax—among other things. He still didn't condone my actions, exactly, but he said he understood my reasons. Sometimes that's enough.

"And he knows when to hand off his costume?" Ishmael went on. "Cass will have time to change?"

I looked at my brother for a long moment. "I never thought I'd be saying this...but Ishmael, you really need to *chill*."

Subject #14, Arnold (Arnie) Hodges:

Oh, we noticed the increased police presence. We knew the government didn't want Oz's product to get out. They'd been watching him for a long time, and they were terrified of what secrets he might reveal.

We were still miles from town, surrounded by woods, when Ishmael slammed on the brakes.

"Dude, did you see that?"

"What?"

He leaned forward and peered through the windshield. I, meanwhile, looked anxiously behind us.

"You realize you stopped in the middle of the road, right?"

"There!" he shouted.

I looked in the direction he pointed and saw a flash of black and white through the trees.

"What is..." I began.

But then I knew.

Ishmael put the Jeep in park and threw the door open. A second later he darted into the woods, shouting, "Muffin!"

The fucking cow.

We were on a sensitive schedule, heading to one of the most important places we'd ever need to be, and my brother took off into the woods after a cow.

I jumped out of the Jeep. "Ishmael! We don't have time for this."

I heard my brother crashing through the woods, but with the deepening evening shadows, I wasn't able to see him. I took a tentative step toward the tree line.

"Ishmael!" I called again.

From the woods, he shouted, "Muffin!"

He was going to make us late. He was going to get stuck in the woods after dark, without a flashlight. He was going to ruin everything. I glanced back at the empty Jeep, still in the middle of the road, engine running.

Then, from inside the woods I heard a loud crash and my brother yelled, "Ow, *fuck*!"

Subject #2, Magdalene (Maggie) Hofstadt:

Mom was helping Oz prepare for the launch and Dad was at the gym, so I asked Gram to drive me to the softball field, where my team was waiting. Gram asked what we were up to, and I said we wanted to practice before Sunday's game. Once she was gone, I gathered everyone in a circle. I asked if they were ready to announce our message of peace to the world and make Oz see the error of his ways—myTality really was such a scam.

Ishmael was on the ground, gripping his right ankle, his face contorted in pain.

"What the hell happened?" I asked.

"She got away, dude."

"To your *ankle*, not the *cow*."

"I tripped," he said, wincing. He rolled up the leg of his pants and to my dismay his ankle was already starting to swell.

"Godammit, Ishmael."

"I didn't do it on purpose!"

He was supposed to be the graceful one. Tripping and twisting an ankle in the woods was something that would happen to *me*.

"You *had* to go after the cow," I said. "What would you have done if you caught her? Shove her in the back seat of the Jeep?"

"Can you just help me get back to the road?"

Ah, yes, the road. Where our Jeep was parked without headlights in the quickly darkening night, waiting for someone to tear around a corner too quickly and ram into it.

Wonderful.

I helped Ishmael to his feet. With him leaning on me for support, we slowly made our way across the uneven terrain.

"Gideon?" he said.

"What?" I snapped, already worn out from the unexpected exercise.

"It's my right ankle that's hurt."

"Yes, I saw."

Ishmael hesitated, then said, "You know I won't be able to drive, right?"

Subject #15, Sofia Russo:

Let's give credit where it's due: *I* was the one who organized the freshman rats. It all happened during the scene when the Pied Piper leads the rats out of Hamelin. Backstage, Cass changed into the Owen's costume because I guess he wasn't into the scheme. Who even knows what the audience thought when "Greta" came onstage dressed as the Piper. Whatever. Cass started playing the pipe and the rats followed her, except they followed her right off the stage and through the audience. People were like, "What's even *going on*?" But then a bunch of Ishmael's friends in the audience got up and followed Cass out of the auditorium. I glanced behind me right before we went outside, and other people in the audience, people who were totally *not* in on the plan, started to follow too. Exactly like Cass said they would. But yeah. None of it would have happened if I hadn't gotten the rats to agree in the first place.

I'd managed to pull the Jeep to the side of the road so, at the very least, my brother and I weren't facing imminent death.

"You can do this," Ishmael said for the third time.

"I can't," I replied tersely. My hands gripped the steering wheel. Sweat beaded on my forehead. "Not only is it illegal for me to drive without an adult, it's also exceedingly dangerous, being that I've had minimal practice and—"

"Dude," my brother interrupted.

"What?"

"Stop using that superior voice. It's okay to be scared."

I swallowed the lump in my throat. I attempted to loosen my grip on the wheel. Pain shot through my jaw and down my neck. I was going to grind my teeth away to nothing.

"I can't do it," I said again, meekly.

"You *can*," Ishmael insisted. "You know how to drive. It freaks you out, but you know exactly how to do it."

"I can't merge."

"You won't need to merge."

"I can't park."

"We'll find an open space for you to pull over."

"I can't make left turns."

Ishmael hesitated. "We'll deal with that when we come to it."

I licked my lips. I took a deep breath. I glanced in the rearview mirror at the road behind me.

"I can't," I said.

"Gideon. Look at me." I complied. Ishmael's expression was

earnest. "You've done harder stuff than drive. Way harder. Setting up everything for tonight was harder than driving. And if you don't drive now, it'll all be for nothing."

He was right.

"Oz will win," Ishmael went on. "He'll *win*. Is that what you want?"

"No."

It was the very last thing I wanted.

"Then put the Jeep in drive, and let's get to the lava lamp."

My hands shook. I'd only driven twice. I'd never driven in the dark. I was absolutely terrified.

But Ishmael was right. I couldn't let Oz win.

Sometimes, no matter how terrifying a thing was, you needed to do it anyway.

I put the Jeep in drive.

"You've got this," Ishmael encouraged.

Slowly, carefully, I eased my foot off the brake.

Subject #6, Arden Byrd:

I stayed home that night because I couldn't bear to see Oz. Plus things still felt a little awkward with Gideon, even though I could tell he was making an effort to be a better friend. Later, I kinda wished I *had* gone. I felt—I still feel—like I missed out on something important.

"I don't mean to pressure you, dude," Ishmael said a while later, "but if you don't go above twenty miles an hour, we're gonna get there too late."

"This road is curvy," I snapped, hunched forward in my seat. "It's dangerous."

"Right... It's just, the speed limit is actually forty-five."

"Surely, they mislabeled it."

"Either way, isn't going too slow kinda just as dangerous as going too fast?"

"I know the rules of the road, Ishmael!" I said.

"Okay, dude. Okay. We'll get there when we get there."

Subject #4, Victor Hofstadt (Father):

I'm at the gym, and suddenly people start gathering around the window. I go over to see what the fuss is about. And there's Cass Robinson, dressed as some kind of court jester, leading a line of people down the street. A couple guys go outside to ask what's happening, and they end up joining the line. Then a few more people do. Next thing I know, I'm the only one left in the gym besides the kid behind the counter. So yeah. I went out and got in the line.

My eyes went to the clock. It was 7:00. Oswald would start in about five minutes, fashionably late as always, I presumed.

"Do you think Cass is already at the square?" Ishmael asked as the Jeep crawled along.

"I don't know."

"Do you think the crowd is going to be really huge?"

"Ishmael. I *don't know*."

I didn't take my eyes off the road. Though driving was getting slightly less daunting, my body was still knotted with tension. And we'd finally made it to town. Which meant stoplights and other drivers.

Though, to be fair, there were few people on the road for a Saturday night. I hoped because all of them were at the lava lamp.

Subject #16, Myrtle Johannsen (tourist):

I was in Lansburg with a group from the senior center. I'd never been before, but Janine from water aerobics had so many nice things to say about the town. Lovely shops and restaurants, and a real, authentic German feel to it. I was absolutely charmed, even with that lava lamp in the middle of it all. Until we got stuck there, that is. Our tour bus got trapped in a parking lot before the streets got blocked off. "What in the world is going on?" I asked Janine. The strangest groups of people had gathered around that silly lava lamp. I'd never seen anything like it in my life.

Later, I saw footage from the beginning of the launch. Some of it gathered by news crews, some posted on blogs by Seekers. So, though I was inching down the street in the Jeep, with Ishmael beside me, moaning, "I could *walk* faster than this," I still saw how the event started.

How the speakers blasting '80s pop music went silent.

How spotlights from the ground were trained on the lava lamp and how the crowd turned their expectant faces upward.

How the Seekers and myTality™ distributors overflowed from the square, and how the Lansburg police department was patrolling, the officers wearing expressions of concern.

How there was a sudden ruckus in the silence, and the crowd turned to look behind them where a teenage girl, dressed in a strange costume and waving a pipe like a baton, joined the gathering, a massive line of people trailing behind her. People from the gym and from the churches, people from the schools and the shops. The town of Lansburg followed the makeshift Pied Piper, and they joined the crowd already formed at the lava lamp until Main Street became a crush of people.

And then, with everyone gathered, the spotlights flashed, and J. Quincy Oswald himself stepped to the rail of the lava lamp's observation deck. He regarded the crowd, a king looking over his kingdom, and from the news footage I studied later, I could see he was pleased.

"My dear distributors," Oswald began, in his smooth, authoritative voice. "How very much I've loved you. How very much good we've done together. And tonight, you'll join me as we embark on a new chapter and invite new people to join our quest to change lives all over the world. Welcome, all!"

Oswald held his arms out, the way a preacher on a pulpit might. He wasn't bogged down by a bullhorn. The sound system worked perfectly, carrying his voice to the very back of the crowd.

"As many of you know," he went on, "for some unexplained set of reasons, I happen to be selected by extraterrestrial Visitors as their ambassador. You may not believe it yet, but I'll tell you, after what you see here tonight, you'll be forever changed."

The crowd roared with approval and watched Oswald raptly.

And in the very back of that crowd, at the end of Main Street, near Ye Olde Fudge Shoppe, no one turned around when a beat-up Jeep slowly rolled to a stop behind them.

Subject #3, Cassidy (Cass) Robinson:

Honestly, I didn't expect *that* many people to get in my conga line. Add that to everyone already at the lava lamp, and practically all of Lansburg turned up. I'm not saying Owen couldn't have done it...but while I was leading everyone, it clicked. I was doing exactly what I was meant to. I knew from the start that the role of Pied Piper was supposed to be mine.

"Holy shit," Ishmael muttered when the crowd appeared in front of us.

"There's nowhere to park." I couldn't keep the edge of panic from my voice.

"Just stop here."

"In the middle of the street?"

"Well, I don't want you getting close to the crowd and forgetting which pedal is the brake. Again."

I gritted my teeth.

I pulled to the side of the road and positioned the Jeep near the curb as well as I could. Ishmael and I climbed out and were immediately met by Oswald's voice, carrying through the speakers.

I'd read his speech already—I needed to know my cue to turn the lava lamp on—so I knew he was close to the unveiling. Too close.

"We need to go, *now*."

But that was easier said than done. Ishmael walked with a pronounced limp and leaned on me for support. We tried to fight our way through the crowd, but people pushed back. Elbows dug into my sides. My feet got stomped on.

We weren't going to make it in time.

"Ishmael, you have to cue the recording on the flash drive," I shouted as we continued to work through the crowd.

"What? I don't know how to do that."

"You *have* to. I can't turn on the lava lamp and get the recording ready in time."

"Laser isn't going to let me touch her equipment," he said. "She's hated me since that time I put up flyers advertising free ice cream to anyone who ordered in a British accent."

"That was *you*?"

Before he could respond, the crowd began cheering, people around us bouncing up and down, and I was barely able to keep from toppling over.

Oswald was explaining the benefits of the Elixir ETernia. Only a few more lines before the lava lamp was supposed to light up.

"Okay," I said. "I'll deal with Laser and the sound system. You turn the lamp on. It's just one switch."

"Now *that* I can handle."

The switch was labeled, and it only took a second to describe where in the boiler room it was. "Just listen for the cue. Oswald will say, *Behold, the Elixir ETernia*, and then you pull the lever marked 'light' and he'll hold up the product at the same time."

"That's all?"

"That's all. The heating element is already on."

Just one lever, then there'd be a long silence as the crowd watched in awe. And that was the moment the recording would begin playing from the speakers.

Hopefully.

Finally, miraculously, Ishmael and I reached the base of the lava lamp. The myTality™ distributor standing at the door nodded to me and unlocked the boiler room. I practically pushed my brother inside.

Then I began fighting through the crowd again, heading toward the sound system.

Subject #17, Laser (last name unknown):

It wasn't my kind of event, but I was getting paid, so I could deal. Until this woman in, I shit you not, a *purple* business suit showed up. She started looking over my shoulder, asking questions like I didn't know what I was doing. What made that Oz guy think I needed a babysitter?

I pushed through to where Laser was set up with her laptop. I panted from exertion, tried my best to stay on my feet. I was so focused on the time crunch, for a moment I didn't notice the person standing behind Laser.

Then I did a double take.

"Mother? What are you doing?"

"Just helping Laser, honey," Mother said over the noise of the crowd.

Laser rolled her eyes. "Yeah. She's a *huge* help."

I was only 12 percent sure I could pull off my plan in time, so I'd have to worry about Mother later. I dug the flash drive from my pocket and held it out to Laser. "I need you to plug this in."

She reached for it, but Mother stepped between us. "What's this?"

"It's an audio file. Oswald wants it to play after the unveiling."

"He didn't mention it to me."

Up on the observation deck, Oswald neared the pivotal moment.

"It was last minute," I said.

"What kind of audio is it?"

"I don't know. A jingle or something."

Mother held out her hand for the flash drive. "Maybe we should have a quick listen first."

That was an astonishingly bad idea.

"There's no time," I said.

"Gideon," Mother said, waggling a finger. "Is this another one of your games?"

I was so close.

I had *driven* to town.

There was no way I was giving up.

As I tried to quickly formulate a plan, Oswald's voice reverberated through the crowd. "And now, the moment has arrived! *Behold*, the Elixir ETernia!"

Subject #1: Ishmael Hofstadt:

I was kinda nervous, I guess. 'Cause the boiler room had some serious-looking equipment, and what if the light didn't come on or something? Gideon would totally blame me. But I listened carefully, and when Oz said his line, I flipped the switch. I only sort of noticed the way the furnace was all steamy—I thought it was supposed to be like that. And I didn't pay attention to the dial on it, the one that had an arrow pointing to red. I figured, if it was important, Gideon would've mentioned it.

The night turned pink.

The glow of the lava lamp lit the square, lit Main Street. It felt bright enough to light up all of Lansburg.

The crowd gasped in amazement. No one moved or spoke. They stared at J. Quincy Oswald and the lava lamp as if witnessing a miracle.

Despite needing to start the recording, I couldn't help but look at Oswald as well. He was poised at the rail of the observation deck, holding up a bottle of Elixir ETernia. I couldn't tell what color the bottle was. Everything was pink.

I knew pictures were being taken. Video was being recorded. Oswald looked exactly like the god he wanted to be.

Except with his free hand, he reached up and wiped his brow. And I realized that even from where I stood on the ground, it was getting hot.

Too hot, a little voice whispered.

Later, everyone talked about what it was like to see the lava lamp lit up. Even the people who knew it was going to happen, like Cass, and Owen—who'd made his way to the square after the theater emptied—were awed. Even Ishmael was awed, when he stepped out of the boiler room and saw his handiwork. Even Father, who hated Oswald nearly as much as I did. No one could look away.

But I had to.

"Laser, put this in," I thrust the flash drive in her direction, hoping Mother was distracted.

Laser mumbled in response but didn't turn from the lamp.

The crowd began to come back to its senses. People murmured and shifted. Any moment, Oswald would start speaking again and the trance would be broken. And with it, my opportunity would have passed.

I was about to reach past Laser to plug in the flash drive myself, when something very unexpected happened.

The lava lamp exploded.

Subject #18, Thomas Ward (fire inspector):

In regular-sized lava lamps, convection currents keep the hot liquid circulating. That wasn't possible in Lansburg's scaled-up version. To keep temperatures steady, a pump had been implemented to push hot water from the bottom to the top of the lamp. It was tied to the lights. Turn on the lights, turn on the pump. That should've happened simultaneously to the boiler being activated. Instead, the boiler was switched on in advance, heating the liquid in the bottom of the lamp for an extended period of time. Far as we can tell, when the light was finally turned on, that pump shot a geyser of near-boiling water straight to the top of the lava lamp. The glass up there was cold, and the sudden heat combined with the force of the geyser cracked it in an instant. You ask me, that lava lamp was a problem just waiting to happen.

The lava lamp exploded *up* not *out*, and later experts would say that was the only reason there weren't casualties.

With a loud pop, the top of the lamp blasted into the night sky, and a geyser of liquid erupted from the top. I froze in horror. Around me, people began to scream, those closest to the lamp ducking and covering their heads.

It was almost beautiful, the way natural disasters can sometimes be magnificent when you distance them from the destruction they cause.

From the corner of my eye, I saw a panicked Oswald running for the observation deck stairs.

I waited for the "lava" to hit the crowd, worried about burns. All that hot water and paraffin and who knew what else. I wasn't the only one thinking along those lines, because the crowd continued to cry out in fear and began to surge.

But as I looked up at the sky, where lava still spurted into the air,

I noticed something incredible. Drops of hot water *weren't* raining on the crowd. Instead, it appeared the lava was turning into...snow?

Of course. Paraffin cooled rapidly. It couldn't survive as a liquid in the autumn air.

I laughed out loud, my face tilted up at the stars and the falling snow-lava, while chaos ensued around me.

Then I snapped back to reality. I looked at Mother. She was staring at the sky, still distracted. I knew I'd never have the opportunity again. I pushed Laser aside, plugged my flash drive in, and opened the audio file.

A moment later, Oswald's voice boomed from the speakers.

Aliens never visited me. The Elixir ETernia is fake.

Subject #5, Owen Campbell:

A hush fell over the crowd. By then everyone realized the water in the lava lamp wasn't going to burn. People quieted down and listened to Oswald saying he was a fraud. And I couldn't help thinking, "Damn, my boyfriend did this. He made a crowd of thousands of people *pay attention*."

It was as if the entire town had been under the spell of a particularly adept Pied Piper and was finally waking up.

With waxy paraffin beneath their feet and a destroyed town landmark rising above them, the crowd shuffled and looked around with shell-shocked expressions.

I glanced at Mother and saw her wipe away a tear.

It struck me then, just how many people had put faith in Oswald. I'd never stopped to consider what those people would feel once he was exposed. How lost and confused they'd be.

Oswald himself stood near the stairs to the observation deck, frozen in place as his own voice played through the speakers, his eyes wide with horror. He looked around frantically, as if there might still be an escape route.

Then the crowd near him parted, letting someone through.

My sister.

Leading a pack of girls.

Serenely, they surrounded Oswald, enveloping him in their circle. Girls on either side of him reached out to take his hands. Solemnly, Maggie approached Oswald and began to speak. I was too far to hear what she said, but I imagined she was preaching to him, the man who'd always been the preacher. Oh, how things had changed.

———————

Subject #8, Special Agent Mike Ruiz:

Kaufman ran the show until that point. She was preparing to arrest Oswald, figuring we could bring him in on destruction of property. But then I saw him surrounded by those teenaged girls—*holding hands* with some of them... We'd heard rumors about him having inappropriate relationships with minors, and I couldn't stand back anymore. I wanted to arrest the bastard myself.

———————

The crowd behind me buzzed.

I glanced around and saw several members of the Lansburg Police Department making a beeline in my direction.

My heart stopped.

But they bypassed me and infiltrated Maggie and Oswald's weird prayer circle. Maggie's friends scattered. Oswald spun around, looking more desperate and afraid by the second.

Kaufman was on a walkie-talkie giving orders and directing her officers, but it was Agent Ruiz who stepped forward to put cuffs on Oswald's wrists.

His arms pulled tight behind him, his face a mask of confusion at his own fall from grace, Oswald scanned the crowd one more time. His eyes locked on me. I couldn't hear him, but I saw his lips move. "You," he said. He struggled against his restraints, but Agent Ruiz pulled him back.

I looked away.

It was my moment. I'd won. Even if it was just for one night, I was the god and Oswald was the starfish. But for some reason, I didn't feel accomplished. I felt more like Oppenheimer,[1] who, upon seeing his work come to fruition, was said to have quoted this line from the Bhagavad Gita: "Now I am become Death, the destroyer of worlds."

Ishmael limped through the thinning crowd and came to stand by me.

"That didn't go according to plan," he said.

"That's one way to put it."

---

1   Robert Oppenheimer (1904–1967): father of the atomic bomb.

"I swear, dude, I did exactly what you said. I didn't mean for anything to blow up."

"I know," I said.

My gaze swept the chaotic scene one more time. I'd lost sight of Mother and Maggie. I knew Father must be somewhere in the crowd too. I wanted to find my family and go home.

I told Ishmael as much, and he nodded in agreement. He leaned on me, keeping his bad ankle off the ground, and I supported his weight the best I could. Together we moved through the aftermath of what was both our greatest success and greatest failure.

———

Subject #12, David O'Grady:

The cops had that health bozo in cuffs, thank Jesus, and I was ready to be on my way, but I heard another shout. I thought, *What now?* I looked over and saw her: my Prudence, running through the crowd, bucking like she had Satan on her heels. People leapt out of her way, not even trying to stop her. And I knew I'd have to go handle it myself. Just like I had to with everything.

NEWSPAPER ARTICLE

The following article was reprinted with permission of the *Lansburg Daily Press*.

POPULAR HEALTH MLM ROCKED BY SCANDAL

By K. T. Malone

November 6

LANSBURG, PA—Details continue to emerge regarding John Oswald, commonly referred to as J. Quincy Oswald or "Oz."

The founder and CEO of the multi-level marketing company myTality™, was arrested Saturday night following his involvement in the explosion of Lansburg's lava lamp.

Daily Press columnist and owner of the blog lightbringernews .com, Adam Frykowski, has taken it upon himself to unearth information about Oswald's past.

"For one, he claims to be from Texas," Frykowski said, "but records cite him being born and raised in California. His birth certificate shows that he's 37 years old, despite his claims to be over a decade older. And that's just the tip of the iceberg."

Lansburg, normally an idyllic place to call home, is still reeling from the loss of the town's most prominent landmark and the pandemonium that followed. Residents wait anxiously to discover what role Oswald played in the event.

EVENT: Family Meeting

DATE: NOV. 7 (TUES.)

For three days, Father didn't speak to me or my siblings. Every time he looked at us, he shook his head with a mixture of fury and disbelief.

For three days, Mother moped around the house, occasionally taking a myTality™ Shake It Up from the fridge, then putting it back with a look of despair.

For three days, we lived in limbo.

From snippets I saw online, I knew rumors were circulating about my and Ishmael's involvement in the alien fiasco. It was a failing on my part—I was so fixated on taking down Oswald I overlooked that my own voice was on the recording. People were putting the pieces together.

I was overcome with dread. I could barely bring myself to eat. I wished someone would hurry up and punish me for the hoax. I deserved it, I knew I deserved it, and waiting only made my guilt and anxiety and fear worse.

It was a relief when Mother finally called a family meeting.

"I don't like the atmosphere in this house," she said once we were all seated in the living room.

Father snorted. "I haven't liked it for weeks."

Mother ignored him and went on: "I think we can agree that many mistakes have been made around here. By *all* of us."

Only Father raised his voice in protest, but Mother silenced him with a sharp look. "Vic, your mistake was quitting the family because you didn't approve of our choices. No one in this house gets to abandon ship."

Father sat back, chastised.

"My mistake," Mother went on, "was ignoring the unsavory aspects of myTality and going along with outright lies, because I was so focused on building my business. I put success before being a good person."

"You never believed Oz, did you?" I asked.

"No, honey. I didn't."

I nodded. I had assumed as much and was glad she admitted it.

Mother turned to Maggie next. "I don't think I need to tell you that it was wildly inappropriate for you to try forming a cult."

Maggie smiled sweetly, but I saw no remorse in her eyes. "Sorry, Mom."

"As for you two," Mother said, to Ishmael and me. "I don't know where to begin. The amount of destruction you caused is astounding, and there will be repercussions."

I leaned forward. "What *exactly* will those repercussions be?"

"That's something your dad and I still need to discuss."

"I'm probably not going on the senior trip, am I?" Ishmael asked glumly.

"No, Ishmael," Mother replied, "I think it's safe to say you're not."

She paused for a long moment and let her words sink in before continuing.

"Now, as I said, mistakes were made, but we're still a family and we'll support one another while we figure out what happens next. Obviously, I won't sell myTality products anymore, and I'll be home with all of you until I figure out what my next career move is."

"Speaking of careers," Father broke in, "I've enjoyed my time out of the house these past few weeks. The kids don't need me full-time anymore. I think I'd like to pick up some more training sessions."

Mother smiled and squeezed his hand. "That sounds lovely, Vic."

I couldn't imagine a life with Father working full-time. I was happy for him, though. Or, at least, I would be once I learned to cook for myself.

"Another matter we need to discuss is that we'll be adding an animal to the farm."

Everyone stared at Mother, baffled.

"I don't know what you did to David O'Grady's cow," she went on, "but he claims she's turned 'feral' and he can't have her behavior influencing the rest of his herd."

"Wait," Ishmael said, bolting upright. "You mean we get to keep Muffin?"

"Not only do you get to keep her, Ishmael, you and your brother get to *care* for her. Now I don't have a clue what that entails, but Gideon, I'm sure you can put your research skills to good use. Ishmael, you'll probably want to get started by building a pen."

Clearly Mother meant it as a punishment, but Ishmael's eyes glowed with joy. At least one of us was happy.

"In addition, Mr. O'Grady has agreed not to press charges for any of your *several* transgressions against him. In return, the two of you will be working on his farm for the next several seasons."

I knew I was getting off light, so I tried my best to not show horror at the prospect of being a farmhand. From Maggie's giggle, I was only 17 percent sure I succeeded.

"Is there more?" I asked with dread.

Mother's face became solemn. "Yes. The police need to speak with you."

EVENT:
Yet Another
Interrogation

DATE: NOV. 8 (WED.)

I'd had several talks with Chief Kaufman in recent weeks, but she always came to the farm. The fact that she asked my parents to bring Ishmael and me to the police station distressed me.

Before we left the house, Ishmael pulled me aside.

"Hey, dude, I think you should let me take one for the team, okay?"

I frowned. "Pardon?"

"You have this bright future ahead of you, you know? Like, you *can't* have a record. And we both know you're in this situation because of me."

"Are you offering to take the blame for everything?"

"Well, yeah," Ishmael said with a shrug.

I stared at my brother for a long time. "You may have started it, but I was there every step of the way. We were *always* in this together. And we will be until the end."

Ishmael began to protest, but I firmly told him the discussion was over.

At the station we were led to Kaufman's office. Agent Ruiz was already there, sitting in one of the two chairs across from Kaufman's desk. When we entered the room, he stood and motioned for Ishmael and me to sit. He leaned causally against the wall and watched us.

"I'll find seats for you," Kaufman told Mother and Father, who hovered behind us.

"We're okay," Father replied. I could hear the apprehension in his voice. He wanted to get the meeting over with as much as I did.

Kaufman took a breath and folded her hands in front of her. She looked back and forth between my brother and me. "You two have had an interesting few months."

Ishmael smiled sheepishly, as if this was fallout from one of his usual pranks and not much, much more serious.

"Why don't you tell us everything from the beginning," Kaufman suggested. "The truth this time."

Behind me, Father cleared his throat. "Are the boys going to need a lawyer, Lisa?"

"That depends," Kaufman replied.

"On?"

"On how willing they are to cooperate."

My eyes flickered to Agent Ruiz. I wondered why he was still in Lansburg, since the aliens had turned out to be a hoax.

As if reading my mind, Ruiz spoke: "The FBI's been watching J. Quincy Oswald for some time. If your sons tell us everything they know about him, up until their involvement with the explosion, the Lansburg Police Department will reduce the charges against them."

"And if they provide you with this information," Mother said, "then what happens?"

Kaufman gave Ishmael and me a long look. "They'll probably get off with community service and maybe a fine."

I was optimistic but wary. It seemed too easy.

"But, like, isn't Oz already in jail?" Ishmael asked. "Why do you need *more* info?"

Ruiz spoke up. "Because John Oswald has spent his life doing terrible things and we need to make sure we can keep him in jail for a long time."

Something struck me. I spoke to Ruiz: "You were never here because of aliens, were you?"

"No."

"You only showed up when Oswald did."

"As I said, we've been watching him for a long time."

I felt oddly defeated. Not that I *wanted* to be the subject of a federal investigation. But I'd actually thought my hoax was so brilliant it caught the eye of government authorities. It hadn't, though. It never would have. It was Oswald from the start.

"So," Kaufman said. "Do we have a deal?"

Ishmael shrugged agreeably. "I'm down."

All eyes turned to me.

"Gideon," Ruiz said, "Oswald has scammed a lot of people out of a lot of money. He conned you too, when he got you to turn that lava lamp on—and believe me, he didn't hesitate to place all the blame for the explosion on you."

"He admitted on my recording that he lied about the aliens and the elixir," I said. "Why isn't that enough?"

"Because lying about aliens isn't a crime, and the elixir hasn't been sold yet. He didn't admit to falsifying claims about any of the products already on the market."

Oh. I'd overlooked that part. I'd overlooked a lot of things.

I couldn't help but feel they were grasping at straws, searching for anything that would keep Oswald behind bars. Not unlike what happened to Al Capone.[1]

I *did* have something to give Kaufman and Ruiz though, information they might be very interested in. But that information wasn't mine to give.

"Can I make a phone call?"

"Gideon!" Mother gasped, as if she couldn't believe my gall.

"I wouldn't ask if it wasn't important."

Kaufman nodded and gestured for me to step out of the room. "Make it fast."

I locked myself in the men's bathroom and called Arden, quickly explaining the situation.

"You want to know if you can tell them about me," she said.

"Yes."

"Will you have to use my name?"

"I think I will," I said apologetically.

Arden was silent for a long time. My gaze wandered around the bathroom, which probably hadn't been properly cleaned since the station had been built. I moved to the center of the room so nothing could touch me.

Finally, Arden said, "He's not a good man, is he?"

"No."

"He tricked all of us."

"He did."

Including me. I'd told myself I was immune to Oswald's charm,

---

1   Al Capone (1899–1947): a notorious gangster who, though suspected in numerous crimes—including murder—eventually went to prison for tax evasion.

but he'd appealed to my ego when he asked for my help with the lava lamp. And I'd fallen for it. He didn't *need* me. Anyone could have figured out the mechanics of the lamp with just a little effort.

Oswald knew I was skeptical of him. It was so easy for him to make people love him, he couldn't handle it when someone refused to bend to his will. And after I caught him with Arden, he had extra incentive to bring me to his side.

He made me complicit in a scam I'd passionately rallied against, simply by making me feel special.

I'd gotten played.

The whole time I was thinking of Oswald as my nemesis, I was nothing but a pawn to him. It was depressing to realize the person you considered a rival never felt the same way about you.

"Okay," Arden said. "Do it. Tell them whatever they want to know."

"Are you sure?"

"Positive," she replied. I heard strength and resolve in her voice that I couldn't help but admire.

Back in Kaufman's office, Ishmael sat casually in his chair, sipping a Coke. How could he be so relaxed?

"All right," I said, sitting down. "We'll tell you everything."

Kaufman asked if she could record the conversation. Ruiz took out a notepad.

"You might want to bring some chairs for my parents," I suggested. "This will take a while."

Five minutes later, we were all settled in.

"Where should we start?" I asked.

"At the beginning," Kaufman replied.

"Well," said Ishmael, and I could tell part of him enjoyed the moment, looked forward to the performance he was about to give. "It started with an explosion..."

AFTERMATH

WORD TRAVELED QUICKLY IN A TOWN THE SIZE OF Lansburg. It wasn't long before everyone found out what Ishmael and I had done.

Adam Frykowski wrote a blog post praising Ishmael and me for being "hoaxer masterminds." Robert Nash, of *Basin and Range Radio*, sadly informed his listeners of the hoax, calling my brother and me "punk kids." Our classmates joked with us, and some asked questions about how we'd pulled off certain things, but we didn't get much flack. After all, a lot of them had claimed to be abducted too.

Really, that went for the whole town. Nearly everyone had

played a part in the alien mania. To call my brother and me out would be admitting their own UFO sightings or abduction stories were fake or imagined. Instead, most people picked up and went on with their lives, leaving a mild air of embarrassment lingering over Lansburg.

The embarrassment was probably exacerbated due to the coverage our town got on the national news. The reveal of the hoax proved to be even more attention grabbing than the hoax itself. Lansburg was famous. My brother and I had done it—we'd left our mark.

Only, sometimes leaving a mark should be called leaving a *scar*. At the center of Lansburg, proudly on display, the town's broken and empty lava lamp was blocked off with sawhorses and caution tape. It would be dismantled and hauled away as soon as town officials figured out how exactly to dispose of a sixty-three-foot-tall lava lamp.

Ishmael and I had plenty of time to look at the lamp and reflect on our actions. Though we hadn't officially been given community service orders yet, Kaufman suggested it would look good if we started ahead of time—by cleaning up the town square.

The myTality™ distributors had fled the day after the explosion and Oswald's arrest. The Seekers had taken a little longer to disperse. I ran into Arnie Hodges as he packed up, loading his step stool into the back of his van.

"We hoped this time was real," Hodges told me, and even his mad-scientist hair looked limp and defeated. "That we'd get hard evidence of extraterrestrials and the world would *have* to take us seriously."

I realized how much I'd offered him and the other Seekers, and how much I'd taken when they found out it was a lie. A surge of guilt ran through me. Why had I thought it was okay to use their faith in aliens to manipulate them?

"What's next for you?" I asked.

"There've been sightings in the Pacific Northwest," he said. "We'll head that way."

So the Seekers departed but left behind a mess in the town square. Ishmael and I spent days picking up trash. Worse than the trash were bits of paraffin that clung to everything. When the lava lamp exploded, it was like candle wax got dumped all over Main Street. I became very adept at working with a paint scraper.

On a particularly cold afternoon, I was removing paraffin from the window of Super Scoop. Inside, Laser stood behind the counter, watching me and smirking.

As I dragged the paint scraper across the glass, I wondered, for approximately the hundredth time, what would happen next. When the strangers were gone, when the town square was cleaned up, when the lava lamp was dismantled, what then? What would happen to *me*?

I'd thought my sociological research would get me noticed by MIT—I needed the edge so badly. Deep down, I'd always suspected I wasn't a good enough candidate on my own. My grades weren't extraordinary, my extracurriculars were minimal, I didn't start a company at age nine or invent a life-changing product at age thirteen. I wasn't special. But maybe, with a sociological paper reporting on an alien abduction, I could be.

When it was revealed to be a hoax, and I was revealed to be behind it, it minimized all of my efforts. I was a fraud. What would

MIT want with some fraud practical jokester? And beyond that, what would NASA want with someone who unabashedly broke the law? My record was marred beyond hope.

In my quest for glory I'd sabotaged the career I'd always dreamed of. And I had no one to blame but myself.

For the sake of absolute transparency, I'll admit that I may have shed a tear or two over this.

I couldn't remember a time when my future was so unclear. I'd always had a path. I'd always had goals and knew the steps I had to take to achieve them. Now what? Where would I be in the coming years? *What* would I be?

The question haunted me. While I cleaned the town square, while I tried to get caught up in my classes, while I tossed and turned in bed late at night. I couldn't stop thinking of my murky future and how, for the first time in my life, I had no direction.

"Hofstadt," said someone behind me, breaking me from my thoughts.

I glanced back and saw Adam Frykowski.

"Have you gotten my messages?" he asked.

"I have."

"And what do you think? About giving me an exclusive interview?"

He looked so eager. I knew he was trying to make a career shift, move away from his paranormal news stories to more serious reporting. I felt a little guilty about crushing his hopes. "I'm ninety-six percent sure that'll never happen."

I moved away from him and toward the next shop, the next glob of paraffin. He followed.

"I visited Oz," he said.

I stiffened. "You did?"

"He had a lot to say about you, Hofstadt."

It didn't matter what Oswald said about me. I'd moved forward. I'd gotten a grip on the unhealthy emotions that had driven me to compete with him.

Except...

How could I *not* be curious?

"Fine, I'll bite. What did he say?"

"I'll tell you if you give me an exclusive."

"Forget it."

"He hates you," Frykowski spoke up quickly, trying to entice me. "He called you his archenemy."

"Interesting," I said as blandly as possible.

I turned away from Frykowski so he wouldn't see the smile that crept onto my face.

"You really don't want to know more?" he practically pleaded.

"Nope," I replied, using the paint scraper to remove another strip of paraffin from the wall. "I'm done with all that."

I *was* done with it.

But that didn't mean I wasn't pleased Oswald finally saw me as a worthy opponent. In the end, neither of us won. But at least he realized I'd been part of the game.

EVENT: Guidance—Part 2

DATE: NOV. 16 (THURS.)

I wasn't surprised when Ms. Singh called me in to "have a chat."

"Things have certainly changed since we last spoke," she said, getting to the point as soon as I was seated in her cramped office.

"That's an accurate assessment."

She held up a printed document. "I have your current grades here."

I winced.

"They're not great," she went on.

"I suspected as much."

"I'm sorry to have to tell you this, but you're probably out of the running for valedictorian."

I nodded. It wasn't a shocking revelation. I'd been thinking of little else for days. It stung, but part of me also felt...oddly liberated. Being a great student had never come naturally. I'd pushed myself because I wanted to be on top, because it was a *competition*, but it never meant as much to me as my own experiments—which was fairly clear, considering how easily I'd ignored my slipping grades for months. Let Sara Kang be valedictorian; she was the one who deserved it.

"MIT might also be off the table," I said. There was no point dancing around the subject.

Ms. Singh seemed thrown off by my calmness. "I'll never say never. But you might want to look into backup colleges."

"I have," I said. "I started a list."

Her eyebrows shot up. "Oh! That's wonderful. Maybe you can bring the list by and we can go over it together."

"Sure," I agreed.

A silence fell in the room and Ms. Singh shifted in her seat, like she wanted to broach an uncomfortable topic. "You seem to be taking this well."

"I'm really not," I admitted. My next words nearly caught in my throat, but I forced them out anyway. I wasn't going back to being the person I was before all of this. If that happened, the hoax would've been a complete waste. "I'm scared about the future."

For a moment, Ms. Singh seemed at a loss for words. Maybe students didn't usually open up to her like this. Maybe she'd just never expected *me* to. "It's okay to be scared, Gideon. It's okay to feel unsure."

"That's what I keep telling myself. I'm actually starting to see a therapist," I said. "Not only because of the hoax, but to work through a lot of issues."

"That's wonderful! Therapy can be so beneficial."

"I hope so."

Ms. Singh smiled as if she was proud of me, which only made me *slightly* embarrassed.

I cleared my throat and brought the conversation back into safer, less emotional territory again. "About my goals, though... I'm not ready to give up yet. I'm still applying to MIT and I'm still hopeful that NASA might eventually hire me. But if not, I'll come up with another plan. Maybe I'll find something even better."

"It's interesting you say that," Ms. Singh said. "I know you previously weren't receptive to the idea of working for Triple i..."

I perked up a bit.

"I hope you don't mind, but I called my friend who works there. I told her a little about you and your situation. She said Triple i is always looking for people who...think outside the box. We discussed possible internship opportunities for you in the future and she'd be willing to put in a good word. Maybe you can spend a summer there and decide if it's really so far off from the career you wanted."

Triple i wasn't NASA. Nothing would ever make it NASA. But there was something to be said for what they were doing. Maybe NASA really was outdated. Maybe Triple i was the future.

Or maybe neither organization was meant for me. It was probably wrong to be so set on one path. I was closing myself off from other opportunities that might arise.

"I'll certainly think about that, Ms. Singh," I said. "But not yet. I need to get myself back on track in the present before I worry about what'll happen in the future."

Ms. Singh smiled. "That's wise of you."

After everything that happened, the last thing I felt was *wise*. But that didn't bother me. I was okay being exactly who I was.

EVENT:
Bonfire

DATE: NOV. 18 (SAT.)

On Saturday, two weeks after The Incident, my parents watched as I packed my lab equipment into boxes. The boxes would be stored in the barn until I "proved I was mature enough to have a lab." Something told me that wouldn't happen before I moved out.

Kepler twisted around my feet as I packed, meowing aggressively. He didn't like the situation either. If he wanted to spend time with me, he'd be forced to venture into the house.

While I dismantled my lab, Ishmael built a pen for Muffin, who'd be coming to live with us the next day. For the first time in decades, there'd be livestock on the Hofstadt Farm. Or, "one livestock," as my brother might say. Maggie watched Ishmael work and made unhelpful comments until Mother told her to go inside.

It hurt to pack up my lab. I didn't know what I'd do with myself without it, where I'd even spend time. But it was a fair punishment. More than fair. Considering the grief we caused an entire town, my brother and I were getting off lightly.

That night, Ishmael and I got to have one last hurrah before being grounded for an unspecified amount of time. We were allowed to invite our friends over for a bonfire.

The boxes of myTality™ products Mother had stored in the barn were dragged into the field, to the very spot where Ishmael and I had blown a crater into the ground. The spot was chosen because damage had already been done, the grass had already been burned away—but it felt fitting.

"All those products are worthless now," Mother said.

"They were always worthless," I replied.

Father stacked wood around the boxes and doused them in kerosene, but Mother was the one to light the match. The boxes immediately went up in flames.

The group of us—my family and the friends we'd invited over for the occasion—stood back, putting distance between ourselves and the noxious chemicals being released into the air. I was close enough to feel the heat of the flames, though. To hear the popping of hundreds of bottles of pseudo-health products combusting.

I looked at Mother and saw her dab a tear away.

Watching the boxes burn probably hurt her as much as losing my lab hurt me. She'd put so much time and energy into the company. And, scam or not, she'd been successful.

I put my arm around her. "I'm sorry."

"Oh, I'm being silly," she replied. "There are always other opportunities. In fact, I was thinking after everything that's happened, this town could really use a wellness center."

"I thought you were taking time off from work," I said.

She laughed. "Yes, well, we'll see."

I should've known. Mother couldn't stop working any more

than I could stop doing experiments. Whether it was a yoga studio or selling myTality™ or opening whatever a wellness center was, she'd always have something on her plate.

I looked around the bonfire where all my family and friends gathered. Cass—wearing a hunting cap with ear flaps despite the heat of the fire—was engaged in a lively conversation with Gram. Father talked animatedly to Owen about baseball. Owen glanced up and grinned at me, making my chest swell and a goofy smile slip onto my face. Arden sat with one of Ishmael's friends and, though I wasn't great at reading body language, they seemed quite interested in each other.

Maggie was alone, near the edge of the fire. She was on her phone, firing off texts and occasionally glancing around furtively. I shuddered to think of what she was plotting. She was more dangerous than Ishmael. She was more dangerous than anyone I'd ever met, maybe.

Speaking of Ishmael, he was the only person unaccounted for. I looked around and finally spotted him standing in the shadows near the barn, gazing up at the sky. I wandered over.

"What are you doing?"

"I don't know. Trying to see the stars the way you see them, I guess."

"Why would you want to do that? Every time I look at the sky I feel insignificant."

"I don't get that," Ishmael replied. "I look up and feel like...like anything is possible."

I followed his gaze upward. It was a new moon, so visibility was excellent, and the sky was as breathtaking as always. It held so much more than humankind would ever know. Maybe that wasn't scary or depressing. Maybe it was inspiring.

"Do you regret anything?" Ishmael asked me.

"I regret lots of things," I said.

I regretted that Mother became disillusioned with her career because of me. I regretted how strained our house had gotten. I regretted how difficult I'd made Chief Kaufman's job. I regretted my behavior with Owen and how I refused to open up to Arden. I regretted how often my pride got in the way of living life.

But did I regret the hoax itself?

Maybe.

Maybe not.

"Are you upset we got caught?" Ishmael asked.

I laughed, startling him. "I think, deep down, I always knew we'd be caught."

"But, like, are you sad your experiment is ruined? Your psychological study, or whatever?"

"Sociological," I corrected. "And it's not ruined. Just different than I thought it would be. It won't get me into MIT, but maybe I'll still compile it into a book."

"That seems like a lot of work."

"Well, I need something to do now that science is banned at the house."

Ishmael snorted.

For a moment we continued to look at the stars together. Then I asked, "Did *you* know we were going to get caught?"

"Well, yeah, dude. What's the point of a prank you can't take credit for?"

A couple months ago that admission would have enraged me. Now, I just started laughing. A second later Ishmael joined me.

"You know, Ishmael, despite our entire lives being turned upside down, I'm glad we did it. I'm glad we did it *together*."

"We kinda make a great team, don't we?" he asked.

A destructive team. Maybe a dangerous team.

But yes.

We were great too.

Of that, I was 100 percent sure.

In Conclusion:

There you have it: the true story of what happened in Lansburg, Pennsylvania, where there were never any aliens, just two teenagers looking for glory and a town that wanted something to believe in.

The fifth step in the scientific method is *draw conclusions*.

I've concluded that it *is* possible to convince people of the legitimacy of extraterrestrial life—and probably many other outlandish things. Possible...but maybe not *advisable*.

A scientist doesn't dictate what others experiment on, though. Everyone has to make their own choices. All I can do is provide enough material for an *informed* choice. Which is why the final step in the scientific method is *report results*.

That's what I've done here. Communicated my experiment through every stage, every failure, and every success. I won't lecture you about hoaxes being a bad idea... Instead, I'll simply hope these pages speak for themselves.

My days as a hoaxer have come to an end, but there will always be new experiments and new discoveries. For me and for the *world*. That's why I implore all of you readers—the skeptics and Seekers, the scientists and sociologists, the gods and starfish—to stay curious, believe in yourself, and never give up.

Go out and find your glory.

Gideon P. Hofstadt
Lansburg, PA
Earth
The Milky Way Galaxy

Acknowledgments

There were times I thought I'd never finish this book. Without the help of some very patient, encouraging, insightful people I probably wouldn't have. A million thanks to:

My agent, the talented Suzie Townsend, for continuing to be my champion and tirelessly helping me navigate this (thrilling, nerve-racking, mysterious) writing journey. I'm so lucky to be part of the New Leaf family.

Eliza Swift, my brilliant editor, who made this book infinitely better. I'm grateful that she shares my weird sense of humor and love of complicated characters—and that she's able to point out my writing flaws in the nicest possible way.

The incredible team at Sourcebooks for putting a tremendous amount of effort into *It Came from the Sky* at every stage, especially: Cassie Gutman, Danielle McNaughton, Jessica Rozler, Nicole Hower, Beth Oleniczak, Valerie Pierce, Ashlyn Keil, Stefani Sloma, and Sarah Kasman. Also, Philip Pascuzzo at Pepco Studio for creating the stunning book cover.

Everyone who read the manuscript in its various (often messy) drafts and gave me valuable feedback: Marley Tetor, Phil Stamper, Anna Priemaza, Jo Farrow, Jilly Gagnon, Lana Popovic, and Bridget Morrissey.

The people in my writing communities who inspire me, entertain me, and push me to be better: Chris, Elizabeth, Gordon, Ilanit, Mandy, Annie, Greg, Jess, Josh, Katelyn, Katie, Kristine, Leann, Morgan, Rachel, and Tasha.

Dillon Battaglia for information about MIT admissions. Ronnie Willard for answering questions about jamming radio signals. Matt Anderson for confusing Robert Frost and Jack Frost. My mom for the constant encouragement and for never joining an MLM.

Evan Sedoti for sharing my obsession with aliens (abductions run in families, after all) and for providing me with lots of sibling-relationship material. Also, for inspiring Ishmael's fashion sense.

Steve Phillips for spending countless hours discussing the Fermi Paradox, seismographs, and the mechanics of lava lamps. *It Came from the Sky* would be much different (and contain far less science) if it weren't for him.

The readers, librarians, bloggers, and booksellers who have continually supported my books (and books in general!). Their enthusiasm motivates me to keep writing.

And thank you to the people who have nurtured my lifelong fascination with aliens, especially: Art Bell, Fox Mulder, Stephen King, George Noory, and the boys from *The Last Podcast on the Left*. Like them, I want to believe.

About the Author

Chelsea Sedoti is the author of the young adult novels *The Hundred Lies of Lizzie Lovett* and *As You Wish*. Before becoming a writer, Chelsea explored careers as a balloon twister, filmmaker, and paranormal investigator. Eventually she realized her true passion is telling stories about flawed teenagers just as strange as she is. When she's not at the computer, Chelsea spends her time exploring abandoned buildings, eating junk food at roadside diners, and trying to befriend every animal in the world. She lives in Las Vegas, Nevada, where she avoids casinos but loves roaming the Mojave Desert.

FIREreads

#getbooklit

Your hub for the hottest young adult books!

Visit us online and sign up for our
newsletter at FIREreads.com

 @sourcebooksfire

 sourcebooksfire

 firereads.tumblr.com